BETWEEN FREEDOM AND DESPAIR

Athas, world of the dark sun. Ruled for thousands of years by power-mad sorcerer-kings, the cities of Athas have become vile centers of slavery and corruption. Only heroes of the greatest strength and bravest heart can stand against the might of these overlords. The Prism Pentad is a tale of such heroes. . . .

Rikus—the man-dwarf whose skill as a gladiator is the only thing that can win him his freedom.

Sadira—the beautiful half-elven slave-girl, caught between her desire to fight for her world and the seductive power offered to her by forbidden sorceries.

Agis of Asticles—the master of psionics and firebrand senator who saw himself as the people's hero . . . until he encountered the true champions of the oppressed, the mysterious Veiled Alliance.

The Verdant Passage
TROY DENNING

THE VERDANT PASSAGE

First Printing: October 1991
Printed in the United States of America
Library of Congress Catalog Card Number: 91-65044

9 8 7 6 5 4 3 2 1

ISBN: 1-56076-121-0

TSR, Inc.
P.O. Box 756
Lake Geneva, WI 53147
U.S.A.

TSR, Ltd.
120 Church End, Cherry Hinton
Cambridge CB1 3LB
United Kingdom

Dedication:

To Andria, for her help and encouragement.

Acknowledgements:

Many people contributed to the writing of this book and the creation of this series. I would like to thank you all. Without the efforts of the following people, especially, Athas might never have seen the light of the crimson sun: Mary Kirchoff and Tim Brown, who shaped the world as much as anyone; Brom, who gave us the look and the feel; Jim Lowder, who came when he was needed; Pat McGilligan, who brought a much-needed sense of drama to the desert; and Jim Ward, who contributed his enthusiasm, support, and much more.

MOUNTAINS

FOOTHILLS

SANDY WASTE

BOULDER FIELD

STONEY BARRENS

FOREST

SCRUBLAND

Great Alluvial
Sand
Wastes

To Urik

To Balic

PROLOGUE

The great ziggurat towered above the squalor of the sun-baked city. Each level of the terraced pyramid was finished in glazed brick of a different color: gleaming violet at the base, then indigo, azure, green, yellow, fiery orange, and, finally, scarlet. In the center of the huge structure, a pair of mighty bastions marked each of the seven levels. The bastions flanked an enormous staircase, which ran straight from base to summit, reaching for the flaxen moons that hovered over the monument's lofty crown and infused the hazy predawn sky with an amber blush.

Thousands of slaves swarmed over the pyramid. Clad only in breechcloths, they toiled to the rhythm of snapping whips, using a web of ropes and pulleys to hoist crates laden with fired bricks up the sheer walls of each terrace.

At the base of the ziggurat stood a diminutive man wearing a long purple robe. Upon his head was a golden diadem, the crown of the king of Tyr. A wispy fringe of gray hair hung from the golden circlet, but his pate was

1

bald and scaly with age. Lines of anger and hate were deeply etched in his brow, a thousand years of bitterness burned in his gaze, and a scowl hung upon his dry, cracked lips. Pallid, wrinkled flesh dangled from his cheeks and jaw, and it looked as if the man had been fasting for a hundred years. For all anyone knew, he had.

Next to the ancient ruler stood an apprehensive man dressed in the black cassock worn by all the king's templars. His auburn hair hung in a braided tail down the center of his back. His features were gaunt, and his face was populated with a hawkish nose, a thin-lipped frown, and beady eyes the color of liver. At five and a half feet, he loomed over the aged king the way elves loomed over men. That fact made him nervous. Tithian of Mericles, High Templar of the Games and sole heir to the Mericles name, would have enjoyed towering over his peers. He was too shrewd to relish standing taller than the king.

Noting that he was casting a faint shadow over his ruler, Tithian stepped forward to examine the violet-hued bricks of the ziggurat's lowest tier. They were embellished with alabaster tiles. A carving on each tile portrayed the Dragon: a stooped beast that walked upright on a pair of massive legs, dragging an immense serpentine tail behind it. An articulated husk of rough chitin covered the Dragon's back and tail. Its arms were two stubs, but its hands were shaped like a man's, and each held a staff that helped support its upper torso. A protective collar of leaf-shaped scales covered its shoulders. From this collar rose a long, powerful neck that ended in a flat head that held narrow, slitlike eyes, no ears, and a huge mouth filled with jagged teeth.

"This workmanship is exquisite, King Kalak," Tithian offered, not taking his eyes from the white tiles. "The detail is amazing."

Kalak reached up and placed his hand on Tithian's shoulder. With its gnarled fingers and swollen joints, it looked more like a claw than a human appendage.

"Did I bring you here to examine artwork?" Without awaiting a reply, the king led Tithian toward a crate of bricks that was being pulled to an upper level of the ziggurat.

Tithian grimaced. This was the first time he had ever seen the king outside the Golden Tower, and he had no idea why he had been called to meet him at such an uncivilized hour. From Kalak's acid tone, the high templar guessed that the meeting would be less than pleasant.

When they reached the rising crate, Kalak grasped the rope that hung from its side. The king's feet left the ground, and he began to float upward. Tithian stifled a scream as Kalak's talonlike fingers dug into his shoulder. An instant later, the ground slipped from beneath the templar's feet. He found himself dangling in the king's grip, staring down upon the heads of the slaves who had been loading more crates at the base of the ziggurat.

The slaves were astonished by the sight of two men rising into the air like wisps of smoke, and they paused to gape at the pair. Their overseers, subordinate templars dressed in black cassocks similar to Tithian's, quickly returned them to work with a few well-placed blows from bone-and-leather whips.

When Kalak and Tithian had risen just above the first terrace, they came face-to-face with four hundred pounds of fur and muscle. The hulking baazrag paused in its difficult task of hauling up the bricks. Creasing its sloping brow, it fixed its eyes on the men, then cocked its high-crested head in confusion. As the beast's glance dropped to the empty space beneath the king's feet, its cavernous nostrils flared in alarm and its muzzle fell open, revealing four sharp, yellow canines. The baazrag stepped back and raised its arms in a defensive display. The rope slipped from its hands.

Stepping onto the terrace, the king barely managed to release the rope and avoid following the crate as it fell to the ground. The bricks crashed upon a human slave, crushing him. The entire load was pulverized by the fall. Kalak stood at the terrace edge, scowling at the rubble and squeezing Tithian's collarbone so hard that the templar expected it to snap at any moment.

When the king finally lifted his gaze, his eyes were blazing with fury. He located a man wearing the black cassock of a templar, then pointed at him. "You!"

The overseer spun around, blanching as he saw who had addressed him. "Yes, Mighty One?"

"This slave just dropped a full load of my bricks!" Kalak snapped, pointing at the wretched baazrag he had surprised. "Whip him!"

The overseer cringed, for the same lack of wit that made baazrags good slaves could result in a murderous rampage when they were beaten. Nevertheless, the man unfurled his whip to obey, for defying the king would mean an immediate and agonizing death.

Before Tithian could see what became of the baazrag's punishment, Kalak ordered another of his priests to throw him a line. Two slaves gingerly pulled the king and Tithian toward another crate of bricks, which was being lifted to the next terrace. With his hand still crushing Tithian's shoulder, the king grasped the rope attached to the crate, and the pair began to rise again. They repeated the process several times, ascending the ziggurat level by level. With each trip, the overseers shouted warnings to their counterparts above, trying to prevent astonished slaves from losing any more bricks.

Most slaves were human, dwarven, or half-elven, but other, more exotic races dominated several terraces. On one terrace labored an entire pack of belgoi, gaunt humanoids nearly identical to men—save for their broadly webbed feet, clawed fingers, and the chinless, toothless mouths with which they chattered.

On another level worked a hundred gith, a grotesque humanoid race that seemed half elf, half reptile. They were lanky like desert elves, with long, slender legs. But the legs protruded from the body at right angles like a lizard's. The gith were so hunched at the waist that they shambled in a perpetual squat. Their bony heads were slender and arrow-shaped, with bulging, lidless eyes that remained fixed on Tithian and Kalak as the two men floated past.

When Kalak and his templar reached the sixth stage of the ziggurat, the king stepped onto the terrace and released Tithian's aching shoulder. They could not continue to rise along the face of the wall, for the seventh, final echelon of the great pyramid was still encased in wooden scaffolds. Over these frameworks swarmed dozens of jozhal, small two-legged reptiles with skinny tails, long, flexible necks, and elongated snouts filled with needlelike teeth. With their small, three-fingered hands, the jozhal were covering the seventh tier with scarlet-glazed bricks. They labored at an amazing pace, running up and down the rickety scaffolds as though they were walking on level ground.

Kalak stepped to the scaffolding and pointed a gnarled finger at the half-completed terrace beyond. "Will my ziggurat be ready in three weeks?"

Tithian dutifully peered through the scaffolding as if to assess the work in progress, but he was hardly the person to ask. Like most people, he had no idea why the king was building the ziggurat. Kalak had not explained its purpose, and those who had inquired about it too often were now dead. In fact Tithian understood less about construction than he did about the ziggurat's purpose. For all he knew, the terrace could be three *days* from completion.

Though he was puzzled by the king's interest in his opinion, Tithian did not intend to allow his lack of expertise to influence his answer. His reply would be dictated by two things: what he thought the king wanted to hear, and what would serve him best politically.

Tithian thought he would be best served by a negative answer. The High Templar of the King's Works, a woman named Dorjan, was his greatest rival. Kalak seemed upset with her, so Tithian sensed an opportunity to add to her troubles.

"Well?"

The templar faced the king and was almost overcome with awe. He had not realized how far they had risen, and from the ziggurat's lofty heights he could only wonder at everything he could see.

At the base of the mighty pyramid lay the sandy floor of the gladiatorial arena. It looked no larger than the courtyard of a minor noble's townhouse, and the great tiers of seats flanking the field seemed no higher than the terraced walls of a garden. Even the Golden Tower of Kalak's palace, which overlooked the opposite end of the arena, seemed an insignificant spire from where Tithian stood.

Beyond the royal palace lay the Templar's Ward. In this part of the city stood the marble palaces of the six high templars, the elegant mansions of their trusted assistants, and the lavish chamberhouses of the subordinate priests. Hundreds of guards patrolled the streets of this district day and night, and a high wall capped with jagged shards of obsidian isolated it from the rest of Tyr. On the far side of the ward stood the fortifications of the city wall, a brick barricade so wide that a military road ran along its crest, and so high that even the Dragon could not peer over it.

From the ziggurat Tithian could see even beyond the wall. There lay Kalak's fields, a three-mile ring of blue burgrass, golden smokebrush, and ground holly, made fertile only by the blood and toil of a legion of slaves. On the far side of these rich pastures lay the orange expanse of the Tyr Valley, a vast sweep of dusty scrubland, speckled here and there with gray-green thickets of bushy tamarisk and spindly catclaw trees.

Through the veil of dust that hung in the air, permanently tinting the Athasian sky in a kaleidoscope of pastel hues, Tithian could even see the stark, ashen crags of the Ringing Mountains. He had heard that on the far side of those impassable peaks there flourished a jungle, but of course he dismissed such absurd tales. From what he knew, all of Athas resembled the wastes of the Tyr Valley, although some regions were perhaps even more desolate.

Kalak interrupted Tithian's reverie with a terse demand. "Tithian, what of my ziggurat? Will Dorjan finish it in time?"

"It looks difficult, but not impossible," Tithian replied, cautiously avoiding an open attack on his rival. "I'm discouraged that there is so much left to accomplish, but perhaps Dorjan has a solid plan."

The king did not reply. Instead, he cast his glance toward a slender templar approaching from the north. It was Dorjan. She was a beautiful woman, with an ivory complexion, straight nose, and high cheekbones. Yet she was not alluring, for her stern personality and cruel temper cast a sharp edge over her features. The high templar moved with a decisive stride, her long, silky hair waving in the wind like a black banner. When she saw Tithian, her dark eyes grew as hard as the bricks of the ziggurat and the full red lips of her wide mouth twisted into a confident sneer.

Behind Dorjan came a pair of subordinates, both burly men with rugged faces and square jaws. Between them they dragged an emaciated slave with dun-colored hair and pallid skin. The slave cradled two broken arms against his stomach. One eye was swollen shut; with the other, he peered at the ground. The man wheezed laboriously through bloody lips, for his nose had been smashed and was now spread across his cheeks like a black-and-purple mask.

"How are my games coming, Tithian?" Kalak inquired casually. His beady eyes were fixed on the slave.

"If the ziggurat were completed today, we could hold the games tomorrow," Tithian replied proudly. "My beast-handlers have trapped a new creature you will find most surprising."

The king raised an eyebrow. "Truly? That *would* be something."

Tithian silently cursed himself. During the thousand years of his reign, Kalak had no doubt seen more exotic beasts than the high templar could even imagine. It was foolish to raise the king's expectations with immodest boasting.

Before Tithian could cover his blunder, Dorjan joined them. Pointedly ignoring her rival, she faced Kalak and bowed. When the ancient king held out his shriveled hand, the templar touched her lips to the withered palm.

"This is the one?" Kalak asked, withdrawing his hand and motioning at the slave.

Dorjan nodded, then reached into her pocket and withdrew a bone amulet covered with runes. "He tried to seal this into the inner passage," she said, offering it to the king. "The runes are meant—"

"To create an invisible wall," Kalak growled, snatching the amulet from her hand. He thrust the bone under the battered slave's nose. "What did you hope to accomplish with this trinket?"

The slave shrugged. "I don't know," he mumbled in a weak voice. "She told me to seal it in the main shaft."

"Who told you?" Dorjan asked, smirking in Tithian's direction.

Before the slave answered, Tithian noticed the king's beady eyes lock on his face.

"I don't know her name," the slave muttered, still not looking up. "A half-elf owned by the High Templar of the Games—"

"Sadira," Tithian interrupted, supplying the name of the only half-elf he owned, before the slave could continue. "She's a scullery maid in my personal training pit. I'm aware of her association with the Veiled Alliance."

Dorjan frowned at Tithian. "I suppose you'll also claim to know that she's trying to disrupt the games celebrating the ziggurat's completion?"

"Of course, but I haven't yet determined the exact nature of the Alliance's plan," Tithian replied, concealing his surprise by gazing at the scaffolding on the seventh tier. "Fortunately, it appears I have more than enough time to complete my investigation."

Giving no indication of whether or not he believed Tithian, Kalak looked to Dorjan. "It does seem that Tithian has several weeks to uncover my enemy's plan, does it not?"

Dorjan reluctantly nodded and did not meet the king's

gaze. "He does."

Kalak scowled. "I thought as much," he said, casually grasping the battered slave by the back of the head. "Let's see if we can help Tithian with his investigations."

"No!" The slave tried to pull away and hurl himself off the terrace, but the king's grip remained secure. Kalak closed his eyes, and the man screamed.

With only casual interest, Tithian watched the king enter the slave's mind, for he had a better understanding than most men of what the king was doing. As a youth, his parents had required him to study the psionic arts for a time, enforcing a strict regimen of self-denial and painful rituals in the name of harnessing the spiritual and mental powers of his being. Under the harsh discipline of his master, Tithian had learned to use these energies to probe another's thoughts, to make objects move with the force of his mind alone, even to picture in his head what lay on the other side of a thick wall. But the Way of the Unseen, as his mentor had called the disciplines, was a difficult path to follow. He had left the school as soon as he grew old enough to make his own decisions, opting for the much easier and more lucrative life of a king's templar.

A slight smile crossed Kalak's papery lips. The slave gurgled incoherently and began to drool, his pulverized face contorting in agony and terror. Then his jaws clamped together violently. The detached tip of his tongue slipped from between his swollen lips and dropped to the floor.

At last, the king opened his eyes and took his hand away from his victim's neck. The slave's one good eye rolled back in its socket. His bloody mouth gaped in a silent scream. Then the wretch tumbled to the brick terrace in a heap.

Ignoring the dying man, the king glared at Dorjan and shook the bone amulet at her. "There are two more somewhere in my ziggurat!"

Dorjan's jaw fell slack. She shook her head in denial, but could not utter any words.

"The slave's thoughts were easily read and quite specific on this matter," said Kalak evenly.

The slender templar moved backward two steps, the color draining from her face. "You'll have them by dusk."

Kalak shook his head. "Not from you."

Dorjan looked away, avoiding the king's gaze in a useless effort to save herself. "Mighty One, give me—"

Her plea ceased in midsentence as the king fixed his narrowed eyes on her face. The power of Kalak's assault was so great that his attack flashed briefly in Tithian's mind as well as Dorjan's. Tithian almost screamed as the image of the Dragon's body appeared in his head. Its immense tail lashed back and forth angrily, and a cloud of yellow gas billowed from its sharp-toothed maw. Its staffs were pointed away from its body like weapons. At the end of one staff, a ball of red lightning crackled. At the end of the other, a small green flame licked the wood.

Just when Tithian feared Kalak's anger would inadvertently destroy him, the Dragon faded from his mind. Dorjan screamed and began to shake her head violently. A wave of astonished murmurs rustled along the terrace as the jozhals and their overseers stopped to stare at the source of the agonized screeching.

The high templar watched his rival's pain in grotesque fascination. Certainly he was happy to be rid of her, but her sudden demise was a sobering reminder of the price high templars sometimes paid for their positions of power.

Dorjan's scream quickly became a feeble wail, then she

abruptly fell silent and lifted her chin. Her eyes went blank, although Tithian fancied for a moment that he could see red lightning crackling and flashing deep inside them. Yellow smoke began to seep from the woman's nose, and a gout of green flame spewed from her mouth. Tithian stepped away, narrowly avoiding injury as a ball of emerald fire engulfed Dorjan's head.

The woman dropped to the terrace in a lifeless heap. Tithian watched her head burn down to a pile of ash in uneasy silence, until Kalak drew his attention away by handing him the bone amulet.

"Congratulations. You're my new High Templar of the King's Works," said Kalak. "Finish my ziggurat in three weeks—and find the other two amulets."

ONE

The Gaj

Rikus slid down the rope and dropped into the fighting pit, anxious to finish the morning combat before the day grew hot. The crimson sun had just risen, sending tendrils of fire-colored light shooting through the olive haze of the morning sky. Already the sands of the small arena were warm, and the rancid odor of blood and decaying entrails hung heavily in the air.

In the center of the pit waited the animal he would fight, a beast that Tithian's hunters had captured somewhere in the desert wastes. It was half-buried in the shallow entrenchment it had dug. Only its scaly, rust-orange shell, about six feet in diameter, showed above the sand. If it had limbs—be they arms, legs, or tentacles—they were either tucked inside this dome or hidden beneath the sand churned up around its body.

Rikus saw the thing's head lift from the sand. Attached to the near end of the shell was a spongy white ball. Compound eyes were evenly spaced in a row across the front. Three hairy antennae crowned the pulpy globe, all of them pointed toward Rikus. Over its mouth dangled six

13

fingerlike appendages, flanked by a pair of mandibles as long as a man's arm.

Caught between these pincers was the savaged body of Sizzkus, a nikaal. He had been the beast's keeper, at least until the evening before. Now the corpse hung between the creature's vicious hooks, partially coated with blood and sand. Sizzkus's pointed chin rested on his scaly chest. From beneath his black mop of hair stared a pair of vacant, lidless eyes. His three-clawed hands were draped over the beast's pincers, which had crushed his shiny green carapace into a splintered tangle. In a half-dozen places, pinkish ropes of intestine looped out of gashes in the nikaal's hide. By the number of wounds on Sizzkus's body, Rikus guessed that he had not died without a hard fight.

Rikus found it surprising that the nikaal had been forced to fight at all, for Sizzkus had been extremely cautious with new creatures in the pit. Not long ago, the nikaal had explained to Rikus that monsters, as well as the so-called "New Races," were developing in the desert all the time, but most quickly died out because they were not strong enough to fight off the other creatures of the wastes. Those that did survive, however, were the most vicious and dangerous of all, and worthy of a beast keeper's caution.

Rikus looked away from the mangled corpse and removed his fleece robe, revealing a scarred, athletic body clad only in a breechcloth of drab hemp. Slowly he began to stretch, for he had reluctantly come to realize that his youth was behind him, and his battle-worn muscles would now pull and tear when cold.

Fortunately for Rikus, his body did not outwardly show its maturity. He took great pride in the fact that his bald pate was still taut and smooth, his pointed ears still lay close to his head, and his black eyes remained clear and defiant. His nose still ran straight and true, and there was not so much as a hint of loose skin beneath his powerful jaws. Below his brawny neck, his hairless body was composed of knotted biceps, hulking pectorals, and bulging thighs. Despite the initial stiffness caused by old wounds and poorly mended bones, he could still move with the grace of a rope dancer when he wished.

Rikus had weathered his decades as a gladiator remarkably well, and there was good reason. He was a mul, a hybrid slave bred expressly for arena combat. His father, whom he had never seen, had bestowed on him the strength and durability of the dwarves. His mother, a haggard woman who had died in the slavehouses of far-off Urik, had given him the size and agility of men. The brutal trainers who had raised him, whom he recalled as hated tyrants and murderers, had coached him in the ruthless arts of killing and survival. But it was Rikus himself who was responsible for his greatest asset: determination.

As a child, he had believed that all boys trained to be gladiators. He had assumed that after they fought their way through the ranks, they became trainers and perhaps even nobles. That illusion had lasted until his tenth year, when the lord who owned him had brought his weakling son to see the practice pits. As Rikus had compared his own tattered breechcloth to the frail boy's silken robes, he had come to understand that no matter how hard he practiced and no matter how talented he became, his skills would never win him the privileged status into which the youth had been born. When he reached adulthood the frail boy would still be a nobleman, and Rikus might still be his slave. On that day, he had sworn to die a free man.

Thirty years and as many brief escapes later, he remained in bondage, but he also remained alive. Had he been anything but a mul, he would have been dead or free by now, either killed as punishment for his repeated escapes or allowed to disappear into the desert after it became too expensive to hunt him down. Muls were too valuable for either option, however. Because they could not reproduce their own kind and because most women died while carrying or giving birth to such big-boned babies, muls were worth more than a hundred normal slaves. When they escaped, no expense was spared to recover them.

Rikus's status was about to change, however. In three weeks, he would fight in the ziggurat games. The king himself had decreed that the winners of the day's contests would be freed, and Rikus intended to be among that number.

As the mul finished stretching, he glanced again at Sizzkus's lifeless body, wondering how such an experienced handler had fallen prey to what appeared to be a relatively slow and clumsy beast.

"Couldn't anyone save him?" Rikus asked.

"No one tried," answered Boaz, the gladiator's current trainer. Boaz had the peaked eyebrows and pale eyes of a half-elf, with sharp, raw-boned features that gave him a rodentlike appearance. As usual, his blue eyes were blurry and bloodshot from a long night in the wineshops of Tyr. "I wasn't about to risk my guards for a slave."

Along with a dozen guards and four other slaves, Boaz stood on the broad deck that capped the rock wall encircling the fighting pit. The small practice arena sat in an isolated corner of Lord Tithian's country estate, amid a cluster of mud-brick cellhouses that served as home to the fifty slaves who staffed the high templar's personal gladiator stable.

"Sizzkus was a good man," Rikus countered, glaring up at the half-elf. "You could have called me."

"The gaj caught him while you were sleeping," Boaz replied, his thin lips curled into a sneer. "And we all know what happens when a gladiator your age fights without warming up."

The guards chuckled at the trainer's affront.

Though they were all husky men wearing leather corselets and carrying obsidian-tipped spears, Rikus glared at them. "I can kill Boaz and six of you before taking so much as a scratch," the mul growled. "I hope you aren't laughing at me."

The guards immediately fell silent, for the mul had made good on such threats before. Rikus had killed his last trainer just two months earlier. Only the memory of the threat he had received on that occasion kept Boaz alive now.

After his previous trainer's death, Lord Tithian had come to Rikus's cell with a young slave and a purple caterpillar. A pair of guards had held the youth down while Tithian carefully laid the caterpillar on the slave's upper lip. In a flash, the thing had crawled up the boy's nostril. He had started screaming and snorting in an effort to dislodge it, but to no avail. A few seconds later, blood had begun to stream from the boy's nose, and then the poor wretch collapsed, unconscious.

"The worm is making a nest in Grakidi's brain," Tithian had explained. "Over the next six months, he'll go blind, forget how to talk, start drooling, and do other things too unpleasant to discuss. Eventually, he'll turn into an idiot, and sometime after that a moth will claw its way out of one of his eyes."

Tithian had paused for a few moments to let Rikus

study the unconscious youth, then had fetched a small jar containing an identical caterpillar from his cassock pocket. "Don't make me angry again."

The high templar had released the slave and left without another word. Today Grakidi was already lame and blind in one eye. He could not speak so much as his own name, and sometimes he lost his way as he went from cellhouse to cellhouse emptying slopbuckets. Still, there was always a grin on his face and he seemed happy in the typical way of idiots. Rikus could hardly bear to look at him, however, for the mul could not help feeling responsible for the slave's condition. He had made up his mind to kill Grakidi as soon as the opportunity presented itself.

Finally responding to the mul's threat against his guards, Boaz glared at Rikus. "I pay these men, so they can laugh at my jokes if they want," he said. "Don't threaten them, slave."

"Would you rather I just killed them?" Rikus asked.

Boaz's bloodshot eyes narrowed. "I should have known better than to reason with a stupid mul," he said, turning his angry gaze away from Rikus and toward the four slaves standing atop the wall nearby. "One of your friends will pay for your disrespect. Who shall I have flogged? Neeva?"

The trainer pointed at Rikus's fighting partner, a blond woman of full human blood, who stared at Boaz with deep, emerald eyes. Her cape hung open in the front, revealing a husky physique almost as knotted with muscles as that of Rikus. With a pair of full red lips, a prominent, firm chin, and pale, smooth skin, she looked both divine and deadly.

Rikus had reason to be glad that her appearances were not deceiving. He and Neeva were a matched pair, which meant that in addition to sleeping together, they fought in games against similar fighting teams. In fact, the contest in which he hoped to win his freedom was a matched game.

When the mul's only response to Boaz's query was a menacing glower, the trainer shrugged. "How about Yarig and Anezka? They're small, so we'll have to whip both of them," he said, pointing at another of Tithian's matched pairs.

Yarig, the male, scowled at the trainer indignantly. Like all dwarves, he stood around four feet tall and was completely bald from head to heel. His features were square and angular, with the distinctive dwarven crest of thickened skull crowning his bald head. Yarig's stocky body was even more muscular and sculpted than Rikus's. The mul had often thought that his friend resembled a boulder more than a man.

"You're not being fair, Boaz," Yarig said firmly. "Size makes no difference."

"I'm not interested in being fair," Boaz snapped, barely granting the dwarf a sidelong glance.

Yarig would not be dismissed lightly. "Size makes no difference to flogging," he insisted. As was typical for a dwarf, he was so caught up in trivial details that he was oblivious to larger issues. "When you're flogged, it hurts just as much no matter how tall you are."

Anezka stepped to her partner's side and tried to drag the dwarf away, frowning at Rikus all the while. She had been lashed as punishment for the mul's defiance once before, and she made no effort to hide her resentment of him. Standing no more than three-and-a-half feet high, she was a halfling female from the other side of the Ringing Mountains. She looked like a scrawny child, save that her figure and face were those of a mature woman. Her hair grew from her head in a tangled bush that had never been brushed, and her cunning brown eyes had a deranged look to them. Her tongue had been cut out before she'd become a slave, so no one had ever been able to determine whether she was truly unbalanced, or just seemed that way. Most didn't debate the question for long, especially since Anezka liked to eat her meat while it was still alive.

Yarig pulled away from the halfling and stubbornly stepped toward Boaz. "You should only flog one of us."

Two of the trainer's guards leveled their spears at Yarig's chest, preventing even the single-minded dwarf from advancing farther. "Boaz isn't going to flog either one of you," Rikus noted.

"Then who will it be?" Boaz asked, his lips spreading into a cruel smile. "If not your pit-mates or your fighting partner, then perhaps your lover?"

Rikus groaned inwardly. He did not hide his dalliances from Neeva, but open discussion of his romantic liaisons never failed to upset her. At the moment, the last thing he needed was an angry fighting partner.

Boaz pointed at the last slave on the deck, a voluptuous scullery wench named Sadira. He motioned for her to come to him. Like the trainer, Sadira was a half-elf, with peaked eyebrows and pale eyes, but there the resemblance ended. Where the trainer's features were sharp and raw, the young woman's were slender and winsome. Her eyes were as clear and unclouded as a tourmaline, and her long, amber hair tumbled over her shoulders in waves.

The wench wore a hemp smock with a wide neckline that hung off both shoulders, and a ragged hem that barely reached the middle of her slender thighs. The smock was the same as those worn by the all the slave girls of the compound, but on Sadira the simple shift seemed as provocative as any noblewoman's most revealing dress.

When the scullery slave reached Boaz's side, the trainer laid a pasty hand on her bare shoulder. Sadira cringed as the trainer ran his lecherous fingers over her smooth skin, but did not dare object to his touch. "It will be a pity to blemish such beauty with flogging scars, but if that's what you want, Rikus—"

"It's not what I want and you know it," Rikus said, stopping short of making another threat. "If you're going to flog someone, flog me. I won't resist."

Smirking at Rikus's submission, Boaz shook his head. "That won't do at all. You're much too accustomed to physical pain," he said. "If we are to teach you anything, your lesson must be of a different kind. So, which one of your friends will pay for your defiance?"

A tense silence followed. "There's no need to hurry your decision," Boaz said, pointing toward the center of the fighting pit. "You can choose after you fight the gaj."

Deciding the trainer's concession would at least give him thinking time, Rikus faced the center of the pit. The gaj waved its antennae in the mul's direction, then opened its mandibles and tossed Sizzkus's body aside with a flick of its head. When the nikaal landed twenty yards away, Rikus made a mental note not to put himself in a position where the beast would be able to throw him around the same way.

"I'll take your cloak," offered Sadira, kneeling at the edge of the wall. "You wouldn't want it torn if the fight moves over here."

Rikus picked up the robe from the ground and tossed it to the slave-girl. "My thanks."

Catching the cloak, Sadira whispered, "Rikus, I don't like the way Boaz is smirking."

The mul smiled, revealing a set of white teeth. "Don't

worry about him. I'll tear him apart before I let him lash you."

Sadira raised her peaked eyebrows in alarm. "No!" she hissed. "That's not what I meant. I can take a flogging if I have to. I only want you to be careful."

The beguiling half-elf's reaction surprised Rikus, for he had thought she would be terrified of being disfigured. Before he could comment on her bravery, however, Neeva stepped to the half-elf's side. Taking Sadira by the arm and roughly pulling her to her feet, Neeva said, "Tell me what weapon you want, Rikus. Our friend is clacking its pincers."

"No blades or points," Boaz interjected, eyeing Rikus. "The gaj is a special surprise for the ziggurat games. Tithian will sell you into the brickyards if you kill it."

He glanced over his shoulder at the gaj. The strange beast's mandibles stopped clacking and remained open. After studying his opponent for several moments, the mul turned back to his trainer. "Are you a betting man, Boaz?"

"Perhaps."

Rikus gave the trainer his most provoking smile and pointed at the gaj. "I'll fight with nothing but my singing sticks. If I win, you flog me instead of someone else. If I lose, you lash us all."

"Those pincers will clip your sticks like straw!" Neeva objected.

Rikus ignored her and kept his attention fixed on Boaz. "Do we have a bet?" When the cruel trainer smiled and nodded, the mul looked to his fighting partner. "Get my sticks."

Neeva refused to move. "They're too light for that thing," she said. "I'm not helping you get yourself killed."

"I'm sure Rikus knows what he's doing," Sadira said, moving away from the edge of the pit. "I'll get the singing sticks."

Neeva started to follow, but Boaz signaled to his guards and they stopped her with the tips of their spears. A few moments later, Sadira returned with a pair of vermilion sticks about an inch in diameter and two-and-a-half feet long. Made from a fibrous wood that contracted instead of breaking, the sticks were extremely light and relied upon speed rather than mass to generate striking power. They had been carefully carved so that the ends were slightly larger around than the centers, and a special oil made them easy to grip.

Sadira dropped the weapons, and Rikus caught one in each hand. The gladiator turned to face the gaj, simultaneously twirling the sticks in a figure-eight pattern. As the weapons sliced through the air, they emitted the distinctive whistle that gave them their name. Although Rikus seldom used singing sticks in contests to the death, they were his favorite sparring weapon, for their effectiveness depended upon skill and timing rather than strength and brute force.

Deciding that his best attack was against the beast's head, Rikus started forward, his sticks trilling as he absent-mindedly traced a variety of defensive patterns in the air.

The gaj waited, motionless, its eyes blank and unresponsive.

"Can that thing see me?" Rikus asked.

The only response was an amused chuckle from Boaz.

The gladiator stopped his advance a few yards from the gaj's head. A sweet, musky odor hung in the air, masking the stench of the entrails that still dangled from the barbs of the creature's mandibles.

Rikus took another step forward, waving his sticks in front of the gaj's eyes. It did not react, so he feinted a strike to its head. When there was still no response, he slipped to one side of its wicked mandibles. Holding one stick ready to parry an attack, he flicked the end of the other at one of the red, multi-faceted eyes, striking it with a light tap.

The gaj jerked its head to one side, smashing the outer edge of its mandible into Rikus's hip and sending him staggering backward. The mul paused and frowned at the beast, trying to figure out what made it so special in Tithian's eyes. There was no doubt that the creature was powerful, but he was far from impressed so far. Had he been carrying a bladed or pointed weapon, the gaj would have been dead when he made his first feint.

"Something's wrong with it," Rikus called over his shoulder. "The hunters must have blinded it when they captured it."

Boaz erupted into a fit of high-pitched laughter.

Neeva called, "Just hit the damn thing and see what happens!"

Gnashing his teeth at his partner's sharp tone, Rikus turned back to the gaj. Pointedly ignoring the beast's vacant red eyes, he strolled to one side of its head. He gave the white sphere a sharp rap, and the stick landed with a dull throb that felt as though he had struck a mattress filled with straw.

One of the hairy antennae lashed out and wrapped itself around the stick, then wrenched the weapon free of Rikus's hand with an effortless flick. The astonished mul leaped away and somersaulted backward to put more distance between himself and the gaj. As he sprang back to his feet, the guards and Boaz roared with glee. The mul frowned, as angry with himself for allowing the gaj to surprise him as he was with the guards for laughing at his carelessness.

The gaj did not move, although it was using its bristly antenna to swing Rikus's stick through the air. After a moment of watching the creature, Rikus realized that it was performing an awkward imitation of a defensive figure-eight pattern—the same pattern he had traced through the air after Sadira tossed him the weapons.

Immediately the mul realized two important things about his opponent. First, it seemed the antennae atop its head were more akin to tentacles, for he had never before seen an animal use an antenna as a grasping organ. Second, the gaj was a lot smarter and more observant than it appeared at first glance. The beast was mimicking a formal fighting pattern, and he doubted that it was mere chance.

Rikus turned, growling, "So, you want to do a little stick fighting?"

He began whirling his remaining stick in a series of randomly changing patterns, then advanced on the gaj behind the blurred, whistling shield he was creating with his weapon.

As the gladiator stepped within striking range, the front side of the gaj's shell rose two feet off the ground. Rikus glimpsed a pulpy white body and a tangle of knobby-jointed legs. Suddenly the beast withdrew its head beneath the shell, taking the singing stick along with it. The shell dropped back to the ground. The gaj's barbed mandibles, all that remained visible of the head, clacked once and reopened menacingly.

"Now what, Rikus?" cried a guard.

"Crawl under there and fight it!" suggested another.

His face reddening with embarrassment, Rikus looked over his shoulder. Only Neeva's face remained serious.

Even Sadira was grinning at his predicament.

"This thing doesn't want to fight," he called. "Why don't three or four of you come down here instead?"

His challenge brought a fresh round of chuckles from the spectators, but none of them volunteered.

Rikus placed his stick between his teeth and circled around to the gaj's side, where its pincers would not be able to seize him. He squatted down next to the shell and grabbed the underside of the lip, then heaved with all his might.

The carapace rose from the ground, and something clattered inside. Rikus heaved harder, pushing it higher. Six canelike legs shot out and planted themselves firmly in the sand, three to a side. The shiny black limbs were about as thick as Rikus's forearm, divided into five segments by a series of knotted joints. Each limb ended in two-pronged claws that now clutched at the sand in a futile effort to hold the shell down.

With the singing stick still clenched in his teeth, Rikus shifted his grip and lowered his body again so that he could push the shell the rest of the way over. This time, it required more effort to raise the beast. On the opposite side of its body, the gaj had extended its legs well beyond its shell and was using them to counter its attacker's efforts. Nonetheless, Rikus was slowly lifting one side. Even a creature like the gaj was no match for the dense muscles of a mul.

The carapace rose higher, and the legs closest to Rikus left the ground. The mul saw that, beneath the shell, the gaj's body was divided into three white sections: the head, a narrow midsection from which sprang all six legs, and a bloated, heart-shaped abdomen. At the end of the abdomen was a ring of red-tinged muscle.

As Rikus pushed the shell perilously close to tipping,

the gaj curled its abdomen forward so that the ring of muscle pointed toward its attacker. The muscles tightened and opened a hole the size of the mul's thumb. There was a loud hiss, and a puff of gas brushed the gladiator's face.

Rikus immediately spat the fighting stick from between his clenched teeth, letting it fall to the sand as he dropped the gaj. He spun away and ran several steps before he dropped to his knees and retched. His throat was filled with such a burning stench that he could hardly stand to breathe, and his skin tingled beneath a moist, foul-smelling substance.

"Think the creature is helpless, Rikus?" asked Boaz, smirking at the stricken gladiator.

Rikus tried to respond, but all he could manage was to gasp a few breaths of fresh air. He grabbed a handful of sand and rubbed it over his face, trying to scour the stinking mist from his cheeks.

"Rikus, you're sick!" called Yarig. "You need help!"

"No!" Rikus yelled, managing to bellow the strained reply. If the mul was to win his bet with Boaz and save his friends a lashing, he could not have the dwarf rushing to his rescue.

Hoping to stop Yarig from rushing to his aid, the mul rose to his feet. To his surprise, he stumbled and nearly fell again. He still felt nauseous, and his head was spinning as though he had just downed a gallon of wine. The thing had poisoned him!

Through his blurred vision, Rikus saw that his efforts had only added to the dwarf's determination. Yarig stepped toward the rope that dangled into the fighting pit. "I'm coming, Rikus!"

"Stay where you are, Yarig!" ordered Boaz. "I'll decide when Rikus leaves the ring."

Of course, Yarig showed no sign of obeying, but through the haze, Rikus saw Neeva intercept him. Though she was no match for the dwarf's strength, the woman managed to detain him long enough for a pair of guards to present their speartips to his throat. The dwarf reluctantly stopped moving.

Rikus's vision was just clearing when both of his fighting sticks sailed over his head and clattered against the rock wall. The mul spun around to face the gaj, his head reeling from the quick motion.

The creature had climbed out of its shallow burrow. Now, standing on all six legs, the crest of its shell was slightly higher than Rikus's head. It was clacking its mandibles and flourishing the hairy tentacles atop its head, and three of its red eyes seemed fixed on the gladiator.

Without taking his eyes off the gaj, Rikus stumbled back toward the wall to retrieve his sticks. On the deck above, the guards and Boaz were talking quietly, but Neeva and the other slaves remained silent.

The gaj scuttled forward, its great pincers opened wide. Not wishing to be trapped against the wall, Rikus moved out to meet his opponent, his sticks whistling through the air as if they were whips. The gaj mirrored his approach, whirling its head stalks in small circles as if they were ropes.

Rikus gave a battle yell and ran forward at the best pace his shaky legs would carry him. He lifted a stick to strike, shifting the other into a middle defense. In the same instant, the gaj's body sank nearly a foot as it gathered its legs beneath itself.

Realizing that it was about to surprise him again, Rikus immediately kicked his feet out from beneath himself. He landed flat on his back with a hard thump. In the same instant, the gaj sprang. The thing's huge body descended on him, its barbed mandibles clasping where he had stood just a moment before.

Holding his sticks like daggers, he jabbed at the underside of the creature's soft thorax. The ends of the sticks sank several inches into the soft tissue. Rikus had no way of telling whether he had injured the gaj, or even whether it had felt the blows.

The gaj lifted the back of its shell, and the gladiator saw the tip of its abdomen curling toward him. Rikus kicked at it with all his might and held his breath. A hiss sounded near his feet. The mul withdrew his sticks and jabbed at the gaj's thorax three more times, then rolled, beating his way through a tangle of slashing legs to pass from beneath the carapace.

As the crimson rays of the sun touched his face and he dared to breathe again, Rikus glimpsed Sadira and the other slaves standing at the edge of the wall, just above the rope that dangled into the pit. The guards who surrounded them seemed more interested in what was happening in the arena than watching the slaves.

The mul scrambled to his feet. "I'm fine!" he called, stumbling backward as he used his sticks to parry a rapid series of wild slashes from a pair of black, jointed legs.

The gaj spun around to face the gladiator with its mandibles. As Rikus feigned a charge, its pincers again closed on empty air. The mul leaped past. He brought his sticks down on the pulpy mass of its head in a rapid cadence of lightning-quick strokes, snapping his wrist as he struck, to add velocity to the blow.

The gaj struck him with its hairy tentacles. Bands of searing agony shot through the gladiator's arms and chest. His entire body seemed to be burning from the inside out, and Rikus feared that he was about to burst into a ball of flame. The mul screamed.

He tried to leap away. His sluggish legs wobbled. Blazing pain seized his shoulders and torso. Rikus ignored the torment, forcing his body to perform his will. It half-obeyed, and the mul felt himself toppling over backward. Letting out a great bellow, Rikus called upon his legs to catch him. They felt as though they were made of stone, but they obeyed and caught him before he fell.

The gaj retracted its head, opening its pincers. Rikus stepped backward and lifted his lethargic arms. The gaj's head shot out from beneath its shell and the mandibles closed around the mul's midsection. He felt four sharp blows as its barbs sank into his abdomen.

Rikus did not attempt to twist free. Even in the terrible pain he was suffering, he realized the futility of struggling against the pincers. Instead, gripping his weapons as if they were a pair of dirks, Rikus jabbed at the closest pair of eyes. As the sticks struck home, the red facets of the compound eyes collapsed inward. A shudder ran the length of the gaj's body.

It gripped Rikus more tightly.

Neeva appeared at the mul's side, a guard's spear in her hands. She jabbed the point at the gaj's head. Rikus dimly heard Boaz screaming at her. As Neeva's weapon descended, the creature intercepted the shaft with a bristly tentacle, then jerked the spear from her hands and flung it across the sand pit.

Yarig appeared on the other side, followed closely by Anezka, who Rikus suspected had entered the fray only to support her partner. The dwarf swung the heft of his weapon at the beast's head as if it were a cudgel. The halfling thrust her spear's point beneath the gaj's mandibles, striking for the underside of the head.

When their attacks landed, Anezka's spear sank well

past the obsidian point. The gaj countered by using Rikus like a mace, whipping him from side-to-side and battering the would-be rescuers with the mul's massive body. The other three gladiators went sprawling.

Rikus glimpsed Sadira sneaking up on the beast's flank, armed with nothing more than a handful of sand. "Get out of here!" he cried, astonished that the slave-girl would risk her life to save him.

He was being shaken so violently that his words were garbled beyond all recognition. Rikus stabbed once more at the gaj's injured eyes. This time, two of the beast's antennae intercepted his blows. The hairy stems wrapped themselves around his wrists. Waves of pain shot up both arms, and the gladiator's muscles contracted so tightly that he feared his bones would be crushed. He screamed and tried to yank the tentacles from their roots, but found his arms could no longer obey him.

The third tentacle slapped him in the side of the head, encircling his brow. His mind exploded in sheer white agony. Rikus could see nothing, hear nothing. He felt his chest contracting and expanding as he screamed, but that was all.

Inside his head, a swarm of thumb-sized beetles appeared out of the chalk-colored emptiness that now isolated him. All of the beetles looked like the gaj. Slowly they scuttled through the air to the surface of his mind and began to eat away at it, leaving behind wispy tendrils of pain as they crawled over its rippled terrain. Gradually they created a net of blistering torment that enveloped Rikus's mind completely.

The net began to draw inexorably tighter, and the mul's panic, his memory, and even his will to fight began to fade. Soon he could feel nothing but the horrid fire of his agony, smell nothing but the bitter odor of his own fear, and taste nothing but the dry ash of his thoughts slipping away.

Finally, even those bitter sensations faded. The mul was left with nothing but the long fall to oblivion.

TWO

The Sorceress

Rikus stopped screaming.

The mul's fighting sticks tumbled from his thick-fingered hands. His shoulders slumped, his knotted knees buckled, and his dark eyes rolled back in their sockets until only the whites showed. The gaj raised its black pincers, displaying the gladiator's limp body as if it were a trophy. One hairy tentacle remained wrapped around Rikus's brow, holding his head upright, and the others still clasped his wrists.

Sadira stopped a dozen yards from the gaj's side. She had to fight to keep from gagging as she smelled the last whiffs of a fetid vapor. The mul's body hung limply in the beast's black pincers, with blood from the barb punctures streaming down his legs and dripping from his toes.

To the left of the gaj, Neeva returned to her feet, clearing her head with a violent shake. On the other side of the beast, Yarig had already stood and was lifting his spear in preparation for a charge. Anezka, whose spear remained lodged in the beast's head, was standing farther away than Sadira, studying the creature with a look of confused

33

anger.

On the wall surrounding the pit, Boaz screamed, "Let the spineless mul die!"

Though it would mean a severe punishment later, none of the slaves obeyed the trainer. When the gaj had lashed the mul with its bristly tentacles, the unfamiliar sound of Rikus screaming and the sight of his retreat had left no doubt that he was in trouble. Yarig had slapped aside the spears pointed at his throat, then slid down the rope to help his friend. Out of loyalty to her dwarven partner, Anezka had followed almost immediately. In the same instant, Neeva had plucked the spears from the hands of a trio of guards and dropped down into the sand, not even bothering with the rope.

To everyone's astonishment except her own, Sadira had slipped past the confused guards and followed the gladiators into the pit. No doubt Boaz and all the others believed she had lost her coquettish head and rushed into the pit out of panic, but that was not the case. Sadira had entered the arena so she would be close enough to cast a spell if there appeared to be no other way to save Rikus.

It now seemed as if the mul would be torn into pieces by the time the other gladiators freed him from the gaj's pincers. If the mul was to be saved, Sadira would have to use her magic—an act that would almost certainly place her own life in peril. In Tyr, as in other Athasian cities, only the king and his templars were permitted to use sorcery. Those who defied this law were put to death.

More importantly, anyone who understood the basics of spellcasting would know that Sadira had not attained such powers on her own. Tithian, her owner and the man who would likely interrogate her, would deduce that she was connected to the Veiled Alliance, the secret society of sorcerers dedicated to overthrowing the king. Doubtless he would want to know why the Alliance had recruited an agent in his pits. If he caught her alive, he would try to force the answer from her through a long and agonizing torture.

Even with all these considerations, Sadira had no choice but to use her magic. Rikus did not know it yet, but the Veiled Alliance had plans for him at the ziggurat games. Too much depended on those plans to let the gladiator die.

Preparing to cast her spell, Sadira took a deep breath and looked for some indication that the fighters were at last gaining the upper hand against their nemesis. She did not find it. The gaj was keeping both Yarig and Neeva at bay by using Rikus's body like a massive hammer, and Anezka seemed at a complete loss without her spear.

"Neeva, Yarig, cover your eyes!" Sadira yelled.

Neeva frowned. "What?"

"Just trust me," Sadira said sharply. "It's for Rikus."

Without waiting for a reply, the half-elf leveled her palm toward the ground and spread her fingers. Shutting out all other thoughts, she focused her mind on her hand, summoning the energy she needed for her magic. The air beneath her palm began to shimmer, then a barely visible surge of power passed through the air, entered her hand, and moved through her arm.

To the untrained eye, it might have appeared Sadira was extracting her magic from the ground, but that was not the case. While it was true that she drew the power for her magic from the life force of Athas itself, like all sorcerers she could only tap this mystic power through plants. The energy flowing into her body came to her from the smoketrees, needlebushes, and hornbushes surrounding Tithian's slave compound. The ground was only a medium for transferring it.

When Sadira had gathered enough power for her spell, she closed her hand and cut off the flow of energy. If she took too much power too rapidly, the plants from which she was drawing the life force would die and the ground holding their roots would become sterile and barren. Unfortunately, few sorcerers were so careful with their powers, and it was their carelessness that had reduced Athas to a wasteland.

Now that Sadira had gathered enough mystic energy, she uttered the incantation that would give shape and direction to her magic, then threw a handful of sand at her target. A flashing cone of scarlet and gold spouted from her fingers and shot toward the gaj's head in a sparkling beam of radiance. As it reached the beast, the stream broke into a froth of emerald bubbles, each of which burst into a spray of red or blue or yellow or any of a hundred other vibrant colors. Even to Sadira, who knew what to expect, the display was dazzling. The brilliance of all the clashing colors set her mind to reeling, and only the fact that she had known what the spell would do saved her from being stunned by the resplendent spectacle.

The gaj's tentacles became flaccid, releasing Rikus's head and wrists. Its red eyes faded to dull maroon. Then it retracted its sticklike legs, and its scaly shell sank to the ground. Unfortunately the pincers remained closed, Rikus's limp body locked in the powerful mandibles. Where the gaj's antennae had held him, red welts covered the gladiator's skin.

Both Neeva and Yarig looked from Sadira to the motionless beast. "What happened?" asked the husky dwarf.

"It's stunned," Sadira replied, stepping toward the thing's mandibles. "I cast a spell on it."

The jaws of both gladiators fell slack. "That will mean your death!" Neeva uttered. "You'd do that for Rikus?"

"I already have," Sadira replied.

On top of the wall, Boaz screamed, "What happened to the gaj? Lord Tithian will have your head!"

The scullery slave ignored him and tugged at a mandible. It did not open. "We've got to get Rikus free," she said. "The gaj will recover soon."

Neeva stepped to Sadira's side and inserted a spear between the mandibles. "Rikus never told me you were a sorceress."

"I try not to tell all my secrets," Sadira answered.

Neeva braced her foot against a mandible and pried with her spear. As the pincers slowly opened, Yarig laid aside his own weapon and started to pull Rikus free. The barbs, still piercing the mul's abdomen, tore at the gladiator's stomach.

"Wait!" Sadira said, laying one of her soft hands on the dwarf's arm. "Neeva must open those pincers farther."

"Can't," came the strained reply.

"What are you doing to the gaj?" Boaz demanded from the wall. "Stop! Don't hurt it any worse."

The guards shuffled toward the rope and started repeating their superior's command to leave the gaj alone, but they did not move to enforce the order. Their hesitation did not surprise Sadira. Their fighting skills could not compare to those of the gladiators, and none of them was anxious to take the initiative in using force against the slaves.

Yarig retrieved his spear and placed it between the pincers, next to Neeva's weapon. As the dwarf lent his ample strength to the effort, the mandibles opened another two feet. The barbs came out of Rikus's stomach and blood poured from the wounds.

Sadira grabbed the big gladiator's shoulders and pulled, but the mul was far too heavy for her.

"Anezka, help me!"

The halfling slowly stepped to her side and took one of Rikus's arms. The two women pulled him from the pincers.

When the unconscious mul was free, Neeva and Yarig abandoned their weapons and allowed the pincers to close. Each grabbed one of Rikus's arms, then dragged him toward the edge of the fighting pit. Sadira and Anezka followed a step behind, both glancing over their shoulders at the stunned beast, checking for signs of movement.

By the time they reached the wall, the gaj's tentacles were beginning to twitch. Yarig grabbed the rope and climbed up, only to find Boaz waiting for him at the top. "I should leave you down there for the gaj," the trainer hissed.

"We'd have to kill it," Yarig replied simply, hesitating at the top of the rope. "Should I go back down?"

Boaz regarded the obstinate dwarf for a moment, annoyed at his own uncertainty. Finally the trainer stepped aside. "No. I'll think of a more fitting punishment for your disobedience later."

As Yarig scrambled out of the pit, Neeva picked Rikus up and lifted him as high as she could. Yarig turned and lowered himself onto his belly, then reached down for the unconscious mul. The dwarf's arms were too short to bridge the gap, but Anezka took care of the problem by scrambling halfway up the rope and passing Rikus's heavy arms to her partner.

"Got him!" Yarig said, struggling to pull the mul toward the deck, with Neeva pushing from below.

Behind Sadira, in the center of the pit, the gaj clacked

its pincers loudly, snapping the abandoned spears with a series of sharp cracks.

Neeva gave a loud grunt, then heaved Rikus up over her head. Yarig seized the opportunity to gather his feet beneath him, then pulled the bulky mul to safety. Immediately, Anezka scrambled the rest of the way up the rope. Sadira dared to look over her shoulder. The gaj had risen to its feet and was pointing its hairy tentacles in the group's direction.

"We've got to hurry," Sadira called. "It's awake!"

No sooner had she spoken than a pair of strong hands seized her by the waist. Before the half-elf realized what was happening, Neeva had passed her to Yarig, who effortlessly hoisted her to safety.

When Yarig set her atop the wall, Sadira spun around. The gaj was scuttling across the sandy floor of the fighting pit and was already halfway to the wall. Neeva leaped up and grabbed the rope, but Sadira doubted that the woman would reach the top before the creature caught her.

Since she had likely exposed herself as a sorceress earlier, Sadira decided she would do no additional harm by using her magic to save Rikus's partner. She pointed toward the gaj and began to recite an incantation, preparing to shoot a bolt of magical energy into the beast's head.

Just before she could cast the spell, Boaz shouted, "Stop her!"

The shaft of a guard's spear came crashing down across Sadira's forearm, misdirecting her attack. A burst of golden energy flashed from her fingertips and blasted into the pit, striking well to the gaj's left. A geyser of sand sprayed thirty feet into the air.

The gaj ignored the blast and continued its charge, loudly clacking its mandibles and angrily waving its antennae. One of Neeva's hands crested the wall, and Yarig grabbed her arm.

As the gaj reached the edge of the pit, it lifted the front end of its shell and began scraping at the base of the stones in a futile attempt to follow. The creature's head lay only a few feet below Neeva's ankles. Her other hand crested the wall, and she started to pull herself free of the pit.

One of the gaj's tentacles lashed out and entwined Neeva's bare calf. The woman cried out in pain and surprise. Her fingers slipped from the wall, but Yarig caught her arm and held it fast. Neeva regained her grip with the other hand. Still screaming in pain, she fought to drag herself up the wall.

The creature's bristly antenna remained about her calf. Neeva jerked her leg upward, twisting savagely. With a loud pop, the stalk separated from the gaj's head. The beast emitted a piercing screech, then scrambled away. A few yards from the wall, it retracted its legs and head, and quickly lowered its shell to the sand.

"Get it off!" Neeva shrieked, violently thrashing about. She tried to reach the tentacle around her leg, but the intense pain caused her arms and legs to jerk with agonizing spasms.

Sadira reached out to help, but found herself facing the sharp point of a guard's spear. "Don't even move," the man threatened.

Ignoring the guard's threat to the scullery slave, Yarig tried to assist Neeva, but Boaz stepped between him and the screaming woman. "I did not give you leave to help her," he said.

The dwarf sneered and tried to sidestep the trainer. A guard lunged forward, pressing his speartip against Yarig's ribs.

As Neeva continued to flail and scream, Boaz looked to the guards surrounding Rikus, who still lay prone on the deck. "Is the mul dead?"

One of the guards shook his head. "He's breathing, but that's about all."

"Then see if you can keep him alive," Boaz ordered. "We can't have our champion dying in his sleep. Lord Tithian would not find that to his liking."

The guard nodded, then bandaged the mul's wounds. Only a few feet away, Neeva continued to cry out in pain. No one assisted her.

Boaz looked to Sadira next. "What are we to do with you, my bewitching little wench? As I'm sure you're aware, the penalty for spellcasting is death."

The scullery slave met the trainer's gaze steadily, though her heart was pounding with fear. "Lord Tithian certainly will want to question me before I'm killed," she said. Feigning confidence, she forced her voluptuous lips into a smile. "But I can see how that might make you uncomfortable. After all, Lord Tithian would not be happy to hear that you sent his prize gladiator to fight the gaj with only a pair of singing sticks."

"So I should just forget what I saw?" Boaz asked, meeting Sadira's smile with a cynical grin.

"That would be in your best interest," she replied, careful to maintain an even tone.

"I have nothing to fear from Tithian," Boaz said. "To him, the mul is just another slave."

As the trainer studied her, Sadira looked for any sign of the doubt she hoped Boaz was feeling. Only the depth of his concentration gave her cause to think she had succeeded. Regardless of what the trainer claimed, Tithian would indeed be upset if he learned how Rikus had been injured. Boaz could be certain that the story would surface if he turned Sadira over to their master for interrogation.

"Perhaps I should kill you now," Boaz threatened. "I could always throw you to the gaj."

"That's your choice," Sadira answered bravely. "But Lord Tithian would be cheated of his opportunity to question me. Eventually he would learn of the magic I used today. Even if your guards keep silent, I'm sure these gladiators will tell him. Or would you kill all of them, too?"

As the trainer considered his next response, Neeva finally ripped the gaj's antenna from her leg and flung it into the pit. Her anguished cries quieted to a moan. The sudden calm seemed to inspire Boaz.

The half-elf gave Sadira a tight-lipped smile. "I'll consider your advice." He looked from the slave girl to the guard beside her, who was now holding the spear at her throat. "Lock her in the Break."

Sadira cringed. The Break was an old storage house with dozens of small silos built into the ground. It was Boaz's favorite punishment. She was not sure what horrors the Break contained, but there were many, many rumors. The one thing Sadira knew for certain was that no slave survived imprisonment in the Break beyond five days.

The guard took the young woman by the arm. As he led her away, the half-elf cast a final look at Rikus. Now two guards attended him. They had ripped the mul's robe into strips and wrapped it around his stomach, but blood still seeped from beneath the bandage at an alarming rate. Sadira was glad to see the bleeding, however, for it was the only sign of life in the mul's inert form.

Boaz motioned to the guard holding Sadira. "See that she is bound and gagged."

Sadira's heart sank with this last order. With bound hands and a gagged tongue, she could not use her magic. It would be impossible to make the gestures or utter the incantations of the spells she would need to make her escape.

The guard nodded, then leveled his spear at Sadira's back. "You know where we're going."

Sadira led the way across the deck to a short flight of steps. Directly ahead were a dozen squat buildings. Their walls were constructed from dun-colored bricks made of mud, and animal hides covered their roofs. Between the buildings shuffled a handful of gaunt slaves. They carried buckets of water and food to the cells that housed Tithian's gladiators and, more importantly, to the pens which held the exotic animals his hunters had captured for the ziggurat games.

Beyond the buildings rose the compound wall, a mud-brick barricade twenty feet high, capped by jagged shards of obsidian. At each corner, a high, flat-roofed tower rose above the wall. The towers' roofs were covered with scaly hides.

A pair of guards stood in each of the four towers. They wore no armor, for anyone dressed so heavily would soon faint in the searing heat of an Athasian day, but each guard was armed with a crossbow, a small supply of steel-tipped bolts, and a steel dagger.

The steel weapons, Sadira knew, were more for intimidation than for actual use. On Athas, metal was more precious than water and as scarce as rain. Tyr was unique among Athasian city-states in that it controlled a working iron mine. For their metal, other cities had to rely on hard-bitten bands of salvagers. These hardy groups of fortune-hunters searched out lost armories and treasure vaults in the ancient ruins which were buried everywhere beneath the sands of the desert.

The fact that Tithian entrusted his tower guards with metal weapons was a sign of the high templar's incredible wealth. Even in Tyr, where iron was relatively abundant, a steel crossbow bolt cost more than a healthy farm slave, and the daggers were worth as much as a good gladiator.

Sadira's guard prodded her in the back with his obsidian spearpoint. "Quit stalling."

Resisting the urge to try a spell immediately, the half-elf descended the stairs leading from the arena deck. At the moment, Boaz and the other guards would be quick to react to the slightest hint of trouble, and Sadira knew better than to think she could fight a half-dozen ready guards. She would have to bide her time, then count on stealth to make good her escape.

Sadira walked to the Break, a small building at the far corner of the compound. Here, a guard gagged her with a grimy cloth and bound her hands behind her back with a rope that bit into her skin. She was handed over to a pair of guards in charge of the Break, who pushed her inside. As she descended a flight of stone steps, the dank stench of offal and unbathed humanity washed over her. She almost retched, then nearly choked on the gag that filled her mouth.

Laughing at her plight, the guards took her by the arms and dragged her forward. The rays of the crimson sun permeated the hide roof, lighting the interior with a ruddy glow that made the place seem even more corrupt and sickening.

The stone floor of the hut was covered with heavy rock slabs. The guards led Sadira to the far side of the room, then pushed one of the stone covers aside. A hushed hissing, not unlike the whispering of a soft wind, rose from the silo below. The cell was as black as obsidian, but Sadira could see the scene below as clearly as if it had been lit by a torch. From her elven ancestors, she had inherited infravision, the ability to see ambient heat when no other light source was present.

By the cool blue of the silo's brick walls, Sadira knew that it was a circular hole about two-and-half feet in diameter and ten feet deep. There was just enough room to stand, but not to sit or lie down.

The cell was filled top to bottom with the green gossamer of a silky web. Throughout this web scurried dozens, perhaps hundreds, of pinkish reptiles that created a soft whisper by rubbing their pliant scales against the silk, the walls, and each other. They were about the length of Sadira's fingers, with soft tubular bodies, arrow-shaped heads, small squarish ears, and compound eyes resembling those of an insect. She was not sure whether to think of them as lizards or snakes, for they had tiny legs and feet in front, but none on their hindquarters.

One of the guards grabbed Sadira beneath the armpits and dangled her over the pit. The half-elf groaned in alarm and braced her feet against the edges of the pit. She knew that struggling was futile, but the thought of being lowered into the squirming mass below was repulsive.

Her captor's companion kicked the slave's feet away from the edges of the pit, and the one holding her released his grip. Sadira plummeted through the web, bringing a shower of slimy flesh and sticky strands down about her as she fell. When she hit the bottom, her knees buckled and her shoulder slammed into the brick wall. Sharp bolts of pain shot through her ankles and knees, and her left arm went numb. She found herself wedged into the cramped silo with her buttocks resting on her heels.

Scaly ropes of flesh began to squirm over her bare legs, her shoulders, even down the back of her neck. Sadira let out a muffled scream of disgust and pushed herself into a standing position. The effort sent renewed streams of pain through her ankles and knees.

At the top of the silo, the two guards chuckled and slid the stone slab back into place.

Sadira stood in the cell, alone save for the repulsive creatures that rubbed their hissing scales against her skin and flicked her with their gritty tongues. She could not decide whether they were welcoming her to the colony or taste-testing the web's latest catch. The sorceress consoled herself with the thought that the greatest danger posed by the reptiles was that they would drive her mad. She doubted that Boaz would tolerate the things if they foreshortened the torment of his victims by killing them.

The half-elf wasted little time panicking or bemoaning her fate, for she knew those were the reactions Boaz desired. Having been born into slavery, Sadira had long ago realized that, while her masters could use threats and violence to keep her in physical bondage, they could not control her mind or her emotions unless she let them. As long as she remained strong and refused to accept their right to enslave her, then she was at least spiritually free. Of course, spiritual freedom was a poor substitute for the real kind, but at least it kept hope alive.

The sorceress had seen too many people give up this last scrap of dignity. Sadira's own mother, an amber-haired human named Barakah, had died apologizing to her daughter for the "crimes" she had committed, crimes that had resulted in Sadira being born a slave. The half-elf did not consider her mother's actions to be crimes, however.

From what the half-elf had pieced together, as a young

woman her mother had supported herself in one of the few outlawed occupations in Tyr. King Kalak had declared it illegal to sell or buy magical components. Naturally a thriving trade in chameleon skin, gum arabic, mica dust, adder's stomach, and other hard-to-acquire items had sprung up in the notorious Elven Market. Barakah had made a living as a runner between the Veiled Alliance and the untrustworthy elven smugglers. She had also made the mistake of falling in love with an infamous elven rogue named Faenaeyon.

Shortly after Sadira had been conceived, the templars had raided the dingy shop where Faenaeyon lived and did business. He had escaped and fled into the desert, but the pregnant Barakah had been caught and sold into slavery. Faenaeyon had simply abandoned his lover and her unborn child, making no effort to buy their freedom or help them escape. A few months later, Sadira had been born in Tithian's gladiatorial pits, and that was where she had been raised.

It was not where she intended to die. Sadira allowed the guards a few minutes to leave, then set about trying to escape. The gag was fairly easy to remove. The half-elf simply leaned her head to one side and rubbed her chin against her shoulder several times. The strip around her mouth rolled off her chin and down around her neck, then she spat the wad out of her mouth.

Next, she attempted to free her hands. Had they not been bound behind her, it would have been a simple matter to gnaw at the rope until she bit through it. Before she could do that, she had to work her hands around to her front. She tried to run her bound hands down her back and around her legs, but her arms were too short. She only strained her already throbbing shoulder.

Realizing that the tight quarters would never allow her

to accomplish this first maneuver, she began to working her wrists back and forth behind her. With time, and she suspected she had plenty of that, she might be able to loosen the knot or stretch the hide enough to slip a hand free.

The repetitive action attracted the lizards. Within moments, the slimy reptiles tickled every inch of Sadira's skin from the elbows down. They writhed over her arms with increasing agitation, their scales whispering as loudly as a strong breeze. The half-elf ignored them and continued to work her hands back and forth.

There was a sharp twinge inside Sadira's elbow. When she felt a warm trickle running down her arm, she realized one of the creatures had bitten her. Dozens of raspy little tongues lapped at the blood, then she felt another twinge on the outside of her forearm. Both wounds bled more freely than they should have, and the lizards' excitement mounted, filling the silo with a soft, steady drone. The half-elf began to fear that her efforts to liberate herself were driving the reptiles into a feeding frenzy.

Fighting to ignore her growing revulsion, Sadira continued to work at the hide. She considered using the lizards to her advantage by trying to get them to chew off her bindings. Unfortunately they seemed more interested in licking blood than gnawing hide.

Soon her wrists began to sting where the thongs were cutting into them, and still more warm blood ran down over her hands. The little reptiles swarmed to the fresh food. A few even crawled into the tight crevice between her bound hands. Repulsed, she groaned and pressed her palms together, successfully crushing a pair of the gruesome things. Their bodies burst with a mushy pop, covering her palms with cool slime.

Noting how slick this scum was, Sadira realized that it

would be useful in freeing her hands. Over the next few minutes, she continued to work her burning wrists back and forth. As they bled, she allowed many more lizards to crawl between her hands, and crushed them each in turn. Periodically, she tried to pull a hand free and found the thongs were still too tight. The reptiles continued to nip at her arms and lick the wounds around her bindings. She squashed several against the wall with a forearm. Soon, her hands and arms were soaked with a mixture of her own warm blood and cool lizard entrails.

Sadira tried again to free a hand. This time, her left hand slipped its loop. Her brief cry of joy echoed off the brick walls of the silo, but she doubted it could be heard outside. The half-elf immediately brought her hands around to her front and brushed the lizards off her bloody arms. Lacking anything better, she cleaned her hands as best as she could against her smock. Next she plucked the lizards from her hair. She didn't bother with the creatures swarming over her legs, for they were too numerous and none seemed to be biting.

At last Sadira prepared to cast the first spell of her escape. Instead of pointing her palm downward to summon the force she needed, the sorceress directed it at the wall. Since she was already underground, there was no need to draw the energy from below before calling it toward her.

After she felt the surge of power enter her body, Sadira took a small ball of web from the wall and placed it under her tongue, then uttered an incantation. When the ball of web disappeared from her mouth, she knew her spell had worked and she would be able to climb the walls as easily as the lizards. The half-elf placed the pads of her fingers on the wall and pulled upward. Her body rose off the ground as though it were as light as a strand of silk.

The sorceress quickly climbed to the top of the silo,

causing a distinct hiss each time she moved. Though her knees and shoulders ached terribly from the drop into the cell, her body seemed so light that its weight caused them no undo strain.

At the top of the cramped cell, Sadira paused to pick a few lizards off her legs, then brushed the rest away. Dangling from the wall as easily as if she were standing on a ladder, she summoned the energy for another spell, then took a deep breath and began to jostle the stone slab covering the silo. She was not trying to move it aside. Rather, the sorceress merely hoped to attract the guards' attention and lure them into investigating the sound.

She did not have long to wait. Within a few moments, the slab began to slide open and a sliver of scarlet light appeared over her head. She retreated down the wall a short way, then waited for the door to open completely.

The first thing to appear in the widening crescent of light was the tip of an obsidian spear. Though the light hurt her eyes, she forced herself not to look away. When the dim silhouette of a guard took form at the other end of the spear, Sadira raised the lizards she had plucked off her legs toward him, then uttered her incantation.

She finished with a comment directed at her victim. "Think about this the next time you drop a nice girl down here."

As she released the spell, the squirming lizards in her hand were transformed into writhing tentacles, each ten feet long and as black as the silo from which they came. They shot from Sadira's hand like bolts of ebon-colored lightning straight for the guard's face. He dropped his spear and yelled in surprise, but the black ribbons cut his scream short as they wrapped themselves around his face and neck. He stumbled away, gasping for air and madly tearing at the stalks constricting his neck.

If her Alliance mentor, a cantankerous old man named Ktandeo, had seen her use the spell, he would certainly have disapproved. He had forbidden her to learn or use magic of such potency. That kind of spell required the drawing of energy from a wide radius; if the radius was too small, the foliage tapped by the spell would die. Ktandeo thought the half-elf had not yet mastered her art enough to attempt such feats. Sadira thought differently, so she had secretly copied the spell and several others from his spellbook during her last clandestine visit. At the moment, she was glad she had.

The sorceress scrambled to the top of the wall. A second guard looked over the edge of the silo, a drawn dagger clutched in his hand. There was no time to cast another spell, so Sadira reached up and grabbed him by the collar.

"Come here," she said, jerking as hard as she could on his shirt. "There's something down here you should see."

The surprised guard pitched forward, raising his knife to slash at Sadira's arm. The half-elf quickly released him and pulled her arm out of harm's way, but the man's counterstrike did not save him. He was already leaning so far forward that he could not recover his balance. He cried out in alarm, and his dagger clattered to the floor. The guard himself followed a moment later, slipping headfirst into the darkness, his hands seizing wildly at the bricks in a futile effort to catch himself. An instant later, he hit bottom. The sharp pop and series of quick snaps that sounded from the base of the silo told Sadira that she need not worry about that particular jailer again.

She climbed out of the silo and picked up the first guard's spear. He was still struggling with the magical tentacles that were wrapped around his face. Though he was hardly in a position to stop her from leaving, she stepped to his side and touched the spear to his ribs.

"This is for all the slaves who didn't climb out," she said, pressing harder on the point.

The guard stopped struggling and turned his tentacle-covered head in her direction. "No. Please!" he gasped, barely making himself understood through his constricted throat. "I . . . have . . . children—"

"So did my mother," Sadira answered.

She pressed all her weight against the shaft and drove the point deep into the man's heart. A short cry of pain escaped his lips and his body trembled. An instant later, he fell motionless. Blood began to ooze from the wound.

After removing the guard's dagger and belt, Sadira dragged his body to the silo. She dumped him on top of his partner without bothering to remove the spear from his heart or the tentacles from his head. As she pushed the stone slab over the pit, her thoughts were already turning to the next phase of her escape.

Sadira strapped the guard's belt and dagger onto her narrow waist, then pulled a few stray strands of lizard web from her smock. She formed these strands into a small wad, then plucked a lash from her eyelid and sealed it in the silky ball. Pointing her palm at the ground, she summoned the energy for another enchantment. As she spoke the words of her incantation, the sorceress slowly rolled the wad between her fingers.

The web and the eyelash disappeared. The half-elf lifted her hand and waved it in front of her eyes. Like the rest of her body, it had become invisible.

Sadira wasted no time leaving the Break. She had only a brief time before her spell expired. In that time, the half-elf had to sneak back to her mud-brick cell and collect her spellbook from beneath the loose stone where she kept it hidden. Afterward, she would leave the estate by walking out the gate, passing beneath the noses of the guards charged with keeping her and her fellow slaves in the compound. By the time her magic lapsed, she hoped to be far away from the walls of Lord Tithian's gladiator pits.

Though she wanted to check on Rikus's condition, she knew that such an act held too many dangers, for guards and healers would surely surround him. She would simply have to trust in the mul's natural hardiness and hope that he survived long enough for her to send help from the Veiled Alliance.

THREE

Old Friends

In a remote corner of his estate, Agis of Asticles sat at the edge of the muddy reservoir that provided water for all his parched lands. On the far side of the copper-colored pool, a dozen slaves marched in an endless circle, pushing four wooden crossbars that turned a creaking waterscrew and filled the small pond with bitter well-water. Every fifty turns, two slaves were replaced by a pair who had been resting and drinking in the shade of a nearby pavilion.

Turning the screw was not particularly strenuous for twelve healthy slaves, but the scarlet rays of the sun cut through the afternoon haze like a shaft of flame. This part of the day was an insufferable inferno, a time when men collapsed simply from walking and when heavy exertion killed others. Nevertheless, the water had to keep flowing, so the slaves had to keep turning the screw.

Unlike the slaves, Agis did not have to pass the hottest part of the day beneath the sun's crimson fury. Yet this was where the robust noble spent most afternoons, sitting crosslegged on the barren ground, his long black hair billowing on an occasional puff of wind. Usually, his brown eyes were fixed on the murky waters of his irrigation pond, staring out from beneath his dark brows with an eerie vacancy. Often the only sign that he was alive was the steady flaring of nostrils at the end of his patrician nose. His firm jaw never flinched, his strong and sinuous arms never twitched, and his solid torso did not fidget.

Like all serious students of the Way, Agis found that extremes of physical sensation, such as suffering the agony of full exposure to the midday sun, aided his meditations. It was only when he hovered on the edge of unbearable torment or unimaginable pleasure that his body, his mind, and his spirit became one, that he felt the immense power of a physical form and intellect so flawlessly joined that he could not tell where one ended and the other began. It was then he fully appreciated the great truth of being: that the energy and vitality of the body could not exist without the mind to give it form and reality and the spirit to give it all a higher meaning.

It was this simple principle that lay at the heart of all psionic power. The individual who truly understood it could tap the mystical energies that infused his own being and shape them however he wished, giving him abilities that were as incredible as they were mysterious.

Unfortunately the Way did not yield its gifts easily. It demanded a high price of those who used it, both in devotion and knowledge. For a student of the Way, enlightenment came most often in times of physical extremes, such as during periods of complete exhaustion or terrible distress. Therefore, like most practitioners of the psionic arts, Agis spent several hours a day in considerable discomfort while he contemplated the unity of body, spirit, and mind. Usually, he chose to perform his meditations on the remote shore of his irrigation pond.

On this particular day, his mind's eye was focused hundreds of miles and more than a decade away, on an oft-remembered place—an oasis that he had visited as a young man. In contrast to the muddy reservoir of his estate, the waters of the oasis pond sparkled blue and clear. It was surrounded by the billowing forms of damson-crowned chiffon trees and creaking canes of black-jointed whip grass. Hanging over the forest were the two golden moons of Athas, Ral and Guthay, secluded from the bloody splendor of the rising sun by a clear expanse of olive sky.

Though he was about to set off across two hundred miles of open desert, Agis was traveling light. Across his back was slung a single waterskin, in his hand he carried a wooden walking staff, and at his waist hung a steel sword with a leather-wrapped hilt. He had just learned from a passing caravan driver that his older sister, the heir to the Asticles family name, had been murdered in Tyr.

Let the spirits of the land guide thee, my love.

The speaker was Durwadala, the druid of the grove. She was not speaking, for she had sworn never to interrupt the music of the wind, but rather waving her four arms through an intricate pattern of gestures that served as a language between her and Agis. She stood nearly seven feet tall, with a tough dun-colored carapace that covered her entire body. Her face was narrow and chitinous, with black, multi-faceted eyes. A pair of small mandibles served as her jaws.

You have taught me well, my lady, Agis answered, moving his arms in a graceless imitation of Durwadala's speech. *Always, your words will be in my heart.*

That is a strange place to keep words, Agis, she observed. *Better to hold them in thy head, where they will do thee some good.*

Agis stifled a laugh, for he knew the sound would upset Durwadala. *I will keep them in both my heart and my head,* he promised.

The druid studied Agis for several moments, then touched his face with one of her antennae. *Walk with the wind,* she said, stepping into the forest. Her carapace instantly changed color and pattern to match the black and gold stalks of cane grass. *The trees will remember thee.*

As Durwadala faded into the underbrush, Agis withdrew from his meditation. There was a serene but hollow feeling in the nexus of his being, that point where the mystic energies of the mind, body, and spirit all converged. The noble blinked his stinging eyes, slowly growing aware of his swollen tongue and the dry, bitter taste of thirst. As always, he felt dizzy and weak from the early effects of heat stroke.

"Caro?" Agis called, bringing the murky waters of his small reservoir back into focus. "I'm ready for my water."

He turned to look over his shoulder, expecting to see his dwarven manservant standing nearby. Instead of the old servant's wrinkled face, Agis found a lanky man dressed in the black cassock of a templar. His features were sharp and bony, and his long auburn hair was pulled into a braided tail. There were deep-etched lines in his furrowed brow, and he had thick, puffy lips that made him look as though he were in a constant sulk.

The templar stepped forward, offering Agis the water he had requested. "So, how goes it along the Way, old friend?"

"Tithian?" Agis exclaimed. He blinked twice and shook his head, fearing he had lost himself in meditation and was imagining things. When the high templar's image remained solid, the noble stood and faced him.

"How did you find me here?" Agis demanded. He glanced over Tithian's shoulder, expecting to see a handful of embarrassed guards or at least Caro's flustered face.

Tithian grinned at Agis's surprise. "Don't blame your slaves," he said. "I used my office to find you."

Agis frowned. Not even Tithian should have been able to sneak up on him unannounced. He would speak to Caro about the lapse at the first chance. "How long have I kept you waiting?"

"Too long," Tithian replied, squinting at the pale green haze in the sky. "You must be quite adept at traveling the Way. Your concentration is impressive."

Agis took the water from Tithian's hand. "One can't master the mind without first mastering the body."

The high templar rolled his eyes. "So I remember hearing, over and over again," he said. "For me, the psionic arts are too much work." He reached beneath his robe and withdrew a ceramic carafe of wine. "I took the liberty of having your servants supply me with refreshment," Tithian said. "I hope you don't mind."

"Not at all," Agis answered, studying his guest's face for some hint as to his mission. Though he and Tithian had known each other since their youth, he was not accustomed to receiving the high templar without notice, especially not during his meditations. "Isn't it rather hot to be wandering around the countryside, Tithian?"

Ignoring the question, Tithian drank directly from the carafe, then smacked his lips with satisfaction. "I saw the most impressive display of psionics this morning. The king discovered that Those Who Wear the Veil hid a number of amulets in his ziggurat."

"The Veiled Alliance?" Agis asked. "Were the amulets magical?"

The high templar said crossly, "Yes, magical. I suppose they're intended to slow down work on the ziggurat, though I didn't see them that closely."

"Or at least you wouldn't tell me if you had."

Tithian continued his story without confirming or denying Agis's reply. "King Kalak was most angry with Dorjan over the matter." The templar paused. "He incinerated her from the inside out."

"That's not how the Way should be used," Agis protested.

Tithian smiled. "You tell that to Kalak. I won't."

"I'm just a senator," Agis said, smiling and shaking his head. "It'll have to be you. You're the high templar."

The joke seemed lost on Tithian, who grimaced and replied, "I'm the high templar, as you say. Now I'm not only the High Templar of the Games, but also of the king's works."

Agis frowned, confused by Tithian's unhappiness over what the senator assumed would be regarded as good news. The templars served the king both as bureaucrats and priests. They performed all of Tyr's civic tasks, such as collecting taxes, policing the streets, supervising public works, and commanding the city guard. They also coerced the populace into venerating Kalak as a deific sorcerer-king, by whose good graces the city was allowed to exist. In return for their worship, the king invested the templars with the ability to use a certain amount of his magic and paid them generous salaries, though they were free to supplement their income through bribery and extortion.

"Those are two very powerful positions," Agis said. "I would think you'd be delighted."

Tithian met Agis's gaze with the first hint of fear that the handsome senator ever recalled seeing in his friend's eyes. "I would be . . . if I didn't have to finish the ziggurat in three weeks, in addition to finding the amulets the Veiled Alliance has hidden inside it!"

"Surely with the king's magic at your disposal you'll have no trouble completing the task."

The high templar scowled. "Do you really think it's that easy?" he snapped. "Cast a spell, find an amulet?"

Agis weathered the storm with a calm countenance, for he had known Tithian long enough to realize that the templar's outbursts posed a danger only to those intimidated by them.

"Isn't it?" the noble countered. "I thought that was why people resorted to magic."

"It's harder than it looks," Tithian replied crossly. "Besides, I tried. The amulets are protected by psionic shields and counterspells. I have people trying to break the safeguards, but if they fail, the only way to find the amulets may be to tear the ziggurat down, brick by brick."

"But you said the amulets were just annoyances?"

The high templar seemed about to speak, then let the topic drop.

Since he had no other suggestions to offer, Agis remained silent, trying to puzzle out why Tithian had picked this afternoon to come visiting. If his guest had been any other friend, the noble would have assumed that the visitor had simply come in search of a sympathetic ear. The high templar, however, was a solitary person who never shared his troubles or his joys with his friends. If Tithian was telling him all this, Agis suspected there was a reason.

"If you want me to do something about the amulets, you'll really have to tell me a little more about them," Agis said at last, deciding to press for all the information he could.

"You?" Tithian asked. "What can you do?"

"Isn't that why you're here?" Agis asked. "I assume you've come to discuss asking the Senate to support an initiative against the Veiled Alliance."

The high templar laughed. "What makes you think Kalak cares about the Senate's support?"

Tithian's reply touched a sore nerve. The Senate of Lords was an assembly of noble advisors who were supposed to have the authority to override the king's decrees. In reality, the body was little more than a paper assembly, for senators who opposed the king invariably suffered prompt and mysterious deaths.

"Perhaps the king should start caring about the Senate's support," Agis said, speaking more openly in front of his old friend than he would have to any other templar. "He's nearly taxed the nobles into ruin building his ziggurat, and he still hasn't bothered to tell the Senate why he's erecting it in the first place!"

The high templar looked away and waved his carafe toward the center of Agis's estate. "May we go back to your house? I'm not accustomed to standing about in the sun." Without waiting for an answer, he began walking with a slow, even pace.

Agis followed, continuing to press. "The caravan captains claim the Dragon is coming toward Tyr, and the king is ignoring our pleas to raise an army."

"Don't tell me you accept all that nonsense about the Dragon, Agis?"

The Dragon was the terror of all travelers, a horrid monster of the desert that routinely wiped out whole caravans. Until recently, Agis had believed it was no more than a myth, dismissing tales of the thing devouring whole armies and laying waste to entire cities as fanciful fabrications. He had changed his mind during the last month, however, when sober and trustworthy men had begun to report glimpses of it at ever-decreasing distances from Tyr.

Agis replied, "I think the king would be well advised to take the threat seriously. He should stop wasting his money and manpower on the ziggurat and start preparing for the defence of our estates and his city."

"If he believed in the Dragon, I'm sure he would," Tithian replied.

They crested the gentle hill that hid the reservoir from the rest of Agis's estate. Below them stretched green acres of tall faro, the dwarf cactus-tree grown as a cash crop by many of Tyr's nobles. The faro itself was almost as tall as a man and had a handful of scaly stems that rose to a tangled crown of needle-covered boughs. The fields were crisscrossed at regular intervals by a network of muddy irrigation ditches. In the center of the farm sat the ancestral Asticles mansion, its marble dome echoing the shape of the distant mountains that ringed the Tyr Valley.

"What's your secret, my friend?" Tithian asked, pausing to run an appreciative eye over Agis's lush fields. "It's all that anyone else can do to produce a few hundred bushels of needles a year, but your farm is covered by an orchard."

Agis smiled at the compliment. "There's no secret to it," he said. "I just took a lesson from a druid."

"And what did you learn?" Tithian asked.

"Treat the land well and eat well. Abuse it and starve." Agis pointed at the tawny plain of barren dust and sand lying beyond the borders of his estate. "If everyone followed that simple rule, the rest of the Tyr Valley would be as lush as my farm."

"Perhaps you should come and explain this discovery

of yours to Kalak," Tithian replied, his cynical tone suggesting that he found what Agis told him difficult to believe. "I'm sure he'd be interested in such a marvel."

"I doubt it," the noble replied. "Kalak's only interest in the valley is draining it of every last ounce of magic-giving lifeforce it can provide, regardless of what it does to the land."

"Be careful who you say such things to, my friend," Tithian said. "That comment borders on treason."

Still carrying the ceramic carafe of wine, Tithian started down the narrow path that led toward the estate mansion. As he descended the slope, Agis was surprised by the total absence of slaves in his fields. It was true that he worked them mainly in the relatively cool hours of the morning and evening, but even in the heat of the afternoon there should have been a few men in the fields to watch the irrigation ditches and clear any blockages. He made a mental note to speak to Caro when he returned to the house, then turned his thoughts to what he might learn from Tithian.

"A week ago, Urik's emissary threatened war if we don't start shipping iron again," Agis said, bringing up a point that he knew the templar could not dismiss lightly. "We can't do it because Kalak has taken the slaves out of the mine to work on his ziggurat. How long does the king think he can continue to ignore the city's problems?"

Tithian stopped and faced Agis. They were now surrounded by snarled faro boughs. "How did you find out about the emissary?" the templar asked, clearly shocked.

"If the high templars have spies in the Senate," Agis responded evenly, "it stands to reason that the Senate has spies in the High Bureaus."

The truth of the matter was that the Senate had been trying for years to recruit a spy in the king's bureaucracy, which, whether they liked to admit it or not, was where the real political power lay in Tyr. Unfortunately, they had always failed. Agis was simply trying to confirm a rumor he had heard from a caravan merchant. If he happened to cause a little turmoil among the templars, that was fine.

"How did Kalak respond to Urik's threat?" Agis asked.

To the noble's surprise, Tithian sighed, then dropped his gaze. "He sent the envoy's head back, carried by a merchant caravan."

"What?" Agis shrieked.

Tithian nodded grimly.

"Is he *trying* to start a war?"

The high templar shrugged. "Who knows? All I can say is that he seemed very pleased with himself."

Agis was almost as shocked by Tithian's candor as he was by the news itself. Normally a high templar, especially this one, would be discreet about such things. "Why are you telling me this, Tithian?" the senator asked suspiciously. "What do you want from me?"

Tithian appeared hurt and did not answer immediately. Instead, he took a long drink from his carafe, then studied the contents for several seconds. At last, he looked up. "I suppose I deserve even your suspicion, Agis," he said. "You must know that you're the only man I have ever considered a friend."

"That's very flattering, Tithian," Agis answered carefully, "but we're hardly in the habit of sharing confidences. Forgive me if I seem skeptical."

Tithian gave Agis a smile. "Believe me or not, it makes no difference. There has always been a certain bond of circumstance between you and me. More importantly, you've always treated me with consideration—even when others didn't."

"I don't think the worst of anyone until I've seen it for myself," Agis allowed cautiously. "Still, you must admit, this is the first time since we were boys that we've truly spoken of friendship."

Because their family estates were near to each other, Agis and Tithian had grown up as friends. They had even attended schooling in the Way of the Unseen together, though Tithian had hardly been an enthusiastic student. Unfortunately, his indolence and rebelliousness had made him something of an outcast with the master and other students, but Agis's friendship had not wavered.

Later, Tithian's father had selected a younger brother to lead the Mericles family. Tithian was so furious that he had committed the ultimate class betrayal and joined the ranks of the templars. Agis's friendship had not wavered even when the younger brother had died under mysterious circumstances and everyone had suspected Tithian—unjustly, the senator had believed—of committing the murder to recover control of his family estate.

Though their friendship had never really come to an end, they had drifted apart over the years. Tithian had risen higher and higher in the templar ranks, Agis had inherited his family's estate, and their interests had grown increasingly opposed to each other. In the end, it had simply been easier to let their close fellowship drift to an end than to strain it by trying to ignore their conflicting concerns.

The templar sipped at the wine in his carafe. When he did not respond to Agis's observation after several moments, the noble continued in a careful tone. "What is it that you need from me?"

Tithian's face clouded with anger. For several moments, he stared at Agis with a sneer upon his lips. Finally he hurled the carafe to the ground. It shattered into a dozen pieces on the hard-packed soil of the path.

"I speak in the king's name!" the templar spat. "I have the power to *take* anything I wish from you!"

Glancing at the smashed carafe, Agis calmly raised an eyebrow. "Why is our friendship suddenly so important?"

Tithian ran his soft, bejeweled hands over his face. "With all that's happening," he said, "I just want you to know how I feel."

As if embarrassed by the emotion, the high templar started back toward the house. Agis followed, silently wondering if he had been treating his boyhood friend unjustly.

A few moments later, Tithian stopped in the middle of the trail. With his eyes fixed on the faro alongside the path, he reached for the dagger beneath his cloak. Following the templar's gaze, Agis saw a two-foot slug inching its way up one of the trunks. It was covered with half-a-dozen green scales that served as excellent camouflage, and it had a long snakelike neck that ended in a narrow head with a beak as sharp as a faro thorn.

Agis quickly caught his friend's arm. "There's no need to kill it."

"But it's a fruit varl!" Tithian objected.

"I can afford to lose a few pieces of fruit." Because faro trees blossomed only once a decade, each piece of the sweet fruit was a delicacy worth almost as much as the tree itself.

Shaking his head, Tithian said, "With thinking like that, I don't know how you pay the king's taxes."

"It's because of such thinking that I can," Agis explained. "All things are linked together in a chain of life.

If you destroy one of the links, then the chain is broken."

Tithian scoffed.

"You commented earlier on my orchard," Agis said. "Would you like to know one of the reasons it grows so well?"

The templar raised an eyebrow.

Agis pointed to the scaly slug. "When the varl eats the fruit, it eats the seed. As the seed passes through its system, its stomach fluids eat away the black coating on the outside. Seeds without black coatings sprout twice as often as seeds with coatings."

"How do you know all this?" Tithian asked.

"I spent a week following varls," Agis replied, allowing an embarrassed grin to creep across his lips.

"Most ingenious," the high templar replied. "You can rest assured that your secret will be safe with me."

"Tell anyone you like. It won't affect the price of faro needles," Agis said. "Too many people would rather sell their fruit today than harvest their needles tomorrow."

"That's certainly true," Tithian said. He smiled and returned his dagger to its sheath, then started toward the house again.

Agis followed.

"You didn't get to where you are today without being as intelligent as you are ruthless, Tithian," the noble said diplomatically. "So I'm sure you've already figured out exactly how you're going to meet the king's deadline for completing the ziggurat."

Tithian nodded, lifting his head so he could glance toward Agis's house. "Why yes, I have."

"Still, since you've come as a friend, it doesn't seem out of place to offer a friend's advice," Agis said.

Tithian paused on a small stone slab bridging an irrigation ditch, looking at Agis out of the corner of his eye.

"And what would that be?"

"Treat your slaves as you would your own family," Agis responded. "Feed them well and give them a warm place to sleep. Not only will they be stronger, they'll work harder."

"Out of gratitude?" Tithian smirked. He shook his head, then resumed walking. "If you believe that, then I've picked a fool for a friend."

"Have you tried it?"

"Agis, for your own good, listen to me," Tithian said, speaking over his shoulder without slowing. "No matter how well they're treated, slaves hate their masters. Maybe they don't let it show, and maybe they don't even realize it themselves. But give them the opportunity and they'll massacre us every time—no matter how tame they seem while we're holding the lash."

"If they're murderers, it's because their owners make them that way," Agis objected.

"Yes," Tithian replied, touching a finger to his forehead. "You're beginning to understand."

Agis bristled at the templar's patronizing tone. "My slaves—"

"Would like to be rid of you as much as you'd like to be rid of Kalak. The difference is that *you* might be foolish enough to give your slaves a chance," Tithian said. "You'll have to be more careful during the next few weeks."

"What do you mean by that?" Agis demanded. He was still talking to Tithian's back and resenting it more with each step.

Tithian ran his hand over the top of his head and down his tail of braided hair. "Nothing threatening," he said evasively. "Things are growing difficult in Tyr; you must be on the watch for treachery everywhere. Just this morning, I discovered that one of my own slaves is in the Veiled Alliance."

"No!" Agis exclaimed, unable to stifle a chuckle. The thought of the Alliance operating right beneath a high templar's nose was too much for him to bear in silence.

"Yes, it's quite amusing, isn't it?" Tithian's voice was tinged with acid.

"I'm sorry," Agis said, suddenly understanding Tithian's comments regarding his slaves. "What did you do?"

"Nothing, yet," Tithian replied, crossing the last ditch between the fields and Agis's house. "I haven't been able to go home to attend the matter."

Tithian stepped out of the faro into the house's formal rear garden. The garden was a comfortable space designed to remind Agis of Durwadala's oasis. In the center of the reserve sat a small pool of azure water, bordered by a sandy bank and a few yards of golden whip grass. It was covered by the gauzy white boughs of a dozen chiffon trees.

Although Agis had designed the garden to serve as a sanctuary when in need of a tranquil place to retreat, he felt anything but peaceful as he entered it now. He heard the subdued murmur of hundreds of hushed voices coming from the other side of the mansion.

"What's that?" Agis demanded, stepping to Tithian's side.

The high templar's face remained impassive. "Perhaps it's your happy slaves gathering to welcome you back."

The mocking tone alarmed Agis. "What's happening here?"

Without waiting for Tithian's reply, the noble closed his eyes and focused his mind on his nexus, that space where the three energies of the Way—spiritual, mental, and physical—converged inside his body. He lifted his hand and visualized a rope of tingling fire running from the nexus through his torso and into his arm, opening a pathway for the mystic energies of his being.

Unlike magic, which drew energy from the land and converted it into a spell, the force Agis was about to use came from somewhere other than Athas—though no one knew exactly where. Some practitioners believed they summoned it from another dimension. Others claimed that living beings were infused with unimaginable amounts of energy, and that they were merely tapping into their own resources.

Agis believed he was creating the power. By its very nature, the Way was a cryptic and undefinable art, relying on confidence and faith instead of knowledge and logic. In contrast to the precise incantations and rigid laws of balance governing magic, which caused Agis and many others to think of it as more of a science than an art, the Way was fluid and malleable. With it, one could do almost anything—provided he could create and control the energies required without destroying himself. A practitioner could call upon the Way as often as he wished or summon as much of it as he needed, without fear of harming the land.

Once he felt the power he needed surge into his hand, Agis focused his thoughts on his sword. It was a magnificent weapon as ancient as Tyr itself, with a beautiful basket of etched brass upon the hilt and its long history etched on the face of its curved steel blade. He stretched his arm toward the sword and saw himself gripping the hilt. He remembered how it felt to hold the smooth, cordwrapped hilt in his hand, and then he lifted the weapon out of its case.

"Very impressive," Tithian said.

Agis opened his eyes again and saw, as he had expected, that the sword was now truly in his hand. Using the energy of the Way, he had simply reached across the intervening distance and picked it up.

Agis moved toward the templar, saying, "You didn't come here as a friend."

"Actually, I did," Tithian said, not retreating. "I'm sure you'll appreciate that . . . if you'll just go to the front of the house."

Agis frowned, still suspicious. "You lead the way," he ordered, motioning toward the garden's exit.

"Of course." Tithian smiled.

The templar led the way around the west side of the house, past a marble colonnade where Agis often received special guests. As they neared the front of the mansion, Tithian went up a short flight of steps onto a veranda that enveloped the front of the house. When they stepped around the corner, Agis's heart fell.

The anterior courtyard was filled with five hundred slaves, nearly his entire work force. They were being guarded by magical human-giant mixes called simply "half-giants." Members of a brutish race, the guards stood as high as twelve feet, with heavy-boned features, sloped foreheads, and long, drooping jaws. They all had chunky, almost flabby builds, with sagging shoulders, round bellies, and enormous bowed legs. The half-giants near Agis's house were dressed in hemp breeches and the purple tunics of the king's legion.

Agis's personal guard, a hundred men and dwarves wearing leather corselets, sat to one side of the courtyard with their hands on their heads. They were being guarded by a dozen of Tithian's subordinate templars, who held their hands forward and high, making it clear that they were ready to deal with any resistance by casting the spells granted to them by the king.

Caro, Agis's dwarven manservant, stood at the head of the slaves, his sagging chin resting on his sunken chest and his cloudy eyes focused on the ground. The ancient dwarf's bald head and hairless face were cracked by age lines, and his black eyes were little more than narrow, dark slits peering out from beneath their baggy lids.

"I'm sorry, master," he apologized in the thick mumble of a toothless old man. "I should of warned you, but I was napping."

"It's not your fault, Caro," Agis said.

"It is," the dwarf maintained. "If I'd have been awake, none of this would have happened."

"Damn it, Caro, if I say it's not your fault, it isn't!" Agis snapped, loosing patience with his stubborn manservant. "Is that clear?"

Caro scowled, staring at Agis for a moment, then finally looked at the ground and nodded.

Agis faced Tithian and demanded, "What's happening here?"

The templar met the black-haired noble's gaze evenly. "The king has need of more slaves to complete his ziggurat," Tithian said, his voice assuming an officious and imperious tone. "The survivors will be returned to you after it is completed."

Agis lifted his sword a few inches. "I should just kill you now and be over with it."

Tithian looked hurt, but did not retreat. "Need I point out that you're threatening a lawful representative of the Golden Tower? This is an act of open revolt, Senator."

"You don't have the authority to confiscate my slaves," Agis said, reluctantly lowering his sword.

"The king issued a decree giving me that authority this morning," Tithian replied.

"The Senate will veto that decree!"

"Not if it knows what's good for it." Tithian's voice grew less formal. "If you try, Kalak will make sure that there aren't enough senators in attendance to achieve a quorum." The high templar started to leave, then paused. "I'll leave the women and children to work your fields. That's more than I'm allowing anyone else, old friend."

FOUR

The City of Tyr

As Sadira approached the rusty, iron-clad gates of Tyr, she cast a wary glance at the templar standing behind the customary pair of half-giant guards. He wore the standard black cassock of the king's bureaucracy, but even in the dim light of dusk she could see the glint of a metal pendant hanging from his neck. The jewelry suggested he was a man of considerable rank, for ordinary templars could hardly have afforded so much metal.

Without slowing her pace toward the city, the sorceress searched the area immediately outside the gate, looking for anything that might explain the templar's presence. From what she knew of Tyr, it was odd for a high-ranking official to assume the mundane duty of supervising guards at the gate.

To one side of the road, thirty porters were unloading a wooden argosy, one of the mighty fortress wagons used by merchants to haul cargo across the vast deserts of Athas. The caravan wagon was too large to maneuver in the streets of Tyr, so it had to be unloaded outside the gate.

The two mekillots that drew the argosy were still anchored in their harnesses. Nearly as long as the wagon itself, the lizards had huge, mound-shaped bodies covered by a thick shell that served both as armor and a source of shade. Sadira gave the mammoth beasts a wide berth, for they were famous for lashing out with their long tongues and making snacks of imprudent passersby.

The other side of the road was clear of argosies and caravans of other sorts. There was a large patch of dusty ground where wagons would wait their turn at loading and unloading, but it was empty now. Beyond this barren patch, dozens of starving slaves were spreading offal from the city sewers over one of the king's fields. As they used their bare hands to throw fistfuls of the foul-smelling sludge over the azure burgrass, or to pack it around the stems of the golden smokebrush that speckled the field, their black-robed overseers whipped them mercilessly with nine-stranded whips.

When her furtive search of the gate area revealed no reason for the templar's unusual presence, Sadira hitched up the huge bundle of sticks on her back and continued at her same slow pace. Though the templar made her nervous, she saw no choice except to trudge slowly forward and hope that his presence had nothing to do with her. Turning away now would have drawn too much attention and, besides, she was too exhausted and thirsty to spend the night in the desert.

After her escape from the Break, Sadira had collected her spellbook and slipped away from Tithian's compound by walking invisibly out the main gate. Her spell had lasted long enough for her to reach a cluster of rocks just beyond the edge of Tithian's lands. Here, she had gathered the large bundle of sticks now slung over her back, put her spellbook in a drab shoulder satchel, and donned a tattered robe over her low-cut smock so that she would draw less attention to herself. She had then gone to the road and trudged to Tyr with the slow, measured pace of a loyal slave who had spent the morning scouring the countryside in search of wooden tool-handles for her master.

The journey had been as uneventful as the other trips Sadira periodically undertook to visit her contact in the Veiled Alliance, save that the road had been emptier than usual because she had been traveling in the afternoon, the hottest time of day. Now, as she approached the eastern gate, the sun was already sinking behind the scorched peaks of the western horizon. Fiery filaments of magenta and burgundy were shooting across the sky, and evening was casting its purple shadow over the city's sand-colored walls.

In the center of Tyr, the setting sun cast a scarlet glow upon the imperious Golden Tower. The spire looked as though it were dripping with blood. Next to the palace loomed the massive ziggurat, its heart blackened by the shadows of evening. In the blazing light that outlined its extremities, Sadira could see thousands of tiny silhouettes swarming over the great structure, and she knew Kalak's slaves were still at work.

Counting herself lucky not to be among them, Sadira stooped a little farther beneath her load of sticks. She fixed her eyes on the dusty road and walked into the gloomy gateway, hoping that if she ignored the gate guards and their overseer, they would ignore her.

A half-giant stepped into her path, and Sadira found herself staring at a pair of hairy, sandaled feet over half a yard long. For a moment, she remained motionless, studying the guard's huge, black-nailed toes. At the same time, she reviewed in her mind the spells she knew, trying to guess which one would prove most useful in this situation.

When the guard did not step aside, Sadira slowly lifted her gaze. Though not particularly muscular, each of the half-giant's thighs were as thick as a tree trunk and probably heavier. Over his round belly, which was solid and powerful despite its shape, he wore a purple tunic emblazoned with Kalak's golden star. He cradled a great club of polished bone across his stomach, at a height about even with the half-elf's eyes.

Sadira tilted her head back and looked upward, setting aside her load of sticks. The half-giant's shoulders were as broad as she was tall. Atop his stout neck sat a huge head with a drooping jaw and baggy, sad-looking eyes.

"Yes, Mountainous One?" she asked, giving him a charming smile.

Instead of answering, the half-giant looked to the templar. Though Sadira's pale blue eyes remained focused on the guard, her mind was on the bureaucrat standing to one side of the road. The man had a portly build and pale hair, with puffy cheeks and tight, pursed lips. His red-rimmed eyes were studying the half-elf with a casual, imperious attitude. The beguiling sorceress quickly judged him to be a lonely, bitter man, just the sort to fall prey to her charms.

"Ask the girl who she belongs to," the templar commanded with exaggerated arrogance. Though Sadira was clearly no girl, it was the habit in Tyr to address slaves as if they were children.

Without waiting for the half-giant to repeat the question, Sadira turned her alluring smile on the templar. "I belong to Marut the tool-shaper," she said in a silky voice.

The sorceress allowed her eyes to run over the official,

finishing by meeting his gaze. When the templar raised his brow at her interest, Sadira coyly looked away and pretended to be embarrassed. A faint blush spread across her high, smooth cheeks. "I have here handles for Marut's axes," she said.

Sadira had no idea who Marut was, or even if such a person really existed. All she knew was that her contact in the Veiled Alliance had instructed her to reply in this manner when questioned. On the few occasions when the guards had interrogated her before, the answer had always secured her release.

"Marut will be happy to loan his slave to the king." The templar's voice was cold and emotionless, but his eyes were studying the half-elf's fine features and surveying the svelte figure beneath her tattered cloak with a covetous air. "Perhaps I shall even present you to him myself, girl."

Both half-giants chuckled lewdly, then the one behind the sorceress moved to grab her.

Sadira eluded his grasp. "I beg you, handsome sir! I'm already late and my master will beat me!"

The sorceress fell to her knees in front of the pudgy official. She surreptitiously opened her tattered robe so it would expose the revealing smock beneath, but was careful not to open it so far that the stolen dagger on her hip became visible. At the same time, she touched the palm of her free hand to the ground, summoning the power for the spell she hoped would save her. It rushed up her arm and gathered inside her swiftly, for there was an ample supply of energy this close to the king's fields.

Under her breath, she whispered the incantation that would shape her spell, at the same time disguising the mystical gestures by bowing her head and hunching her shoulders. It was risky to employ magic against templars, for it was always possible that they would recognize when a spell was being cast and interrupt it.

A huge hand seized the half-elf's shoulder. "Come here, slave, or you won't even make it to the king's pens."

As the guard lifted her off the ground, Sadira fixed her eyes on the templar's. She released the spell by pursing her full lips as if blowing him a kiss.

The man narrowed his beady eyes and frowned. He ran his plump hand over his face and shook his head, but when he looked back to Sadira, there was a warmth to his gaze that had not been there before. Her spell had worked. Now the templar would want to help her, as long as it posed no risk to him. All she had to do was find the right words to convince him that no harm would come to him if he did.

With her feet dangling off the ground, Sadira pleaded, "Please, at least let me take these handles to Marut. I'm sure he'll allow me to return to you."

The templar bit his lip indecisively, then shook his head stubbornly. "I don't know this Marut. I have no reason to believe he'll send you back."

"Marut is a trustworthy man, a loyal subject of the king," Sadira countered, grimacing against the pain of the half-giant's grip.

The templar scowled at the guard holding the slender sorceress. "If you bruise the girl, I'll have your head!"

The half-giant nearly dropped her. The jaw of the other one, who was standing next to the templar, fell slack.

As Sadira's captor put her feet back on the cobblestones, the templar said, "Letting you go is out of the question. I'm to confiscate every slave that comes through this gate."

Sadira realized that the templar's fear of his superior was stronger than his desire for her. The half-elf could hardly believe it, but decided it might be wiser to press along a different course. She pointed at the bundle of sticks she had dropped in the road. "If I don't deliver those handles to my master tonight, Marut won't be able to make the picks he's supposed to give the Ministry of Works tomorrow."

"You said the handles was for axes," rumbled a half-giant.

Without looking away from the chubby templar, Sadira hastily explained. "He usually makes axes, but the ministry needs more picks for the brick pits."

To her relief, the templar nodded. "I've heard that."

"Without my master's tools, the ministry will be short of bricks," she said, locking her clear blue eyes on those of the portly man. "Maybe *you* should escort me to Marut's shop, then bring me back here after we've delivered the handles. I'm sure your superior would be most grateful for your initiative, and so would I."

She gave the portly official a promising smile, but did not allow it to linger too long on her lips. The key to bringing him entirely under her influence was to make him believe that she was truly attracted to him, which wouldn't be too difficult since it was something he clearly wanted to believe anyway. She just had to be careful not to alert him to her act by overdoing it.

"Don't listen to her, Pegen!" said the half-giant next to the templar. "You can do as you want with the girl, anyhow."

Sadira lifted her peaked eyebrows and allowed her mouth to fall open as if in fear. She stepped away from the templar, saying, "What does he mean, Pegen? What are you going to do to me?"

This tactic worked perfectly. The templar scowled at the half-giant, angered that Sadira's attraction had suddenly turned to repulsion. "Quiet or you'll be hauling bricks on the ziggurat tomorrow!" He turned back to the half-elf. "Don't worry. I'm not going to do anything to you."

Sadira backed away another step. "I don't understand what they're saying," she said, glancing at the guards. "What do they think a small slave-girl like me could do to a strapping man like you?"

Bristling at the imagined insult, the templar scowled at the two brutish guards. "Close the gate when dark falls," he ordered. "Then wait for me to return."

"But—"

"Do as I say, Tak!" Pegen commanded, scowling at the reluctant sentinel. "No more arguments!"

After he had finished chastising the half-giant, Pegen nodded to Sadira. "Lead the way, girl. I hope your master's shop isn't too far."

Sadira picked up the bundle of sticks and hoisted them onto her back. With Pegen following a step behind her, she walked past the rusty gates and through a gently sloping tunnel that passed beneath the city walls. At the other end, a monstrous block of granite rested to one side of the exit. Every year or two, when another of Athas's cities ran out of food and sent an army to steal what it could from Tyr's poorly stocked granaries, a high-ranking templar would levitate the block and it would be pulled into place to block the tunnel until the war was over.

Upon stepping past the barrier, the half-elf found the inside of the city more surprising than the templar's presence outside the gate. In contrast to the cacophony of squeaking wagons and strident voices that had greeted her on previous trips, Tyr seemed as silent as the desert. The great boulevard that circled the inner perimeter of the wall was empty save for a handful of artisans and well-robed merchants dashing along with their eyes focused steadfastly on the cobblestones. The food and wineshops opposite the city wall, usually lit by torches and oil lamps until the early hours of morning, were uniformly dark. The rich aromas she remembered—fried rotgrubs, spicy silverbush, fermented kank nectar—were absent. In their place, she smelled only fetid animal dung and the acrid smoke of burning black rock.

Sadira turned left along the great avenue, following a route that she had traveled not more than two dozen times in her life. Pegen walked at her side, his heavy boots ticking an even cadence on the cobblestones. A few minutes later, as night was falling over the city, Pegen laid a hand on Sadira's shoulder. He pointed down an avenue snaking its way between two rows of three-story mud-brick buildings.

"Aren't we going to the Tradesman's District?"

Sadira paused and looked down the avenue. It was a broad street, well-lit by flickering torches in door sconces. The half-elf had no idea where the avenue led.

"Marut's shop doesn't lie that way," she said, pointing down the boulevard they were already traveling on. "It's farther down here."

Pegen frowned. "If you say so."

After another three hundred steps, Sadira paused, then looked down a dark lane weaving its way into a ramshackle region of dreary tenements and crumbling shanties. Though the windows and doors of the mud-brick buildings were dark, the slave-girl's elven eyes allowed her to see the sinister-looking residents who were watching the alley from every fourth or fifth building.

"Doesn't this lead toward the Elven Market?" Pegen asked.

"My master's just a short distance down the way," Sadira said. She stepped into the dark alley before the templar could object.

The half-elf had gone no more than a few steps into the lane before she heard Pegen stumbling over the loose cobblestones in the street. He laid his hand on her burden and tugged.

"Wait!"

Sadira obeyed instantly, dropping her bundle on his feet. She reached beneath her cloak and drew the obsidian dagger she had stolen from the guard in the Break. The human templar, unable to see in the dark, stumbled over the sticks and fell. Sadira spun, raising her dagger to strike.

The templar sprawled over the bundle face-first, cursing and struggling to push himself back to his feet. Sadira realized that it would be a simple matter for her to disappear into the labyrinth of shabby tenements in this part of the city. Certainly that was what the Veiled Alliance would have wanted, for her contact had instructed her never to antagonize the king's bureaucracy unnecessarily.

"Help me up, you clumsy girl," Pegen ordered. "I could have you lashed for this!"

"Wrong thing to say," the half-elf said, deciding that "unnecessarily" was a relative term.

With her free hand, Sadira grasped his bronze pendant. She jerked it up so that the chain lifted his double chin and exposed his corpulent neck. Pegen's eyes opened wide and looked toward her face, but remained unfocused and fearful in the darkness. "What do you think you're doing?" he demanded in a gasping voice.

"Seeing if this knife is sharp enough to cut through your fat throat," Sadira answered, laying the edge of her weapon's blade to the thick folds of skin beneath his chin. She had to press hard, but the blade was sharp enough.

The feel of warm blood covered her hand. Pegen gurgled and clasped his hands over his throat. He rolled off the bundle of sticks and lay on his back, his life slowly seeping from between his fingers and his astonished eyes staring up at the night sky. Without waiting for him to die, Sadira cleaned her hand and the blade on his cassock, then ran down the dark streets at a sprint.

The half-elf did not slow her pace until she had slipped between a pair of tenements into a small square where five lanes met. The plaza was bathed in bright yellow light, for it was surrounded by six wineshops, two brothels, and a gambling house, all of which had burning torches in the sconces outside their doors. Dozing men, mostly humans and elves, lay slouched against the sides of the buildings, and half-naked women were wandering to and fro looking for someone in need of companionship.

Sadira stopped at the edge of the square and removed the blood-spattered cloak she was wearing. With the inside of a sleeve, she wiped the dust and sweat from her face, then stuffed the cloak into the satchel that held her spellbook. She ran her fingers through her amber hair in a half-successful attempt to remove the tangles. Despite her efforts, she knew she could not look even close to her best. Her recent run had left her chest heaving and her slender legs trembling with fatigue. Still, once she had done all she could to make herself presentable, she crossed the square to a wineshop whose entrance was adorned with a picture of a drunken giant.

Inside, a brawny man with a balding head and an unkempt red beard stood behind a marble counter, using a ladle of carved bone to serve fermented goat's milk to three bleary-eyed patrons. As Sadira entered the shop, she caught the barman's eye, then casually drew her hand across her full lips and delicate chin. He nodded toward the back of the shop, then whispered something to one of his customers. The patron immediately rose and stumbled out of the shop.

Sadira went to the back and sat on a small granite bench, placing her shoulder satchel beneath it. To her surprise, the red-bearded server brought her a mug of tart-smelling sapwine. As he approached, she smiled and said, "You know I don't have any money."

"I know, but I can see you need something to eat and drink," the brawny barman said.

"Why?" Sadira demanded, feeling embarrassed. She touched her fingers to her cheeks, suddenly frightened that she had missed a spot of blood. "Do I have something on my face?"

The barman chuckled and shook his head. "No, you just look like you're thirsty," he said, motioning to two drunks sitting at the counter. "At least that's what those fellows must have figured. They're paying."

Sadira gave the two men an enticing smile, then downed the mug of fermented tree resin in a single gulp. As the drink's powerful kick hit her, she closed her long-lashed eyelids and shook her head. Handing the mug back to the barman, she announced, "I'll have another."

"I think I'd better have a look at their purses," the barman laughed, accepting the mug. Before he returned to the counter, though, his face grew serious. "Are you in trouble?"

Although the half-elf and the red-bearded man were familiar to each other by sight, she did not know how much to reveal. The only thing she knew about him was that he could reach her contact in the Veiled Alliance. Otherwise, both he and she had deliberately avoided prolonged conversations, for if the king's men caught one of them, the less they knew about each other the better.

"A templar tried to seize me for the ziggurat," she said, leaving the matter with a simple explanation.

The server nodded. "They've been confiscating slaves all day. Press gangs have been through here three times arresting drunks. That's why the square is so quiet this evening." He fetched Sadira another mug of bitter wine, then asked, "Should I expect the templar that was after you?"

The half-elf shook her head. "Not until the dead can walk."

The man relaxed, his face betraying his relief. He handed the mug to Sadira, then sat the carafe next to her. "I'll pull the curtain just to be safe. By tipping that bench over, you'll open an escape tunnel. Use it if you hear anything strange out here."

Sadira glanced at the stone couch. "Where does it lead?"

"To UnderTyr," he said, "and a Temple of the Ancients."

"No!" Sadira gasped. She knew very little about the ancient temples, except that they had been built before Athas had become a desert. According to rumor, most were filled with vast amounts of metal treasure defended by the ghosts of those who had worshiped long-forgotten, or long-dead, gods. "Under this wineshop?"

"Not directly under it," the barman answered. "But if something happens and you use the escape tunnel, don't be in a hurry to find that temple. From what I hear, you'd be better served giving yourself over to Kalak's templars."

With that, he stepped away and pulled a drape across the back of the shop. The drape was made entirely from snake scales that had been pierced and threaded together.

Each scale had been sealed with shiny lacquer to preserve and heighten its natural color. The result was a scintillating curtain of many different hues—sandy yellow, rusty orange, cactus green, and a half-dozen others.

Sadira drank her second mug of sapwine more slowly, forcing herself to sip the powerful drink. Although she felt like gulping the entire mug to quench her thirst, with the curtain closed, she doubted that a refill would be forthcoming. The fermented resin was the foulest drink available in the wineshops of Tyr, but the half-elf still wanted to savor it. On Tithian's estate, all she ever received to drink was water.

As the half-elf sipped the last of her wine, an old man stepped around the edge of the curtain. He had robust, proud features, with a heavy forehead accented by coarse white brows, a large, hooked nose between shrewd brown eyes, and a firmly set jaw. His beard was long and snowy. He wore a white, knee-length tabard, and over his shoulders hung an ivory-colored cape fastened at the throat with a copper clasp. In one hand he carried a mug filled with thick brown wine, and in the other a cane of dark wood. The cane's pommel, a ball of polished obsidian, was both unusual and striking. Sadira found it difficult to tear her gaze from the beautiful black sphere, but she did, for she knew its owner did not like people staring into it.

The old man eyed the half-elf carefully, taking a long drink from his mug. At last, he pointed his cane at her and asked, "What are you doing here, young lady? I didn't send for you."

"It's good to see you, too, Ktandeo," Sadira replied, smiling warmly. She rose and wrapped the man in her willowy arms.

"Watch my drink!" he snapped, holding his mug away from his body as a few drops of its contents sloshed over the edge. "This is the good stuff."

Sadira was unintimidated by the old man's peevishness. She was as close to him as any man and knew that beneath his surly manner lay a kind heart.

A few days before Sadira's twelfth birthday, Tithian had hired a cantankerous old animal handler to train beasts for the arena. Ktandeo, who had sought the position in order to find a spy in the high templar's household, then chose the young girl to be his helper. Over the next year, he had examined Sadira's character, subtly presenting her with moral quandaries and tests of courage. The most vivid instance she recalled was when the old man had "accidentally" locked her in the cage with a hungry takis to see if she would panic. While he had fumbled with the latch, she stood motionless and let the bearlike creature sniff her from head to toe with its slime-oozing trunk. Ktandeo had not opened the door until the hulking animal bared its dagger-shaped fangs and started beating the floor with its bony tail-club. The only time Sadira had ever seen her mentor laugh was during the angry lecture that she gave him following her escape.

Then, one High Sun morning after they had sent the current lot of animals to the games celebrating the new year, Ktandeo had come to help her clean the empty pens. He had asked her if she wanted to learn magic. Over the course of the next few weeks, he had taught her to fill the air with dancing lights. When she had asked to learn another spell, he had hesitated, saying he had already taught her too much. Only after weeks of her begging had he agreed to teach her another spell. This time, however, he had placed a condition on his gift. She would have to join the Veiled Alliance and serve it no matter what was asked of her.

Of course Sadira had agreed, for she saw in magic an

avenue to escaping her bondage. Over the next four years, Ktandeo had taught her many spells, but he had also instilled in her a sense of purpose that went beyond simple escape. He began to speak of revolution, of overthrowing the king and giving the slaves their liberty. It was not long before Sadira shared his dream and had dedicated herself to liberating all of Tyr.

When Sadira reached sixteen and began to blossom into full womanhood, Ktandeo had brought his "daughter" to stay with him. Catalyna had been anything but a daughterly figure, with provocative eyes, a flirtatious smile, and a shapely body. Under her tutelage, Sadira had learned to make the most of her own beauty, and it was not long before she could procure an extra helping of faro needle gruel or a little extra water, using only the flash of an eye and a warm smile.

Once her training was complete, Ktandeo had helped her sneak out of the compound, then had taken her into Tyr and shown her how to find him by coming to this wineshop. Shortly afterward, both he and Catalyna had vanished from Tithian's estate. Sadira had remained behind, quietly spying on members of the compound for the next five years. Mostly, her duties had consisted of using the techniques Catalyna had taught her to loosen the tongues of guards and overseers. Twice each year, she ventured into Tyr to report the little she had discovered and to learn a new spell or two.

The young sorceress had finally decided to ask if there wasn't someplace she could be more useful. Then Rikus had appeared in the gladiatorial pits. She had duly reported the mul's presence to Ktandeo. A short time later, he had sent word to her to "become as close as possible" to the new mul, suggesting the Alliance needed his cooperation for a very special project. She had since learned that the special project meant having Rikus attack Kalak with a magical spear during the ziggurat games.

Clearing his throat, Ktandeo took a seat on the stone bench and folded his hands on the pommel of his cane. "Well?"

Sadira remained standing. With a quaver in her voice, she said, "Rikus is injured. He may not live."

The old man's face darkened.

Sadira told her contact all that had occurred since morning, omitting only her use of the magical tentacles against the first guard at the Break. By the time she had described her attempt to charm Pegen, and her eventual escape, her wine was gone.

For several moments, Ktandeo sat frowning in thought. Finally he looked up, his brown eyes dark with anger, and sharply rapped her knuckles with his cane's black pommel. "You are playing a dangerous game, girl."

Sadira's slim jaw dropped at Ktandeo's accusatory tone. "What?" she gasped, rubbing her aching hand.

The old man gave her a disapproving scowl. "Is your control so good that you can cast a half-dozen spells a day, all under stress, and maintain the balance? Someone of twice your experience wouldn't have the stamina. I shudder to think of the damage you did."

Sadira was glad she hadn't mentioned the tentacle spell along with the others. Ktandeo would probably have declared her a defiler, a sorcerer who abused the land. According to the traditions of the Veiled Alliance, members who became defilers were executed.

"And was it really necessary to murder three—"

"A templar and two slave guards!" Sadira objected.

"Still human beings," Ktandeo countered. "You sound as though you're proud of yourself."

"What if I am?" the half-elf demanded, rising to her

feet. "Any one of them would have flogged, raped, or murdered me in an instant. As far as I'm concerned, I got to them before they got to me. Why shouldn't I be proud?"

The old man also rose. "Listen to yourself!" he snapped, angrily waving his cane over her head. "You sound like a templar! What's the difference between you and them?"

"The same as the difference between you and Kalak," she retorted. "If *you're* going to assassinate the king, why am *I* wrong to kill his men?"

"Kalak is the source of our evil. He's the one who has outlawed magic, who defiles the land, who makes slavery a way of life, who rules his subjects with murder and fear—"

"You can't believe that once Tyr is rid of him, his templars and nobles will suddenly become servants of good?"

Ktandeo shook his head vigorously. "Of course not," he said. "But Kalak is the foundation. Knock him out and the rest of the structure will fall."

"Even without Kalak, you're not going to topple the bureaucracy and the nobility without bloodshed," Sadira objected. "So I don't see what's wrong with fighting now."

"Nothing is wrong with fighting, or even with ambush and assassination—as long as you're freeing a group of slaves, destroying a brickyard, or working toward another worthy purpose. But to kill out of hatred . . ." Ktandeo let the sentence trail off. "It isn't worthy of you, girl."

Sadira lashed out with her lean arm and swept their mugs off the bench. They hit the stone wall and smashed into dozens of pieces. "Don't *you* address me like a slave!" she spat, her pale eyes flashing with fire. "And don't judge me. What do you know about being a slave? Have you ever felt the whip upon your back?"

After a tense pause she said, "I thought as much."

The red-bearded man stepped around the curtain, a pair of flagons in his hands and a small blackjack tucked into his apron. "I thought I heard someone drop a mug," he said, eyeing the earthenware shards on the floor. "Here's refills." He cast a meaningful glance at Ktandeo, then added, "Try not to spill them."

"Now look what you've done," said the old man after the barman had gone. His voice was gentler than it had been a few moments before. He sat back down and carefully laid his cane across his lap so that he wouldn't be tempted to swing it around. "Now that you've exposed yourself, you'll have to go to another city."

"I'm not leaving," Sadira replied, struggling to keep from raising her voice. "I'm not ready to leave Rikus."

"Rikus? What about him?" Ktandeo asked. He took a long draught from his mug.

"I haven't asked him to throw the spear," Sadira answered. "In fact, he still doesn't know I'm in the Veiled Alliance."

"At least you followed those instructions," the old man said.

"I *do* try." Sadira felt a tear running down her cheek and quickly turned away to wipe it off her face. Ktandeo was the closest thing to a father she had ever known. Despite the fact that she thought he was being overly sensitive about the guards she had killed, the confrontation with him distressed her more than she liked to admit.

When she turned her attention back to Ktandeo, the old man's brown eyes had softened, but he still held his jaw firmly set. "Once Tithian hears how you saved

Rikus, he'll know you wear the veil. He'll look under every cobblestone in Tyr to find you."

"But if I leave, who'll ask Rikus to throw the spear?" she objected.

"Right now, I don't even know if there's going to be a spear to throw," Ktandeo said. "I haven't fetched it, and the way things are going, I won't be able to."

"Why not?" Sadira demanded, alarmed.

Ktandeo ran a large, liver-spotted hand over his wrinkled brow. "The king is striking at us," he said. "Already, his men have stormed the houses and shops of fifteen members. In defending themselves, they have killed fifty templars and a dozen half-giants, but the enemy is trying to capture our people alive. Each time they succeed, the king's mindbenders learn another name or two, and a little more of our network is exposed. Sooner or later, they'll get a grand councilor. When that happens . . ."

Sadira resisted the temptation to ask what could possibly be more important than killing Kalak, for if there was a legitimate answer, it would be better not to know it if she was captured. Instead, she said, "I'll get the spear for you. By the time I return, things will be calmer and I can talk to Rikus then."

Ktandeo shook his head. "The spear is being made by a halfling chief. If I send anyone else to get it, he'll kill them."

"I'll take that chance," Sadira offered. "You just send a healer to make sure Rikus is alive when I get back."

"I'm not sending you to a certain death; I'm sending you away to safety," Ktandeo said, automatically reaching for his cane. He thumped the tip on the floor, then added, "And why this doting on Rikus? There are plenty of other gladiators."

"Not like Rikus," Sadira returned.

Ktandeo raised an eyebrow. "And what's so different about the mul?"

Sadira felt hot blood rise to her cheeks. "He's a champion," she said, taking a gulp of wine and setting her mug back on the bench. "He's the only gladiator you can be sure will live long enough to get a clean throw at the king during the games."

"We'll find another time and place to attack," Ktandeo answered, looking away with an unconcerned expression.

"If that were possible, you would have attacked him by now," Sadira said, realizing that Ktandeo was toying with her, probably in an effort to determine the extent of her attraction to Rikus. She rose, continuing, "You're the one who told me to get close to Rikus and I did. If that upsets you, I'm sorry. It doesn't change the fact that we need him. You've got to send help to him, and I've got to stay here until he's conscious again."

"No! You're letting your emotions cloud your judgment!" Ktandeo growled, also rising. "Think! If you stay in Tyr and Tithian tracks you down, what can you tell him? Not only can you identify me and this wineshop, you can describe our whole plan to him!"

"Then make sure I don't get caught!" Sadira answered.

"That would be impossible, especially considering the way you've been talking tonight," Ktandeo snapped, thumping her in the chest with his cane. "As for Rikus, if I sent him a healer and that healer got caught, which would be likely, Tithian would know we're planning something for the mul. He'd guess what it was in an instant, and then our plan would be no good at all."

The old man paused to scowl at Sadira. She could feel her lips trembling, but she did not know how to respond to Ktandeo. What he said made sense, but she could not accept the old man's cold logic. Rikus was more than a hulking mass of muscle who they hoped would kill Kalak, and she was more than a lifeless puppet to be discarded when she was no longer of any use.

"You're treating us no better than our master does!" Sadira snapped. She reached beneath the bench and snatched her shoulder satchel. "I'm not leaving Tyr until Rikus is well and I've spoken to him!"

Before the old man could make a move to stop her, the half-elf threw the curtain aside and rushed toward the front of the wineshop. As she pushed past the patrons who had bought her first two mugs of sapwine, Ktandeo's voice boomed, "Come back here!"

Sadira ignored him and rushed into the plaza, instinctively starting back down the street in the direction from which she had come. Before she had taken three steps, she saw several half-giants blocking the alleyway a short way ahead. The leader wore a helmet with a huge purple plume, a corselet made from the scaly underbelly of a mekillot, and a wide belt with a massive obsidian sword dangling from it. In his hands he held a pair of leashes.

At the other end of the leashes strained a pair of cilops. The giant centipedes stood as tall as Sadira and were more than fifteen feet long. Their flat bodies were divided into a dozen segments, each supported by a pair of thin legs. On their oval heads were three sets of pincerlike jaws, a single compound eye, and a pair of prehensile antennae that ran back and forth over the ground before the creatures.

Sadira immediately backed out of the alleyway, for the cilops were an escaped slave's worst nightmare. She had heard stories of the horrid things tracking men across ten miles of stony barrens—more than a week after the slaves had passed and a wind storm had covered their trail with two inches of dust.

"That's the girl!" cried a half-giant's familiar voice. "She's the one who killed Pegen!"

Sadira's first instinct was to run for the wineshop before the half-giant released the cilops. As she spun around and looked toward it, she saw both Ktandeo and the red-bearded barman watching her from its doorway, their curious faces betraying no hint that they knew her.

"Stop, slave!" cried the lead half-giant. "Stop or I'll let me babies go!"

Sadira quickly realized she could not return to the shop with the half-giants so close behind. Not only would she be likely to expose it as an Alliance rendezvous, she would be risking Ktandeo's capture. As angry as she was at him, she knew that was a risk she could not take.

Instead she turned away from the shop and rushed for another dark alley. There was not much likelihood that she would escape, but she knew her best chance lay in luring the cilops into the labyrinth of alleys in this section of the city and trying to confuse them by crossing and recrossing her own path.

Behind her, the half-giant cried, "Last chance!"

Sadira glanced over her shoulder and saw that the leader and his tracking beasts had stepped into the plaza. Beneath the sign of the Drunken Giant, Ktandeo and the barman were still watching with calm looks of curiosity on their faces, though the old man was anxiously tapping his cane on the ground.

"Girl, over here!"

When Sadira returned her attention to the direction she was running, she saw a seven-foot figure poking his lanky torso and gaunt-featured head from an open door. He had pale, yellowish skin, dark hair, and pointed ears, with smooth, almost feminine cheeks and lips. His fleece cloak was obviously expensive, as was the garish feathered cap on his head.

"Of all the terrible luck," Sadira cried.

The elf flashed a broad grin, then drew a flask from beneath his cloak. "This will throw even the cilops off your scent," he said. "I promise."

Sadira looked over her shoulder again, considering what her chances of escape might be without the elf's help. The half-giant had moved several steps into the plaza and was just withdrawing his pets' leashes from their collars. Behind him, the two gate guards and several more half-giants were rushing from the dark alley.

Sadira ran toward the elf, whispering, "I know I'm going to regret this."

FIVE

Shadow Square

The old man paused at the entrance to a narrow alley and peered down the shadowed corridor as if gauging the likelihood of being attacked there. Agis caught up to the fellow and gently tapped him on the shoulder. The man spun around, raising his wooden cane as if to strike with its pommel, a remarkable ball of polished obsidian.

"What?" the old man demanded, thumping the noble on the chest with the cane's tip. He had robust, proud features with a hooked nose and a long mane of white hair.

"Pardon me," Agis said. He lifted his hands so it would be clear he intended no violence. "I'm not familiar with the streets of the Elven Market. Would you be kind enough to direct me to a suphouse called the Red Kank? It's located in Shadow Square."

The old man frowned, then asked, "What do you want in a place like Shadow Square?"

Agis raised his brow, for the Elven Market was not the kind of place where strangers asked those sorts of questions. "The same thing as anyone else who goes there," he answered evasively.

Though the noble didn't have a clear idea why most people went to Shadow Square, the answer was the only one he would give. He had no intention of telling the old man his true reason for going to the Red Kank, which was to meet an influential group of his fellow senators. They wanted to discuss the Senate's response to Kalak's slave confiscations, and all of them had agreed it would be best to meet in a place templar spies were not likely to frequent.

The stranger studied Agis for several moments without replying. The noble was just about to leave when the fellow finally said, "You'd be well-advised to avoid Shadow Square. It's no place for someone of your class to go—especially alone."

"Your concern is well-taken," Agis said. "If you'll direct me to the Red Kank, I'll no longer be alone."

The old man shook his head in resignation. "I hope your companions have more sense than you do," he grunted, pointing his cane down the street. "Walk down this street until you reach the pawnshop, then take the alley to the left. It opens into Shadow Square."

"My thanks," Agis replied, reaching for his purse.

The man laid his cane sharply across the noble's hand. "I don't want your coin, son," he said. "If you expect to leave the market alive, don't flash your gold around."

Agis took his hand away from his purse, ignoring the dull ache in his knuckles. "Any other advice?"

"Yes," the white-haired man said. He moved his cane to the noble's back, then tapped the steel dagger concealed beneath his cloak. "No matter what happens, keep that thing in its sheath. You'll live a lot longer."

In light of the stranger's earlier advice to avoid Shadow Square, this last comment seemed deliberately ominous.

"Is there some reason you're trying to keep me out of Shadow Square?"

"Not really," the old man replied. "It makes no difference to me whether you live or die." With that, he turned and stepped into a nearby alley.

Agis frowned at the stranger's parting words, then signaled Caro to join him. He had instructed the dwarf to wait behind so the old man would not be alarmed by the approach of two strangers. After the blows his knuckles and chest had suffered, the noble was glad he had not startled the old fellow any more than he had.

As the valet hobbled forward, Agis marveled again at the aged dwarf's ingenious escape from Tithian's press gang. A thirsty and bruised Caro had returned to the Asticles estate the same evening that the high templar had confiscated Agis's male slaves. According to the dwarf's report, he had pretended to collapse after a few miles of walking. When the templars kicked and lashed him to get him moving again, Caro had refused to budge or even look up. Finally Tithian had ordered the dwarf abandoned at the roadside. After the column had moved on, Caro had walked back to the estate.

Agis was surprised that such a simple escape plan had worked, but not that Caro had returned. The old slave had devoted his entire life to serving the Asticles family and, in typical dwarven fashion, he was willing to endure any hardship rather than break his commitment.

Once Caro reached his side, Agis pointed down the alley and said, "The old man warned me not to go to Shadow Square. Have you ever heard that there's anything particularly dangerous about it?"

"No, but I doubt that your friends would have suggested you meet there if that were the case," Caro replied, squinting up at Agis.

On one of Caro's wrinkled cheeks was a yellow bruise the size of a fist. Hidden beneath the dwarf's robe were several similar marks and a few lash wounds. Though the evidence of his valet's beating angered the noble, he was relieved that the old servant had not suffered more. From the violence Caro had described, Agis had expected his slave to have any number of broken bones and deep, purple bruises from head to toe. Still, the senator knew even a minor wound could be painful, if not dangerous, for someone as old as Caro.

"It's only been two days since your escape," Agis said. "Are you sure you're up to this?"

"Didn't I say I was?"

"Yes, but I know how dwarves are," the noble replied. "You'd die before you admitted you need to rest."

"I'm fine," Caro replied. "Let's go."

Agis started down the cramped street, his servant walking a step behind to watch for pickpockets. Though the midday sun could have baked bricks, the heat did not hamper the bustle of activity in the Elven Market.

The street was lined by two-and three-story buildings that had not been plastered or painted, but simply left the natural grayish brown of their bricks. The first story of every building contained a shop with a broad door and a pass-through counter that opened to the sidewalk. The sly, leathery faces of elven merchants leered out of every window or door, inviting passersby inside to examine the exotic wares their tribes had brought to Tyr: unbreakable giant-hair ropes from Balic, fingerbone necklaces from Gulg, shields of impenetrable agafari wood from Nibenay, even fleece from the legendary Silt Islands.

Sometimes an elf stretched his slim torso over a counter to tug at the sleeve of a well-dressed human or to pinch the purse of an unwary wanderer. Other times, one of the seven-foot shopkeepers blocked the path of an intimidated customer, babbling in a melodious voice about some worthless trinket.

In the center of the street, men and women of all races scurried along in a tight-packed stream, their hands clutching their purses and their eyes alert for trouble. Here and there, the stream temporarily parted as it passed a pile of debris or a pair of brawling elves, no doubt serving as bait for cutpurses working the crowd.

Agis walked down the middle of the avenue, for he had no interest in anything the elves had to offer. Most represented nomadic tribes that bought goods plentiful in one city and hauled them across the desert to sell in another place where such items were rare. In theory, this was what any merchant did, but the shifty elves were seldom satisfied with an honest profit. Elven tribes usually bought inferior goods and sold them at outrageous prices, or they raided legitimate merchants in the deep desert and sold the stolen cargo as their own.

After several minutes of struggling through the crowd, Agis reached the point the old man had indicated—a dilapidated pawnshop, identified by the three ceramic spheres hanging over the door. He slipped out of the throng and stepped toward the alley, pausing to make sure Caro followed.

"Hey, fellow!"

The voice belonged to a golden-haired elf who leaned against a wall just outside the alley. Taller even than most of his kind, the elf wore a tawny burnoose wrapped around his lanky body and had a bronze, weatherbeaten face with cloudy blue eyes. "You lookin' for magic components? I got glowworms. I got wychwood. I even got powdered iron."

"Isn't that stuff against the king's law?" Agis asked,

hoping to silence the huckster.

The elf raised his peaked chin. "You a templar?"

"No."

"Then what d'you care?" He looked away indignantly, leaving the noble to stare at a pointed ear caked with dirt.

Agis stepped into the alley, Caro following behind. The tall buildings provided some shade from the sun, but little relief from the oppressive heat of the day. Nevertheless, paupers and beggars had taken refuge in its shadows and lined both sides of the narrow corridor. As Agis picked his way through their legs, they silently extended their bony hands and filled the lane with desperate pleas for water and money.

Resisting the temptation to part with a handful of coins, Agis glanced over his shoulder at Caro. "This is what comes when a king cares more about magic than he does his subjects," he said angrily. "If Kalak hadn't rejected my proposal to set up relief farms outside Tyr, these people would have food, water, and beds."

"They're free," Caro replied. "At least they have that."

"Freedom won't wet their throats," Agis snapped. "You've been a servant for most of your life. You know that such service means you'll always have enough to drink and eat, and a soft bed to sleep in."

"I'd be glad to go hungry and thirsty a few days in exchange for my liberty," Caro replied, stepping to Agis's side.

"Ever since you escaped from the press gang, you've been talking like this. Why?" Agis demanded. "Is there something you need? Just ask and you know I'll give it to you."

"I need my liberty," Caro answered stubbornly.

"So you can join these wretches? I won't do it. You're better off as my servant," Agis said. He swept his hand at the alley of derelicts. "They'd all be better off as my slaves."

"But—"

"I won't discuss it any further, Caro," Agis said, reaching the other end of the rank-smelling lane. "Don't bring the subject up again."

"As you wish," the dwarf said, once again falling a step behind his master.

The alley opened into a plaza, as the old man had promised. The scene in Shadow Square seemed more chaotic than the merchant row on the other side of the alley, but Agis saw nothing particularly dangerous. Dozens of tents had been pitched by elves either too poor or too cheap to rent a storefront. These elves were vainly accosting the dozens of half-elves, dwarves, and humans who carried large ceramic pots toward the center of the square.

There, a templar and a pair of half-giant guards collected a small tax from the pot-bearers for the privilege of filling a jug from the public fountain. It was a slow and tedious process, with a long waiting line, for the fountain consisted of a single trickle of water spilling from the mouth of a stone statue. The artist had shaped a braxat from the stone, a huge, hunchbacked creature resembling a cross between a baazrag and a horned chameleon. It walked on its hind legs and had a thick shell covering its back and neck. Agis could not imagine why the king's sculptors had selected such a grotesque beast for a fountainhead, save that the city populace was always curious about the seldom-seen creatures that roamed the wastes.

Looking away from the fountain, Agis walked along the edge of the square, carefully studying the symbols painted above the building doorways. There was no writing on the signs, for in Tyr, as in most other Athasian cities, only nobles and templars were permitted to read or write.

At last, Agis came to a red sign portraying a man mounted upon a kank, one of the giant insects that caravan drivers often used as beasts of burden. The insect had an abdomen from which was suspended a globule of honey. Judging that he had reached the Red Kank, Agis entered the suphouse, Caro close behind.

Lit only by a handful of narrow windows, the interior of the building was quite dim. As Agis stood near the door, waiting for his eyes to adjust to the darkness, the babble of voices inside quickly died.

Once his eyes were accustomed to the shadows, he found himself standing in a small square room. Dozens of surly-looking elves stared at him with intolerant expressions, their hands firmly closed around mugs of fermented kank-nectar, known locally as broy.

A beefy man wearing a filthy linen apron hitched his thumb toward a set of stairs. "Your friends are upstairs, my lord."

Agis nodded his thanks to the proprietor, then ascended the stairs and stepped out onto a second-story veranda overlooking Shadow Square. In the background rose Kalak's mountainous ziggurat, looming over the plaza like a dark cloud.

Four nobles, easily identifiable by their haughty bearing and careful grooming, sat at a table on the edge of the balcony. Like Agis, they were all senators, each the informally acknowledged leader of a different faction. A half-elf serving wench with fire-colored hair and a low-cut bodice stood beside the table, gamely laughing at a ribald joke.

As Agis stepped toward the table, a fair-skinned man with a square-set jaw noticed him. "Welcome Agis!"

Beryl called. "Tell me, did you manage to arrive with your coins?"

Agis placed a hand on his hip and felt his purse still hanging from his belt. "As a matter of fact, I did."

"Good!" bellowed Dyan, a lord with a jowl-heavy face and a rotund build. "You can pay!"

A lanky man with long blond hair offered Agis a stool at his side. "You may as well spend your money here, my friend. You'll never leave the Elven Market with your purse strings intact." Kiah's tone was warm, as always when he was spending someone else's money. He was the leader of a formal association of business-minded nobles.

Agis accepted the stool and ordered a mug of broy, leaving Caro to stand behind him. No other servants were present, undoubtedly because Tithian had confiscated them all.

As soon as the serving wench left to fetch Agis's drink, Dyan nodded toward Caro. "Perhaps it would be wise to send your boy downstairs."

Realizing that the other nobles would feel more comfortable discussing their sensitive agenda without a slave present, Agis nodded to Caro. "Wait downstairs. Have whatever you eat or drink charged to me."

The old dwarf inclined his head and left without a word.

"You're too kind to your slaves," Kiah said. "It makes them insolent."

"To the contrary," Agis replied. "It makes them loyal. I guarantee that Caro will not abuse the privilege I just offered him."

"Let's get to our business while the serving wench is away," Dyan said. "Mirabel may be no friend of the templars, but she's no friend of ours either. I wouldn't put it past her to earn a coin or two by selling what she hears of our conversation."

Agis began immediately. "We all agree that Kalak is driving Tyr to ruin. Closing the iron mine was bad enough, but by confiscating our slaves, he's condemned the entire city to starvation."

"What do you propose?" asked Jaseela, the only person who had not yet spoken. She was a sultry beauty with silky black hair hanging to her waist, a shapely figure, and a regal face dominated by huge hazel eyes. Jaseela's speeches were seldom taken well in the Senate chamber, for they often bordered on the seditious. Still, even her greatest rivals admired her courage in so consistently speaking out against Kalak.

"Given that everyone's interests in this matter are similar, I thought we might work together toward a solution," Agis said. "Between the five of us, we have enough influence to insure that any resolution passes virtually unopposed in the Senate."

The other three men nodded, but Jaseela rolled her hazel eyes and looked out over the square.

Agis continued, "Let's convene an emergency session at sunrise. We'll co-sponsor a resolution demanding that the king return our slaves and reopen the iron mine. With our influence, we're sure to get unified backing. Even the king won't be able to ignore us."

"He won't ignore us, that's true," returned Dyan. "He'll have us assassinated."

Beryl added, "Even if we survive, Kalak hasn't listened to the Senate on any matter dear to him in a thousand years. What makes you think he's going to start now?"

"If he doesn't, we'll withhold our taxes. We'll burn our fields," Agis said enthusiastically. "We'll revolt!"

"We'll commit suicide is what you mean," Dyan said, shaking his head. "You're talking madness. We can't force the king to do something he doesn't want to. He'll kill us all."

"Then what are we going to do?" Agis demanded.

Beryl glanced toward the ziggurat. "Nothing. Kalak's been building the ziggurat for a hundred years. Our grandfathers and our fathers managed to survive his mismanagement, and so will we. Now that the tower's less than a month from completion, we'd be fools to oppose it."

"In a month, my faro will be withered and dead," Agis said. "Without enough slaves to work my wells and irrigate the land, my fields are baking. The rest of you can't even be as well off as I am."

"So what? Are any of *us* going to starve?" Dyan asked, shrugging his plump shoulders. "I, for one, have no intention of risking my life to feed slaves and derelicts."

Kiah placed a hand on Agis's shoulder. "You're overreacting, my friend," he said. "If you look at it in a certain light, the situation is advantageous to us." He paused and smiled at the other nobles. "I'm sure we all keep crops stockpiled against famine. Once the effects of the confiscations hit, those stockpiles will be worth ten times what they are now. If we can reach some arrangement among ourselves and the other nobles, we might even drive the price much higher."

Agis shrugged Kiah's hand off his shoulder and stood. "Are we concerned about nothing but gold and protecting our own fat necks?" he demanded. "By the moons, I can't believe what I'm hearing!"

Mirabel stepped out of the door with Agis's broy. He quickly returned to his seat, pretending to laugh at some abusive jest. Once she placed the gummy liquid in front of him, Dyan immediately handed an empty mug to her and said, "Be a good wench and fetch me another milkwine."

As soon as Mirabel went back into the suphouse, Agis resumed his appeal. "If we allow our fear of Kalak to intimidate us, we're no better than his slaves."

"If you give me a course of action that will work, I'll go along with you," said Dyan. "But I won't risk my life and my estate by sponsoring a meaningless resolution that Kalak will ignore anyway." He shook his head to emphasize his point.

"He's right, Agis," Beryl said, not lifting his eyes from his mug. "The Senate can do nothing."

"Perhaps we need to do something outside the Senate," Jaseela said, commanding the senators' attention by ending her long silence.

"Such as?" asked Kiah.

"Kill him."

The balcony fell quiet. Finally, Dyan asked, "Kill who, exactly?"

"You *know* who I'm talking about," she countered, fixing her hazel eyes on each of the men in turn.

"Regicide?" gasped Dyan, pushing his stool away from the table. "Are you mad?"

"He's too powerful," objected Beryl.

"What would happen to the city?" demanded Kiah, waving his hand toward the merchant emporiums on the other side of the ziggurat. "The political and economic structure of Tyr would collapse. We wouldn't be able to sell our crops."

Agis remained thoughtful, trying to decide if Jaseela could be right. Perhaps the only way to save Tyr was to kill the king. It was a difficult thing for him to accept, for it meant destroying the foundation of the city's ancient social order. He could not deny that there was much that was wrong in the city—the corruption of the templars, the poverty of the masses, the injustice of Kalak's laws—but he had always believed that those things could be corrected by working from within the established order. He wasn't sure that he was ready to give up that notion.

Jaseela's mind, however, was made up. "Gentlemen, all of your objections can be worked out," she said, bracing her elbows on the table. "The question is, do we let Kalak ruin our city or don't we?"

Kiah shook his head. "No. The situation is more complex than that. What about the templars? How will they react when Kalak is killed? How will—"

"The question before us is simple," Jaseela interrupted, rising to her feet. "Are we nobles, or are we slaves?"

When no one answered, the noblewoman turned her hazel eyes on Agis. "What about you?" she demanded. "You're the one who wanted to resist the king. Is your courage limited to the Senate chamber, or are you willing to fight for what you believe?"

Agis met her demanding gaze with a calm countenance. "I've spent ten years in the Senate fighting—"

"Can you point to a single resolution that we've passed in that time that has actually made Tyr a better place for anyone but ourselves?" Jaseela demanded.

Agis pondered the question for a moment, then looked down into his mug of broy.

"Of course not," she said for him. "The templars are corrupt, the Senate is corrupt, and so is the nobility."

"So we should destroy it all and start over?" Agis asked. "You're beginning to sound like you're in the Veiled Alliance!"

"I wish I was," Jaseela said bitterly. She turned to leave. "At least they've made enough trouble for Kalak to attract his attention."

Agis rose to intercept her, but before he left the table he

caught sight of a tumult in the square below. "Don't leave just yet, Jaseela," he said, moving to the edge of the balcony. "Something's happening in the square."

Jaseela and the other nobles joined him. Dozens of paupers were pouring into the square from the narrow alleys that led away from it. From the elves' tents rose a drone of apprehensive voices as the merchants hurriedly packed their goods into bundles. Confused residents were casting aside their water pots and trying to push through the mass of paupers rushing into the square.

Kiah searched the sky above the tenements surrounding the plaza. "There's no sign of smoke, so I don't think it's a fire."

The five nobles watched in silence for several more moments. The scene grew more panicked and more confused, with beggars and paupers continuing to stream in from all directions. Soon, hundreds of people jammed the small plaza, half of them crowding toward the center and the other half pushing toward the tenements surrounding it. Most of the elves had wrapped their wares in their tents and, in groups of two and three, were beating their way through the crowd.

Agis turned to peer down an alley running alongside the Red Kank. He found himself staring down at a half-giant, his menacing eyes as big around as plates. Below the eyes, a huge nose ran down to a misshaped, thick-lipped mouth.

"In the king's name, stand away from the wall!" ordered the half-giant, tilting his head back only a little to look up at Agis.

Agis obeyed, reaching for his mug of broy. The guard turned his attention back to the alley, gleefully kicking at the beggars, driving the poor wretches into the square.

Once the half-giant had passed the Red Kank, Dyan,

Beryl, and Kiah immediately disappeared into the suphouse. Agis and Jaseela stayed where they were to watch what happened next.

From each alley emerged one of the king's huge soldiers, using his feet and a club of polished bone to drive a small group of terrified paupers before him. Behind the half-giants came templars armed with whips and long black ropes. As Agis and Jaseela watched, the templars moved to the edge of the square and started separating people into two groups. They released one group to leave the square, then they bound the hands of those who remained into loops on the black ropes. As far as Agis could tell, the only thing that determined whether the templars released a person or bound him into a rope was whether or not the captive could produce a bribe.

"Tithian is certainly a clever fellow," remarked Jaseela sarcastically. "I would never have thought to solve the worker shortage by enslaving beggars."

"I wonder if it has occurred to Tithian that the king's half-giants would do much better on the ziggurat than our slaves or these paupers?" Agis asked, glancing at Jaseela.

"I'm certain it has, but have you ever known a half-giant to give an honest day's labor?" Jaseela countered. "Besides, if he made slaves of the king's guard, who would keep the Veiled Alliance in line?"

Below the Red Kank's balcony, a pauper broke away from the slave rope and sprinted for the alley. A half-giant lumbered after the escapee, roaring with excitement. He caught the unfortunate wretch in front of the suphouse, knocking the starving beggar into the wall with a well-aimed blow of the bone club.

The guard stopped a few feet from the balcony and peered up at the nobles. "Nice smash, eh?" he chortled, displaying his bloody club.

At that moment, a silver flash flared behind the guard and a clap of thunder rolled across the square. Agis looked toward the sound and saw a different half-giant crashing to the cobblestones, a smoking hole in the center of his back.

The guard in front of the Red Kank slowly turned and searched the square. "What's happening?"

An alarmed murmur rustled across the square, and the king's men stopped collecting slaves to look at their fallen comrade. Suddenly golden bolts of energy shot from shop windows and alleys all around the square, striking templars and half-giants with unnerving accuracy. Several black-robed bureaucrats collapsed. Others disappeared into the crowd. Some of the half-giants took the attacks without falling. They only roared in pain and clutched at the hideous burns that marked them wherever the golden beams had struck.

The guard in front of the Red Kank stood with his back to the nobles, looking from one side of the square to the other.

"Look!" Jaseela pointed at a form standing behind the counter of a nearby shop.

The figure wore a blue robe with a white veil pulled across his face. From beneath the veil protruded a small yellow tube, directed at a wounded half-giant a quarter of the way across the square. As the nobles watched, a handful of shimmering balls streaked out of the tube. When they hit the wounded guard, they erupted into sprays of brilliant flame. The half-giant dropped with without making a sound.

The guard in front of the Red Kank raised his club and started toward the figure, but paused when Jaseela called, "There's another!"

She pointed at a nearby alley, where a crackling flame streamed from the outstretched fingers of a blue-robed figure to scorch another guard's head.

"Sorcerers!" Agis gasped. "It has to be the Veiled Alliance!"

A nearby templar scooped three stones off the ground. "In the name of Mighty Kalak, let these missiles strike dead the enemies of the king!"

The templar tossed the stones at the wizard attacking with the fire stream. As soon as he released them, all three shot through the air like arrows and struck their target square in the forehead. The sorcerer collapsed, spraying the alley walls with great gouts of effulgent flame.

The half-giant in front of the suphouse stepped toward the first sorcerer that had revealed himself. In the same instant, Jaseela pulled a steel stiletto from beneath her cloak.

"What are you doing?" Agis asked.

"Joining the fight," Jaseela returned. "How about you?"

With that, she hopped onto the wall and dropped down onto the guard's back. As the noblewoman landed, she threw her free arm over the half-giant's shoulder and reached around his massive neck, burying her stiletto deep into the guard's soft throat.

The half-giant bellowed in rage. After dropping his club, he grabbed at Jaseela's head with one massive hand and at her stiletto with the other.

Agis watched the noblewoman's attack with a sense of detached shock. In the flash of an eye, Jaseela had declared herself in full rebellion against Kalak. If someone later identified her as a participant in the ambush, which seemed likely given the number of people in the square, her lands would be confiscated and orders issued to kill her on sight.

Jaseela ducked the half-giant's clumsy grasp, then slipped down his back, still clinging to her dagger. The blade opened a long gash in the guard's throat, then suddenly came free. The noblewoman dropped the rest of the way to ground, her arm soaked with dark blood.

The half-giant spun around. He held a massive hand across the gash in his throat, but could not stop the flow. Bright red bubbles appeared between his fingers. He gurgled an unintelligible threat and lifted his free hand to strike.

Realizing that even a wounded half-giant could crush the noblewoman with just one blow, Agis took a deep breath and prepared to help her. With a little bit of luck, he could use the Way to save Jaseela and no one would ever know.

The noble focused his thoughts on his energy nexus, then made a fist and turned the knuckles toward the guard's chest. In his mind he imagined a mystical rope of energy flowing from his nexus into his arm. Agis mentally shaped the energy he had summoned into a huge fist. He drew his arm back and punched at the guard, simultaneously releasing his psionic attack.

The invisible fist struck its target square in the chest. The half-giant rocked back on his massive heels, but did not fall. Instead, he shook his ponderous brow and peered more closely at Jaseela, then slapped her with the heel of his open hand. An astonished cry escaped the noblewoman's lips as the blow sent her crashing into the suphouse wall. She collapsed to the ground, and the half-giant reached down to pick her up.

Agis cursed himself for being tentative and subtle when he should have been bold. He had used the Way not because it was the best method of saving Jaseela, but because he was afraid to overtly involve himself in the revolt. Jaseela had shown no such hesitations. She had seen what was right and done it in an instant.

As the half-giant's fingers closed around Jaseela's limp body, Agis drew his dagger and climbed onto the edge of the balcony. "Up here!" he called.

The half-giant looked up, blood still seeping from between the fingers clasped about his throat. Agis dropped off the balcony. He landed on the guard's shoulder and stabbed at his foe's eye with all his might. The dagger sank to the hilt. The half-giant screamed and spun away, spilling Agis onto the cobblestones next to Jaseela. The huge brute plucked the dagger from his eye and stumbled away in pain and shock. A few steps later, he finally dropped to the ground.

Agis turned to Jaseela. The noblewoman's eyes were closed and her breathing shallow. He ran his hand over the back of her head and felt a huge knot forming where it had struck the wall. She was covered with blood, but he could not tell how much of it was hers and how much was from the dead guard.

Agis poked his head into the shadowy door of the Red Kank. "Caro!" he yelled. "I need you!"

Though he had no doubt the other three nobles were also inside the suphouse, he did not bother calling them. If he was disappointed in himself for letting Jaseela attack alone, he was disgusted with them for abandoning her altogether. Besides, he and Caro would have an easier time getting the noblewoman out of the Elven Market if there was more than one group of nobles for greedy pickpockets and vengeful templars to follow.

As Agis turned away from the Red Kank, he saw that the elven merchants had fallen upon the templars. He knew the elves were more interested in stealing the bureaucrat's fat purses than resisting Kalak's oppression, but he was glad for the diversion. The more chaotic the scene in Shadow Square, the less likely templar informers would be to take note of him and Jaseela.

Agis gently stretched the noblewoman out on the cobblestones, then kneeled at her side and checked once more for obvious wounds. As far as he could tell, all of the blood had come from the half-giant.

Caro stepped out of the suphouse. "What happened?"

"No time to explain now," Agis said. "I'm going to need you to keep Jaseela from being jostled as we leave. Do you feel well enough for a little pushing and shoving?"

The dwarf nodded. "I'll do my best."

Without further comment, Agis laid his hands on the ground next to the noblewoman, then called on his psionic powers to create an invisible bed of pure force beneath her. His fingers and hands began to tingle, and Jaseela's body rose off the ground. Agis laid a palm on her stomach to keep her stable and used his other to take her hand. He stepped toward the alley through which he had entered the square, thinking he might be strong enough to keep her levitated until they had left the Elven Market.

When Agis lifted his eyes from Jaseela's unconscious form, he found himself facing a large man wearing a blue robe, a white scarf pulled across his face. The brown eyes peering out from beneath the white brow seemed as ancient as Caro's, but there was a depth and power to them that Agis found both alarming and awe-inspiring. In one hand, the wizard held the noble's bloody dagger, and in the other he carried the obsidian-pommeled cane that Agis recognized as belonging to the old man who had given him directions to Shadow Square.

The figure offered the dagger to Agis without saying a word.

"You?" the noble gasped.

The sorcerer ignored the question and placed the dagger in Agis's hand, then turned to go. The senator caught him by the shoulder. "Wait. We're part of this now. We want to help."

Using his cane, the sorcerer knocked Agis's hand away. "We don't need your help."

With that, he took a single step away from the nobleman. Before Agis's eyes, the old man's body grew translucent and faded from sight.

SIX

Debt of Honor

Rikus stood atop a peninsula protruding from a cliff of orange shale. A cool breeze danced over his face, and tall, wispy rods of ruby thornstem scratched his bare shoulders. At his back lay a vast plain of rusty desert, mottled by delicate clumps of white brittlebush and green globes of tumbling spikeballs. Before him hung a void filled with still, ashen haze that stretched from below the cliff to the zenith of the sky.

The mul had been peering into the gray murk for a long time, he couldn't say whether it had been minutes or hours or days, hoping for some glimpse of what lay on the other side. So far, the curtain had not parted, and he was beginning to think he was looking at the Sea of Silt.

Rikus did not remember crossing the desert at his back, and he had no idea how he had come to be standing on this cliff. The last thing he recalled was seeing his friends rush to his rescue as the gaj burned his mind. He feared that his lapse of memory was due to damage caused by the creature's attack.

To the mul's right, the gray haze finally stirred, churn-

121

ing itself into an oval eddy as tall as a man. Rikus stepped away and raised his fists to a fighting guard, prepared to defend himself. The eddy simply continued to whirl.

"Step through," spoke a voice at Rikus's back. It had a smooth, melodious timber that was neither male nor female.

The mul turned. A vaguely human shape stood beside him. The figure wore a gray burnoose with the hood pulled over its head so that neither its face or eyes were visible. It held its arms before it, its hands neatly folded into the opposite sleeves.

"Who are you?" the mul demanded. His heart was suddenly beating hard with confusion and fear, and he did not like the feeling.

"No one," came the reply. The figure lifted an arm and pointed toward the swirling eddy. There was no hand at the end of its sleeve. "What are you waiting for?"

"Nothing," Rikus answered, staring at the sleeve.

"Then you have found it."

Rikus stepped toward the figure. "What's happening here?"

"Nothing," came the reply.

The mul scowled and peered beneath the shadows of the hood. When he saw only empty darkness, he reached up and pulled the hood away.

The figure had no head. Even the burnoose's collar was as empty as the sleeves and the hood.

With a start, Rikus realized why he could not remember crossing the desert. "Is that it? I'm dead?" he demanded, waving a hand at the curtain of grayness. "This is all a lifetime of pain and bondage comes to?"

"This is all everything comes to," the figure replied, its dulcet voice sounding from the empty space above its collar. With its empty sleeve, it gestured toward the swirling eddy.

Rikus shook his head. "It's not enough," he said. "Not for me." He turned toward the desert plain and started walking.

The gray figure appeared in front him. "There is nothing more," it said, raising its empty sleeves to block his way. "You can't escape."

"I can try," the mul hissed, reaching out to clutch the cloak. "Besides, what's to stop me?" He wadded the empty robe into a bundle and tossed it over his shoulder. "Nothing."

He walked for miles, then tens of miles. The terrain never changed, save that the gray curtain at his back grew more and more distant. Ahead of him, an endless plain of orange shale stretched to the horizon, the dreary monotony broken only by the white caps of brittlebush, the green dots of spikeballs, and the barren stalks of thornstem waving in the breeze.

Finally Rikus's legs grew weary. He sat down to rest, then yawned and realized he could not remember the last time he had slept. The mul leaned back, ignoring the sharp edges of shale that poked him in the shoulders and ribs. There was no sun in the yellow sky, only an ethereal haze that radiated an amber glow. Rikus closed his eyes.

When he woke, he was no longer in the desert. Instead, he lay in the center of a square room. Over his head hung a ceiling of mekillot ribs, lashed together to form a grid of squares. Above the bone grid, the twin moons, Ral and Guthay, shone through a scaly roof of stretched hide, filling the room with dim, yellow light.

The walls and floor were of solid stone, save that there was a large gate of iron bars in one wall. Once unlocked, the gate could be raised into a special slot by means of a sturdy giant-hair rope and pulleys located outside the cell.

"What am I doing here?" Rikus asked no one in particular.

Beneath him lay a pile of dirty rags that had been serving as his bed. The cell stank of offal and sweat, and through the gate came the roars, chirps, and shrieks of a dozen kinds of beasts.

Rikus sat up and shook his head, sending waves of throbbing pain through his skull. His back, arms, and legs were stiff and sore, and his abdomen burned where the gaj's barbed pincers had punctured his skin.

The mul groaned, taking his first good look around the pen. In one corner, Yarig and Anezka lay curled up together. At Rikus's side, Neeva's massive form was stretched out on the stone floor, covered only by her heavy cape.

"I'm alive," Rikus said.

"So it would seem," answered a familiar, sarcastic voice. "What a pity."

Rikus lifted his eyes to the gate. Boaz stood in the corridor beyond. The half-elf wore a cape of blue silk and carried an open carafe of milkwine. His eyes were blurry, and he stood awkwardly braced on stiff legs, as if he would pitch forward at any moment. At his waist hung a ring of keys and a steel dirk.

"No guards?" asked Rikus. In his mind, the mul saw the trainer standing atop the practice pit wall, wanting to know which of the mul's friends should be flogged in punishment for his disrespect. The memory filled the gladiator's heart with bitter anger. "That's careless of you, Boaz."

"I'm safe enough with that between us," the half-elf replied, gesturing at the iron gate. His words were slurred. "Besides, my guards have all passed out. Not enough to do in this tedious compound, so they drink too much."

"If there's nothing to do here, why aren't you all in Tyr?" Rikus asked, stepping to the gate.

Boaz lifted the carafe to his lips, then spat a mouthful of milkwine over Rikus's face. "Because of you—you and Sadira," the trainer said, taking the precaution of moving out of arm's reach. Behind him, something stirred in the pen opposite Rikus's. "I'll see to it that you're punished in the morning."

"For what?" Rikus demanded, wiping the white froth off his face. Even if he could have reached Boaz, he doubted that he would have killed the half-elf at that moment. Doing so would have meant giving up the chance to win his freedom, and he wasn't prepared to do that over a mouthful of wine.

Boaz lifted the carafe to his lips again. Rikus stepped away from the gate, but this time the only wine that left the half-elf's mouth was what dribbled down his chin. In a rambling speech, the trainer told Rikus how Sadira had saved him from the gaj with her magic, then killed two guards to escape the Break. "Lord Tithian was furious with me and my fellows," Boaz finished. "He confined us all to the pits."

"You're lying," Rikus said. "Sadira would never—"

"He's not lying," Neeva interrupted. She stepped to Rikus's side and leaned against the gate, wrapped in the same cape she had been using as a blanket. "What part don't you believe—that Sadira's a sorceress or that she left you behind?"

"That I was saved by a scullery wench," Rikus answered.

"She's no ordinary slave girl," Neeva replied, giving the mul a sarcastic smile. "It's surprising that I'm the one who has to tell you that."

Boaz snorted at Neeva's jealousy.

Rikus ignored the trainer. "What happened to her?" he asked. "Where is she now?"

"What does it matter?" Neeva demanded, narrowing her emerald eyes. "You weren't in love with her, were you?"

"Of course not." Rikus looked away and noticed that both Yarig and Anezka had also awakened. The dwarf and his halfling partner were doing their best not involve themselves in the conversation. "I owe her a debt of honor. That's all."

"There have been other slave girls and you haven't lied to me yet," Neeva said, thumping Rikus in the chest. "Why start now?"

Rikus found that he could not look his fighting partner in the eye. Instead, he cast a meaningful glance at Boaz and asked, "Do we have to talk about this here?"

"Yes," Boaz chuckled. "It's best to air these things immediately. Hidden resentments have ruined many a matched pair."

"Well?" Neeva asked. "Is Sadira so different from the others?"

Rikus forced himself to meet his partner's gaze. In his own mind, the mul did not know whether what he felt for Sadira was gratitude or something deeper, and the uncertainty made him uncomfortable. "Sadira risked her life to save mine. I guess that makes her different."

Neeva turned away, tears welling in her eyes.

Rikus grabbed her shoulders. "My feelings for Sadira—whatever they are—have nothing to do with us. I just need to know what happened to her."

Neeva pulled away and stepped into a dark corner of the pen.

"I wish I could help you two lovers," Boaz sneered.

"Unfortunately, nobody knows what happened to her. My guess is that someday I'll run into her in the Elven Market. In a brothel, no doubt."

Rikus thrust an arm through the iron bars, clutching at the half-elf. Boaz watched the gladiator's fingers close a few inches shy of their target, then clucked at the mul. "Anezka will pay dearly for that."

No sooner had the trainer finished his threat than Rikus felt an earthenware mug smash against his back. He glanced over his shoulder and saw Yarig grab his half-ling partner, who was just reaching for a wooden bowl to throw. The dwarf shrugged, but made no apology for her.

Rikus shook his head and faced Boaz again. Before he could say anything, he heard a wispy voice inside his head.

He lies.

"What?" Rikus demanded, grabbing his ears. He turned to Neeva. "Did you hear that?"

When she ignored him, Yarig asked, "A voice inside your head?" The dwarf still had not released Anezka.

Rikus nodded.

"No, I didn't hear it just now," he answered facetiously. "But I have in the last few days."

Rikus furrowed his hairless brow and shook his head. "If—"

Boaz laughed at the mul's confusion. "It's the gaj, you buffoon. It was talking to you."

"Talking to me?" Rikus gasped, half-disgusted and half-frightened. The gaj's stinging tentacles and the way it had scorched his mind glowed fresh in his memory.

Yes. I am learning to speak well, the gaj reported.

Boaz looked toward the pen opposite Rikus's. The beast inside had moved in front of its gate, and the tips of its pincers protruded between the iron bars. Rikus could barely see the gaj's bulbous white head inside the murky pen.

"We've learned a lot about the gaj over the last couple of days, haven't we?" Boaz said. "It doesn't eat bodies, it eats minds." He took a step toward its pen.

The beast scuttled back into the shadows. *Boaz knows an elf called Radurak,* the gaj said in Rikus's mind. *Radurak has your woman.*

Rikus turned to Yarig. "Did you hear that?"

The dwarf shook his head. "It only talks to one person at a time," he said.

Boaz will tell Tithian where to find her.

"How do you know?" Rikus asked.

It's in his thoughts, the gaj replied.

In the corridor, Boaz picked up a loose stone and threw it into the gaj's cage. "How come you don't talk to me anymore?"

Rikus was stunned. Should he believe the gaj, or was this some sort of trick on Boaz's part to get him to reveal what he knew of Sadira? Rikus had heard of the Way, of course, and knew that it could be used to speak telepathically. What he had trouble accepting was that an overgrown bug like the gaj might be intelligent enough to use it. Still, he had no choice except to believe what he heard inside his head.

Boaz drained the last of his milkwine, then threw the carafe at the gaj. "Stupid beast!" He started to stumble out of the animal shed.

"Tell me, Boaz, do you think telling Tithian about Radurak will make the high templar forgive you?" Rikus called.

Boaz stopped dead. "Where did you hear Radurak's name?"

Any doubts about what the gaj had told him vanished from Rikus's mind. "I don't think it'll help you," the mul continued, ignoring the trainer's question. "Lord Tithian will still blame you for not noticing Sadira's powers, and then for letting her escape."

Rikus heard Neeva shuffle in the dark corner to which she had retreated. He glanced at her and saw that, although she still glowered at him, she had dropped the cape from her shoulders and watched him closely. The mul breathed a sigh of relief. He didn't know what would happen next, but he was happy to see that she would back him up.

Boaz returned and stood in front of Rikus's pen, safely out of reach. "You had better hope my confinement is lifted," the trainer said. Though he stank of fermented milk, the half-elf suddenly appeared almost sober. Rikus feared it would be difficult to lure him close enough to the gate to strike.

"Life is growing tedious on this estate," Boaz continued. "When I get bored, I get irritable. Things could go very hard on you and your friends if Tithian is not in a forgiving mood."

"Perhaps I should put in a good word for you with the high templar," Rikus offered sarcastically.

Behind Boaz, the gaj, too, moved forward, pushing its pincers through the bars of its cage in an effort to snag the trainer. The mandibles were too short to reach the half-elf, but an idea occurred to Rikus that might make it possible to kill Boaz and save Sadira, without sacrificing his dream of freedom.

The trainer sneered at Rikus's offer of aid. "I doubt that I'll let you live long enough to speak with Lord Tithian."

Gaj, if you want Boaz, here's what to do, Rikus

thought, hoping the beast could hear his thoughts as it
had heard Boaz's. He laid out a simple plan.

He must be alive, came the reply. *If he dies before my
antennae touch his head, his mind will be spoiled for me.*

Yes, Rikus agreed. He grabbed the bars of his gate,
then said to Boaz, "After I'm free, the first thing I'm going to do is track you into a dark street—"

The mul did not have a chance to finish his threat. Behind the trainer, the gaj threw itself at its gate. A tremendous crash echoed through the animal shed as the beast's
carapace struck the iron bars, triggering an immediate
chorus of alarmed squeals and roars from the other pens.

As Rikus had hoped, the startled trainer leaped away
from the gaj, straight into the mul's waiting arms. Rikus
grabbed Boaz by the collar, pulling the half-elf toward
the gate. The astonished trainer started to cry for help,
but Rikus slapped a massive hand over the man's mouth.

"Rikus!" gasped Neeva. "What are you doing?"

"Repaying Sadira for saving my life," the mul responded. "Get his keys and unlock our gate."

Don't kill him! the gaj urged, settling back into its pen.

"You'll have him alive—more or less," Rikus answered,
squeezing Boaz's mouth with all his strength. He felt a
series of satisfying pops as the half-elf's front teeth broke
away at the roots.

Boaz groaned in pain, then reached for the dirk at his
belt. Rikus grabbed the trainer's wrist with his free hand.
"Wrong move," he said, pulling the offending arm
through the gate. He pressed the forearm against an iron
bar until he heard a sharp crack. A muffled wail escaped
Boaz's covered lips.

"You'll get us killed," Neeva said, stepping to Rikus's
side. She removed the key ring from Boaz's belt.

"Not if my plan works," Rikus replied, giving his fighting partner a confident wink. "They'll think the gaj did it."

"They'd better," Neeva said, moving to the gate lock and fitting keys into it.

Rikus looked at the dwarf, who still held onto Anezka, though it no longer appeared that she needed to be restrained. "Yarig, you'll have to lift the gate for Neeva to crawl under."

"I don't like it," the dwarf said. "You shouldn't have done something like this without asking us first."

Boaz tried to pull free. Without looking away from Yarig, Rikus slammed him back into the gate. "Don't you think asking would have ruined the surprise?"

"That doesn't matter," Yarig answered stubbornly. "This affects all of us. I don't care if you are the champion. You can't make decisions like this on your own."

Rikus rolled his eyes, then let go of Boaz's broken wrist. "You're right," the mul said. "I'll let him go."

Anezka shook her head urgently.

Neeva turned a key in the gate lock and a loud click echoed in the cell. "Make up your mind, Yarig," she said.

"We'll push Boaz over to the gaj, lock ourselves back in, and toss the keys in front of its pen," Rikus said, once more slamming the half-elf into the gate—this time only because he enjoyed doing so. "Everyone will think he was drunk, wandering around in here, and got too close to the cage."

Yarig released the halfling and slowly lifted the gate. Once he had raised it high enough for Neeva to crawl beneath, she went into the corridor and restrained Boaz from the outside while Rikus left the pen.

In both directions, the long corridor was lined with steel gates similar to the one from beneath which the mul had just crawled. In a few places, he could see claws or tentacles or vaguely humanlike hands protruding from between the bars, but otherwise every pen appeared identical.

As Rikus stepped into the corrider, Neeva shoved Boaz toward a cage a short distance away. A powerful, acrid odor rose from the pen.

"Rikus, maybe we should feed Boaz to a raakle instead of the gaj," Neeva said.

No, Rikus! the gaj whined. *You promised!*

The trainer cringed, and his eyes glazed with horror. Rikus did not blame him for being frightened. Raakles were brilliantly colored birds the size of half-giants, but their mouths were short tubular beaks no larger around than a man's fingers. They digested their prey by gripping it with their powerful, three-clawed feet, then spitting sticky acid over it. This fluid reduced bone and flesh alike to a pulpy ooze that the bird sucked up through its small mouth.

Though he would have enjoyed hearing Boaz scream in the terrible agaony of being digested alive, Rikus shook his head. "I gave my word," he said. "Besides, being eaten by a raakle can't compare to the pain the gaj will cause Boaz's mind."

"If you say so." Neeva shoved the trainer toward the gaj's pen.

Rikus laid a hand on his fighting partner's shoulder and shook his head. "I'll take him," Rikus said. He substituted his hand for the one that Neeva had been using to hold Boaz's bleeding mouth closed. "I want the pleasure of feeding him to the gaj myself."

The gaj thrust its mandibles as far into the corridor as they would go. Rikus stepped toward the pen.

Boaz mumbled something at the mul. Though the trainer was doing his best to appear menacing and confident, fear and panic softened his sharp features.

The gladiator moved the hand covering the half-elf's mouth just far enough to hear what he had to say. "You'll never get away with this," Boaz hissed. "Tithian will know what happened, and Neeva will be the one who pays."

"You're the only one who's going to pay," Rikus interrupted. The mul smashed a fist into the half-elf's rib cage. Boaz cried out, then began to wheeze.

Please, Rikus, the gaj asked. *Give him to me now.*

Boaz tried to call for help, but with his broken ribs and teeth, only incoherent mumbles came from his mouth. Rikus smiled, then pushed the half-elf across the corridor. The gaj's barbed mandibles closed on the trainer's abdomen, and a pair of whiplike antennae lashed out of the pen, entwining themselves around its victim's brow.

Despite his injuries, Boaz found the strength to scream.

SEVEN

A Bidding War

The instant Agis stepped into the hastily erected slave-yard, his eyes fell on a white-haired man standing amidst the crowd of nobles who had gathered there. Though the old fellow was only a few inches taller than the people around him, he stood out from the jabbering throng by virtue of his silent demeanor. Over his broad shoulders he wore an ivory-colored cape, and in his hand he carried an obsidian-pommeled cane that left no doubt in Agis's mind that the man was the sorcerer who had returned his dagger to him in Shadow Square.

"What's he doing at a slave auction?" Agis murmured.

"Buying slaves, I suspect," Caro replied sarcastically. "Isn't that what one does at these iniquitous affairs?"

"You asked to come, Caro. If you don't intend to be good company, perhaps I should send you home," Agis replied.

Along with fifty other lords and the sorcerer, Agis and Caro stood beneath the Elven Bridge, an ancient structure spanning the dusty bed of the Forgotten River. According to legend, the magnificent bridge had once crossed a broad, slow-moving estuary of glistening water. Now the edifice was no more than a useless relic, for all that remained below it was a short bend of dry gulch sealed at both ends by piles of rubble. The only signs of water in the riverbed were white crusts of calcium and lime left on the bridge piers two decades past—the last time it had rained in Tyr.

Currently an enterprising tribe of elves was using the area below the bridge as a slaveyard. They had created a small square by erecting four walls of dirty hemp and had invited a select group of nobles to attend a surreptitious auction. Judging by the bulging purses hanging from the nobles' belts today, the elves' trade promised to be a brisk one.

Agis turned his attention to the old man. "Come along, Caro," he said, starting across the square. "Let's have a word with our friend."

In the days following the uprising in the square, there had been no indication that the templars knew about Agis's participation in the affair. Neither had Jaseela been questioned. Agis might have banished the memory of his involvement in the whole matter, save that he found that he did not want to. In killing the half-giant, he had crossed some intangible line. Now, for better or worse, he was a rebel.

With his aged manservant close behind, the noble worked his way through the crowd. Several acquaintances invited him to stop and gossip, but he risked seeming rude by giving them brisk replies and moving along.

By the time he reached the sorcerer's side, a pair of seven-foot elves had already stepped into the makeshift square. They politely cleared a space in which they could display the slaves.

"We meet again," Agis said, smiling at the sorcerer.

The old man gave him a blank stare. "Do I know you?"

Though Agis was certain the sorcerer recognized him, he decided to play along. "You were kind enough to give me directions to the Red Kank a few days ago."

The old man's face remained sour and blank, but he said, "I see you survived your little expedition."

"Yes, thank you," the noble replied, offering his hand. "I'm Agis of Asticles."

The sorcerer ignored the introduction and looked away. "Don't give me reason to regret what I did for you."

"It surprises me to see you here," Agis noted casually, ignoring the affront.

"Nobles aren't the only ones who need slaves," the old man commented.

"I didn't think the Veiled Alliance condoned slavery."

The sorcerer raised an eyebrow. "You have mistaken me for someone else," he said. Without waiting for a response, he muscled his way through the crowd and left Agis behind.

For a moment, the noble considered pursuing the old man to brooch the subject of a coalition between himself and the Veiled Alliance. Unfortunately, he suspected that pursuing the subject in a public place would make the sorcerer even less inclined to listen. The noble decided that if the old man was attending a slave auction, there was a good reason. By watching carefully, he might learn something that would enable him to approach the Alliance, and under better circumstances, as well.

A pale elf with black hair stepped into the square. Instead of the typical desert burnoose that most elves favored, he wore a fine cloak of brushed fleece. The elf lifted his hands to quiet the crowd. "Gentlemen and gentlewomen, welcome. I am your host, Radurak, and it gives me great pleasure to present to you a collection of slaves brought all the way from Balic—"

"Your tribe hasn't been away from Tyr in six months," called a noble.

Radurak tipped his hat to the noble. "The Runners of Guthay have many warriors," he said, grinning slyly. "A few of us have been to Balic more recently than you think."

Several nobles expressed open skepticism at the statement. Though what Radurak claimed may have been true, it would have been difficult to move a sizable number of slaves across such a vast distance with only a few warriors. It seemed more likely that the elves had stolen the slaves from legitimate traders. Had it not been for the old man's presence and his own desperate need of slaves, Agis would have left at that moment. He did not like doing business with thieves.

"I'm sure all of the commodities you offer come from legal slave stock," called another noble.

"Of course," Radurak replied. "Unfortunately, the seals of ownership were taken by raiders, not fifty miles outside Tyr. You have my word that every one of the fine specimens I sell today is my tribe's property."

This brought a round of laughter from the skeptical lords. Finally a voice called, "Let's just get on with it! I want to have my slaves tucked safely inside my townhouse by nightfall."

Agis looked toward the speaker and saw that it was Dyan. He elected not to greet the portly noble, as he no longer felt a kinship with the cowards who had deserted him and Jaseela in the square.

Radurak bowed. "By your request."

For the rest of the day, Radurak and his elves presented a motley assortment of paupers, sots, and cretins they had assembled for the auction. After the first hour, Agis had no doubt that the entire bunch had been gathered from the alleys of the Elven Market. At one point, the sorcerer lifted a hand to wipe the sweat from his brow and Agis glimpsed a fat purse hanging from the belt beneath his white tabard. He had, indeed, come to buy something, though Agis could not figure out what.

As the afternoon wore on, the nobles began to grumble about the quality of the stock and complain bitterly that half the slaves would die before they reached the estates. Radurak took their protests in stride and continued to smile, as well he might. The slaves were drawing ten times their value. Some desperate nobles were even bidding on men so feeble they had to be carried into the yard.

Finally, as dusk began to fall and the square was plunged into swarthy shadows, the elves brought no more slaves into the makeshift yard.

"I'm afraid you have depleted my stock," Radurak said.

A disappointed murmur ran around the courtyard. As bad as the elf's slaves were, they were all that had been available in Tyr since Tithian's confiscations had begun.

The pale elf smiled warmly, then raised his hands, "As a way of thanking you for your patronage, I have a special treat."

Radurak clapped his hands twice. Immediately a pair of elves escorted a lithe half-elf female into the yard. For the benefit of their human customers, the elves carried a pair of torches that cast an enchanting yellow light over the slave-girl. Agis could see that she was as beautiful as any noblewoman, with a willowy figure and elegant features. Her long amber hair spilled over her shoulders in silky waves, and her pale blue eyes were as clear as the finest gem. Had Agis been the sort of man to take concubines, she was the woman he would have wanted.

Radurak had dressed Sadira in a gossamer gown that revealed just enough of her charms to make any man want to see more, but she deliberately moved with an awkwardness that she hoped would make her seem inept and stupid. She was far from happy about being sold in Radurak's heinous auction and intended to do everything she could to bring him a small price.

It had been Radurak who had offered Sadira refuge from the king's men three nights past. As soon as the half-elf had passed through the doorway from which the elf had hailed her, he had emptied a vial of noxious liquid on the threshold, filling the air with mordant fumes. They had stepped away from the doorway just before the cilops reached it, but Sadira had heard the animals let out terrible screeches of pain. The square then erupted into frightened screams as the beasts rushed blindly about, attacking anything they touched.

Radurak had taken advantage of the confusion to lead Sadira through a tangle of halls and rooms, emerging in an alley on the far side of the building. As the sorceress had stepped out the door, several of the elf's tribesmen had seized her, binding and gagging her. Shortly afterward, Radurak had discovered her spellbook and taken it away, threatening to destroy the volume if she gave him any trouble. He had also offered to return it if she did not try to escape before she was sold. Sadira had reluctantly agreed to his terms, for her spells were too valuable to lose—though she had her doubts about whether or not he would keep his word. If not, she would think of a way to make him pay.

"I personally bought this slender beauty in the slave markets of Gulg," Radurak lied, "where it was said that she is the daughter of the chieftain of the great Sari tribe—"

"Master, you have me confused with someone else," Sadira interrupted, smiling sweetly and batting her eyes at the repulsive elf. "I've never been out of the Tyr Valley."

Her interruption brought a round of laughter from the nobles gathered in the yard, but Radurak was not amused. He stepped to her side and, cuffing her with the back of his hand, hissed, "Remember your book, wench!"

Before Sadira could respond, Ktandeo's voice asked, "How much?"

"Fifty gold," Radurak replied. It was elven practice to run an auction by naming a price and selling to the first person to match it, or failing that to sell to whoever came closest.

"I'll pay it," Ktandeo replied.

Sadira breathed a sigh of relief. Ktandeo had no doubt seen her accept Radurak's help, so she was not surprised that the old man had tracked her down. Neither was she surprised that he was coming to her aid, for as he himself had said, it would be disastrous if she fell into the templars' hands. The sorceress was shocked to see him taking the elf's price so quickly, however, for he had always struck her as a shrewder fellow than that.

Radurak smiled at the old man. "You are a gentleman who appreciates quality, sir."

An astonished murmur rustled through the crowd, for the price was five times what had been paid for any slave that day. It had grown too dark for Agis to read the sorcerer's expression, but he had no doubt that the slave girl was the reason for the old man's presence.

"I'll pay fifty-five gold," Agis called, breaking with established bidding protocol.

A charge of excitement shot through the crowd, and Caro hissed, "You have fallen to a new low, Master."

"I don't want her for myself," Agis explained, motioning his dwarf to be silent.

"Sixty gold," the old man replied, his voice rock steady.

Radurak looked from one man to the other, then shrugged and smiled. "It seems I have underestimated the value of my merchandise. My tribe is open to any offer."

Agis started to speak again, then abruptly changed his mind. Suddenly, bidding against the old man seemed a foolish thing to do. He found himself thinking that he already owned hundreds of slaves and this one was really not as special as she looked. The thought also crossed his mind that Radurak had waited until dusk in order to conceal some flaw that would become readily apparent tomorrow morning.

"Will you bid again on the right?" Radurak asked. "She is a true beauty. I'm sure you won't be sorry."

The elf's words brought Agis back to his senses, and he realized the thoughts that had been going through his mind were not his own; they had been planted by some outside influence. His training in the Way told him that the influence could not have been psionic in nature. He would have felt it entering his mind had it been so.

With a start, Agis realized that the old man had cast an enchantment on him. He started to complain, but realized that at an auction being run in such a place by a tribe of elves, his protest would have seemed absurdly naive and comical. Instead, he said, "Sixty-five gold."

Agis turned to Caro, then whispered, "Keep up the bidding. Whatever you do, don't let the half-elf get away."

"But she's only—"

"Just do it!" Agis ordered. "You'll see why later."

The noble closed his eyes and visualized a solid wall of faro trees rising out of the ground to surround his intellect, their spine-covered boughs intertwining so thickly that it was impossible for something so small as a needle-worm to crawl through the hedge without being ripped to shreds. This living barrier kept growing and arched over the top of his mind like a bower, protecting him against attack from above as well as from the side. He imagined the roots of the trees reaching deep inside him, drawing upon his energy nexus for the power to make the defenses strong. The hedge was not impenetrable—nothing was to a master of the Way—but Agis knew that the sorcerer would find it difficult to slip any more spells past it.

Once his own mind was defended, Agis set about attacking his opponent's. Normally he would not stoop to using the Way to win an auction, but if the old man was calling upon magic, Agis saw nothing dishonorable in using his own abilities.

The senator opened his eyes and looked across the courtyard. Though it was too dark to see the sorcerer's face, in his mind Agis pictured the old man's shrewd brown eyes. Closing his mind to anything but those eyes, he summoned enough psionic energy to create a psychic messenger—in this instance, an owl. He gave the owl feathers that matched the color of the sorcerer's eyes and sent it flying silently toward his opponent. As the owl approached its target, its brown feathers disappeared against the irises of the old man's eyes, then slipped into what lay beyond.

A fragment of his intellect moving with the owl, Agis was staggered when they entered the sorcerer's mind.

From the old man's curt manner and constant frown, the noble had assumed he would find a stormy, harsh place as violent as the Athasian desert itself, with fiery flashes of anger and cold bolts of disdain shooting in every direction. Instead, it seemed more like a blissful oasis on a still night, its pool filled with blue waters and its perimeter surrounded by a forest of stalwart trees strong enough to withstand any wind. Agis was so surprised that he hesitated before sending his owl down to claim control of the place.

In that moment, the old man realized that his mind was being invaded. Suddenly, a thousand white shrikes appeared out of the trees and flew toward Agis's owl. Each of the little birds screeched a tremendously loud and shrill warning call. The noble tucked the wings of his raptor and dropped toward the pool, but the shrikes attacked, tearing at the larger bird's tailfeathers and pecking at its eyes.

Even as Agis prepared to change his probe to something less subtle and more powerful, the shrikes tore the owl. The noble glimpsed a beak and a handful of feathers settling over the oasis pond, then Agis found himself staring across the murky courtyard at his opponent.

The noble gasped several times, for the battle and the loss of the owl had cost him a considerable amount of energy. Nevertheless, though he doubted he could enter the sorcerer's mind again, he had plenty of stamina left and there were as many ways to use the Way as there were men who walked the face of Athas. He would find another way to attack and try again.

"What's the bidding, Caro?" Agis asked.

"Seventy-one gold."

From across the courtyard, the old man's sonorous voice called, "Seventy-five."

"Eighty," Agis replied automatically.

A murmur rustled through the courtyard. Mul gladiators could be had for eighty gold.

No response came from the other side of the courtyard. The slave girl regarded Agis with her icy blue eyes, then cast a glance in the old man's direction.

"Are you finished bidding?" Radurak asked, directing his gaze to the old man.

"I withdraw my offer."

To the astonishment of Agis, the voice had come from close at hand. Had Caro spoken? Agis looked down and saw that a pair of lips had formed in the dust at his feet. There was no nose or chin or face of any sort, just a mouth.

As the nobleman watched, the lips parted and said, "I withdraw my offer."

Radurak's brow sank in disappointment as he looked to Agis. "Did I hear you right?"

Planting his boot square in the mouth on the ground, the senator shook his head. The mouth tried to speak again, but all that emerged was a muffled garble. When it was clear that the sorcerer's magical lips would not interrupt him again, Agis called, "I said eighty-five gold."

"A bold maneuver," Radurak said, smiling in relief. He turned back to the old man. "Can you match his bid?"

This time, the noble was ready to pay the sorcerer back in kind. He used the Way to create an invisible tunnel that ended directly in his opponent's mouth. As the old man spoke, Agis silently mouthed the words he wanted to come from the other man's lips.

"I do not have that much." The voice was the old man's, but the words were Agis's. The noble was particularly proud of the way the voice cracked with disappointment.

"How unfortunate," Radurak cooed sympathetically. He motioned Agis forward.

The old man started to protest, but again Agis put his own words into the sorcerer's mouth. "Perhaps you would trust me for the rest—"

This brought a roar of laughter from everyone assembled beneath the bridge. The sorcerer scowled in Agis's direction, but the noble ignored him and stepped forward, taking his purse off his belt. He found his fingers trembling with fatigue as he untied the knot. His contest with the sorcerer was taking its toll on his energies.

The slave-girl looked in his direction, an expression of contempt on her face. She mumbled something under her breath, then motioned for Agis to return to his place. "You'll never lay a hand on me, spawn of a misbegotten mekillot!"

Agis's foot struck an invisible obstacle, and he found himself sprawling face-first into the dust. He barely managed to tuck his heavy purse of gold away before his body struck the hard ground.

More than a few of his fellows made lewd comments suggesting Agis should wait until returning home to think about what he was going to do with his prize. The noble accepted the jibes with good-natured humor, then gathered himself up.

The sorcerer's voice called, "I found a few more coins, Radurak. My bid is raised to ninety gold." The old man glanced at Agis, gesturing at him as if motioning him away.

Agis stood, calling, "Ninety-five!"

The bid elicited a puzzled look from Radurak.

The elf frowned, then asked Agis, "*Have you ever seen Ral and Guthay dance a two-time jig?*"

"What are you talking about?" the noble demanded.

This time, the elf scowled angrily. "*You should walk on your hands to Gulg.*"

With a sinking heart, Agis realized the sorcerer had cast another enchantment on him. Whatever anyone said to him reached his ears in the form of utter nonsense. Judging from Radurak's expressions, the reverse was also true.

The elf motioned Agis back to his place, then invited the sorcerer forward. When the noble did not obey immediately, two tall tribesmen stepped forward to enforce their chief's order. Agis decided he would accomplish nothing by arguing in his present state—except, perhaps, starting a fight. He reluctantly retreated, then watched the old man shuffle forward.

As the sorcerer moved into the torchlight, Agis saw the old man's purse bulging beneath his tabard. A last desperate idea occurred to him. He slipped his empty hand beneath his cloak and imagined it disappearing from the end of his arm, calling on the Way to make it happen. A sharp pain sliced through his wrist, and then he felt nothing below the wrist.

The old man paused in front of Radurak, reaching beneath his tabard. Keeping the stump of his arm beneath his robe, Agis reached toward the sorcerer's gold. Once again calling on the Way, he visualized his hand appearing beneath the old man's cloak, clasped onto the purse. Suddenly he felt the heavy bag in his hand, just as if his hand were still attached to his own arm—save that there were many yards of numbness between his forearm and his fingers.

The sorcerer untied his purse strings. Agis jerked on the leather sack, at the same time ending the expenditure of psionic energy which kept his hand separated from his wrist. The feeling below his wrist returned to normal, and he now held a heavy sack of gold clenched in his fist.

As the purse was ripped from the sorcerer's hand, the old man spun and pointed a thickset finger at Agis. "*You'll find that water from the black well tastes best,*" he snarled.

Agis shrugged at the nonsensical words. Still holding the old man's purse beneath his cloak, he raised his eyebrows at Radurak. Before the elf could respond, the sorcerer said something to him, pointing an accusing finger at the noble.

While the old man was turned away, Agis took the opportunity to stand body-to-body with Caro and slip the purse he had just stolen to the dwarf.

Of course, what the old man said made no sense to Agis, but he was counting on the legendary greed of elves to do his arguing for him. Since there was no gold in the old man's hands, the noble hoped Radurak would dismiss him quickly.

As Agis had anticipated, the elven chief shrugged at the sorcerer's complaint, then motioned Agis forward. "*Bring me the lungs and kidneys of your favorite goat.*"

Without taking the chance of a reply, the noble went to the elf's side. He counted out ninety-five gold coins while the other nobles left the slaveyard with their purchases. Once Agis had paid the full amount, Radurak had his assistants bring the slave-girl forward, offering her hand to the noble with the words, "*Take this woman to the nearest mountaintop. The moonlight there will be good for her skin.*"

The half-elf cast a dismayed glance in the sorcerer's direction. The old man angrily regarded Agis for several moments, then turned to the slave and said, "*In the faro fields are whopping great windows. For now, you'll be safe with him.*"

Agis breathed a sigh of relief; the second half of the old man's comment made sense. Apparently the spell had been a short-lived one and he could now hear and speak normally. He stepped toward the old man. "Before you go—"

The sorcerer cut Agis off by jabbing the tip of his cane into the noble's chest. "The answer is no," he spat. With that, the old man turned sharply away and stepped out of the makeshift slaveyard.

Motioning Caro to come forward with the sorcerer's purse, Agis started to follow. "At least hear me out."

The noble was stopped by his new slave. "My name is Sadira," she said, stepping in front of him.

Agis tried to move around her, but she once again blocked his way. Fixing her icy blue eyes on his, she added, "I don't know why you bought me, but I assure you, it was a waste of good gold."

EIGHT

Kalak's Treasure

Tithian and three subordinates stood in the lowest room of the ziggurat, staring down at an iron trapdoor that had once been hidden beneath two layers of bricks. The low-ranking templars had discovered it a few hours earlier, while searching for the last of the Veiled Alliance's hidden amulets.

"Go ahead," Tithian said, motioning to the door.

One of the assistants, a half-elf named Gathalimay, kneeled on the floor. He released the lever holding the circular door closed, and it fell open with a loud creak. Gathalimay took a torch and peered into the darkness below.

"It's a tunnel!" he called.

"We'd better see where it leads," Tithian said.

He ordered one of the templars to stay behind, then took the other two and descended into the tunnel. They found a circular, man-sized corridor running eastward beneath the gladiatorial arena. It was lined with bricks of black obsidian that made the strange passageway seem supernaturally gloomy and dark.

"Who dug this, the Veiled Alliance?" asked Stravos, a wiry, gray-haired human.

"We'll see soon enough," Tithian said, motioning his two assistants forward.

After walking a time in the strange corridor, Gathalimay stopped and looked up. Above his head rose a small shaft, also lined with obsidian. He held his torch close to the cavity, but they could not see the top.

"Where does that go?" he asked.

"There's only one place it can go," Tithian replied. "We're underneath the fighting floor of the arena. It must lead to a trapdoor concealed under the sand."

The half-elf glanced around. "We aren't near the prop room for the games, are we?"

Tithian shook his head. "We've gone too far. Those chambers and the shafts that lead up to the arena are closer to the middle of the field."

"Why would the Veiled Alliance build a shaft like this?" asked Stravos.

"What makes you think the Alliance built it?" Tithian countered, motioning him and Gathalimay forward. "We're heading toward Kalak's palace."

A short distance later, the tunnel ended. In the ceiling hung another trapdoor with a bas relief of the Dragon's head molded into it. The beast's sunken eyes seemed fixed on Tithian's face, and its jagged-toothed muzzle gaped open as if ready to seize anyone who attempted to open the door.

Despite his curiosity, Tithian was tempted to leave the trapdoor closed. He had no doubt that they were somewhere beneath Kalak's Golden Tower, which meant the tunnel could only be a secret passage connecting the palace and the ziggurat. He doubted that the king would be happy to know it had been discovered.

Unfortunately, he and his men had only recovered one of the two amulets that remained secreted in the ziggurat. He could not afford to ignore the possibility that the other had been planted in this tunnel or on the other side of the door. Besides, Tithian was curious. As the High Templar of both Games and the King's Works, it seemed suspicious to him that Kalak had not mentioned this secret passageway. He wanted to find out as much about it as he could.

Tithian stepped away from the door and motioned to the half-elf. "Gathalimay, give Stravos a lift so he can open the door."

Stravos's wiry face went ashen.

"We'll have a look around and cast a few detection spells," Tithian said, more to reassure himself than the human templar. "If the last amulet isn't there, we'll close the door and forget we ever saw this place."

Gathalimay created a stirrup with his pudgy hands, then Stravos swallowed hard and stepped up. When the gray-haired templar released the latch, the rusty door fell open with a loud creak. Dim white light shone down into the tunnel.

Tithian motioned the man through the doorway, then passed his torch up and followed himself. As Stravos reached down to help Gathalimay through the trapdoor, Tithian lifted his eyes to examine their surroundings.

He saw that they had come up facing the wall of a gloomy chamber. Suddenly a melon-sized globe of yellow-green light appeared in front of him. The sphere hovered four feet off the ground, a fuzzy, undulating, indistinct ball of glowing haze shaped vaguely like a bald head with a sagging chin.

"Lord Tithian?" asked the shaky voice of Agis's aged valet, Caro.

Beneath his breath, Tithian swore at the spy's bad timing. "I'm busy. Contact me later."

The ball changed hue to deeper green and blurred even more. "This is the first chance I've had to sneak away in three days and it might be the last for another three. You'll have to listen now or take your chances on hearing from me again."

Tithian sighed, cursing the combination of dwarven obstinacy and Agis's leniency that made Caro so insistent. He had turned the old valet to his cause after confiscating his old friend's slaves. It had been an easy matter to undermine the dwarf's loyalty to the Asticles family, for the high templar understood the power of both bondage and liberty as few other free men did. When presented with the option of dying in the king's brick pits or earning his liberty by spying on Agis, Caro had opted for freedom.

"Hold the crystal away from your face," Tithian ordered. "We'll be able to see each other."

He had given Caro a magical crystal of olivine that the dwarf could use to communicate with him. Just as he could see Caro in the ghostly light, he knew that his spy could see his own face in the crystal itself. Tithian's words would sound like no more than a faint whisper to anyone except the person holding the crystal.

As Caro obeyed, the heavy furrows of the dwarf's withered face came into focus. The old slave was squinting into the crystal, his wrinkled brow folded in concentration and his toothless mouth hanging open.

"What is it?" Tithian demanded.

The high templar listened impatiently as Caro told him about the meeting between Agis and the other four nobles, as well as the attack that had resulted in Jaseela's injury. Tithian was not surprised by anything the dwarf told him, for he had expected his friend to respond to the slave confiscations by doing something foolish.

When the dwarf related the story of Agis's purchase at the slave auction, Tithian's impatience changed to interest. "What's the girl's name?" he demanded, temporarily forgetting where he was standing.

"Her name is Sadira."

"Don't let her out of your sight!" Tithian exclaimed, motioning for Stravos to stand up. "Where are you? I'll send someone to watch her immediately."

"That will do you no good," Caro replied. "A few minutes after he bought her, Lord Agis gave the girl a bag of gold and set her free. He told her he wanted to aid the rebellion and that she should contact him when Those Who Wear the Veil needed his help."

"I have the luck of a blind desert runner!" Tithian snarled. "What did the other bidder look like?"

With growing frustration, the high templar listened as the dwarf offered a portrait that, save for the obsidian-pommeled cane, could have fit half the craftsmen in Tyr. Once Caro had finished his description, Tithian questioned him briefly about the auction and the elves who had run it.

"You'll be a free man soon," Tithian said, as the conversation wore to a close. "Besides, with your help, it'll be much easier for me to keep Agis out of trouble. You're doing the Asticles family a great service."

"I know what I'm doing," Caro replied, the black pits of his eyes fixed steadily on Tithian's face. "Don't make a fool of me by pretending that it's anything but betrayal."

Tithian shrugged. "Think of your service however you wish," he said. "If you see Sadira again, contact me immediately. You'll have your freedom the same day I capture her."

"I will," Caro replied. He closed his fingers over the crystal, and his shriveled face disappeared from view.

Tithian turned to his subordinates. "Forget you heard a word of this."

No sooner had he issued the command than he wondered if there had been any need. Both Stravos and Gathalimay were staring at the room with gaping mouths. Tithian joined them in inspecting their surroundings.

They had entered an immense chamber in the bottom of the Golden Tower. Copper-plated rafters hung high overhead. In the squares between the beams were carved shadowy figures of beasts that Tithian did not recognize. At the edges of the ceiling, fluted columns of granite supported the gilded rafters. Between these pillars stood row after row of wooden shelving. Most of the planks were empty, save for a few ceramic urns and metal boxes filled with coins and glittering jewels. In a few places, the murky outline of an ancient steel sword or battle-axe occupied an otherwise empty shelf. On one shelf rested an entire suit of dust-covered armor.

A translucent, alabaster panel through which shone a filmy white light provided the chamber's weak illumination. Beneath the alabaster panel sat a black, glassy pyramid taller than a full giant and more than a dozen paces across at the base. The entire structure had been carved from a single block of obsidian, the surface polished to icy smoothness. It seemed to Tithian that he was staring into the heart of darkness itself, and he felt more curious than ever about the significance of the obsidian corridor.

The top of the pyramid was flat, forming a small deck large enough for several men to stand upon. Along the edge of the deck sat two-dozen balls—also of polished obsidian—ranging in size from that of a piece of fruit to as large as a half-giant's head. As strange as they were, the ebony globes were not what caught the high templar's eye. A magnificent silver-gilded throne stood at the front of the deck.

On the arms of the throne sat a pair of human heads with topknots of long, coarse hair, their faces turned toward a diminutive figure perched at the edge of the seat. Tithian could just make out the gleam of a golden diadem ringing the old man's head and see that deep-etched lines of age creased his withered face. The high templar had no doubt that he was looking at Kalak.

At Tithian's side, Stravos gasped as he turned and saw who was watching them. The aged templar stepped toward the exit. The trapdoor suddenly swung shut with an ominous clang, sealing them all in the vault with Kalak. Stravos faced the king and fell to his knees, an action quickly mimicked by Gathalimay.

"Mighty One," Stravos began, inclining his head toward Kalak. "Forgive our intrusion—"

"Quiet!" Tithian ordered, cuffing the templar across the head. He had no idea how Kalak would respond to their presence, but he did not want to make the king angry by having his subordinates behave disrespectfully. "How dare you speak without permission!"

After a short silence, Kalak turned one of the heads so that it faced the three templars. "Look, Wyan. Intruders."

Tithian could make out just enough detail to see that Wyan's head was sallow-skinned and sunken-featured. Its leathery lips were curled into a sinister grin, revealing a broken set of yellowed teeth. Fixing its gray eyes on the trio, it said, "Filthy murderers come to assassinate their king, don't you think, Sacha?"

The other head asked, "Why do you always think of

murder, Wyan? Perhaps they're greedy thieves, come to steal what's left of our treasure."

"My treasure!" Kalak stormed, sweeping Sacha off the throne's arm.

The head rolled down the pyramid and landed in front of the intruders. It was grotesquely bloated, with puffy cheeks and eyes swollen to narrow, dark slits. It stared up at Tithian with a grisly snarl.

"Our treasure," Sacha insisted to the high templar. "Kalak spent it all on his ziggurat. A millennium of prudence and thrift, thrown away in a mere century."

Tithian studied the thing in ghastly wonder. There was a glow of intelligence in its dusky eyes, and the spiteful expression on its face seemed as lively and spirited as any he had ever seen on a templar's face. The heads, he realized, were no mere zombies that Kalak had animated for his own amusement. They were alive, at least after a fashion.

Kalak grabbed Wyan's head by the topknot and stepped to the edge of the deck. He crept down the smooth surface of the pyramid as easily as he would have crossed a level floor. As the king came closer, Tithian saw that the skin of Wyan's missing neck had been gathered up beneath the jawline and neatly stitched into a straight seam.

When Kalak reached the bottom of the pyramid, he dropped Wyan next to Sacha. The two heads fell to arguing about whether the three intruders were murderers or thieves, and Kalak moved close to Gathalimay.

"This one was thinking of stealing," said the ancient monarch.

"No, Mighty One," Gathalimay answered, not daring to lift his eyes from the floor. "I was merely awed—"

"Don't lie to your king!" Kalak snapped, glaring at the

half-elf.

"I'm sorry, Great King," Gathalimay answered, his voice trembling. "The thought crept into my mind, but I would never—"

"What you would have done doesn't matter," the sorcerer-king interrupted.

Kalak stepped behind the kneeling templar, grabbing Gathalimay's chin with one hand and placing the other on the back of the half-elf's head. He jerked the chin to one side and pushed forward at the base of the skull, snapping the neck with a single crack. The body slumped to the floor in a flaccid heap.

The only emotion Tithian felt at the loss of his subordinate was fear for himself. It seemed entirely possible that the king would kill him as well.

Kalak stepped to Stravos next. "This one is frightened."

"Kill him!" urged one of the heads.

"Please, Mighty One. I only opened the door because the High Templar ordered it," he said, his voice quavering. "I've done nothing wrong."

"Are you not frightened of me?" Kalak demanded.

"M-most certainly, Great King."

"That is wrong," Kalak responded. "You are mine. If I choose to kill you, you should be happy because that is my will. You should not be frightened because your insignificant existence is about to end."

"Yes, my king. I understand that now," Stravos said.

"Let us see if you do."

The king reached down to Stravos's belt and drew the templar's dagger, then smiled as he saw that it had an obsidian blade. "Feed the dagger," he said, handing the weapon to Stravos.

The templar stared at the knife in horror, but made no

move to do as the king ordered.

"Feed the dagger," echoed Sacha and Wyan, their bloated gray eyes sparkling with anticipation.

As Tithian watched the scene, his fear for his own life mounted. So did his interest in the sorcerer-king's seemingly insane actions. Obsidian was so common that it was used to make weapons and inexpensive jewelry. He was surprised to see Kalak and the heads treating the stone as if it had magical properties.

At last Stravos directed the blade toward his own heart, but he froze there. His lips began to quiver and tears welled in his eyes. "My king, show pity on a poor subject."

"I thought as much," sneered Kalak, fixing his black eyes on the dagger.

Stravos suddenly gripped the hilt more tightly. The muscles on his arms tensed as he struggled against the king's mind. "No, please!" The blade moved closer and closer to his chest, though the templar fought to hold it back

A crooked grin crossed the king's lips. The hilt slipped from between Stravos's hands and plunged deep into his stomach. The gray-haired templar grasped at the dagger, then pitched forward and rolled onto his side. He lay groaning on the marble floor, lacking the strength to pull the blade from his gut.

"You should have done it yourself," Kalak chuckled. "You could have chosen to die a lot faster."

Tithian watched a stream of blood spill out of the wound and spread over the marble floor.

The king looked at Tithian next. "I didn't summon my high templar," he said. "What is he doing here?"

"Robbing," said Sacha.

"Spying," said Wyan.

Though he had not been given permission to speak, Tithian decided to explain before the two heads convinced Kalak to execute him. Trying to keep his fear from showing, the high templar met the king's gaze. "Mighty One, we were searching for the Veiled Alliance's last amulet when we discovered the secret passage between the ziggurat and your palace. We only opened the door to be sure—"

Kalak raised an eyebrow. "Does he really believe that Those Who Wear the Veil hid an amulet in my treasure vault, Wyan?"

"I had to be certain," Tithian answered before the undead creatures could speak.

"He's disrespectful," said Sacha.

"Kill him, too," added Wyan.

Kalak shook his wispy-haired head. "Not Tithian," he said. "I have need of him."

Tithian breathed a sigh of relief.

"Tithian of Mericles?" demanded Sacha. "This snake-faced runt can't be a descendant of mine!"

Tithian's jaw fell slack, and he stared at the bloated head in astonishment. "Who are you?"

With an amused chuckle, Kalak lifted his disembodied companions by their topknots. He brought Sacha over to the high templar and held the head out to him. Tithian accepted it with both hands, and was surprised to discover the head seemed as warm as any living body.

"I present Sacha the Beastly, progenitor of the noble Mericles line," the king said to Tithian. "Sacha and Wyan were the two chieftains who accompanied me when I conquered Tyr."

"You mean the chieftains who conquered it for you," Sacha spat.

Kalak ignored the comment and stooped over Stravos's

groaning form. He pulled the dagger from the templar's wound. The man cried out as blood began to gush from his shredded stomach.

Tithian stared at the head in his hands. He felt nothing but disgust toward his ancient ancestor and could not bring himself to accept that the thing's blood ran in his veins.

Kalak moved to Stravos's side and placed Wyan in front of the templar's wound. The sallow head extended its ash-colored tongue and began lapping up blood.

Kalak handed the dagger to Tithian and motioned toward Gathalimay's inert form. "Feed your ancestor," he said. "Then we'll discuss some things I want you to do for me."

Tithian tucked Sacha under one arm and went to the half-elf's body. "Where would you like me to cut him?" he asked the head.

"The throat," Sacha said anxiously. "Prop his feet up. The blood will flow more freely."

Tithian placed the bloated head near the dead templar's throat and did as his ancestor instructed. He left the dagger lying on Gathalimay's barrel-shaped chest.

Kalak gripped Tithian's arm and led him to the base of the pyramid, squeezing the high templar's elbow painfully. "You saw the shaft leading down from my arena into my tunnel?"

Tithian nodded. "Yes, my king." His arm began to throb beneath Kalak's grip.

"Good. During the games commemorating the completion of the ziggurat, you must place this obsidian pyramid over the shaft you passed, but only when the last match of the day begins. Make it look like part of the contest."

Tithian studied the enormous structure with an eye toward moving it. Teleporting the pyramid would require more magic than the king had granted him, but he thought he could shrink it just long enough to move it. "What about the throne and the balls?" he asked. "Should I place them in the arena as well, Mighty One?"

"No!" Kalak hissed. His long fingernails broke the surface of Tithian's skin and drew blood. "Don't touch anything else. The globes and the throne stay here with me!"

"As you command," Tithian replied evenly. "Forgive me for asking. Is there anything else?"

Kalak nodded. "When the last game begins, I want you to lock all the gates to my stadium."

"Until when?"

"Don't worry about opening them," the king said. "You'll need to make special preparations so they can't be burned down."

"How long will we keep the gates closed?" Tithian asked. "It won't be an easy matter to provide food and water for forty thousand people."

"You won't have to feed them," Kalak said. "Just keep them inside."

Tithian frowned, puzzled by the unusual order. "Perhaps it would help if you could tell me—"

"You don't need to know anything else, High Templar," Kalak snapped. He glared at Tithian from beneath his aged brow. "All you need to know is that I want the gates closed and the spectators kept inside."

"Yes, Mighty One," Tithian replied, looking at the floor. Clearly, Kalak had more in mind for the games than celebrating the ziggurat's completion. He suspected that whatever it was, it would not be pleasant.

"We'll need a security force to keep the spectators in their seats after my games end," Kalak continued. "I've placed Larkyn in charge of that. You are to coordinate with him regarding how the gates are sealed, but don't question anything else he wants done. Is that clear?"

"As you wish," Tithian replied. He was not happy to learn that this particular task had been given to someone outside his sphere of influence. The high templar wondered how many other similar, regrettable assignments the king had made.

Kalak flicked a wrist at the trapdoor, and it clanged open again. "From what I heard of the conversation with your spy, it appears you're having trouble discovering the plan being hatched by the feeble sorcerers in the Veiled Alliance."

Tithian took a deep breath, then said, "They won't disrupt the games. You have my word, Mighty One."

"I don't want your promise," Kalak replied sharply. "I want them dead."

"Yes, my king," Tithian said as calmly as he could. His heart was pounding so hard that it muted his words in his own ears.

Kalak studied his servant for a moment. "These sorcerers are as wary as jackals," he said. "Perhaps it is time to offer some bait to lure them into the open."

"Into the open, Mighty One?"

The king nodded. "Use that simpleton senator, Agis of Asticles. You're his friend, are you not?" Kalak said. "Think of something the Alliance wants and offer it through him."

"He has no connections with the Veiled Alliance!" Tithian protested.

"Do not lie to me, Tithian. Agis has more of a connection to Those Who Wear the Veil than anyone within your grasp. Besides, the good senator participated in an open revolt against my servants," Kalak replied, narrowing his eyes to dark slits. "Use him or kill him!"

Tithian bowed his head. "Yes, my king."

Kalak studied Tithian for a few moments, then nodded. "Good. Now, who else knows about my tunnel?"

"Only the guard I left at the other end," the high templar replied.

Kalak smiled. "Have him lay the bricks back over my door when you return to the ziggurat."

"As you wish," the high templar nodded. "And after he's done that, I'll kill him personally."

"Yes, Tithian," Kalak said, looking back to his obsidian pyramid with an eerie smile. "We must keep my tunnel a secret."

NINE

Tin Gates

Sadira stood beneath a portico across the street from Tyr's gladiatorial arena. The immense structure's high walls were supported by four stories of marble arches, with those at street-level covering short tunnels that ran into the stadium. Though the crimson sun had just risen, these entryways already swarmed with slaves cleaning the stones in preparation for the coming games. From inside the passageways echoed the creak of pulleys and a constant din of strident hammering, high-pitched and sharp.

"Can't you at least tell me why I'm doing this?" Agis asked. He stood next to Sadira, along with his manservant Caro. "I'd hate to think I'm risking my life for the sake of a test."

The sorceress shook her head, sending waves of rosy light dancing through her hair. "That's not the way we work," she said sternly. Though her statement was technically true, what it implied was not. The Alliance had not authorized her to contact the noble. Asking Agis for help was Sadira's idea. "If you can't convince Tithian to do as you ask, it'll be better if you don't know much."

On his master's behalf, Caro demanded, "Better for whom?"

"Better for the Veiled Alliance," Sadira replied. "If Lord Tithian realizes Agis is trying to influence him through the Way of the Unseen, nothing will save your master."

The shriveled dwarf looked at Agis, creasing his hairless brow against the ruddy rays of the morning sun. "You deserve to know why you're risking your life," Caro declared, casting a caustic glance at Sadira. "She's playing you for a fool."

"Agis said he wanted to help the rebellion," the half-elf replied. "Here's his chance."

The dwarf shook his head. "You should tell us why—"

"That's enough, Caro," Agis interrupted. "I'm the one who's taking the chances here. If I don't need to know the reason, then neither do you."

Caro glared at Agis, but pressed the matter no further.

Sadira took the noble's hand and squeezed it warmly. "Be careful. When you return, don't stop to talk to us. Walk down the street six blocks, then wait for us there. Once I'm sure you haven't been followed, we'll join you."

Agis smiled. "You are careful, aren't you?" Without waiting for a response, he set off across the street.

Sadira watched him go, hoping she was not making a terrible mistake. Two days earlier, when Agis had set her free, she had feared the noble's generosity was a templar plot to locate the Alliance. Instead of trying to find her contact, she had taken a room and spent the night waiting for the sorcerer-king's guards to break the door down.

Sadira had spent the next day trying to look suspicious, striking up conversations with perfect strangers and sneaking into the back entrances of a dizzying array of shops and taverns. During the whole time, she had kept a careful watch for templars or anyone else who looked like he might be following her, but had seen no one. At last, she had come to the conclusion that Agis's offer was sincere.

It was then that the sorceress had made her most difficult decision: not to return to the Veiled Alliance. Ktandeo would have bustled her out of the city immediately, giving no further thought to Rikus or to convincing the mul to kill Kalak, so Sadira had decided to accept the senator's offer of help.

The sorceress had approached the noble in the Alliance's name, hoping he could use his status to arrange a safe meeting between her and Rikus. Unfortunately, she had soon realized that even Agis could not organize a rendezvous without the possibility of alerting Tithian to what was happening. Nevertheless, Sadira had asked him to try. Unless she spoke to Rikus, the Alliance's plan for assassinating Kalak was doomed anyway.

On the other side of the street, Agis paused at an entrance to the stadium. A sour-faced templar met the noble at the open gate, a steel-bladed glaive in his hands. "You're not permitted inside," the man said flatly.

"I'm Agis of Asticles," the noble replied.

"So?"

"Tithian—er, the High Templar of the King's Works—asked me to meet him here this morning."

The templar's scowl deepened. "Why didn't you say so?" he demanded, stepping aside. The man turned and called over his shoulder, "This is the one."

Another templar, this one a woman in her mid-thirties, stepped from the shadows. "This way," she ordered, waving him forward.

Agis stepped beneath the arch and was temporarily blinded by the stark contrast between the morning light and the shady stadium. The smell of burning charcoal hung heavy in the air, and the sound of striking hammers echoed down stone passageways opening to both sides of the corridor.

"I said, this way," the female templar repeated, grabbing Agis's arm and roughly pulling him forward.

They emerged onto a cobblestone terrace that ran along one side of the stadium. Far below the terrace lay a huge field of sandy ground that would have taken even a mul half a minute to sprint across. At one end of the field stood Kalak's immense palace, with its large balcony overhanging the arena. At the other end loomed the rainbow-hued ziggurat, still shrouded beneath a web of ropes and swarming with an army of slaves.

Below the terrace, tier after tier of stone benchwork descended toward the sandy arena floor. Behind Agis rose more grandstands, with an immense balcony overhanging them. Though the senator was not fond of the sport played in the stadium, he had to admit that the structure itself was an impressive feat of architecture.

Agis's guide led him along the terrace, stepping around several large braziers filled with glowing charcoal. Sweating smiths heated ingots of tin over the coals while others worked nearby to hammer out thin sheets of the light metal.

Just past the smiths, the templar stopped and motioned Agis into one of the entryways that led back out into the street. "The high templar will meet you in here."

Agis stepped into the dark corridor. Although he could see a templar guard silhouetted against the light coming from the street, there was no sign of Tithian. To either side of the small tunnel, a stone stairway ascended into the inner sections of the stadium hidden beneath the grandstands. Down these stairways rolled such a din of hammering and whip snapping that his ears began to ring.

Agis walked toward the guard, thinking that the templar might know where Tithian was.

The hammering ceased. A muffled command sounded in the stairway to the left, then the clatter of chains echoed through the stones. The templar at the end of the corridor leaped into the street, barely avoiding a large gate as it dropped out of the ceiling and crashed to the ground with a deafening roar.

Agis found himself staring at a distorted, silvery reflection of himself. He walked to the gate. It was as solid as a wall, and its entire surface was covered by a layer of tin. The sheets had been so carefully joined together that Agis could not have slipped the tip of his dagger into any of the seams.

The noble heard footsteps from the stairway behind him. He turned just in time to see Tithian lead a small party of templars into the tunnel. The high templar's beady eyes gleamed with delight, and his bony features seemed unusually cheerful.

When he saw Agis, Tithian smiled broadly and stretched out his arms in greeting. "My friend!"

The high templar walked forward and clasped his hands onto Agis's shoulders. Instead of hugging the noble, however, Tithian spun him around to look at the tin-sheathed gate. "What do you think?" he asked. "That should keep them from burning it, shouldn't it?"

Agis nodded. "I suppose it should," he said. "Who are you trying to keep out?"

"In," Tithian corrected. Behind the high templar, the jaws of several subordinates fell open. "If we were trying to keep someone out, wouldn't we be putting the tin on the outside?"

"High One!" clucked a subordinate templar, "Is it wise to tell this to a noble?"

Tithian spun on the man savagely. "I decide what is wise and what isn't, Orel," he snarled, laying his arm over Agis's shoulder. "My friend is as loyal to the king as I am."

Agis could not help but grin at the irony of that statement.

Tithian motioned his templars back up the stairs. "Go and tell them to retract this gate. Agis and I wish to talk."

After the templars left, Agis said, "Thanks for seeing me, Tithian."

"It's my pleasure, old friend," the high templar replied, motioning him toward the terrace. "What can I do for you? Our last meeting was not very pleasant, and I'd like to make up for that."

Agis forced himself to keep smiling, for the reminder of losing his slaves sent a surge of anger through him. Instead, he thought of two boys—himself and Tithian three decades earlier—creeping through his father's faro field on a hot afternoon. He looked directly into the other man's eyes and sent this thought drifting toward his mind, probing ever so gently for an opening that would allow him to slip into Tithian's head without alerting the high templar to his presence.

The noble had chosen his attack carefully, giving it the form of a pleasant memory that both he and Tithian shared. He hoped it would serve as a hunter's blind, concealing his presence while he guided the high templar's thoughts in the direction he wished.

The shadow of a sentimental smile formed on Tithian's lips, and Agis knew he had made contact. He did not press the probe any farther, giving the high templar's mind time to adjust to its presence.

"With all of your duties, it must be difficult to attend to your lands," Agis said casually.

"It can be difficult at times," Tithian replied.

"Perhaps I can help you."

Tithian raised an eyebrow. "How?"

Inside Tithian's mind, the high templar's subconscious noticed the memory Agis had planted and began supplying its own details. Young Tithian's auburn hair was suddenly pulled into a short pony-tail, for he had just turned twelve and won the right to groom himself as he pleased. Agis's own black hair was cropped almost to the point of baldness, much shorter than he had ever worn it, and his ears stuck out at an embarrassing angle.

The sweet scent of faro blossoms filled the noses of the two boys, for it had rained that year and all of the spiny plants boasted at least one of the huge red flowers. Short swords with obsidian blades appeared on the boys hips and crossbows in their hands. They were near the top of the gentle hill that separated the fields from the irrigation pond, hunting varls.

Agis suppressed a shudder at this memory. Not realizing how important the scaly slugs were to the orchard's health, his father had sent him to hunt them at every opportunity. It was a wonder there had been any trees left when the estate finally came into Agis's hands.

The young Tithian, standing near the top of the hill, suddenly dropped to his belly and motioned for Agis to do the same.

To the men standing in the gladiatorial stadium, all of this occurred in the blink of an eye. It was the moment Agis had been waiting for.

"Let me manage your fields," the noble said to his old

friend. "I'll make them as fertile as mine."

At the same time, from behind the screen inside Tithian's mind, he sent out a single, compelling message: *That is a wise suggestion.*

Tithian's subconscious continued to unfurl the memory. The young Agis called and asked what was wrong. Tithian silenced his friend with a finger to the lips, then peered over the top of the hill toward the irrigation pond.

Here Tithian's memory diverged widely from what Agis remembered. The noble recalled lying on his belly in the dirt with the hot sun beating down on his back for what seemed like an eternity. He had heard a faint rustle in the faro ahead, but had not even caught a glimpse of what caused it. Agis had cocked his crossbow and waited, wondering what danger his friend had seen lurking in the fields ahead.

Tithian's memory was different. In the high templar's mind, he was peering over the hilltop. His eyes were fixed on Agis's curvaceous sister Tierney as she swam nude in the pond.

The noble didn't know whether to be angered or amused at the memory. In all the years since, Tithian had never revealed what he had really been watching over the top of the hill.

In the stadium, the high templar asked, "And what do you get in return for managing my fields?"

The tone of the question was amiable, but cautious. Of course Agis had no intention of telling the high templar what he really wanted, which was the opportunity to arrange a meeting between Rikus and Sadira.

"The use of your gladiators for part of each week," he replied. "As kind as it was to leave my women and children, they can't keep the scavengers out of the fields. In a day or two each week, a few gladiators could kill enough thieves to eliminate the need for field patrols, and it would be good practice for them."

Returning to Tithian's mind, the memory became more familiar, though it still varied slightly from what Agis recalled.

Suddenly three bony gith scampered through the faro, each clutching a sackful of stolen needles in one four-fingered hand and a huge spear in the other. Through Tithian's memory, Agis saw himself jump up and fire his crossbow, killing the leader. Young Tithian reacted more slowly, for his attention had been fully absorbed by the beautiful young woman right up until the moment he'd heard the scavengers.

Tithian struggled to bring his crossbow to bear. Agis drew his sword and charged the second gith as it dropped its needle sack. Tithian inadvertently triggered his weapon. The quarrel shot straight for his friend's head. Agis swung his sword, separating his target's skull from its neck. The momentum carried him off his feet, and Tithian's bolt sailed over his head. The quarrel took the last gith square in its bulging eye.

The high templar's memory of the event surprised Agis. For the last twenty-five years, the senator had believed that his life had been saved by a well-timed and skillful shot. Nevertheless, Agis was experienced enough in the Way that the discrepancies would not interfere with his plan. The noble sent the message he had come to plant in Tithian's head: *Say yes. Loan Rikus and Neeva to Agis.*

Before his old friend could voice the agreement the noble hoped to hear, a female templar stepped to Tithian's side with a message. As she whispered into her superior's ear, Agis tried to listen from behind his memory screen. He heard a faint echo of the woman's voice saying something about an urgent message. The thought passed too quickly for him to grasp, but he didn't send a probe after it. The more active he became, the more likely it was that Tithian would detect his presence.

"You'll have to excuse me for a moment, my friend," Tithian said, moving down the terrace. He spoke with the woman for several moments, pausing once to give his guest an apologetic shrug.

Agis waited patiently, maintaining his presence in the high templar's mind by slowly adding to the memory: Tierney appearing at the top of the hill, now dressed in a fleece robe and proclaiming the two boys her saviors; the young Agis telling her how Tithian had spotted the gith from the hilltop, and describing the incredible feat of marksmanship that had saved his life.

The messenger continued to speak with the high templar for several moments. Tithian's expression grew concerned, but Agis resisted the urge to expand his presence in his old friend's mind. It was simply too risky.

When Tithian returned, he said, "My thanks for your offer, Agis, but my farm manager has been with me since I inherited the Mericles estate. He's not as good as you, of course, but I have no need to boost my land income. I'm sure you understand. It would be a shame to put out a loyal retainer."

Inside Tithian's mind, Agis found his memory screen isolated by a vast plain of silent, white emptiness. Whatever the woman's message, it had put the high templar on the alert, and he was now carefully suppressing his memories. For a moment, the noble worried that Tithian had somehow detected his presence, but realized this could not be. If that had happened, dozens of templars would be rushing to arrest him.

"I didn't mean to imply that I would take your man's

place," Agis said. "I intend to show him better ways—"

Tithian raised a silencing hand. "He's quite touchy about his expertise," the templar said, taking Agis's arm and walking him toward the ziggurat. "I'll have a young gladiator sent to your estate as a gift. He should keep the scavengers off your land."

Agis locked eyes with the high templar. "This has nothing to do with your farm manager," he said, changing approaches. "You just don't trust me."

As he spoke, he sent a black snake of guilt slithering across the empty plain around his probe. Soon, the noble saw a mountainous form looming on the horizon. It was a flat-topped pyramid with sides as black as night and as smooth as ice. With a start, Agis realized that the pyramid was something Tithian had seen recently, something that weighed heavily on his mind.

Glassy black balls began rolling off the pyramid, threatening to crush the snake-probe. Grimacing at the energy it required, Agis attached wings to his serpent, and it lifted off the white plain. For a moment he wondered if the avalanche had been a counterattack from Tithian. When the balls reached the bottom of the pyramid, however, they kept going without regard for the fact that they had missed him. A black shaft appeared in the plain, and the balls rolled into it. Agis dropped his winged snake closer and saw that the hole was lined by obsidian bricks.

A boiling mass of memory came shooting out of the shaft. Agis found himself staring into the sunken black eyes of a small, haggard man wearing a golden diadem—Kalak. Fearing Tithian had lured him into a trap, Agis turned his probe away and flapped its wings with all of his flagging strength.

The snake started to carry him out of Tithian's mind,

but the noble paused when Kalak's voice spoke in a conversational tone. "You saw the shaft in my tunnel?"

Agis turned his probe in the pyramid's direction. He saw the king's shriveled form standing next to the obsidian structure. Kalak ran his gnarled fingers over the glassy surface, his eyes fixed on Tithian, who now stood before him. It was not a trap, but another memory.

Tithian nodded. "Yes, my king."

"Good. During the games commemorating the completion of the ziggurat, you must place the obsidian pyramid over the shaft you passed, but only when the last match of the day begins," Kalak said. "Make it look like part of the contest."

"What about the throne and the balls?" Tithian asked. "Should I place them in the arena as well, Mighty One?"

"No!" Kalak hissed, scowling as though he would kill the high templar. "Don't touch anything else. The globes and the throne stay with me!"

"As you command," Tithian replied. "Forgive me for asking. Is there anything else?"

Kalak nodded. "When the last game begins, I want you to lock all the gates to my stadium."

"Until when?"

"Don't worry about opening them—"

In the memory, Kalak's form stopped speaking in midsentence and faded away. Tithian faced Agis's flying snake, then the black pyramid rose off the white plain and sailed toward him. Now completely certain that the high templar had discovered his presence, Agis changed his snake to an arrow and shot across Tithian's mind like a bolt of lightning.

An instant later, he broke contact with the high templar.

"A man in my position can trust no one, not even his

friends," Tithian said, continuing the conversation where it had left off only a moment earlier.

Agis was in no condition to follow Tithian's words, for he had all but exhausted himself inside the high templar's mind. He stumbled and nearly fell, then felt his friend gripping his arm to prevent him from tumbling into the seats below.

"Easy," Tithian said. "I wouldn't want you to fall."

Agis blinked several times. "Thanks for your concern," he said, only a little sarcastically. When he glanced to both his right and left, he saw no sign of the guards he had expected the high templar to summon.

"Why aren't you arresting me?" Agis demanded, still leaning against the wall ringing the terrace.

"Why should I?" Tithian asked, giving Agis a forbearing smile. The templar pulled the noble away from the wall, then gently turned him so that he faced the immense ziggurat. "Tell me, Agis, why do you suppose Kalak is having that thing constructed?"

"You're the one who's building it," Agis said bitterly, recalling all his slaves whom the high templar had confiscated. "You tell me."

Tithian shrugged. "If I knew, I would," he said warmly. "The king hasn't even told me what it's for. I've shown you all that I know, and frankly, it scares me."

Agis rolled his weary eyes. "Save your pathos for someone else," he said. "I know you better than that. The only life you're concerned with is your own."

"Even to me, the possibilities of what Kalak's plan might mean are horrifying. What does he need forty-thousand people locked in a stadium for?" Tithian countered. "Of course, if I wasn't going to be one of the forty-thousand, it might be less horrifying, but that's hardly relevant. I'm in this along with everyone else."

Agis frowned. "What are you saying?"

Tithian raised his brow in a satiric look. "I think you're intelligent enough to figure it out—and if not you, then certainly those of your friends who do not like to show their true faces in public."

Though he was shocked to discover that Tithian knew of his tentative association with Veiled Alliance, he tried not to show his surprise. "Assuming I do know someone who might be interested in Kalak's plans, why did you show me the pyramid, and why do you want the king's enemies to find out about it?"

Tithian took Agis's arm. "I want to survive," the high templar said, guiding the noble toward an exit. "To do that, two things must happen. First, Those Who Wear the Veil must tell me where they hid their amulets. If I don't find the last one soon, Kalak will kill me. Second, they must stop whatever the king has planned for the games. I'm going to be there, too. I've seen no reason to think he intends to spare his high templars."

"And what will you do in return?"

"Anything I can without getting myself killed," Tithian answered. "To start with, I'll allow Sadira to speak with my slave, Rikus—but only after I've recovered the amulets."

Agis stumbled. Though it was difficult, he refrained from asking how Tithian knew of Sadira. Obviously the high templar had a spy—either close to him or high in the ranks of the Alliance.

"Apparently you're still fatigued from the exercise of your powers," the high templar said, chuckling at Agis's clumsiness. He paused at the gate through which the noble had entered the stadium. "Would you like to use my litter for the trip home?"

"No offense," Agis said, "but I'd rather crawl on my

hands and knees."

As the noble stepped into the tunnel, Tithian caught him by the arm. "By the way, there's one thing you should know about my proposal."

"What?"

"It isn't a truce," Tithian said, releasing the noble. "Watch yourself."

TEN

Decisions and Promises

It was dusk in the animal shed. The beams of the descending sun rained down upon the roof of stretched hide, setting the whole interior ablaze with crimson light. In their pens, vicious animals paced, scuttled, or slithered back and forth impatiently, roaring, yowling, and clacking their mandibles in anticipation of the evening meal.

"Be quiet out there!" Rikus stormed, knowing that his command was futile even as he gave it.

It does no good to make noise, the gaj informed him. *The feeders won't come faster.*

I don't care about the feeders, the mul replied. *I just want some peace.*

Rikus sat on a cushion of rags in one corner of the pen, gingerly poking at the deep bruises he had received while cudgel-sparring with Yarig earlier. The dwarf had fared little better. Also covered head-to-toe in purplish marks, he sat in the opposite corner of the pen, rewrapping the leather thongs that bound the head of his warhammer to its shaft.

The young templar who had replaced Boaz allowed his charges to keep their weapons at night. He realized that fighters who took care of their own equipment would have more confidence in it. He also knew that, if the four gladiators wanted to escape, their weapons would be of little use against the magic-wielding templars whom Tithian had stationed around the compound after Sadira's escape.

Rikus winced as he probed his side and felt the cartilage shift between two ribs. "Were you trying to kill me today, Yarig?" the mul joked.

"Why would I kill a friend?" the dwarf demanded, his square jaw set in its customary seriousness. "That makes no sense."

"You have no business complaining about how Yarig fights," Neeva interjected. She sat in the center of the pen, using a piece of curved antler to chip a new blade for Rikus's short sword.

When the mul did not answer, the woman continued, "Serving wenches brawl harder than you've been fighting lately." She pressed the point of the antler against the obsidian edge she was shaping. A tiny chip popped loose and tumbled onto a pile of similar shards. "If you don't get your mind off that scullery girl, we'll both suffer more than a few bruises in the games."

"We'll win our contest," Rikus growled. "Don't you worry about that, Neeva."

The mul offered no further argument. There was no denying that he had been preoccupied with thoughts of Sadira over the past few days. He felt responsible for the half-elf's fate, yet unable to aid her. The conflicting emotions filled him with guilt and interfered with his concentration.

Gradually Rikus realized that the din in the animal

shed had reached a fever pitch. The increasing tumult usually meant the feeders had arrived, but it still seemed too early. A moment later, the mul heard murmuring voices approach. The other three gladiators continued to work, but he rose and stepped toward the iron gate just as six men wearing black cassocks stepped into view. Rikus recognized only one of them, a sharp-featured man with a long tail of auburn hair: Lord Tithian.

No food, Rikus! complained the gaj.

The feeders will come later, Rikus answered. *Be patient. Leave me to speak with these people.*

The gaj withdrew its presence and remained quiet.

"I don't suppose you've come to return us to our cells?" Rikus asked.

"You can't be serious. The least I can do for Boaz is let his punishment stand," Tithian replied. "Actually, I've come to speak with you. My new trainer tells me your performance has been pitiful since Sadira's escape."

"I'm still sore from fighting your gaj," Rikus said, trying to avoid the topic of the slave girl. The less the high templar knew about his feelings for her, the better. "I'll be fine in a day or two."

Neeva gave the mul a chiding glance, but did not rebuke his statement.

"In that case, you probably wouldn't be interested in hearing what happened to the wench," Tithian said sarcastically.

"Of course I would!" Rikus growled. Sensing that he had shown his opponent an opening, he added, "I owe her a debt of honor."

"Honor is an overvalued commodity," Tithian said coldly.

"It's all a slave has, my lord," Yarig said, not moving from his corner. "Knowing what happened to Sadira might help Rikus's fighting."

"Well spoken for a dwarf," Tithian replied, stepping forward to peer toward Yarig.

It occurred to Rikus that he could reach through the cage and snap the high templar's neck. The thought was such a pleasant one that the mul allowed himself to savor the imagined feel of his owner's spine cracking in his hands, but he made no move to attack. Rikus still wanted to win his freedom in the ziggurat games.

The mul's predatory expression was not lost on Tithian, who stepped back. "My guards would kill you in an instant."

"They might," Rikus allowed, smiling slyly. "And they might not. What happened to Sadira?"

The high templar chuckled. "First, you must tell me what the Veiled Alliance wants with you."

Rikus ran a hand over his hairless scalp. "I didn't know that they wanted anything with me," the mul replied. An image of Sadira came unbidden to his mind. Was the sorceress tied to the Veiled Alliance somehow? "Those Who Wear the Veil are not the sort to fix the games," the mul added quickly.

Tithian looked to one of his subordinates, an emaciated young man with bulging brown eyes. "Is he telling the truth?"

The young man nodded. "He also knew she was a sorceress."

Realizing he had been tricked, Rikus shot his arm through the cage.

"Mindbender!" the mul hissed, closing his fingers on the astonished fellow's cassock. Swiftly he pulled the youth to the gate and slammed his face into the bars. As the other templars moved forward to help, Rikus clasped his free hand on the mindbender's larynx. "I'll rip out his throat."

The young templar began trembling. "Stay back," he begged, barely choking out the words.

Yarig and Neeva moved to Rikus's side. Anezka hid in the shadows, probably hoping to avoid the punishment that was sure to follow Rikus's brash act.

The other templars looked to Tithian, who calmly removed a small jar from his pocket. It contained a purple caterpillar. "Don't kill him, Rikus."

The mul stared at the worm, but did not release the frightened templar. "Keep your part of the bargain."

Tithian feigned a look of disappointment. "Have I ever broken a promise to you?" When Rikus did not counter him, the high templar continued. "I'm not sure how, but a friend of mine bought her. There's no need to fear on her account. Agis of Asticles cares for his slaves the way most men care for their children."

Rikus smiled, then patted the templar on the cheek and shoved him away. "Lucky boy."

Tithian put his jar in a pocket, then stepped away from the pen. "By the way, the mul's little outburst will mean a week of half-rations for you all."

Anezka threw Neeva's chipping antler at Rikus's head. He knocked it aside, narrowly avoiding losing an eye. The mul was getting tired of being attacked by the mute halfling, but he could understand her anger.

As soon as the templars were gone, the gaj said, *Your female—Sadira—is not safe, Rikus.*

The mul smashed his callused fist against the stone wall. He barely noticed as blood began to stream from his knuckles. "Tithian was lying?" he asked aloud.

Tithian did not lie, but he spoke only some of his thoughts, the gaj answered. *Agis has your female, but Tithian has a watcher in Agis's burrow. He is looking for her veiled friends.*

"The Alliance?"

"What are you talking about, Rikus?" Neeva demanded.

He explained what the gaj had told him.

"Sadira in the Veiled Alliance?" Yarig scoffed. "It's impossible."

"Then where did the girl learn her sorcery?" asked Neeva.

The dwarf scratched his bald head. "It's impossible," he growled stubbornly. "We would have known."

What does Tithian want to do with Sadira's friends? Rikus asked the gaj.

Kill her, the gaj replied.

Rikus cried out in anger, leaping up to grab the mekillot ribs that served as the ceiling of their pen. The effort tore at his bruised cartilage, but he did not let go. He swung his legs upward and kicked at one of the thick ribs, attempting to break it.

"What are you doing?" Yarig demanded.

"Escaping," Rikus groaned.

Before the feeders come? asked the incredulous gaj.

The mul kicked at the ceiling again.

"What about the games?" Yarig demanded. "You can't just forget them!"

"This is more important," Rikus gasped, cringing at the pain in his ribs.

As he lowered his legs to prepare for another kick, Neeva grasped his waist. "Let me do it," she said. "You're too weak to break through a straw roof, much less a mekillot rib."

"You'll help me save Sadira?" Rikus asked, astonished.

"Would it change anything if I said no?"

When Rikus did not answer, Neeva jumped up and

grabbed the overhead grid. "That's what I thought," she said, swinging her legs toward the ceiling. She smashed a rib with each foot, opening a hole as wide as the mul's shoulders.

Yarig watched their efforts with a perplexed and hurt look.

As Neeva dropped back into the fighting pit, Rikus said, "You know, Yarig, you and Anezka could come with us. After we warn Sadira, we'll join a slave tribe somewhere in the desert. We'll be free."

"Free?" the dwarf echoed. His eyes clouded over, and Rikus could see that he was struggling with an internal conflict.

Anezka stepped to her partner's side and took his hand. Yarig looked at the mute. "Is that what you want, Anezka?"

The halfling nodded eagerly.

Yarig looked at the floor and took a few deep breaths. "You go ahead," he said. "I can't go with you. I just can't."

Anezka's wild eyes betrayed her disappointment, but she shook her head and clung to the dwarf's arm.

"Go on!" Yarig ordered. "There's no reason for you to stay."

The halfling stayed at her partner's side.

Neeva glanced at the pair with the closest thing to a sympathetic expression Rikus had ever seen on her face. "Yarig, just this once, can't you change your mind? If you don't go, neither will Anezka."

"I can't help it," Yarig answered. "She's free to go, but I've got to fight in the ziggurat games. It's my focus."

"Focus?" Neeva asked.

"Dwarves choose a purpose for their lives," he said. "I've chosen to fight in the ziggurat games. If I abandon

that purpose, I'll become an undead creature after I die."
Yarig gazed into Anezka's feral eyes. "Go with Rikus and
Neeva. You're a halfling, not a dwarf. You were meant to
be free."

Anezka shook her head and clung to Yarig.

Ignoring the pair's sentimental moment, Neeva said,
"We'll need a plan, Rikus. With templars lurking all over
the place, we can't expect to walk out of here easily."

After the feeders, I'll help, the gaj offered, clamoring at
the gate of its cell. *You must take me.*

"No," Rikus said. "We can't fight our way out, so we'll
have to use stealth. With you along, we wouldn't have a
chance."

I'll hide us, it countered.

Wishing that the gaj could communicate with more
than one person at a time, Rikus relayed to Neeva what
the beast wanted. She shook her head.

"We're doing this on our own," the mul declared.

No! Take me or I'll tell the feeders where you're going.

Rikus frowned and relayed the threat to his partner,
then they studied each other for several moments. "We
have no choice," Rikus growled.

"We need a better plan," Neeva complained. "There's
no way under the two moons we'll sneak that thing over
the wall."

After feeders, I'll hide everyone, the gaj repeated.

"How?" Rikus asked.

Trust me.

"I don't trust you," Rikus insisted.

The gaj did not answer, but an idea occurred to Rikus.
"One set of feeders will come into the animal shed, and
one set will leave," the mul said. "We'll use their wagon
to haul the gaj out of the compound."

Both Neeva and Yarig smiled. "Just because I'm not

going with you doesn't mean I can't help you escape," the dwarf said.

Neeva used her hands to make a stirrup for Yarig, boosting him high enough to slip out of the gap in the ceiling. He used the rope and pulleys to open the gate. The four gladiators left their pen, taking with them Neeva's trikal and Anezka's cudgel. They did not bother with Rikus's sword or Yarig's warhammer, for both were in disrepair.

Outside the pen, the shed was nearly dark, with only a few faint rays of flaxen moonlight shining through the hide roof. The wild clamor of the impatient animals was louder than ever.

"Neeva, you and Anezka sneak over to the entrance and take a look outside," Rikus said. "See if you can find the templars."

Neeva nodded, then she and Anezka started down the path toward the entrance.

Remember me, the gaj demanded. *Leave, and I'll tell the feeders where you're going.*

Rikus grabbed the rope in front of the gaj's gate and began pulling. "We're not leaving you, but you must do as I say."

Yes. I promise.

Rikus peered through the iron bars. The gaj crouched on the other side of the gate, two of its antennae flattened against its head. Where Neeva had torn off the third one, a new, small stalk waved tentatively. The gaj had closed its mandibles, and its compound eyes were staring at the floor.

Hoping the creature's meek demeanor meant it would be as cooperative as it had promised, Rikus pulled on the rope. A wave of pain shot through his injured rib cage, causing him to groan.

Yarig stepped toward the gate to help. Before he grasped the iron bars, he peered at the gaj and ordered, "Back to the other side!"

The creature obediently scuttled across the stone floor. With a deep groan, the dwarf lent his strength to assist with raising the heavy gate.

Without warning, the gaj leaped, shooting across the pen in a rust-colored streak. It struck Yarig straight on, its barbed pincers snapping shut around the dwarf's neck before he could scream.

Rikus released the rope. The heavy gate crashed down on the beast's shell, trapping it halfway out of the pen. Its canelike legs scraped madly at the stones of the pathway.

Oblivious to his sore ribs, Rikus leaped toward the gaj's head. Blood poured from the barb punctures in Yarig's throat.

"You lied!" Rikus yelled, smashing his fist into one of the gaj's eyes.

Lying is a useful thing, it replied, unimpressed by the blow.

Rikus struck again, aiming for a spot just behind the three stalks. The beast countered by slapping the gladiator with a antennae, sending a bolt of searing agony down the mul's side and paralyzing his left arm. He punched with his right hand.

The gaj slapped Rikus across the face. Images of gray, empty nothingness floated through the mul's mind, and he felt himself stumbling. The beast clubbed him with its mandible, knocking him halfway across the corridor.

Rikus glimpsed the gaj as it wrapped its stalks around Yarig's head. Painfully gasping for breath, the mul returned to his feet.

He has no thoughts! the gaj exclaimed, disappointed. *He's dead.*

With a casual flip of its head, the beast tossed the dwarf's limp body aside. It turned toward Rikus, then pumped its shell up and down in an attempt to dislodge itself from the gate.

Gathering his strength, the mul rushed for the gaj. As it opened its pincers, Rikus leaped into the air. He sailed over the huge mandibles and planted both feet in the center of the beast's head. The flying kick dislodged the gaj and knocked it back into its pen. The mul threw himself to the left, landing on his belly as the gate crashed down only inches behind him.

Rikus crawled away and lay on his stomach. He could do nothing but force his throbbing ribs to draw breath. The animals in their pens screeched madly, stirred into a frenzy by the sound of fighting and the smell of blood.

At length, the mul saw torchlight farther down the pathway. Anezka rushed past, pausing to drop a black bundle of cloth in front of Rikus. She kneeled beside Yarig's body and closed the dwarf's lashless eyes, touching her brow to each one in some halfling sign of affection that Rikus did not understand.

Neeva stepped to the mul's side, a torch in one hand. In the other she held a pair of spears and an obsidian dagger. She wore a black templar's cassock similar to the one Anezka had dropped.

"What happened?" she asked, laying the weapons aside and helping her partner to his feet.

Rikus pointed at the pen. "The gaj attacked Yarig," he said. "It was lying about coming with us."

"A little trick it learned from Tithian," Neeva observed. She touched her heart, then held her hand out to Yarig in the gladiator's traditional gesture of farewell.

Rikus motioned at the equipment Neeva had brought. "What's this?"

"We met the feeders and a pair of templar escorts at the door," she reported. "They didn't last long."

Rikus picked up a spear and went to the gaj's pen. The beast crouched in the corner, it eyes and lethal stalks turned toward the gate.

"This is for Yarig," the mul said, flinging the spear through an opening.

The shaft struck the gaj in the center of its antennae. It let out a high-pitched squeal and pulled its head beneath its shell.

"Will that kill it?" Neeva asked, holding her torch over the cage so she could see inside.

"Not for a few hours, I hope," Rikus answered.

You have not beaten me yet.

The squealing did not cease as the gaj sent its message, but the creature lifted its shell and pointed the tip of its abdomen at Rikus and Neeva.

"Time to leave," the mul said. He pulled his partner away from the pen just as the gaj sprayed the corridor with fetid vapor.

Neeva helped Rikus don the black cassock she and Anezka had procured for him. It was a snug fit, but the mul hoped it would get him as far as the gate. If someone came close enough to notice how tight the robe was, Rikus felt confident he could handle any problems that might arise.

When they were ready to leave, the mul picked up Yarig's body, certain that the dwarf would not want to be buried in Tithian's slave pits. "Are you coming with us, Anezka?"

The halfling nodded.

The three gladiators started toward the entrance, Anezka holding the spear, and Rikus and Neeva each carrying obsidian daggers in their pockets. They left their customary weapons in their cells. Trikals, staves, and warhammers would have drawn unwanted attention to the trio.

When they stepped out of the shed, Rikus pulled the cassock's hood over his head. Though it was still early, neither of the moons sat very high in sky, so the evening was reasonably dark. In each of the towers, the mul saw the shadowy forms of a templar and two guards.

The feeder's four-wheeled cart sat to the side of the door. A putrid stench rose from the various dead and almost dead animals lying in its wagon. "Let's get this unloaded," Rikus said. "We'd better feed the animals so they'll be quiet."

They quickly did as the mul suggested, blindly throwing different sorts of meat into the pens without regard for the beasts inside. A few minutes later, the cart was empty. Rikus laid Yarig's body in the wagon, then traded his dagger for the spear that Anezka carried and instructed her to lie down next to her fighting partner's corpse.

Rikus went to the front of the cart, where a single kank was lashed into the yoke. The docile beast stood a little higher than the mul's waist. Its chitinous body was divided into three sections: a pear-shaped head topped by two wiry antennae, an elongated thorax supported by six thin legs, and a bulbous abdomen hanging from the rear of the thorax.

Though Rikus had never driven one of the creatures, he had ridden in kank-drawn wagons enough to understand the basic principal. In his free hand, he picked up a long switch lying on the front of the cart, then tapped the kank between the antennae. To his surprise, the beast took off at a trot.

"How much attention are you trying to draw to us?" Neeva demanded, jogging to keep up with the cart.

"Slow down!"

"How?"

The blond gladiator snatched the switch from his hand and passed the end over the beast's antennae several times. It immediately slowed to a more acceptable speed.

They plodded down the lane, then turned right on the broad road leading to the back gate. Several tower guards paused to peer down at the wagon, but no one showed any sign of alarm.

At last, the gate itself loomed before them. It consisted of a large wooden door hinged between a pair of small towers. This evening, each tower was manned by one guard, with a single templar supervising them both.

Neeva steered the cart directly for the gate, not varying the kank's pace. The tower guards and the templar watched the disguised gladiators approach without comment. A guard turned a wheel inside his tower, and the gate slowly started to open.

The escapees passed into the dark shadows between the towers.

"Wait!" called the templar.

Neeva glanced at Rikus, and the mul nodded to indicate she should obey. The brawny woman passed the switch over the kank's antennae until the cart stopped.

"Did I see bodies in there?" the templar demanded.

"Yes," Rikus confirmed. "They insulted Tithian. We're taking them out for the raakles."

"I'd better have a look," the templar sighed, climbing down the ladder.

Neeva gave Rikus a questioning look. He shrugged, then peered over his shoulder at Anezka. She was playing dead, with one hand tucked awkwardly beneath her back.

The templar reached the ground, then went to the side of the cart. He was a human with a three-day growth of beard.

"What have we here?" the templar muttered, reaching over the wagon toward Yarig's neck. When his fingers came back sticky with blood, he grumbled with disgust and held his hand away from his body as if he didn't quite know what to do with it. "They're dead."

"Of course," Rikus answered. "I killed them myself."

The templar regarded the mul with a disgusted look, then motioned the cart through the gate. Neeva hardly waited for it to open the rest of the way before she moved the little cart out from between the towers.

A vast plain of rocky barrenness, purple-shrouded and as silent as death itself, lay before them.

"Where do we go now, Rikus?" Neeva asked, urging the kank into a trot.

"The estate of Agis of Asticles," the mul answered. "Wherever that is."

ELEVEN

UnderTyr

Ktandeo tapped the bench with his cane. "Sit."

Sadira obeyed immediately, but Agis ignored the command and remained standing. The three of them were gathered around the stone bench in the back the Drunken Giant wineshop. They had drawn the shimmering curtain of lizard scales for privacy.

"At last, we meet formally," Agis said, holding both hands palms up in a formal gesture of greeting. "I am Agis of Ast—"

"I know who you are," Ktandeo said, pointing to the bench. "Now sit."

Sadira pulled Agis down next to her, anxious to avoid angering her contact any further. She and the noble had been trying to see Ktandeo since Agis's conversation with Tithian. After two days of the pair making nuisances of themselves in the wineshop, the old man had finally come.

As soon as the senator touched the stone, Ktandeo scowled at the sorceress. "I'm certain you know what you've done."

Sadira was not sure whether he was referring to her efforts to arrange a meeting with Rikus or to bringing Agis to the rendezvous point, but she nodded anyway. To the Veiled Alliance, both were grave offenses. "When you hear what Agis has to say, you'll be glad I did."

"You'd better hope that's so," Ktandeo replied. "Otherwise—"

Agis interrupted the old man's threat. "Something terrible is about to happen in Tyr, and only you can stop it."

Before Ktandeo could reply, the red-bearded barman slipped past the curtain with a carafe of thick red wine and three mugs. Agis reached into his purse and withdrew several coins, but the old man laid his cane across the noble's wrist.

"I wouldn't drink what your coins buy," the sorcerer said.

"You can drink what Agis offers you," Sadira snapped, laying a hand on the senator's firmly muscled knee. During the last two days, the sorceress and the noble had not spent more than ten minutes apart, and she had come to know him well. "He's a better man than his peers."

"Is my hearing bad?" Ktandeo asked, sticking a thick finger into his ear as if to clean it. "I could have sworn I just heard a woman who kills templars defending a slaveholder's reputation."

Sadira's cheeks reddened. "The men I killed were petty, murderous scum, and they would have been the same whether they were free or slave," she said. "Agis is a good man, and being born into a corrupt nobility doesn't change that."

"Whether he's noble or slave is all the same to me," said the barman, holding out his hand. "His money is what matters."

Agis dropped a few coins into the server's hand. The

barman examined the coins briefly, then returned a small bronze disk to Agis. "If you think I'll take this instead of good Tyrian currency, you're mistaken. That's no coin I've ever seen."

Agis slipped the disk into his robe pocket with an air of chagrin, then retrieved two proper coins to replace it. "I've no idea how it came to be in my purse. Please accept my apologies."

As the burly man left, Ktandeo raised an eyebrow in Sadira's direction. "Didn't you storm out of here the other night because you love that gladiator?"

"What if I did?" Sadira demanded.

Ktandeo waved his cane in Agis's direction. "You're talking as though you care for this one, too."

"I might," Sadira answered, giving Agis a warm smile. He returned her gesture by looking slightly distressed. "What's wrong with that?"

Sadira understood why Agis and her contact seemed disturbed, but she did not share their prudish attitudes. Nothing in her background had taught her to consider romance an exclusive commitment. Tithian had used her mother as breeding stock, and Catalyna, the woman who had taught her the art of seduction, had warned the young sorceress against becoming attached to a single man.

"Perhaps we can discuss my visit with the high templar?" Agis suggested.

"That's what you came here for," Ktandeo grumbled, eyeing Sadira coldly. "And it had better be important."

As Agis recounted his meeting with Tithian, Ktandeo grumbled about the liberties Sadira had taken by recruiting the noble in the Alliance's name. He frowned at her when Agis revealed that the high templar knew the Veiled Ones wanted to meet with Rikus. However, when the senator described the pyramid and balls he had seen in Tithian's memory, Ktandeo's mood changed from one of petulance to one of apprehensive distraction.

"Tithian knows too much about what you two have been doing," Ktandeo said, his eyes thoughtfully fixed on the pommel of his cane.

"There's no doubt Tithian has a spy close to one of us," Agis said.

"It's your manservant, Agis. I'm sure of it," Sadira added.

The noble disguised his reaction to the statement by lifting his mug and taking a swallow of wine. This was one area where they were not in complete agreement. When Agis had gone to meet Tithian two days ago, Caro had excused himself on the pretense of relieving his bladder. He had not returned until just before Agis left the stadium. Even then, Sadira had been suspicious of the dwarf's prolonged absence. When she had heard about the interruption that ruined the assault on the high templar's mind, she had immediately concluded that the dwarf was a spy and pulled Agis aside to warn him.

"The dwarf who was with you at the slave auction?" Ktandeo demanded.

Agis put his wine aside with a sour face. "When you look at what Tithian knows and what Caro could have told him, it seems likely," Agis said. "I still find it difficult to accept. Caro's been loyal to my family for two hundred years."

"You're overestimating the strength of a slave's loyalty," Sadira said.

"Perhaps, but Caro's focus is serving the Asticles family. Do you know what it would mean if he betrayed me?"

"Eternal damnation seems a high price to pay for betrayal," Ktandeo agreed. "Still, Athas is full of dwarven banshees, and we have no way of knowing what Tithian may have offered him. I hope you had enough sense not to tell your servant where you are now."

Agis nodded. "I sent him home the same day of my meeting with Tithian. He hasn't seen us since."

"Let's hope so," Ktandeo answered. He stared at his cane's pommel. "What you saw in Tithian's memory is worrisome." He looked to Sadira. "I owe you an apology, my dear. You were right—nothing is more important than killing Kalak, and as soon as possible."

"Why?" Sadira and Agis asked the question simultaneously.

Ktandeo raised his hand and shook his head. "Let us pray you never learn the answer," he said, switching his gaze to Agis. "Now, what do you make of Tithian's proposal? Surely you don't think the high templar can be trusted?"

"Only to do what is best for himself," Agis replied. "But I do think he's sincere about working with you."

"Then you're a fool," answered Ktandeo.

"Perhaps not," Agis countered. "Kalak has put Tithian in a hopeless situation. He has no choice except to turn to the king's enemies for help."

Sadira added, "At the same time, he warned Agis to watch himself, so—"

A handful of muffled cries sounded in the plaza outside the wineshop, interrupting Sadira. Though the curtain remained drawn, it was not thick enough to muffle the panicked voices. The half-elf was rising to investigate the noise when the barman stuck his head around the edge of the curtain. In his hand, he held the satchel in which Sadira had been carrying her spellbook when Radurak captured her.

"Templars!" the barman hissed. He shoved the satchel

into her hands and left.

Sadira turned to Ktandeo. "Where did he get this?" she gasped, slinging it over her shoulder. She was so delighted to have it back that she was hardly concerned about the templars.

"From Radurak, of course," the old man answered curtly. "There's no time to discuss that now. Tithian's offer was bait, and you two swallowed it!"

The sorcerer tipped the stone bench onto its side. Beneath it, a cobweb-filled stairway descended into the murky earth at a precariously steep angle. To Sadira's elven vision, the first few feet of the stone stairs were outlined in blue tones emitted by the cool rock. Beyond that, the passage was as dark to her as it was to her human companions.

"Where does this go?" Agis demanded.

Before anyone could answer, the harsh, demanding voice of a templar sounded outside the curtain. Without waiting for Ktandeo's command, the half-elf took Agis's hand and led him into the stairwell. As the old sorcerer followed, he pulled the bench back into place, plunging the stairwell into darkness. The red hues of her companions' warm bodies and the blue hues of the cold stone provided all the illumination Sadira needed, but she knew her human friends would be completely blind in the darkness.

"I can cast a light spell," she whispered.

"Absolutely not!" came the old man's reply. "Go!"

The half-elf started down the stairs, guiding Agis by the hand. Ktandeo followed a step behind, his cane quietly tapping each stair before he stepped on it. As they descended, the silky filaments of the cobwebs slipped over Sadira's bare shoulders like a gossamer shawl, sending shivers of trepidation down her spine. Several times, imagining that something had crawled beneath her chemise, she had stifled the urge to slap at her back.

Worse than the cobwebs was the thick layer of dust covering the stairs. With each step, small puffs billowed up to tickle her nose and throat, vexing her with the urge to sneeze and cough. The dust was so deep that the edges of the stairs were slick and treacherous. Several times, Sadira slipped. Only the strong grip of Agis's warm hand prevented her from tumbling into the murkiness.

After many moments of hurried descent, they reached the bottom of the stairwell. There the passage changed into a corridor, which then ended almost immediately at a stone wall. Sadira turned around, conscious of a musty smell and the refreshing coolness of subterranean air.

"We're at the bottom," she whispered.

A loud clunk echoed from the upper end of the stairs. Far above, a narrow shaft of light poured into the stairwell. A black-robed templar appeared at the entrance.

"Go on," Agis whispered.

"It's a dead end," Sadira replied.

"Wrong," Ktandeo hissed. "Be quiet while I take care of our friends."

The old man calmly waited as the templars lit torches and began descending the stairs. The heat of the small flames overpowered Sadira's elven vision with painful white light, but her eyes quickly adjusted back to normal.

As the first templar reached the halfway point, a crooked smile crossed Ktandeo's lips. "Cover your ears."

The old man pointed the tip of his cane up the stairwell and uttered a single word, "Nok." A deep red light blossomed in the heart of the glassy pommel.

Sadira gasped as a strange tingle stirred deep inside her belly. The half-elf clasped her hands over her ears just as Ktandeo whispered, "Ghostfire."

A tremendous blast slammed through the corridor. Dust and stone chips showered down on the trio, and the air itself beat against them. A geyser of nebulous light shot up the stairwell. At first it merely washed over the men on the stairs, illuminating their frightened faces in a roiling, ruby-hued stream. For more than a second, the astonished templars remained motionless inside the crimson ray, their mouths gaping open and their hands clutching their short swords.

The spell began to fade. The skin of those caught within its beam grew ashen and flaky. Flesh poured off their bodies in a fine powder, and screams filled the stairwell. Some men tried to flee up the stairs, and others charged downward. Their efforts did little good, for as the light grew dimmer, their hair, eyes, and even their entrails turned to ash. By the time the stairwell returned to darkness and Sadira was once again relying on her elven vision, all that remained of the templars was a mass of charred bones clattering down the steps.

"The cane drew its energy through us!" Agis gasped.

"What kind of magic is that?" Sadira demanded. Ktandeo had never told her it was possible to draw magical energy from animal life.

Ktandeo let out a fatigued gasp. He reached out for Agis's shoulder, but could not find it in the darkness. Sadira stepped past the noble and slipped her shoulder under the old man's arm. To her eyes, the color of his body had faded from deep red to pink. Ktandeo's magic had apparently drawn most of its energy from the old man himself.

Supporting himself on Sadira's shoulder, the sorcerer staggered to the end of the corridor and tapped his cane against a stone. "Push there," he gasped.

With her free arm, Sadira guided Agis forward, and he

gave the stone a shove. A door-sized slab pivoted open in front of them as more templars stepped into the top of the stairwell. The king's men descended rapidly, cursing and kicking at the bones of their dead fellows.

"Take them alive!" yelled a commanding voice.

Sadira prodded Agis through door. "We should have killed Caro when we had the chance."

"This only proves it wasn't him," objected Agis. "He doesn't know where we are.

"Quiet!" Ktandeo gasped, pushing Sadira through the door. Once they were clear, Sadira quickly inspected their dark surroundings while Agis closed the door. Ahead lay a silent cavern smelling of mildew and decay. It was filled with the round, cool-blue shapes of rocky pillars rising more than ten feet overhead to disappear into a yellowish mass of gauzy filament that hung from the ceiling.

"Nok," Ktandeo said again, speaking the word that activated his cane, then named the spell he wished to use. "Forestlight."

The pommel of his cane began to glow. Sadira blinked, and then she saw that the obsidian ball was surrounded by a small circle of eerie violet light. She felt a faint tingle in her gut as the cane drew energy from her.

Muffled voices began to sound through the stone slab at their backs. Ktandeo led them away, moving at a painfully slow pace. Sadira knew he would never be able to outrun the templars. Fortunately the trio had already traveled many yards into the pillar forest by the time the hidden door behind them began to scrape open.

The old sorcerer ran the palm of his hand over his cane's pommel, and the violet light faded away. Behind them, the torchlit forms of templars began to pour into the cavern.

"You're our eyes now," Ktandeo whispered, pulling Sadira to the front of the party. "I'll hold your hand. Agis, you hold my cane. Keep on eye on what's happening behind us."

Sadira glanced over her shoulder and saw that the number of templars gathering outside the door had risen to more than a dozen. "Where are we going?"

Grasping her by the shoulders, Ktandeo oriented her so that she faced exactly the same direction as him. "Straight ahead. Count fifty pillars and stop."

The half-elf took her master's hand and started walking at the fastest pace she judged Ktandeo could endure.

A templar's strident voice echoed through the quiet cavern. "They went this way! Ten silver for every man here if we catch them alive. Ten lashes if they escape!"

"Agis?" Sadira asked, continuing forward. She did not look back, for she did not want her elven vision washed out by the heat of the templars torches.

"They're following our path," he reported.

"Run!" Ktandeo hissed.

"But—"

"Do it!" he ordered.

Holding Ktandeo's hand, Sadira set off at a jog, her steps falling silently on the cold stone floor. Behind her, the old sorcerer stumbled and scraped along, his breath coming in unsteady, rasping wheezes. Agis brought up the rear, his footfalls muffled and steady. Though their passage could hardly be called hushed, the half-elf did not worry about the noise they caused. Their pursuers were making so much noise that she and her friends could have spoken aloud without concern.

After Sadira passed the correct number of pillars, she stopped. "This is it," she said. "How close are they, Agis?"

"Three city blocks. Maybe less," he answered. "It's hard to tell."

"How are they following us?" Sadira asked. "Cilops?"

"I don't see any sign of handlers or animals," Agis said, scraping his foot along the rocky floor.

The old sorcerer hefted his walking stick. "Let's see if I can't slow them down a bit."

Fearing Ktandeo was too weak to use the cane again, Sadira pushed it down. "Allow me."

Kneeling at the base of the pillar, the sorceress fetched a piece of charcoal from the shoulder satchel that held her spellbook, then traced a series of flame-shaped runes at the bottom of the column.

"We'd better hurry. They're running hard," Agis advised. "I can almost see their faces. They must be only a block or two back by now."

Sadira pointed at the ceiling and summoned the energy she needed for the spell. To her surprise, a large circle of the gauzy filament overhead shriveled up and turned black. The filament had to be some sort of strange plant. Thankful that Ktandeo could not see what she had done, Sadira spoke her incantation and rose.

Agis whispered, "They'll see us soon."

"I'm ready," Sadira answered, also whispering. "Now where, Ktandeo?"

"Twenty pillars to the right," the old man gasped.

"Let's go!" Agis said.

Sadira took Ktandeo's hand and led him away. They had traveled only six pillars when a templar cried out, "I see them!"

"I hope your spell works," Ktandeo huffed.

"You'll be proud," Sadira promised, continuing forward.

A few seconds later, a loud crack echoed behind them.

Sadira looked over her shoulders and saw a pillar of golden, fluidlike flame consume the leader of the templar column. The man screamed and whirled in a wild dance of agony, throwing great globs of golden flame all around.

The commander shouted orders for the rear of the column to circle around and take the lead. As the templars obeyed, more sprays of flame erupted from the base of the pillar, shooting directly for the nearest men. More templars burst into flame. Within moments the cavern was glowing with golden light and echoing with anguished screams. The templars fell into complete disarray.

"Let's go," Agis said. "Their confusion won't last forever."

"Wait a moment," Sadira replied, motioning her companions to hide behind a pillar.

She pointed a hand upward and summoned the energy for another spell. Again, a circle of the gauzy flora overhead shriveled and turned black. This time, the small skeleton of some long-dead cavern animal tumbled from the ceiling and landed at Ktandeo's feet. The thing had a flat, circular skull with four eye sockets and six legs.

Ktandeo's eyes went from the skeleton to the ceiling, then the old man gasped. "Look what you did!"

Sadira cringed at the reprimand, knowing it would eventually result in a long lecture, then cast her spell. A glimmering yellow light, resembling a distant torch, appeared amidst the pillars to the right of the templars. It slowly began to drift away.

For the next few moments, Sadira held her breath and hoped the simple conjuration would be enough to fool the templars. She had intended to enhance the deception by adding ghostly voices to the phantom torch, but that was out of the question now that Ktandeo had seen how delicate the strange plantlife on the ceiling was.

At last, a templar noticed the light. "What's that?" he cried, barely making his voice heard above the general clamor.

Sadira gestured at the light, and it danced away as if running. The templars followed, screaming orders at each other and leaving their burning companions behind to die.

"Now we can go," Sadira said.

She led her companions forward until she had counted twenty pillars, as Ktandeo had instructed. "Now where?" she asked. The templars were no more than distant voices of turmoil, and Sadira was once again relying on her elven vision to see in the dark.

"Turn half a step to the left," Ktandeo panted, barely able to speak.

"I think we can rest for a minute," Agis said, supporting the old man. "We seem to have lost them."

"What are all these strange columns for?" Sadira asked, inspecting the pillar closest to her. It had a woodlike grain, but the thing felt like solid rock.

"I assume you're looking at the pylons," Agis replied, blindly facing Sadira's voice. "Those are the foundations of the city. This is UnderTyr."

"Tyr is built on pillars?" Sadira asked. "Why?"

"According to legend, Tyr once sat in the middle of a vast swamp—"

"That's more than legend," Ktandeo said weakly, his voice lacking its customary strength. "But we have more important things to discuss—such as the destruction Sadira's spellcasting caused."

"What was I supposed to do, let them catch us?" she demanded.

"Yes," Ktandeo answered, fixing his eyes on the darkness over Sadira's head. "You must maintain the Balance at all costs. Once you become like the sorcerer-king and his minions, there's no coming back to our way."

"I thought you said killing Kalak was more important than—"

A pair of fine-featured men with the arched brows and slender features of half-elves jumped from behind the pillar at Ktandeo's back. Both wore the heavy cassocks of templars. One of them stood nearly as tall as a full elf, and the other had an unusually stocky build.

"Behind you!" Sadira yelled, grabbing Ktandeo and pulling him toward her. "Templars!"

The tall half-elf tossed a rope net in her direction. The square mesh settled over her shoulders before she could react. Immediately the templar cinched the drawline, and the bottom of the net contracted, pinning her arms against her body.

Ktandeo activated his cane's violet light.

Though she had little chance of freeing herself, Sadira continued to struggle, hoping to keep the tall half-elf busy.

"Commander!" cried one of the half-elves. "Over here!"

Ktandeo raised his arms to use his magic, but the stocky templar called the king's name and pointed a finger at the old sorcerer, casting a spell of his own. Ktandeo's hands grew stiff, and his incantation came out in a jumble of meaningless phrases. The sorcerer tried to shrug off the templar's magic, but could do no better than to move at half the speed of everyone else.

Agis drew his steel dagger. He sent the stocky half-elf reeling with a kick to the stomach, then stepped toward Sadira and slashed the rope holding her prisoner.

The tall templar dropped the net and backed away before Agis could strike again. The noble whirled on the other ambusher, catching the stocky half-elf just as he was recovering from the first kick. Agis drew his dagger across the man's throat before his sword left the scabbard.

The effects of the enchantment upon Ktandeo ended. He took two steps forward and stumbled over the half-elf Agis had just killed. The old man fell to the ground in a heap.

By the time Agis turned to face the tall half-elf again, the templar had fled into the dark. Instead of attacking, the noble finished cutting the sorceress free.

"We'd better move," Ktandeo groaned, slowly returning to his feet. "Look."

He pointed back the way they had come. Sadira could already see torches moving in their direction.

"How are we going to escape?" she asked.

"Follow me," Ktandeo said.

Wheezing and gasping, the old man led the way at a slow run, lighting their path with his glowing cane. The templar commander's harsh voice echoed behind the trio as he shouted orders to his subordinates. Each time, the voice was louder.

"Maybe you should darken your cane, Ktandeo," Sadira suggested. "It's making us easy to follow."

"It's not my cane they've been following so far," he huffed. The sorcerer braced his hands on his knees and looked ahead, to where the pylon forest ended. From there the ground sloped down at a steep angle. "Besides, we're almost safe."

Ktandeo took a deep breath, then led them down a bank to a small cobblestone courtyard. Although she was surprised to see such a thing under the city, Sadira had no

time to puzzle over its origin. As they crossed the courtyard, she kept her attention focused over her shoulder,
glancing at the ground only occasionally to look for ob-
stacles. By the time they reached the other side of the
small courtyard, the first templars were standing at the
top of the embankment. They were close enough that she
could distinguish between the ones who had mustaches
or beards and those who did not. Many of them had
stopped pursuing and were staring over her head with
their jaws drooping open.

Sadira looked forward and saw the reason for their
shock. Ktandeo's cane was illuminating the facade of an
immense building of granite block, the likes of which she
had never seen before. A great apron of stairs led up to
several pairs of ornate doors, each set into a high arch
covered by a gabled porch. Beautiful windows of colored
glass adorned the gables, each depicting a tall man with
the head of an eagle, a huge pair of leathery wings, and
the lower body of a coiled serpent.

"What is this place?" Sadira asked, awestruck.

"It's the Crimson Shrine," Ktandeo wheezed, slowly
climbing the stairs. "A temple of the ancients."

Sadira and Agis froze, for such places were rumored to
be the homes of wraiths and ghosts.

"Beneath Tyr?" Agis asked.

"Before Tyr was a swamp, it was a sacred wood,"
Ktandeo replied, not bothering to turn as he spoke.
"That was two thousand years ago. The city was built
around this temple."

On the far side of the courtyard, the templar commander barked, "Don't waste time gaping! If they get inside, I'll send you in after them!"

Sadira and Agis started after the old man. "How do you
know all this?" Agis asked.

"I've spoken with those who inhabit the temple," the old man answered, reaching the top of the stairs.

As Sadira stepped to Ktandeo's side, the purple light of his cane illuminated the wall high above them. Four pairs of tall, dagger-shaped windows flanked a statue depicting the eagle-headed figure in flight. In the windows the figure was captured in flight, too, and from a bucket carried beneath its arm, it was sprinkling rain over a green forest.

As she studied the wall, Sadira glimpsed a black, man-shaped shadow passing behind one of the dagger-shaped windows. It peered down at Sadira and her companions, setting the slave girl's heart to pounding with fear.

"You aren't thinking of taking us in there?" she asked.

"The pure of heart have nothing to fear in the Crimson Shrine," Ktandeo said.

Agis followed the sorcerer toward the door, but Sadira did not move. "What do you mean by 'pure of heart'?"

Ktandeo pointed his cane at the square below. "You can face the crimson knights or Kalak's mindbenders. Only you know which choice to make."

Seeing that a dozen of the king's bureaucrats had already moved halfway across the courtyard, Sadira said, "I'll try the knights."

Ktandeo motioned for Agis to open the doors of the temple. The noble obeyed, then stepped backward in alarm. "By Ral!"

In the doorway stood a wraith dressed head to foot in steel armor. Its visor was open, revealing two red eyes that looked out from a mass of churning darkness. Over its breastplate hung a pearly tabard decorated with the eagle-headed figure so prominently depicted in the temple's facade, and from the crown of its helm rose a fantastic red plume. The wraith held a tall halberd, and its burning eyes were fixed on Agis.

Beyond the guard lay a cavernous room lit by a thousand candles flickering with a brilliant red flame. It seemed that every inch of the church had been carved with bas reliefs of fantastic creatures.

"It's amazing!" Agis gasped. "What keeps all those candles lit, magic?"

"There is no magic in this temple," Ktandeo said. "Faith keeps the candles burning."

Sadira cast an anxious eye behind them. The twelve templars had reached the bottom of the stairs. On the far side of the square, the templar commander was shouting orders to the rest of his men, sending them along the edge of the embankment to encircle the area.

"If we're going inside, let's do it," she said.

Ktandeo slipped past the wraith and entered the temple, the violet glow of his cane dying as he crossed the threshold. The area outside the door grew dim but did not fall entirely dark. The light of the shrine's candles illuminated the entire stairway.

Agis motioned for Sadira to enter next, but she shook her head. "You first," she said.

The noble stepped toward the door with his customary confidence and poise. As his foot crossed the threshold, the wraith struck him across the brow with the butt of its halberd.

"No!" Its deep voice echoed far into the pylon forest.

Agis let out a surprised cry, then stumbled backward holding his bleeding brow.

"Cursed nobles!" Ktandeo growled, half-stepping out of the door.

"Why won't it let him in?" Sadira demanded, addressing her question half to her master and half to the ghostly guard.

"Because he owns slaves, perhaps, or for some other

vice," the old sorcerer said, raising his cane and pointing the tip toward the twelve templars on the stairs. "Get down, both of you."

As Sadira and Agis obeyed, Ktandeo uttered, "Nok! Quietstorm!"

Sadira felt her stomach tense, then a beam of white light silently shot from the cane's tip. It illuminated the face of the closest templar. The man's torch went out, and he quietly crumpled to the ground in a lifeless heap. A second bolt of light shot from the cane, and Sadira felt more energy being drained from her body. Another templar fell dead. A third flash followed, and then a fourth and a fifth. Each time, another torch went out, another templar died, and Sadira felt a little weaker.

By the time the cane flared the twelfth time, Sadira lay on the stones gasping for breath and fighting to keep from retching. When she could finally lift her head again, she saw that Ktandeo still stood bathed in light from the interior of the temple. He was hunched over and struggling to support himself by hanging onto the door. Agis lay to her right, holding his bleeding head and drawing slow, even breaths.

"You chided *me* for killing a little ceiling moss?" she gasped.

Ktandeo looked up, seeming immeasurably old and feeble. His whole body heaved with the simple effort of breathing.

"I have taken nothing that cannot be replenished," the sorcerer wheezed. "What you did destroyed—" He broke into a fit of coughing. When he finished, he said, "You know the difference. Now come. If we close the door, perhaps Agis can sneak away in the darkness."

Agis nodded. "Go on," he said. "My strength is coming back. I'll be fine. Even if they capture me, I doubt

Tithian will let them do me any harm."

"I'm not taking that chance," Sadira insisted, her strength also returning. "We have to change the guard's mind and get Agis inside."

"The guard has no mind to change," Ktandeo answered weakly. "All it has is faith in its god's teachings, and those teachings prohibit Agis from entering this temple."

On the far side of the courtyard, another half-dozen templars started down the steep bank. Agis rose and started to leave, but Sadira caught his arm.

"The god can't still be alive! Kalak would never stand for that beneath his own city," Sadira objected. "The guard has nothing to lose by making an exception."

"You don't understand," Ktandeo said, pulling himself completely upright. "The gods of the ancients aren't sorcerer-kings. They were much more powerful, and those who worshiped them did so with all their hearts—not the way the templars worship Kalak."

"What happened to these ancient gods?" Agis asked.

Ktandeo shook his head. "Like all glories of the past, they faded away. No one knows why."

Sadira pulled Agis toward the doorway. "I don't care about the decree of some dead god or a wraith's blind faith in it."

Ktandeo blocked her way. "To let Agis in, the guard must break its faith," the old man said, his voice growing stronger. He pointed toward the interior of the shrine. "Every time a crimson knight breaks its faith, a candle goes out. Does it look like many lights have died in the last two-thousand years?"

Sadira did not have time to study the room, but at first glance she did not see any unlit candles.

"If you must stay with Agis, then stay with him,"

Ktandeo said, pulling the door closed until only a sliver of red light escaped the temple. "Leave me here and go. I'll be safe until my strength returns, and you two will stand a better chance of escaping without me."

"Where will I find you again?" Sadira asked.

"I'll find you," Ktandeo answered, motioning them away. He kept the door cracked open so he could watch them leave.

Sadira took Agis's hand and fled down the left side of the temple's stairs. It appeared that the line of templars ahead of them was fairly spread out. She hoped to sneak through one of the dark places between their glowing torches.

The commander's voice suddenly rang across the square. "They've changed directions!" he called. "They're moving toward the left side of the square!"

The six templars in the square adjusted their approach accordingly.

"How can he track us from up there?" Agis asked, frustrated. "It's as if he can smell us!"

"Not smell us, but feel us!" Sadira exclaimed, suddenly realizing how the templars had tracked them both to the Drunken Giant and through the dark caverns of UnderTyr.

"What?" Agis asked. "What do you mean?"

"Magically! He can feel where we are by using magic," Sadira answered. "Do you still have that bronze disk you tried to give the barman?"

"Yes, right here." He placed the token in the half-elf's hand.

Sadira smiled in the darkness. "This is what's leading them to us," she said, reversing their course and leading Agis back up the stairs. If she was correct about the bronze disk, she thought it would be possible to virtually guarantee their escape.

"Caro must have slipped it into your purse before you sent him home the other day," Sadira whispered as they reached the top of the stairs. "The templars tracked us to the Drunken Giant with it, then waited for Ktandeo to show up before springing their trap. With this little trinket to help them keep track of us, they could afford to be patient."

On the far side of the square, the commander yelled a curse, then cried, "They've reversed directions! They're heading toward the temple doors!"

The six templars in the square turned back toward the center of the shrine. Fortunately, the six men's little detour had delayed their progress, and they were only halfway across the square.

"Dozens of men went in and out of the wineshop every day," Agis objected. "How would the templars know which one was your contact?"

"Caro again," Sadira answered, working her way back toward the sliver of red light where Ktandeo still held the temple door cracked open. "He was there when you bought me at Radurak's auction. He would have been able to describe Ktandeo from that incident."

Ahead of her, the flickering shaft of light widened as the door opened. Ktandeo stuck his head outside. "I'll cover your escape, Sadira," he called in a throaty rasp. In the dim red glow shining from the doorway, the sorceress saw him point his cane at the six templars in the square. "Run."

"Wait—"

In the same instant that Sadira spoke, Ktandeo activated his cane, then called, "Groundflame!"

A glob of fluorescing green gas spewed from the cane and wafted over the center of the square. The templars stopped moving as the cloud descended in their midst. The stones began to sizzle, and the glowing haze spread out across the square like a ground fog. In the blink of an eye, it changed color to vibrant blue. There was a blinding flash, and the templars screamed once. When Sadira's vision cleared again, the square was completely dark.

Ktandeo groaned and grasped at the door to keep from slumping to the ground. The sorceress moved to catch him, but a tremendous thunderclap reverberated off the cavern's rocky ceiling and floor. A bolt of lightning flashed across the courtyard and slammed into the open door.

"Ktandeo!" Sadira shrieked, momentarily blinded.

As her vision cleared, the sorceress saw that the bolt had not even scorched the church door. She dared to hope Ktandeo had escaped injury, then she saw the old man's crumpled figure lying between the double doors.

Sadira rushed forward and snatched his cane from where it had fallen. As she kneeled at the old man's side, she saw warm blood streaming from his ears and mouth. Though the lightning bolt had not even scorched the temple's door, it had crushed Ktandeo's ribs.

The sorceress slipped the cane into her master's hand. "Will this help?" she asked. Tears began running down her cheeks and dripping onto the old man's face.

Ktandeo pushed the cane away. "No, that wand only takes life." He suffered a fit of violent coughing and spewed up a gob of bright red fluid. When he could finally speak again, he said, "Sadira, you must go to Nok."

"Nok?" she asked. "Where—"

The old man grasped her wrist. "Listen! Take my cane, go to Nok in the halfling forests. Get the spear and kill Kalak. Tithian betrayed you, but the danger he showed

Agis is real."

"What about that danger?" Sadira asked. "Tell me."

"Nok, he will—" He fell into another fit of coughing, and Sadira waited patiently for him to stop. She did not even try to suggest that the old man would survive. The lie would have been obvious to both of them, and she would not insult the man who had taught her magic that way.

When Ktandeo stopped coughing, he motioned her close to him. "You'll learn the answer there," he said. "There is one other thing I must tell you, Sadira."

She leaned over to hear his final words. "Yes."

"Be careful," he said, gesturing toward the satchel that contained her spellbook. "If the templars hadn't come, I wouldn't have given that back to you. You're walking too close to the edge. Step off, and you will fall so far you'll never see the light again."

With that, he gave one last cough and closed his eyes forever.

TWELVE

Asticles Wine

Rikus didn't care much for Asticles wine. The pale golden color reminded him of something he'd rather not drink, and the tart, dry scent made his nose tingle. It had a thin, light taste that left him with a dry mouth, and after each swallow he had a thirst for something richer and sweeter. Still, compared to the fruit syrup doled out in Tithian's slave pits, Asticles wine was at least drinkable, and it was a lot more potent than its watery appearance suggested. Besides, drinking it made the gladiator feel like he was stealing something from a nobleman, and he liked that feeling.

The big mul lifted his crystal goblet and asked, "How about some more?"

"Have all you like. My master won't care," replied Caro, who had introduced himself as the valet of Agis of Asticles. The wrinkled old dwarf picked up a carafe and refilled the goblets of his guests.

Rikus, Neeva, and Caro were in the western courtyard of the Asticles mansion, sitting on a pair of benches sheltered beneath a vine-covered bower. The bower stood upon a small patio-island located at the center of a deep pool. A narrow bridge ran from the island to the marble colonnade that ringed the pond, and the colonnade was in turn encircled by a granite privacy wall.

Enormous lily pads covered the surface of the pond. Round, with upturned edges, they resembled green serving trays set out to float on the water. Between the pads drifted pink-hearted blossoms with pearly white petals.

Every now and then, a flower bobbed once or twice, then Anezka's wooly-haired head appeared as she treaded water and gulped down a few lungfuls of air. The halfling had been in the pond since they arrived, when she had astonished both Caro and her companions by stripping off her dusty clothes and jumping into the pool.

Rikus and his companions had spent the previous four days skulking about the desert, sneaking into faro orchards to ask directions of unguarded slaves. They had met with little success, for most fields were deserted, having been ravaged by scavengers or burned by marauders. On the two occasions when they had found someone, the slave had mistaken them for raiders and had run off screaming the alarm. Finally the trio of gladiators had gone to the road, where they had ambushed a templar. He had told them what they needed to know in exchange for a mercifully quick death. After the four-day ordeal, Rikus was so tired and thirsty that he would have joined Anezka in the lily pond, had he known how to swim.

"How will your master feel about a halfling bathing in his pond?" Rikus asked.

Caro watched Anezka's small form slip beneath a lily pad, then smiled crookedly. "Don't worry about my master," the dwarf said. "If we wanted to, we could drink the last drop of his wine and swim in his pond for days. He'd never say a word to us, I promise."

"Then here's to Agis of Asticles. May his fortunes prosper!" Neeva said, raising her goblet. When Caro did not match the gesture, the woman asked. "What's wrong? It's only proper to drink to your host's health."

"To toast him would be to toast my bondage," the dwarf replied, his face unreadable.

"There are worse things than this sort of bondage," Neeva said, waving her hand around the lavish courtyard. "This is paradise!"

"Compared to our slave pits, perhaps," Rikus allowed, rolling his crystal goblet between two grimy fingers. "But slavery is slavery. I doubt that Caro's master views him much differently than he does this colonnade or his house. It's all property."

Caro nodded. "I couldn't have put it better, my friend."

"Forget I offered that toast," Neeva said, starting to empty her glass on the ground.

Rikus grasped her wrist. "Don't waste the wine!" he said. "Slaves get too little of it. We just have to think of something better to toast."

Caro lifted his glass. "To your freedom," he said.

All three of them downed their wine in a single gulp. The dwarf refilled their glasses, then casually tossed the empty carafe into the pool. It landed on a lily pad and came to a rest in the center of the enormous leaf.

"Have you given thought to where you'll go from here?" Caro asked.

Rikus nodded. "After we find Sadira, we'll join a slave tribe," the mul said.

"I'm afraid you may have to wait for quite some time before you speak to Sadira," Caro replied. "She's with Lord Agis in the city, and I don't know when they'll return. Perhaps you should leave the message with me. I'll see that she gets it."

Rikus shook his head. "We'll have to wait—"

"We can't wait long," Neeva interrupted. "The cilops are probably already on our trail. If we're going to have any chance of escaping, we've got to keep moving—and get to the mountains before they catch us."

"It's not fair to burden Caro with this particular message," Rikus said.

Neeva met Rikus's eyes evenly. "Tithian's spy is watching Sadira. If Caro's here and Sadira's in Tyr, then Caro can't be the spy, can he?"

"Spy?" Caro gasped, his jaw dropping. A moment later, he closed his mouth again. "How did you find out there's a spy in my master's household?"

"That's a long story not worth the telling," Rikus said, far from anxious to dredge up memories of Yarig's death by discussing the gaj. "If you'll tell us where your master and Sadira are, we might reach her before we go to the mountains."

"I'm afraid it would be impossible to find them. The last time I saw my master and Sadira, they were going to a rendezvous. They never returned," Caro explained, a sudden frown accentuating the deep crow's feet around his eyes. "I'm afraid something may have happened to them."

"We're too late!" Rikus yelled, hurling his goblet across the pool. It smashed against the outer wall, causing a light tinkle of shattering glass to echo all around the colonnade.

Neeva reacted more calmly. "How long ago was this rendezvous?" she asked. "Where was it to take place?"

"Agis and Sadira disappeared three days ago," Caro reported. "Neither would say where they were going, but both were acting rather nefarious about the whole thing.

I suspect their destination was somewhere in the Elven Market."

Rikus stood. "That's where we're going."

The old dwarf slipped off the bench and dropped to the ground. "I have something in the house that might help you."

"What?" Neeva asked.

Caro smiled. "It's a surprise," he said. "I'm sure you'll find it quite remarkable."

After the dwarf left, Rikus and Neeva retrieved the weapons they had stolen during the escape from Tithian's estate. They secured the daggers to the belts of their breechcloths, then Rikus kneeled at the edge of the pool to catch Anezka's attention.

Just as the mul glimpsed her form gliding toward him, several sets of thudding steps sounded outside the colonnade. Rikus looked up and saw the stout form of a half-giant blocking the arched entrance. His brown hair hung over his ears in long greasy strings, and he had a protruding brow set above a pair of drooping eyes. The half-giant wore a purple tunic emblazoned with Kalak's golden star, and in one hand he carried a polished bone club taller than a dwarf. The guard's thighs were as big around as the pillars of the colonnade, and he had to stoop to keep from scraping his head on the ceiling.

"In the name of King Kalak, stand where you are!" the half-giant bellowed. His voice rumbled over the still waters of the pond and echoed off the opposite wall encircling the colonnade. As the guard lumbered toward the bridge, another half-giant, a little stockier and shorter than the first, stepped into the entrance.

Anezka briefly stuck her head up from between a pair of the lily pads. When she saw Rikus's shocked expression and the half-giant guards, she slipped back beneath the water and disappeared beneath the floating leaves.

"Neeva!" called Rikus, returning to his feet. "Hand me the—"

The mul had spoken too late. Even as he reached for the spear, it whistled past his head. The shaft took the first half-giant square in the rib cage and sank to half its length. The guard dropped to his knees, then pitched forward onto his face.

The second guard began to climb over the still body of the first. A third half-giant moved through the entrance and, upon seeing the blockage ahead, circled around the other way.

Rikus searched the area beneath the bower for something to use as a weapon. Both he and Neeva had obsidian daggers, but the knives did not seem like effective weapons against half-giants.

When the mul's eye fell on the bench, an idea occurred to him. He gave his dagger to Neeva, then nodded toward the closest half-giant. Rikus did not need to say a word for his fighting partner to know he wanted her to cover the attack he was about to make.

The second half-giant finished climbing over his dead comrade, then stepped onto the bridge. Rikus wrapped his massive arms around the bench and picked it up, groaning with the effort. He turned toward the bridge.

The half-giant stepped a third of the way across in one stride. "Stop!" he cried.

Rikus charged, holding the bench like a battering ram. The half-giant grinned and lifted his club.

From behind the mul, Neeva's dagger flashed overhead in a black streak. It hit the guard in the brow, striking hilt-first. It bounced harmlessly away and landed on a lily pad with a hollow thump. Nevertheless, the attack served its function—stunning the half-giant long enough to keep him from swinging his club before Rikus drove the end of the bench into the guard's chest.

A great crack sounded from the half-giant's sternum. A heavy groan escaped his lips. He whirled his arms, and his club went crashing into the bower. With a tremendous bellow, the guard fell backward, slamming into a pillar. The marble column broke into the three pieces, and the half-giant landed among the sections, cursing and vowing vengeance.

As the guard started to sit up, the roof collapsed, dumping half a ton of rubble on his head. His death cries were lost amid the thunderous clatter.

Rikus dropped the bench and turned around. He saw that the third half-giant had decided against the bridge and was approaching the patio through the pond. Neeva already faced him. Armed only with a dagger, she was moving forward to meet him at the edge of the island.

To one side of the bridge, Anezka emerged from the water long enough to grab the dagger that had fallen on the lily pad. Guessing that she intended to attack from under the water, Rikus retrieved the second half-giant's club and stepped to his fighting partner's side. When Neeva lifted her arm to throw her remaining dagger, Rikus laid a restraining hand on her wrist.

"Not yet."

"Maybe I'll get lucky."

The mul did not reply, but held onto her throwing arm, waiting for Anezka's attack. When the half-giant lifted his club to swing at Neeva, Rikus finally released her.

"Thanks a lot!" the blond gladiator exclaimed, preparing to dodge instead of throwing her dagger.

The half-giant paused in mid-stroke. He stared at his feet, then screamed in pain. The guard plunged his hand into the water behind his ankle.

Guessing that Anezka had severed the tendons at the soldier's ankle, Rikus swung his club at the half-giant's head. He made contact, but the shock jarred him to the soles of his feet and his hands went numb from vibration. It felt as though he had struck a marble column instead of a skull.

The only effect on the half-giant was to draw his attention away from his feet.

"Now, Neeva!" Rikus yelled. "Throw your dagger!"

The guard's massive fist shot out of the water and hit Rikus in the face. The mul tumbled a dozen yards across the patio and smashed into one of the posts supporting the bower.

As Rikus struggled to focus his eyes, Neeva threw her dagger. It struck blade first, ripping a long slice in the guard's cheek. The half-giant roared and lifted his weapon to strike. Neeva threw herself in Rikus's direction.

As the club smashed into the patio, the guard bellowed again, then reached into the water and grabbed at his other heel. He took a panicked step toward the colonnade. He stumbled and fell into the pond, spraying water and scattering lily pads everywhere. Rikus could see the half-giant flailing and clutching at the pillars to keep himself from drowning.

A moment later, clenching her bloody dagger in her teeth, Anezka slipped out of the pond and went to retrieve her clothes.

*　*　*　*　*

The bellowing and roaring of the battle inside the colonnade had reached even the faro fields surrounding the Asticles mansion. Agis and Sadira surmised that someone was fighting in the courtyard, but they could determine little else.

They crouched at the edge of a dusty field, staring over the coppery field of rockstem that separated the farm from the mansion grounds. The meadow was one of the most ancient features of the Asticles mansion, for rockstem was a leafless, hard-skinned plant that did not grow so much as accumulate in one place over the centuries, forming fantastic, twisted shapes.

From across this tangled heath, the white marble colonnade looked like nothing more than a wing of the mansion. The two half-giants and the templar standing outside it were silhouettes the size of insects.

The two watchers were protected from view by both the rockstem and the faro trees, but neither plant shielded them from the oppressive afternoon sun. Both Agis and Sadira were dizzy from the heat, and their throats were so swollen with thirst that they sometimes found themselves choking on their own tongues.

They had been prowling about in the faro fields since mid-morning, when they had returned to Agis's estate from UnderTyr. After Ktandeo had died, a crimson knight had taken the old sorcerer's body inside the temple. Sadira had thrown the bronze disk by which the templars had been tracking them into the shrine, then she and Agis had crept away and hidden at the edge of the dark courtyard.

Shortly afterward, the templar commander had ordered his men to storm the shrine. The crimson knights had met them at the entrances, and Agis and Sadira had taken advantage of the resulting battle to flee. They had retraced their path to the Drunken Giant. After finding the wineshop wrecked and abandoned, they had returned to Agis's house to gather supplies.

Fortunately, Sadira had insisted that they take the morning to reconnoiter, reasoning that Tithian might well have ordered Agis's house watched. After several hours of waiting, it had become apparent that the half-elf's caution was warranted. Four figures, two tall and two short, had entered the colonnade. Agis had been able to identify the shuffling gait of one of the short figures as that of his manservant Caro. A short time later, Caro had left the colonnade and fetched five half-giants and a templar from main house. Three of the half-giants had gone into the colonnade, and that was when the fighting had begun.

"The time has come to reclaim my home," Agis said, staring at Caro, the templar, and the two half-giants still waiting outside the colonnade. "I think we're looking at all that remains of the group Tithian sent to watch my house."

Sadira nodded. "If we stay out here much longer, my tongue will be too thick to cast spells."

Agis studied the scene for a few more moments, then asked, "Can you disable the two half-giants?"

The half-elf started to shake her head, then looked at the cane in her hand and changed her mind. "I can probably kill everybody, but we'd better get a little closer."

Agis scowled at Ktandeo's cane. "Are you sure that's wise?" he asked. "We don't know much—"

"I know enough," the half-elf insisted. "Besides, it's dangerous to use normal magic so close to your rockstem. Such slow-growing plants might not recover from the drain."

Agis pursed his lips, but nodded. "Just leave Caro alone."

"You can't believe he didn't betray us!" the half-elf objected.

"No, I can't even *hope* that any more," Agis said. "I still don't want him killed."

Sadira shrugged, then looked toward the colonnade. "If you want to save Caro, you'll have to kill the templar standing next to him. The more distance there is between my targets and Caro, the better."

Agis nodded, then unsheathed his dagger and held it in the palm of his hand. The noble closed his eyes and focused his concentration on his energy nexus, opening a pathway from his body through his arm and into the palm that held the dagger. Agis let out a short breath, at the same time closing his fingers around the dagger. He pictured them melding with the hilt and ceasing to exist as separate digits. The weapon became a part of his body that he could control and direct as easily as he could his arms or his legs.

When Agis opened his eyes again, to him it appeared the dagger had taken the place of his hand at the end of his wrist. He felt the leather hilt wrapped around the cold steel of its tang in the same way he felt his skin covering his bones. "Ready?" he asked.

"As ready as I'll ever be," Sadira replied. "Let's go."

"We'll rely on their curiosity to get us closer," he said, leading the way out of the faro.

They moved through the waist-high rockstem formations casually, Sadira walking several paces to the noble's left and swinging her cane as if it were any normal walking stick. As he approached, Agis could see that the templar, Caro, and the half-giants all faced the colonnade, their backs turned toward him and Sadira. So tightly was their attention focused on the small courtyard that they never noticed him and the sorceress.

When they had closed to within fifty yards, the templar motioned to the two half-giants as if sending them into the colonnade.

"Attack now!" Agis said, anticipating it would be difficult enough to flush out the templars and half-giants already inside the colonnade without allowing more to join
them.

The noble whipped his arm toward the templar. The
dagger separated from his wrist, leaving a bare stump behind. As it streaked toward its target, Agis kept his arm
pointed at the man's head. To him, the cold steel still felt
as though it were attached to his arm and he was guiding
the weapon's flight just as though he were using his hand
to plunge it into his victim's back.

The dagger slipped into the base of the templar's skull.
In his wrist, Agis felt the scrape of steel against bone. A
warm liquid enveloped the blade as it entered the man's
brain.

Agis broke the connection. He had little interest in experiencing a man's death from the viewpoint of a weapon.

The templar fell forward, dying before he hit the
ground and probably not aware of it. Caro, who had been
talking to the man, stared at the body in confusion.

Sadira's attack was more spectacular. She pointed the
cane at the two half-giants, then spoke two words Ktandeo had once uttered when he used it: "Nok" and
"Ghostfire."

The obsidian orb flared a brilliant orange, then a thunderous boom rocked the field. A stream of fiery light shot
from the cane and enveloped the two half-giants. Agis did
not see what happened next, for in the same instant he
felt a cold hand reach inside him and draw away a portion
of his life energy. It was a feeling similar to the one he had
experienced when Ktandeo used the cane, but many
times stronger.

A tremendous shudder ran through the senator's body. His knees buckled, then he crashed through a brittle rockstem formation and pitched face-first onto the ground. He rolled onto his side and looked toward Sadira, but otherwise he felt too nauseous to move.

The sorceress had sunk to her knees and was holding Ktandeo's cane in both hands, staring at it with a look of indignation and confused astonishment. A faint scarlet light glimmered from the depths of the black pommel, squirming and crawling over the surface as if it were alive. The scarlet gleam slowly faded, and Sadira's body swayed uncertainly. When the red light disappeared entirely, she toppled forward into a coppery fan of rockstem.

Agis forced himself to his knees and looked toward the mansion. Caro was staring at the ground where the half-giants had been standing only a moment before. The noble took his horrified expression as a sign that they would not have to worry about those two half-giants, at least.

Finding the strength to crawl to the sorceress's side, Agis found her curled into a ball and gasping for breath. Her skin was as pale as bone, her face was haggard, and the luster was gone from her amber hair. Her eyes were focused on the old man's cane, which lay in front of her.

The noble put a hand under her elbow. "Sadira? Can you hear me?"

The half-elf's gaze slowly shifted to Agis's face. She cried out in shock.

"What is it? Are you hurt?"

"I'm fine," she gasped.

Agis helped her to her knees. She continued to stare at him. "Is something wrong?" he asked.

Sadira shook her head and seemed to return to her senses. "No. Everything's fine," she said, brushing the hair around his temples. "You don't see any gray streaks in *my* hair, do you?"

"No, of course not. Why?" Agis had no sooner asked the question than the answer occurred to him. He looked at the black-pommeled cane in shock. "That thing turned my hair gray?" he gasped.

"Just a few streaks, around the temples and the top of your head," Sadira replied defensively. "It makes you look distinguished."

Agis heard heavy footsteps approaching. He looked up to see a large mul dressed only in a breechcloth. Like all muls, this one had small, pointed ears, was completely bald, and below the neck appeared to be nothing but bulging muscles. He was unusually handsome for a man-dwarf, for his rugged features were generally well-proportioned and appealing. He had a sturdy brow with dark, expressive eyes, a proud straight nose, and a powerful, firmly set jaw.

Agis was about to ask Sadira if she knew the mul when the half-elf struggled to her feet. "Rikus!" she said, opening her arms to hug him as he rushed to her.

As they kissed, the noble winced inwardly. Though Sadira had made no secret of her feelings for the famous gladiator, Agis had not expected to meet him so soon—and he was certainly not prepared to deal with the jealousy he was experiencing.

After Sadira finally removed her lips from the mul's, she asked, "What are you doing here?"

Rikus smiled at her, then, giving Agis a wary glance, leaned close to her ear and whispered. Feeling as though he were intruding, Agis rose to his feet and looked away.

Behind the gladiator, two women also approached from the colonnade. One was a full human almost as husky as the champion himself. She had pale, smooth skin and a full, firm shape. The other was the size of a child, with a head of wild hair and a wiry figure. Trapped between the two women was Agis's manservant, Caro.

"We don't have to keep secrets from Agis," Sadira said, taking the noble's arm and standing between him and Rikus. "He knows all there is to know about me."

"Is that so?" Rikus asked, raising an eyebrow at the senator.

Sadira smiled coyly and let the mul's question drop. "Rikus escaped Tithian's slave pits to warn me about Caro," she said, turning to the senator.

"That was very courageous," Agis offered, uncertain as to whether he should greet the gladiator with the traditional double handclasp of the higher classes or dispense with it as would have been appropriate with any other slave. He decided instead to wait for the mul to take the initiative. "You needn't have troubled yourself, Rikus. We're already aware of Caro's treachery, and your escape comes at a most unfortunate time."

The mul bared his teeth. "What do you mean by that?"

"Nothing, I assure you," Agis said, raising his hands reassuringly. "It's just that Sadira is safe with me, and you would have been more use to us where you were."

Rikus reached out and grabbed the sorceress's arm. "Well, now she's safe with me," he said. "I warn you, if you try to follow us, I'll kill you."

Sadira pulled free of the mul's grasp. "Rikus, where do you think you're taking me?"

The gladiator frowned. "We're escaping," he said. "You're coming with Neeva and Anezka and me to the mountains."

"I don't need to escape!" the half-elf said. "Agis set me free. Besides, there's someplace he and I have to go."

Rikus's face showed his disappointment. "Free?" the

mul echoed, half-dazed. "He set you free, and you're still with him?"

Sadira squeezed the mul's hand and rose onto her toes to kiss him on the cheek. "It's not forever, Rikus," she said. "I told you, he and I have someplace to go."

Rikus studied Agis, then returned his attention to Sadira. "We'll come with you."

"Thanks for offering, but we can get along fine ourselves," Agis said.

"I wasn't asking permission," the mul insisted. "We're going with you."

"Rikus has a right to go along," Sadira said, giving Agis an imploring smile.

"We're going to have enough problems without Tithian's slavehunters chasing us alongside his templars," Agis said.

Sadira shook her head. "What's the difference?" she asked. "Being hunted is being hunted. Besides, it won't hurt to have three gladiators along, and I wouldn't be surprised if Anezka could take us to Nok, whoever he is."

The two women escorting Caro arrived at the gathering, putting an end to the debate. The blond, who Agis guessed to be Rikus's well-known partner Neeva, glanced at Sadira's grip on the mul's hand and sighed.

Without commenting on the affectionate hold, she turned her attention to Agis. "This belongs to you, I think," she said, shoving the aged dwarf at him. At the same time, the halfling held out a square crystal of green olivine, and Neeva added, "He's a thief as well as a traitor. Anezka caught him trying to slip this into his pocket."

Agis took the green crystal from the halfling. "This doesn't belong to me," he said, examining it closely.

The noble was startled by the sound of Tithian's voice

in his ears. "How many times must I tell you to hold the crystal away from your eyes?"

Raising an eyebrow, Agis obeyed the command. A tiny image of Tithian's face appeared inside the crystal. As the high templar's sharp features came into focus, his jaw slackened. "Agis?"

The noble nodded. "Yes, Tithian. It's me."

"How did you get Caro's crystal?" Tithian asked. "You're supposed to be trapped inside the temple of the ancients!"

"We escaped, no thanks to you," Agis said bitterly. In his peripheral vision, he could see everyone except Caro staring at him as if he were mad.

"Didn't I warn you that I wasn't proposing a truce?" Tithian demanded defensively. "If you'll recall, I *did* tell you to watch yourself."

Though Agis had to agree, he was far from pleased with his friend. "I suppose that justifies using me to hunt for the Alliance?"

"You're the one who involved himself in the revolt," Tithian countered. "Don't blame me if that causes you trouble."

"I suppose what you showed me about the obsidian balls and pyramid was just bait?" the senator asked.

"No. It was real enough," the high templar said. Though it was difficult to read facial expressions on the tiny image in the crystal, Agis thought Tithian appeared frightened. "Tell me, how did the Veiled Ones receive the news?"

"Why should I tell you anything?" Agis demanded.

"Because my offer still stands," Tithian replied.

"Forgive me if I seem skeptical."

"You can't afford to dismiss me lightly!" the high templar said. "You have no idea what I've done on your behalf. Kalak knows about your adventures with the Veiled Alliance. If I hadn't used you, you'd be dead by now!"

"I'm gratified by your thoughtfulness," Agis noted sarcastically.

"If you have Caro's crystal, you must know that Rikus and Neeva escaped and went to your estate to look for Sadira." Tithian raised a single finger into view. "This is how many days it would take me to track them down. As you can see, they're still free. I've kept their absence a secret and didn't send out any trackers or cilops. I even had the guards who found their empty cell killed."

This last detail convinced Agis that his old friend was telling the truth, for it seemed exactly the sort of ruthless thing the high templar would do to protect a secret.

"Whatever the Veiled Alliance wants with my gladiators is still possible," Tithian continued. "No one knows they're gone except me and my most trusted subordinate."

"That's all very nice," Agis replied, truly relieved that no slavehunters would be hounding them into the mountains. "But you're still hunting down the Alliance with all your resources. Where *do* you stand?"

"Wherever my footing is the most solid at a given moment," Tithian answered frankly. "I'm trapped in the middle. If I don't make progress against the king's foes, Kalak will kill me. At the same time, I'm terrified of whatever he has planned for the ziggurat games."

"So you'd be willing to assassinate him?" Agis asked, deciding to see just how far his friend would go.

"It can't be done," Tithian countered.

"If it could?" Agis pressed.

Inside the crystal, Tithian closed his eyes for a moment. When he opened them again, he said, "I wouldn't prevent someone from trying."

Agis smiled. "That's all I need to know," he said, moving his hand over the crystal.

"Wait!" Tithian shouted. The senator removed his hand, and the high templar smiled. "For me to play along with you until this attack on Kalak succeeds, I need to know the location of the third and final bone amulet inside the ziggurat."

"I knew we couldn't trust you," Agis sighed.

"That's hardly true," Tithian noted. "You can trust me to take care of myself. Just be certain that your side always offers me what I seek." The high templar paused and tapped his chin in thought. "You'd best have Sadira let Those Who Wear the Veil know that it is in *their* best interest to reveal the location of the amulet. You'll figure out how to get the information to me somehow."

Without offering a reply, Agis closed his fist over the green gem. The noble explained what had just passed between him and Tithian, then returned the stone to Caro.

"It might be best to let Tithian know about the amulets," Sadira ventured. "I know where the three were hidden. Could you tell the high templar, Caro?" When the dwarf nodded, she quickly told him where the magical amulets had been secreted. "They weren't very powerful anyway," she concluded with a shrug. "Just a few wards to stall the king's works."

At last Agis turned to his servant. "How long have you been Tithian's spy?" he asked gently.

The dwarf looked away, his withered lips quivering with fear or regret—Agis could not tell which. "Not long, only since your slaves were confiscated," Caro said. "The high templar sent me back to you. He promised to give me my freedom after the games."

"And your focus?" Agis asked. "It never changed?"

Caro shook his head. "No. Until the moment I broke

it, it was to serve you and the Asticles family."

"Why did you give that up?" Neeva asked.

Caro met the woman's gaze evenly. "I would have died on the ziggurat, and I didn't want my life to end without a taste of freedom."

"I can't tell you how sorry I am, Caro," Agis said, a deep sense of regret welling inside his breast. "If I had realized how much your freedom meant, I would have granted it gladly."

Caro looked at Agis. "I don't need your sympathy," he said bitterly. "Just kill me and be done with it."

"If I were you, I wouldn't be so anxious to die," Rikus said. "Won't you come back as a banshee?"

The old dwarf looked at Agis, then a crooked grin crossed his lips. "That's right," he said, his black eyes sparkling with bitterness. "I'll come back to haunt the Asticles estate—the site of my failure."

"Then it will be quite some time before we meet again, I hope," Agis said.

"What's that supposed to mean?" Rikus asked.

"Every man is born with a desire for freedom in his breast, just as he is born with a desire for food and drink. Anyone who has ever kept slaves knows this."

"As does any slave," Rikus said.

"Depriving a man of freedom is like depriving him of food and water," Agis said, his gaze still fixed on Caro's withered face. "If a man has no food or water, his body dies a lingering death. If he has no freedom, it is his spirit that dies."

"So?" Rikus demanded. "What noble cares about his slave's spirit or his life?"

"I do!" Agis replied hotly, thumping his own chest. "I've never taken a slave's life!"

"Then you are a rare slaveholder," Sadira said.

Agis looked to the half-elf. "Perhaps, but no better than the others. Now I see that my philosophy merely made me a hypocrite. That's why the wraith wouldn't allow me into the Crimson Shrine."

"What are you going to do about it?" Sadira asked, her pale eyes fixed on his.

Agis turned to the ancient dwarf. "Caro, I have no right to ask anything of you," he said, unfastening the purse attached to his belt. "Still, I would like you to perform one last service for the Asticles house. Go to the slaves that remain in my pens. Tell them they're free to go or stay as they please."

The dwarf's face showed his surprise. "And me?"

"Go and enjoy your freedom."

Taking the purse Agis offered, the dwarf walked away without a word to his former master. As he watched Caro trudge along under the blistering sun, Agis realized how little his gesture must have meant to one who had lost his whole life to servitude. Perhaps there would be others like Caro he could save from a slave's life; Agis let that hope assuage his stinging conscience, but only for a little while.

THIRTEEN

The Verdant Passage

"Get up!" Rikus called, fixing his stern gaze on Agis. "It's not time to rest!"

The handsome noble looked up at the gladiator for a moment, then spoke in an even voice. "I don't need your permission to sit," he said, once more propping his head in his hands. "Or to do anything else."

They were high in the Ringing Mountains, struggling up a narrow stone terrace. On one side, a cone-shaped spire of granite loomed thousands of feet overhead, and on the other a sheer precipice plunged more than a mile straight down. Below the cliff lay the Tyr Valley. Their goal lay hidden before them: the magical spear Ktandeo had mentioned to Sadira. It, of all the weapons on Athas, offered them the power to strike against the sorcerer-king.

"We're moving too slowly," Rikus said, shivering in the cold mountain wind. He was wearing only his customary breechcloth and a pair of sturdy sandals, having refused Agis's gentlemanly offer to loan him something warmer. In his hand, the mul carried the one item he had condescended to borrow, a bone axe with twin blades set side by side.

Rikus pointed ahead to where the stone terrace ended at the edge of a deep chasm. "Where's Anezka?" he asked. "If we lose her now, we'll never find Nok or Sadira's damned spear."

"She'll be back," Agis said, rubbing his temples. Though he was dressed in what Rikus considered a foppish manner—calf-high walking boots, leather breeches, and a rust-colored corselet with a matching fleece cape—the mul had to admit that at least the noble's outfit appeared warm.

Agis looked toward Sadira and Neeva, then added, "The women need to rest."

Rikus followed his gaze and saw that Sadira was a few yards behind the noble, dressed in leather pants and a fleece shawl. Somewhere in Agis's house, she had also found a crownlike hat with a pair of stylish straps that descended along her nose and crossed beneath her cheeks like a mask. The mul had seen noblewomen dressed in similar hats, and it bothered him to see Sadira proudly imitating their inane fashions.

Behind the half-elf came Neeva, struggling up the mountainside at a plodding but steady pace. Of course, the only clothing Agis had been able to provide for a woman of her proportions had come from his slave pens. Still, she looked comfortable enough in a pair of hemp pants and a coarse wool cloak, and seemed completely at ease with the steel-bladed trikal in her hand. She had been absolutely delighted when Agis gave it to her as a gift, and that bothered the mul even more than Sadira's love for her new hat. This Agis of Asticles was working too hard to make himself popular with a group of escaped slaves.

"The women look like they're doing better than you," Rikus said, sneering at the noble's weakness. "At least they're still moving."

Despite his callous attitude, Rikus knew what Agis felt. When they had first started climbing, the companions had all noticed a certain shortness of breath and unusual weariness. As Anezka had led them higher into the mountains, this feeling had continually grown worse. Their heads throbbed with blinding pain, the mere effort of breathing racked their lungs with searing torment, and the muscles of their legs were numb with fatigue. The difference between Agis and his companions was that the noble was unaccustomed to prolonged deprivation and hardship, whereas the others had known it all their lives.

Ignoring the mul's barb, Agis reached into his satchel and withdrew his waterskin. It was half-empty, for the group had not come across any fresh water since entering the mountains three days ago.

As the noble opened the neck, Rikus cried, "It's not time to drink. Save that for later."

Agis sneered at the mul. "I'm carrying it. I'll drink when I like."

"We're running short on water," Rikus growled, stepping toward the noble.

"Our stores are far from depleted," Agis countered. "Besides, I've spent time in the desert. I can find more water when we run out." The noble looked around at the barren mountainside surrounding them, then added, "Well, before we're in danger of dying, anyway." He lifted the skin to his lips again.

The mul reached for the waterskin. "Your soft ways are going to get us killed!"

Agis pulled the skin away. "What are you doing?"

"Protecting us from you!" Rikus replied. He lunged

for the waterskin again, this time grasping it around the open neck.

Agis pulled in the other direction just hard enough to prevent the mul from taking it. "Rikus, if we continue this, we're going to spill what's left of the water," he said, speaking in a patronizingly calm tone.

"What are you two doing?" Sadira cried as she got close.

Rikus ignored her. "I'm not going to let you drink it all," he said, refusing to yield to what he perceived as a veiled threat. "I'll pour it on the ground first."

Agis released the waterskin. "You're a big enough fool to do it, aren't you?"

"I ought to split your skull for you," Rikus countered.

Unimpressed with the threat, Agis turned to Sadira. "I don't think Rikus could have illustrated my point any better, do you?"

"Don't get me involved," she said, rubbing her temples. "This is between you."

Neeva joined them. "If you two spent less time arguing, we'd probably be in the halfling forest by now," she said. Rather than trying to stand next to Sadira on the narrow ledge, she stopped behind the half-elf. "Maybe what we need is a leader."

Rikus smiled at his fighting partner, then smirked at Agis. "Good idea," he said, retying the neck of the waterskin. "We drink when I say."

The noble frowned. "Neeva said we need a leader, but I didn't hear anyone say it should be you."

Rikus regarded Agis disdainfully. "Who else could it be?" he demanded. "You're too soft."

Agis's eyes flashed. "I spent more than a year learning the ways of the desert," he said in a controlled voice. "I doubt that your background allowed for the same opportunities."

"We're in the mountains, not the desert," Rikus insisted, not quite sure whether the noble had meant his comment as an observation or as an insult. "Besides, I don't care how much time you spent in the desert. You're still too soft."

"You're too simple," Agis countered hotly. "You mistake bullying for leading, and the only way you know to solve a problem is to kill it."

Rikus stared at Agis without speaking. There was probably some truth to what the noble said, for he had never been trained to do anything but fight. This realization did little to decrease his desire to grab Agis and pitch him over the cliff.

"Neither of you should be the leader," Neeva said, stepping around Sadira.

"What are you saying? We should follow you?" Rikus asked.

"Maybe," Neeva answered. "At least my mind is on Nok and the spear."

"When did you get so interested in the spear?" Rikus demanded. "Don't tell me *you're* joining this crazy plot to assassinate Kalak?"

Neeva met his gaze steadily. "What do you think I'm doing here?"

Rikus frowned, unable to answer. He had assumed that Neeva was making the journey just because he was. It had not occurred to him that she might have another reason.

"If you're not here because you want to kill Kalak, why did you insist on coming along?" Agis asked pointedly.

The mul motioned to the half-elf. "To protect Sadira," he said. "She saved my life, so I owe her a debt of honor. I must defend her life until that debt is paid."

The senator smiled. "In that case, there's no need for you to continue. I'm perfectly capable of defending the young—"

"Forget it," Rikus snapped, glaring at Agis. He had not explained the real reason he was here: he simply wanted to be with Sadira.

"Why don't you both turn back?" Neeva asked. "We'll travel a lot faster if we don't have to stop and wait while you two fight over Sadira every few miles."

"They're arguing, not fighting," Sadira noted. "Besides, there's nothing to fight over. A woman can have feelings for more than one man."

Neeva rolled her eyes.

"Just like Rikus loves both you and me," Sadira went on. "No one sees *us* arguing."

"We're not exactly friends," Neeva replied coldly. "And I wouldn't say what Rikus feels for me is love." With that, she looked toward the end of the terrace. "There's Anezka. If we're going to reach Nok, we'd better keep up with her. Soon, she'll grow tired of waiting for us."

Rikus gave Neeva an angry glance, but did not say anything. As usual, his fighting partner had cut to the heart of the matter with a few biting comments.

When the mul looked forward, he saw Anezka standing at the end of the terrace watching him and the others with a disgusted expression. She turned toward the peak on the right, then stepped over the edge of the terrace and was gone from sight.

The mul followed and saw that she had stepped onto a small shelf of rock. This ledge was so narrow that, at first glance, it appeared to be nothing more than a dark line crossing the shadowy side of the peak. It ran along the granite face until it disappeared around the far side of the mountain.

Rikus took a moment to secure his twin-axe to his satchel, then stepped onto the ledge. It was barely wider than his feet and was covered with a layer of loose dirt. Nevertheless, Anezka moved along it as casually as if she were walking down the corridor leading into Tyr's great stadium. Rikus followed, half expecting the shelf to collapse under his weight.

To his surprise, he discovered that the ledge itself seemed quite sturdy, but the thick layer of dirt covering it posed a constant threat. Twice in the first few steps, the slick soles of his sandals slipped on the loose ground and nearly plunged him into the dark abyss below. He looked back to warn the person behind him about the treacherous ground, but held his tongue when he saw it was Agis. Even if Rikus had felt like protecting him, he doubted the noble would have taken the advice in a friendly manner.

Rikus faced the mountain so that he could use both hands to brace himself. Slowly he shuffled across the ledge, kicking the dirt away before he took each step. He had always heard that one shouldn't look down from a high place, so he tried to keep his eyes turned toward the summit of the peak.

After a time, he realized this was a terrible mistake. The endless sky overhead filled his mind with images of a bottomless abyss beneath his feet. When he had gone about a quarter of the way across, a picture of his body tumbling into the chasm below flashed through his mind. Every now and then, he saw himself bounce off a craggy wall, his musclebound figure growing smaller every second and the echoes of his terrified scream more distant. Finally his body shrank to a speck and simply disappeared into the dark abyss.

Rikus ignored the vision as best he could and continued to shuffle along the ledge. Halfway across, the mul pictured not his own brawny form falling into the chasm, but Neeva's. He saw her bounce off the cliff once, twice, then silently plunge head-first into the abyss. He shook his head to clear it, then continued forward. To his surprise, he found that the muscles in his knees were quivering.

When he was most of the way across, Rikus's lead foot slipped as he placed his weight on it. He let out a short yell, then his fingers caught hold of the rocky handholds and prevented his fall. Rikus's legs began to tremble. He found himself breathing hard and fast, and his vision was filled with white spots. The mul closed his eyes and held onto his handholds so tightly that his forearms ached.

Agis crept up beside Rikus. "What's wrong?" the noble asked. "Do you need help?"

"No!" he hissed, keeping his eyes closed. "I'm fine. How are Neeva and Sadira?"

"Better than us, I think," Agis replied. "They've tied themselves together."

"What? That's stupid," Rikus said, opening his eyes. "If one of them falls, she'll pull the other off."

Agis's grim face was perspiring with the bitter sweat of fear. Like Rikus, he gripped the rocks so tightly that the veins on his forearms bulged. The noble's knees were also shaking, though not nearly as badly as the mul's.

Although it made him perilously dizzy, Rikus tilted his head back so he could see the two women. They had roped themselves together and were working their way across the ledge in a much calmer fashion than the men. First Neeva moved ahead the length of the rope. Sadira waited behind, watching the other woman intently, prepared to cast a spell that would save them both from falling. When Neeva neared the end of the rope, she found a suitable place to brace herself. As Sadira came along behind, the gladiator took up the rope and remained ready to catch the smaller woman the instant she misstepped.

"Not a bad idea," Rikus said approvingly.

"I wonder if we should try something similar," Agis replied.

Rikus glanced over his shoulder at his satchel, then looked between his feet at the darkening depths of the abyss. "You feel like digging your rope out of your bag?"

Agis also looked down. "I don't think so."

"Me neither," Rikus replied. "We'll just have to do the best we can alone."

The mul returned to shuffling across the ledge. Soon, Rikus smelled a strange fragrance, an earthy odor he had never known before. It seemed sweet and sour at the same time, with undertones of both perfume and decay. Rikus looked westward. Anezka waited a short distance ahead, where the ledge crossed the corner of the mountain.

Behind her, a fuzzy silhouette ran the entire length of the ridge. It looked like a roiling, greenish cloud hanging close upon the ground. At certain times, the shapes protruding from it reminded Rikus vaguely of the rare tree he had seen in the Tyr Valley, but he had never seen one writhe and twist as these seemed to be doing.

As he came closer, Rikus heard the wild cackles and squeals of strange creatures. The wind now carried something the gladiator had never before felt on his skin: a cold mist. The air was heavy with the scent of a recent rain, and the mul could see now that the strange silhouette running along the top of the ridge was, in fact, the crown of a forest—a forest that seemed to be dancing, but a forest nonetheless.

The mul could not count the number of times they had crested similar ridges or saddles in the last week. Each time they expected to see the great halfling woodland spread out before them, but discovered only the rocky slopes of an even higher mountain hidden behind the one they had just crossed. Filled with joy and excitement now, Rikus looked back and gave Agis a broad smile. "We're there!" he said, pointing toward the ridge.

The mul's foot slipped, unexpectedly shifting half of his weight onto the hand still clinging to the rock face. His fingers peeled away from the handhold. Painfully they scraped along a series of tiny sharp ridges on the rocky face, vainly clutching at each minuscule rib as they passed.

Rikus toppled backward.

The cliff fell out of reach as the mul found himself looking straight up into the azure sky. The peak's distant summit flashed before his eyes. Agis called his name.

Rikus watched his feet tumble over his head, then the maroon depths of the chasm were rushing up to meet him. Distantly he heard Neeva and Sadira screaming, and even thought he heard a soprano trill from Anezka's direction. Rikus somersaulted again and glimpsed Agis glowering with intense concentration, pointing one long finger at him.

It seemed to Rikus that his heart stopped beating. A sick, giddy feeling of terror gorged his stomach, and the sound of his own screaming filled his ears. He wished for the only thing that a man could wish for under such circumstances, to die of fright before his body erupted into a red spray on the boulders far below.

As the mul tumbled over again, a circle of blackness opened beneath him. He plunged into it. An icy blast knocked the air from his lungs. Passing through the dark tunnel, Rikus had enough time to wonder where the circle had come from. An instant later his body smashed in to the ground.

His breath shot from his lungs, and his body erupted into agony. The mul curled into a fetal position. To his surprise, the pain continued. He felt himself sliding down a steep slope. When he opened his eyes, he saw green ferns and black, rich soil beneath his cheeks.

A pair of tiny strong hands gripped his shoulders and stopped his descent. Rikus looked up. The soft, familiar features of a small, wild-eyed face greeted him.

"Anezka?" he gasped, finding to his amazement that he could still breath.

The halfling scowled, then nodded. Bracing her feet on either side of Rikus's shoulders, she pulled him into a more or less seated position. The mul gasped at the sight before his eyes.

The mountains on this side of the range were even steeper than those facing Tyr. Instead of barren yellow-orange rocks, the slopes were covered by a dense forest of indigo-needled conifers. These towering trees looked as though they were performing some primitive, gyrating dance. Their red trunks were segmented by pivoting joints that creaked and groaned as the powerful wind contorted them into an endless succession of shapes.

There were also smaller trees—at least Rikus assumed them to be trees—with large, white-barked trunks shaped like balls. From the tops of these globes rose sprays of huge fronds covered with heart-shaped leaves.

Long strings of moss dangled off the boughs of both kinds of trees. From these damson strands sprouted an astounding array of colorful mushrooms, most shaped like bells and as big around as Rikus's fist. On the ground flourished a puffy, billowing mass of yellow undergrowth. In the distance, more than a dozen steep ridges covered with the same profuse vegetation reared up, presenting themselves to Rikus.

A great cloud covered the base of the mountains like an immense blanket of cotton, glowing rosy pink with the light of the setting sun. This cloud sent tendrils of thick mist creeping into every one of deep valleys lying between the ridges ahead.

Rikus barely noticed when Agis stepped up behind him. "Sorry for the rough landing."

The mul paid no attention to the apology. "It's a good thing Anezka came with us," he said, pointing at the vast forest below. "Without her, we'd never be able to find Nok in all those trees."

FOURTEEN

Singer

Agis woke to a peculiar serenade of dulcet chirping, underscored by the gentle patter of a soft rain. Without opening his eyes, the noble rolled over on his bed of groundcloud—the name they had given to the forest's undergrowth of puffy fungus—and yawned. Languidly he reached out to embrace Sadira. Instead of her soft skin, he touched something plump and warm, covered with coarse bristles. The chirping grew softer and more melodious.

"Who's there?" Agis asked. As his grogginess cleared, he remembered that in order to reduce the jealous tension in the group, they had all agreed to sleep alone.

The noble opened his eyes and, in the pale dawn light, found himself staring at a row of six sapphire eyes. Below the gemlike orbs, a pair of flexible fangs grasped a wad of groundcloud and stuffed it into a hairy mouth. As the creature ate, it rubbed two pairs of shiny forelegs together, producing the serenade that had awakened the noble. Four more legs supported the drum-shaped body upon which his hand rested, and a great lemon-colored abdomen hung suspended from its rear quarters.

Gasping in alarm, Agis jerked his hand away and reached for his sword. The huge spider reacted by scurrying up a silk cord running from its abdomen to a white web overhead. There it remained, dangling upside down and rubbing its forelegs together to produce gentle, soothing tones.

The noble sat up, carefully watching the singing spider. He was astonished to see that, as he had slept, the creature had woven a solid, tentlike web high overhead, anchoring it to the jointed trunks of four dancing conifers. Although the web rolled and undulated as the wind twisted the trees into different shapes, Agis could not complain about the shelter offered by the spider's handiwork. Outside his tent fell a steady drizzle, but he remained as dry as if he'd been sleeping beneath the roof of his own mansion.

There were a dozen similar canopies in the area. Below each, a chirping spider fed on the groundcloud. Sadira, Neeva, and Rikus were each covered by web. Only Anezka lay exposed to the rain, curled into a wet ball and shivering in the cold. Apparently the halfling had fallen asleep during her watch, for she rested on the ground some distance from her bed.

The spider above Agis chirped tentatively, then reached for the ground with two legs. Chuckling at his instinctive revulsion to the creature, the noble put his sword away. To his surprise, the spider descended on a thick strand of silk and landed at his side. It resumed feeding, chirping in a contented tone that made Agis appreciate just how peaceful the forest morning was. In contrast to the ruddy sunrises of the Tyr Valley, the dawn light here was soft and lush and green, the cruel sun hidden behind a thick morning fog.

Growing reflective, the noble looked at his dozing companions. Their bodies were tense and restless, as if even in their sleep they were cringing against the lash—or, more likely, dreaming of the day they would kill those who held them in bondage.

"What am I doing here, Singer?" Agis asked, assigning a name to the arachnid. He suddenly felt acutely aware of the vast differences that separated him from his fellows. "My ancestors would think me crazy to risk the Asticles estate and name for the sake of slaves."

The spider chirped a few playful notes, then moved closer to Agis and rubbed its bristled body against his leg. The noble guessed that the thing wanted him to rub its back, but he could not bring himself to touch it again. He felt slightly chagrined for letting the spider's appearance put him off, but no matter how friendly the beast was, it remained repugnant.

Instead he said, "Still, we know what's right, don't we? If my ancestors had acted on principle instead of fear, perhaps we wouldn't need to worry about what Kalak is planning for his games."

As Agis spoke, a curtain of moss parted on the other side of camp. A pair of halflings slipped into view and silently crept toward a nearby spider tent, their footsteps muffled by the patter of morning rain. They resembled Anezka in size and appearance, save that they were both male and clothed only in shaggy breechcloths. The rain washed the filth from their bodies in long streaks of black mud. In their hands they gripped flint-tipped spears, and on their belts hung short daggers of sharpened bone.

The noble was about to wake his friends when the two halflings gently laid their spears aside and rushed the spider they had been sneaking toward. They did not snap a branch or create any sound that Agis could hear, and even their target seemed unaware of their presence.

Grabbing his sword, the noble crawled toward the exit of his tent. Singer scuttled around to face the direction he was going. It chirped what seemed an inquisitive tone and followed, but neither it nor any of its kin paid any attention to the halflings' presence. Agis paused, wondering why the spider at his side did not seem alarmed. Either it could not see that far, or its kind was some sort of halfling pet or herd animal.

An instant later, he had his answer. The halflings' target whirled around to meet its attackers. The spider's chirping changed to a single screech of alarm, then it fell silent and frantically tried to climb into its web. Simultaneously, Singer and all the other spiders scrambled into their webs, continuing to chirp in agitation.

The halflings' prey was not fast enough to reach its web before the two hunters tackled it. As the little men wrestled their prey to the ground, Agis stepped into the cold rain and called, "What are you doing?"

The halflings, who had both drawn their bone daggers, looked toward Agis. The noble motioned toward his shoulder satchel. "If you're hungry, we have food enough to share."

Though Agis spoke in a congenial tone, the halflings obviously took the stranger's words as a threat and rushed out the back side of their quarry's tent. They disappeared into the forest as silently and as quickly as they had come, leaving their spears behind.

Behind Agis, Rikus cursed, then Neeva cried, "Get away, you hairy brute!"

Sadira was apparently the last to awaken and see the spiders. She screeched once, then called, "Where'd *these* come from?"

Agis did not answer, for he was still trying to catch a

glimpse of the halflings. Unfortunately, it appeared that would be difficult. He did not see so much as a branch waving in their wake. The only sign that they had even been near the group's camp was the spider they had attacked, which had climbed into its web and was chirping angrily. The other spiders relaxed and began to rub their legs together in lively, spirited songs.

Rikus was the first to reach the noble's side. "What's all the noise about, Agis?" the mul demanded, his bone twin-axe in one hand and his satchel in the other. "You're not scared of a little spider, are you?" He gestured at a nearby tent, where the spider had already dropped back to the ground on its silk cord.

"The spiders and I get along well enough, especially since I like to sleep dry," Agis answered, holding one hand palm-up in the icy rain now soaking him. "I scared away a pair of halflings."

"Halflings?" Neeva asked, stepping to their sides.

Before Agis could answer, Sadira joined them, her satchel already slung on her back and Ktandeo's cane in one hand. She was using her free hand to brush at her shoulders and hair.

"You can stop preening," Neeva said. "After a few minutes in this drizzle, you're going to look as bad as the rest of us."

Sadira regarded the others with an air of distaste. "I can live with that, I suppose. You don't see any webs on me, do you?" she asked. "I can't stand webs."

Neeva rolled her eyes, but turned the half-elf so she could inspect the sorceress's shoulders. "No webs."

"Good," Sadira answered, breathing a sigh of relief. "Now, what's this about halflings?"

"They were over here," Agis said. "I scared them off, but maybe we can coax them back out."

"Halflings are too skittish for that," Rikus grunted. "Anezka would have a better—"

The mul was interrupted by another spider's screech, this time from where Agis had been sleeping. He turned and saw Anezka beneath his silken canopy, wrestling with Singer.

"Anezka, no!" Agis shouted, rushing toward the small woman.

He was too late. She lifted the steel dagger he had given her, then plunged it into the spider's abdomen. Singer stopped struggling, but continued to rub its legs together in plaintive, agonized tones.

As Agis approached, he saw that the spider lay on its back. Anezka sat astride its thorax, having opened a long gash in its abdomen. Pushing at the halfling with the four legs closest to her, Singer weakly struggled with its attacker and chirped out its agony.

Anezka plunged her arm into the slash she had opened in the spider's abdomen. She felt around for a moment, then gave a quick jerk and pulled out a handful of froth-covered eggs. Singer's legs moved more frantically, filling the air with a loud howl. The other spiders responded with sad melodies.

Agis grabbed the halfling by the shoulders. "What are you doing?"

Anezka's arms were covered with green slime from the spider's abdomen. She scowled at him and, by way of explanation, began to eat the eggs.

This was more than the noble could stand. He grabbed the halfling and threw her to the ground as far away as his strength allowed, paying no attention to where she landed. Next, he turned to the spider, which was now chirping a pained lyric. Intending to put Singer out of its misery, he unsheathed his sword—but found he had no idea how to kill the spider quickly and painlessly.

"Agis, your back!" cried Rikus.

The noble spun around and saw Anezka raising her dagger to throw at him. Rikus leaped to the halfling's side and slapped her arm as she released the weapon. The knife plunged into the ground at Agis's feet.

The noble looked from the dagger to Rikus. "Thank you."

"I'm only paying you back for what you did at the cliffs. Now we're even," the mul answered gruffly. At the same time, he grabbed the halfling to prevent her from making another attack. She growled incoherently and struggled against Rikus's grip.

"It's not very smart to throw our guide around like that," Neeva said, fixing her green eyes on Agis's face. "What are you so upset about, anyway? It was just a spider."

"Spiders or not, these are friendly creatures," Agis said, gesturing at the canopies over their heads. "It would have been just as easy for them to string their webs someplace else, and then we would have had a wet, cold night."

"I suppose so," Sadira said, joining them. "But we don't need any more hard feelings in the group right now. If Anezka wants to eat a spider, let her. After all, it's her forest."

Once again, Agis was reminded of the differences between himself and his four companions. The gladiators had spent their lives fighting for the amusement of others, so to them the spider's agony must have seemed a small matter. No doubt, even Sadira had seen—or even suffered—much worse on Tithian's estate. It was no wonder that they regarded the beast's pain with indifference, whereas the noble, who had purposely shielded himself from such unpleasantness, regarded it with horror and revulsion.

Even considering the differences in their backgrounds, Agis was outraged at the halfling's cruelty. Having someone in his company behave so callously made him feel as he thought Tithian must, simply doing what was necessary to survive. If he was going to risk life, property, and name, the noble was determined to do so in the cause of principle, not practicality.

"I don't care if Anezka *is* our guide," he said. "I won't stand for needless torture, by her or anyone else."

"If it will make you happy, ask her to kill her breakfast before she eats it, but don't start a fight over it," Neeva said. She pointed at the center of Singer's body. "Now, if you want to put this spider out of its pain, strike there—deeply."

Agis did as she suggested. As his sword plunged through the spider's body, its legs stopped writhing and it died quickly. "Thanks," he said, cleaning his blade on the groundcloud. "How did you know where I should strike?"

"We've often fought giant spiders of one sort or another in the arena," she explained, turning toward where she had left her satchel. "Let's get on with our journey."

Agis picked up the dagger Anezka had thrown at him, then went to where Rikus held the halfling. "In my company, I'd appreciate it if you'd be more selective about what you eat and how," he said to the small woman.

Rikus shook his head in derision. "Only a noble would be soft enough to worry about eating a spider."

"Perhaps," Agis replied, not taking his eyes from Anezka. "But I'm serious about what I say."

The noble put the halfling's dagger in his satchel. He had intended to return it to Anezka as a sign of good faith. From the way she had stared at him, however, he knew the halfling would only have used it to attack him the first time his back was turned.

After Agis slipped his satchel onto his shoulder, Rikus released the halfling. Anezka angrily gathered her things, then led the party down the crest of the ridge, moving through the forest as effortlessly and as silently as though she were walking on barren, level ground. Behind her, Rikus and Neeva crashed through the trees with all the grace of a matched pair of boulders tumbling down the hillside. Sadira followed the gladiators, carrying Ktandeo's cane in one hand and grasping at tree fronds with the other as she fought to keep her footing. Agis came last, carefully weighing each step, yet cursing under his breath as he slipped with every fifth or sixth footfall.

They descended along the top of the muddy ridge for over an hour before it abruptly ended in a sheer cliff. Without pausing, Anezka simply changed directions to avoid the precipice. She moved down the side of the ridge, descending its steep slopes with the grace of a rock leopard. The others followed more laboriously, punctuating the soft patter of raindrops with the sounds of their passing: snapping sticks, tumbling rocks, and occasional cries of alarm as they slipped and fell to the ground.

After some time, they heard a faint hiss coming from the gully at the bottom of the ridge. Rikus and Neeva drew their weapons, carrying them at the ready position. Agis unsheathed his sword, and Sadira silently considered the spells she had memorized at the moment.

Anezka laughed at them and continued down the hill. The hiss grew louder, changing into a steady, loud sizzle that echoed off the trees. Agis tried to imagine what kind of strange creature could be making the noise, but he had never heard anything like the sound and failed to think of a single possibility.

At last they came to a break in the underbrush. Rikus and Neeva stopped dead in their tracks. Sadira and Agis quickly stepped to either side of the two gladiators, then also stopped, their eyes wide with shock.

A twenty-foot ribbon of water blocked their path, flashing silver and white as it ran down a narrow, rocky channel. Agis stood at the stream's edge, listening to it roar and gurgle as it flowed down its jumbled course. Anezka waded out into the stream and began to drink.

"Where does it all come from?" Rikus asked, taking his satchel off so he could fish out his waterskin and fill it.

"From the rain," Agis answered, also fetching his waterskin.

"There's too much water for that," Neeva said. "It would have to rain every day to keep this gully full."

"What makes you think it doesn't?" Sadira asked, waving her hands at the dense forest around them. "Plants need water. This many plants must need a lot of water."

"Rain every day?" Rikus scoffed. "That's impossible. I've seen five rainstorms in my life, and that's a lot for someone my age."

"Perhaps the rain is attracted by magic," Agis suggested, his mind wrestling with the problem of how something as wondrous as a forest could exist. "If sorcerers draw their magic from plants, maybe plants can make magic that causes it to rain."

"There's no doubt that something magic is at work here," Sadira said. "But who can say what? It could be the forest itself, or it might be something else. I'm not sure we'll ever understand—and maybe we shouldn't."

"No, that's where you're wrong," Agis countered. "If the forest can exist in the mountains, then it can exist in other parts of Athas. For that to happen, we need to understand what makes it grow first."

Rikus finished filling his waterskin. "The noble's soft in his head as well as his body," the mul mumbled.

"I don't know about that," Neeva said. "Did you see his faro orchards? If anyone could grow a forest, I think it would be Agis."

"My thanks, Neeva," replied Agis, encouraged by her support. "If I could just live in the forest for a year—"

"Whatever Kalak has planned for Tyr would be done and over," Sadira said. "Maybe we can make Athas green with trees someday, but not now." She pointed downstream. Anezka had left them and was already far ahead, picking her way silently along the stream bank. "Let's try not to lose her again. I'm afraid she won't come back for us."

They quickly closed their waterskins, then crashed down the gully in pursuit of the halfling. Eventually the ravine descended into a deep, steep-sloped canyon, and the stream transformed into the frothing waters of a wild river. The whole canyon trembled with the power of the mighty watercourse, and the thunder of its torrents overwhelmed every other sound within the valley.

Although the drizzle had finally let up and the sun was baking the rocky shoreline, Anezka continued without letting the party stop to marvel at the river. The halfling led the way along the shore, and eventually they came to a trail overhung by mossy tree boughs.

As they stepped onto this path, Agis caught sight of a quaking branch out of the corner of his eye, then glimpsed the silhouette of a halfling hiding behind the tree itself. The halfling was pointing a small bow at Rikus's back.

"Rikus, down!" Agis called.

The mul obeyed just before a twang sounded from the

small man's hiding place. A tiny, foot-long arrow sailed over Rikus's head and lodged in the bulbous trunk of a frond tree. When Agis looked back to the attacker's hiding place, the halfling was no longer in sight. Neeva and Sadira swung around with their weapons ready. When Agis drew his sword, Anezka disappeared into the forest on the opposite side of the trail.

"Where are they?" Rikus demanded, returning to his feet.

"I only saw one, and he disappeared," Agis reported.

"You lost sight of him?" the mul snapped angrily.

"*You* didn't even see him," Agis pointed out, his eyes still searching the trees.

Neeva plucked the arrow from the white bark. "They're not going to do much damage with this thing."

Rikus snatched the arrow from her hand and peered at the tip. "It was coated with something," he said. "There are still traces above the tip."

The other three spoke at the same time. "Poison!"

Another twang sounded from the side of the trail. This time, the arrow struck Neeva in the thigh. She let out a frightened scream and slapped it off her leg. With her other hand, she pointed her trikal at a clump of trembling conifer boughs. "There he is," she said, stepping in the direction she pointed.

Her knees buckled on the second step, and she pitched face-first onto the ground. Sadira kneeled at her side. Screaming in anger, Rikus leaped over the two women. Ignoring Agis's and Sadira's panicked cries to be cautious, he disappeared into the shadowy forest.

Agis started to follow, but almost immediately Rikus yelled, "Got the little varl!"

A sharp smack sounded, then the mul stepped back into the trail with the halfling's unconscious body in one hand. "Maybe a hostage will discourage—"

Another twang sounded from the other side of the trail. An arrow lodged in the mul's bare chest. Rikus brushed it away with a quick swipe, then hurled the unconscious halfling at his attacker. He charged toward the underbrush again, cursing and growling, but collapsed before he left the trail.

Sadira pointed her cane over the mul's head, but Agis called, "No!"

Without explaining further, he pointed a hand to each side of the trail and closed his eyes. Opening an energy path from his nexus to both of his arms, the noble imagined an invisible cord that ran from deep inside him to his fingers. An instant later, his hands tingled with psionic power.

Remembering the halfling taste for giant spiders, Agis decided to use a pair of mental constructs to seek vengeance in Singer's name. He visualized each of his hands changing into a huge spider, but not the chirping kind Anezka and her fellows liked to eat. These were black and shiny, with great bulbous bodies and carapaces as hard as rock.

The spiders had no physical existence, for they lived only in the noble's thoughts. After the halflings turned their attention on Agis, however, the spiders would seem as real to the little warriors as anything else in the forest.

Assuming that the warriors were watching him by now, Agis visualized the illusionary spiders leaping off the ends of his arms. When they landed, each was as large as Rikus. They scurried into the forest on eight sturdy legs equipped with claws as sharp as a rock leopard's nails and as long as a dagger.

By fixing their attention on Agis, the halflings created a

faint mental contact between themselves and the noble. The enormous spiders located two of these tenuous threads and followed them like silky strands of web back to their sources. Through his spiders' eyes, the noble saw the two halflings who were watching lift their bows. They each nocked a black-tipped arrow into the bowstring.

As the halflings took aim, Agis's hunters entered their minds. Both halflings screamed and released their bowstrings, shooting their tiny arrows into the ground. They dropped their weapons and reached for their daggers, totally convinced that the psionic creatures were real. Agis visualized the spiders' fangs dripping black poison, then the two beasts struck. The astonished halflings cried out and clutched at the enormous fangs they believed to be piercing their bodies. They struggled briefly, arms flailing wildly as they tried to free themselves. Finally the warriors grew lethargic and fell silent, convinced that they had been killed.

That belief would not last, Agis knew, for he had not penetrated his targets' minds deeply enough to persuade them that they were truly dead. Doing so would have taken valuable time and energy. Besides, killing the small warriors hardly seemed wise, considering that the halflings were the ones who possessed the spear he and his friends needed.

After the two halflings stopped struggling, the noble allowed his hunters to roam the forest a little longer, waiting for more ambushers to focus their thoughts on him. After a moment, he felt reasonably sure that he had eliminated the remaining ambushers.

Agis cut off the flow of energy to his spiders, then placed his hands on his knees and gasped for breath. The attack had been one of the most powerful he knew, and it had placed a considerable strain on his body. "We're safe—for now," he huffed.

Sadira looked doubtful. "What do you mean?"

"The Way," Agis explained simply. "What of Neeva and Rikus?"

"They're still breathing," Sadira replied. "They seem to be in no danger of dying."

"Can you wake them?"

Sadira tried shaking, slapping, and yelling at them. Nothing worked. "We'll just have to wait until they're conscious."

"We can't," Agis said, shaking his head. "The halflings will recover within an hour or so."

Sadira looked at the two gladiators. "Why couldn't this have happened to us instead of them?" she complained. "We'll never move them."

"Can't you do something?" Agis asked, finally bringing his breath under control.

Sadira shook her head. "I don't know any spells for carrying people."

"What good is magic?" Agis sighed, stepping toward Rikus's inert form. "See if you can find Anezka."

"There's no use trying," Sadira answered. "I saw her running down the trail after Rikus fell."

Agis closed his eyes and let out a long breath of disappointment. "Now what are we going to do?"

Sadira shrugged and gestured toward the pathway. "This must lead somewhere. There's as good a chance that we'll find Nok there as anyplace."

With Sadira's help, Agis rolled the unconscious gladiators onto their backs and laid them side by side, securing their weapons beneath their belts. He grasped them each by the wrist and closed his eyes, then opened a pathway from his power core into their bodies. He pictured them becoming clouds and rising off the ground of their own accord.

Once the two gladiators began to float, Agis stood. Being careful not to lose contact with their bodies, he looked down the trail and said, "Let's go, and fast. I don't think I'm going to last more than a few hours. Besides, we should be as far away from here as possible when the halflings wake."

With Sadira in the lead, they walked until midafternoon without incident. At last, the valley broadened into a wide basin and the trail left the edge of the roaring river.

The half-elf suddenly stopped and stared at her feet.

"It's about time we rest," Agis gasped thankfully. "I'm so tired I can hardly tell the trail from the forest any more."

"I didn't stop to rest," Sadira said, pointing at a small strand of brown string stretched across the trail. "Our friends have set up a surprise."

She started to step over the string, but Agis called, "Wait!" He nodded to Neeva's trikal. "Probe the ground on the other side," he said. "That tripwire is too obvious."

The half-elf raised an eyebrow. "My, aren't you the cautious one?"

Nevertheless, she took the trikal and did as Agis suggested. A mat of woven fronds, covered by a thin layer of dirt, collapsed and dropped into a deep pit with a muffled crash.

Sadira swallowed, then faced Agis. "It doesn't look safe to walk the path any longer."

Agis was about to answer when a halfling stepped onto the trail behind Sadira. "Look out!" he cried.

The noble dropped the two gladiators' wrists and

grabbed Sadira. As he pulled her aside, he heard the twang of a bowstring. Something sharp bit into his neck.

In the same instant, the astonished sorceress stumbled over the tripwire. A loud crack sounded overhead, then a log crashed down out of the trees and swooped toward them.

The noble stepped forward, intending to shove Sadira to safety. Instead, his knees buckled. As he fell, he spun around in time to see the log strike the young slave girl in the head. He reached out, but found himself falling slowly backward, almost as if the air itself had grown thick. Agis realized that the poison had taken hold of his mind and that he was dropping into the pit they'd uncovered. The last thing he saw before he disappeared into the earth was Sadira's limp body collapsing into the underbrush.

FIFTEEN

The Living Bridge

Sadira's head pounded as though it contained a dozen drummers, all beating the same primitive rhythm. Her ears ached, her temples throbbed, even her teeth hurt. Her eyes were too sore to open, and she felt sick to her stomach. She was so dizzy that she didn't think she should be standing, yet, to her surprise, that was exactly what it felt like she was doing.

The sorceress tried to lift a hand to her aching head and found it an impossible task. For some reason she did not understand, she could not move her right arm. She tried with her left and discovered that it, too, was immobilized. There was a terrible, sharp pain in both wrists.

Fearing that she was paralyzed, Sadira opened her eyes. As her vision began to clear, she saw that the sound of the drums came from outside her head, not inside. Ahead of her lay a small meadow covered by soft moss, tinted pink by the light of the afternoon sun. At the edges of the clearing stood a dozen halfling men dressed in breechcloths, their eyes round and glazed as they beat a feral cadence on tall drums.

In the center of the meadow, a mound rose high into the air. Sadira squinted at the structure and, despite her blurred vision, saw that it had been built entirely from large blocks of gray rock. A steep stairway ran up the center, but otherwise the structure was perfectly smooth, with only tiny seams where the blocks met.

Atop the mound sat a small house of white marble, with a smoking copper brazier outside the door. Next to the brazier lay the weapons and satchels that Sadira and her friends had brought into the forest. In front of the pile stood Anezka and a wild-looking halfling male. He was covered with green paint, and a crown of woven fronds ringed his tangled mass of hair. In his small hands, the man held Ktandeo's cane.

Sadira's heart sank. After using the cane at Agis's estate, she had realized that it was far more dangerous than she had suspected. Still, the sorceress did not like seeing it in the hands of a forest-dwelling savage. She and her companions would need it to battle Kalak.

Looking to the bottom of the mound, she saw that a single oak tree grew there. The majestic oak looked oddly misplaced in a meadow surrounded by dancing conifers and frond trees, but its isolation had not prevented it from growing up straight and strong.

Scattered around the oak's trunk were dozens of halfling men and women, all holding wooden bowls. Some had adorned their arms or legs with brightly colored feathers, but otherwise none of them wore anything except loincloths. They all watched the top of the mound with an air of anticipation.

"You're awake." The voice came from Sadira's left.

"I *feel* like I'm dead," Sadira answered shakily, turning her aching head toward Agis.

A few feet away, the noble hung on a stone slab that had

been planted upright in the ground. His hands and feet were lashed into place with leather ropes running through a set of special holes. At the bottom of the slab was a large, semicircular catch basin, stained brown with old blood.

"What happened?" Sadira asked. Her head had finally cleared, and she realized that she hung on a similar stone. The pain in her wrists was caused by her bindings.

Agis told her about their capture. When he explained how she had stumbled into the tripwire as he tried to save her from the poisoned arrow, he added, "I'm sorry about your head."

"She's alive and conscious," said a woman's voice. "There's nothing to be sorry about in that."

Sadira turned her throbbing head to the right and saw that Rikus and Neeva were also hanging from stone slabs.

"It was Anezka who led us into the ambush, not Agis," agreed Rikus. "Maybe she did it because of that business with the spider—"

"And maybe not," interrupted Neeva. "I doubt we'll ever know, but now isn't the time to worry about it." She tilted her chin toward the granite mound. "I think we're finally about to meet our captor."

Sadira looked in the direction Neeva indicated. The green-painted halfling stepped off the mound into mid-air. Instead of falling, he slowly drifted down toward the sorceress and her friends. He carried Ktandeo's cane in both hands, like a full-sized man would carry a fighting cudgel.

Behind him, Anezka climbed down the steep stairs. When she reached the bottom, a half-dozen halflings with feathered armbands joined her. One of them handed her a wooden bowl, then they walked toward Sadira and the others.

As the floating halfling settled to the ground in front of Sadira, the slave girl saw that a large ring of gold hung in his hawkish nose. Bands of hammered silver ringed his ears, and a large ball of obsidian dangled from a chain around his neck.

The halfling looked at Sadira with an air of indignation. "Where did you get this staff?" he asked.

"Who wants to know?" Sadira responded.

The halfling stared at her menacingly, obviously shocked at her challenge to his authority. When Sadira met his gaze evenly, he said, "I am World Tree, whose roots bring forth fruit so that my people may eat. I am Rain Bird, whose wings shower the land with water so that my people may drink. I am Time Serpent, whose tail is the past and whose head is the future, so that my people will live forever. I am Nok, the forest."

Nok raised the cane. "Now, tell me how you came by this staff."

"A man named Ktandeo gave it to me."

Nok narrowed his eyes. "I made this for Ktandeo. He would not have given it to an impudent young woman."

"It was his dying act," Sadira said, regarding the halfling in a new light. Anyone who could make such an item was no ordinary savage. "He gave me the cane so you would know we came in his name."

The halfling's posture grew less menacing, and he closed his eyes. "Now I know why the moons have been weeping. Ktandeo was a worthy friend of the forest," he said, touching one hand to the gold ring in his nose and the other to a silver ear-band. "He brought many fine offerings."

Anezka arrived with the six halflings wearing feathered armbands. They stood behind Nok, patiently holding their bowls in both hands. Rikus and Neeva fixed angry glares on Anezka, but said nothing. Agis also remained silent, studying Nok with a thoughtful expression.

"Ktandeo sent us for his magical spear," Sadira said.

"I have been growing a spear," replied the halfling, meeting Sadira's gaze with warmer eyes. "I cannot give it to you."

"Why not?" the sorceress asked. "Isn't it ready?"

Nok glanced over his shoulder at the oak tree. "It's ready . . . but you are not worthy of it."

Assuming he meant she was not strong enough to throw it, Sadira pointed her chin at Rikus. "He's the one who will use the spear. Not me."

Nok regarded the mul with an appraising eye, but shook his head. "There is more than strength to throwing a spear," he said. "The aim must be accurate, the heart true. Without Ktandeo to guide his hand, the hairless one will fail."

"What do you mean?" Rikus bristled. "The spear hasn't been made that I can't handle."

"You cannot wield this one!" Nok snapped.

"You haven't seen him fight. How is it that you know this?" Sadira asked.

"Because you hang on the Feast Stones," the halfling replied, tapping the cane against the basin at Sadira's feet. "If you were worthy of the Heartwood Spear, you would not be there. Your blood would never yearn to fill these basins."

"Feast Stones!" Rikus exclaimed, tugging at his bindings.

"We came as friends!" Agis objected.

"You'll become part of the forest. What could be a greater gift for one's friends?" Nok asked, smiling sincerely.

"Anezka didn't bring us here to be eaten!" Neeva

growled.

"Of course she did," Nok said. "You are her offering."

"Offering!" Rikus cried, looking to Anezka. "That's not why you brought us here, is it?"

Anezka nodded, giving the mul a reassuring smile.

"Nok, my friends and I would be honored to join your forest," the sorceress lied. "Unfortunately, Ktandeo sent us for the spear because the need in Tyr is great."

"What need?" the halfling asked.

"Kalak has a small pyramid made of obsidian," Agis explained, his eyes fixed on the halfling's pendant. "He also has many obsidian balls, and a tunnel lined with obsidian bricks. Do you know what this means?"

Nok's eyes opened wide. "It is too soon," he said, shaking his head sadly.

Agis went on to tell the halfling about the memory he had seen inside Tithian's mind and about the king's plans to seal the stadium during the gladiatorial games.

When the noble finished, Sadira asked, "Now will you give us the spear?"

Nok shook his head. "You couldn't even reach me without being captured," he said. "How can you hope to stop a dragon?"

"Dragon?" Sadira uttered. Her companions echoed her astonishment. "We're talking about Kalak, not the—" Sadira stopped herself, the implication of Nok's question striking her with the force of a half-giant's club. "Kalak is the Dragon?" she gasped.

"No. There are many dragons throughout the world," the halfling said. "Kalak is not yet one of them."

"But he's about to become one," Sadira said, her mind racing as she began to understand the wicked nature of Kalak's plan. "That's what the ziggurat is for."

"Yes," Nok agreed. "He needs it for his changing."

"The time to strike is before he changes!" Neeva exclaimed. "Give us the spear before it's too late."

Nok regarded the woman thoughtfully, then shook his head. "I cannot entrust the Heartwood Spear to someone who is not worthy."

"We're worthy!" Rikus growled. "I've won more than a hundred matches."

Nok seemed unmoved. In vain Sadira searched her aching head for another approach that would make the halfling listen. The more she learned about Kalak, the more he terrified her and the more determined she became to stop him.

"If you were willing to help Ktandeo against the sorcerer-king of Tyr," Agis said, "it must have been because you feared for your forest."

The halfling nodded. "One dragon—the one you foolishly call *the* Dragon, as if it were the only one—already claims Tyr, as it does everything from Urik to Balic. When another appears, one of them will be forced across the Ringing Mountains."

"And what does that mean to the forest?" Agis pressed.

"The same thing it means to Tyr: annihilation," Nok answered. "The dragon that passes over these mountains will devour every living thing it finds: plants, animals, people. It will allow nothing to escape."

"Why?" Sadira asked.

"Dragons grow more powerful when they kill," Nok answered. "And dragons covet power above all else, or they would not be dragons."

The four companions remained silent for a time. Nok also remained quiet, patiently studying them as if waiting for them to perform some customary act of obeisance. At last, Agis looked toward the dome, where the group's possessions were piled, and said, "We apologize if our previous gifts were unworthy, and we ask for them back. Instead, we offer our lives in defense of the forest."

"We *will* stop Kalak before he comes across the mountains," Sadira added.

Nok considered the offer, then said, "I am still not certain that your gift is worthy of the Heartwood Spear, but we shall see."

The chief turned to the halflings gathered behind him and spoke a few words in their own tongue. With crestfallen expressions, they set aside their wooden bowls and stepped around behind the Feast Stones to undo the lashings.

Once the four companions were free, Nok led the way toward the granite mound. The halflings in the area parted, jabbering to each other in peculiar, nasal words punctuated by birdlike shrieks and squeals. Nok paid them no attention until he stood at the tree itself, when he silenced them with a harsh command.

With the meadow quiet, Nok cradled Ktandeo's cane in one arm, then opened his other hand and touched the oak. He spoke a few phrases in his own language. The tree's boughs shuddered, and Nok's fingers melded into the bark. Slowly he pushed his hand deeper, until his arm had disappeared clear to the shoulder.

Nok closed his eyes and stood next to the oak in silence. His lips were tense and turned down at the ends, giving him a stoic and slightly remorseful expression. He remained perfectly still. Sadira wondered if he was having second thoughts. At last, the chief opened his eyes, then looked at the tree and spoke to it in a conciliatory tone.

Another shudder ran through the oak's boughs, and a terrible, sonorous creak sounded from its core. Leaves began to rain down on the people below. To Sadira it seemed that the bark paled to a lighter shade of gray. Nok slowly stepped away, pulling his arm from the tree as he retreated.

In his hand, the halfling held a thick spear colored deepest burgundy. The shaft tapered to sharp points on both ends, with a grain so fine it was hardly visible. Sadira thought at first that the weapon pulsated with magical energy, but when she looked directly at it, the impression faded. It seemed no more than a normal, finely crafted weapon.

Nok stepped away from the oak, sending a few halflings to fetch the party's belongings. Motioning for his prisoners to follow, he led the way to a small trail winding into the gloomy depths of the forest. As they traveled along the path, Sadira realized the halflings had carried her and her companions a considerable distance from where she and Agis had fallen. In addition to the dancing conifers and bulb-trunked fronds, the trail was lined by immense, slanting hardwoods. These trees had waxy, ruby-colored leaves and ripe, sweet-smelling fruits with the shape of daggers and the color of sapphires. The constant drone of insects underscored the shrill whistles and chirps of the jungle birds, and the shadows were so thick that, at times, Sadira felt as though she were walking through UnderTyr. Presently, the rumble of a nearby river began to drown out the sound of the insects and birds.

At last they stepped out of the forest. Before them, a narrow suspension bridge spanned a rocky gorge so wide that Rikus could not have thrown his axe across it. The bridge was made of flowering vines woven together to form a V-shaped channel. A densely braided cord of the woody plants served as the walkway, two smaller cords as handrails, and a plethora of bud-covered vines as netlike walls. A round boulder blocked the other end, so it was impossible to tell if the trail continued on the other side of the canyon. The whole scene had an eerie red hue, for the setting sun hung in line with the gorge, bathing it in fiery light.

Nok stopped at the edge of the bridge. Without putting down Ktandeo's cane, he hefted the Heartwood Spear and threw it. A concerned cry escaped Sadira's lips, but the spear sailed across the gap as though borne on a cushion of air. It sank half its length into the trunk of a ruby-leaved tree growing behind the boulder on the other end of the bridge.

Nok faced the four companions and used Ktandeo's cane to gesture across the gorge. "There is the spear you seek. To prove you are worthy of it, you must pull it from the tree."

After studying the bridge, Rikus said, "This thing doesn't look sturdy to me. Maybe we should go across one at a time."

Agis shook his head. "I don't think so. There's more to this test than crossing a bridge cautiously," he said. "Kalak is surrounded by guards every bit as powerful as you. I wouldn't be surprised if he or some of his people are masters of both the Way and magic. To defeat him, we're going to have to work together."

"Four people can't throw a spear," Rikus countered.

"True," Sadira said. "But the spear won't strike unless we coordinate our efforts to overcome Kalak's defenses. I think Agis is right—Nok is testing our ability to work together."

The mul cast a wary eye at the vine bridge, then nodded and looked down at the halfling chief. "We need our weapons and some rope," he said, gesturing at the warriors who had brought their property along.

"Rope, you can have," Nok said. "You won't need weapons."

Rikus looked doubtful, but accepted the rope without protest. "I'll lead the way," he said, tying one end of the line around his waist and passing the other to Sadira. "Sadira and Agis will follow, and Neeva will bring up the rear."

"Rikus, I'm hardly vulnerable, and it might be best to have my skills in front," Agis said, stepping forward. "I'll lead."

Sadira caught the noble's arm, afraid that the discussion would deteriorate into an argument. "Rikus is right. If you're in the middle, you can protect us all. If you're in front, it'll be impossible for you to protect us against an attack from the rear."

Reluctant, Agis nodded, then stepped back into line. Once the four companions had all tied themselves into place, Rikus led the way onto the bridge. Sadira followed next, with Agis and Neeva behind her. They moved slowly and carefully, holding onto the handcords and keeping a careful eye on the braided vines beneath their feet. Though the bridge swayed and rocked with each step, it showed no sign of coming apart under their weight.

They were about a third of the way across when Rikus suddenly stopped. He stared at the walkway, gripping the handcords so tightly that his knuckles were white.

"What's wrong?"

No sooner had Agis asked the question than they all saw why Rikus had halted. The vines were writhing and twisting at his feet, re-growing in a different pattern before their eyes. The bridge wasn't coming apart; it was reforming itself into two separate pathways, each running in a slightly different direction.

Without releasing the handcords, Rikus took a tentative step. His foot sank through the writhing mass of vines. Only his secure grip saved him from plummeting into the river that snaked like a silver line far below.

"Don't move!" Agis cried. "The bridge isn't changing. It's a psionic illusion!"

"Where is it coming from?" Sadira asked, looking over her shoulder.

She did not need to finish the question, for the noble was already facing Nok. The two men had locked gazes and were staring at each other like gladiators in a death match. Agis gripped the handcord with tightly closed fists, but his legs trembled and lines of perspiration ran down his neck. On the other side of the noble, Neeva stared at her feet in horror.

Sadira looked down. There were three separate bridges beneath her feet. "Don't turn around, Rikus. Neeva, when I say to, cover Agis's eyes and close your own."

Plucking a handful of flower buds off the vines forming the wall, the sorceress pointed a hand toward the forest behind Nok to summon the energy for a spell. She had hardly opened her palm before she felt the incredible power from the massive trees rush into her body. For the first time in her life, she found it necessary to close her fist and cut off the flow of energy before it overwhelmed her.

Pushing aside her shock, she cried, "Now, Neeva!"

The gladiator cover Agis's face with a hand and shut her eyes. Sadira tossed the buds at Nok and spoke the incantation that would shape her magic.

The buds disappeared in midair, and a spray of brilliant hues blossomed before the halfling's eyes. It was the same spell she had used to save Rikus from the gaj, but with the forest's energy, the effects were more spectacular. The colors were deep and dazzling, competing with each other for splendor, mesmerizing in their radiance. Nok's eyes went glassy. Though Sadira had not directed the attack at the halflings behind the chief, even they seemed shocked.

The spell faded almost immediately, but Nok and the other halflings remained stunned. It would take them at least a few moments to recover from its effects.

As his mind was released from combat, Agis's knees buckled. Neeva opened her eyes and caught him. "Are you well?" she asked.

Agis gripped the handcord and nodded. "Thanks to Sadira. I've never faced such a powerful mind!"

"Kalak's will be stronger," Neeva answered.

At the front of the line, Rikus called, "I see one bridge again! Let's go!"

They continued forward faster than before, but also with more apprehension. With each step, Sadira expected Nok to recover. When they passed the midway point of the bridge without another attack, she hazarded a glance over her shoulder. The halfling chief stood on the far side. His eyes were clear, and he was studying the companions with an air of detached interest.

Rikus yelled, "Get ready! We've got trouble!"

Sadira faced forward. The group's weight had depressed the bridge enough to create a steep slope between the center and the ends. The granite ball on the far side of the bridge had left its resting place. It was rolling down the V-shaped channel, picking up speed as it traveled. Rikus braced himself to catch it.

"Rikus, down!" cried Agis.

The mul cast an angry glance over his shoulder. "Are you mad?"

"Do it!" Sadira snapped.

Rikus looked back at the boulder. It was shooting down the trough with terrifying speed. Taking a hard gulp, he dropped to his belly and wrapped his arms around the walkway. Sadira did the same, craning her neck to watch Agis.

The noble closed his eyes, then held out an arm as if he intended to let the boulder roll up it. He cupped his palm, then tipped it toward the side of the bridge.

The sorceress looked forward again. The ball was almost upon them. Rikus flinched and dropped his face into the vines, yelling, "Never trust a noble!"

The ball lifted into the air, passing just above the mul's bald pate. By the time the boulder reached Sadira, it was even higher in the air. It arched up before drifting out over the handcord, then plummeted into the gorge below.

For a moment, Sadira lay motionless, trying to slow her pounding heart.

"What was that about trusting nobles, Rikus?" asked Agis. Though his voice was weak with fatigue, there was a wry grin on his face.

Rikus looked over his shoulder. "You sure took your time to—" He broke off in midsentence. Sadira heard the throb of huge wings beating the air, then the mul called, "Duck!"

Two gigantic dragonflies zipped past overhead, their hooked feet slashing through the air. The sorceress rose to her knees and peered over the handcord. The two insects had already flown past. Nevertheless, she could see that a halfling sat behind each beast's glittering compound eyes. The riders pulled the mounts into a steep, banked turn.

"Crawl, Rikus!" yelled Agis.

The mul obediently moved forward on hands and knees. The others followed close behind, keeping their heads below the handcords. The two insects streaked past again, their gossamer wings shimmering with the ruby light of dusk.

Sadira made the whole line pause while she peered through the side of the bridge. The halflings were again banking their mounts. Unfortunately, this time the riders were holding their palms toward the forest, collecting the energy to cast a spell.

"Magic!" she hissed. They crawled forward as quickly as possible.

"I hear them behind me," Neeva shouted, looking fearfully over her shoulder. Yet the dragonflies and their riders were nowhere in sight. An instant later, Sadira heard the throb of wings at the back of their line.

"Oh no," the sorceress cried. "They're invisible!"

A dragonfly appeared above Neeva, the spell that had hidden it from sight negated by the suddeness of its attack. The halfling on the creature's back shouted a series of strident commands. The beast dropped onto the woman and locked its six legs around her body.

"Help me!" Neeva shouted, struggling to turn so that Agis might have a clear attack on the giant insect or its rider.

The noble formed a short loop from the slack in the rope connecting him to Neeva. Stepping past the dragonfly's long tail, he flipped the noose over the rider's head and jerked the halfling off his mount. The warrior landed screaming on the handcord. Agis shoved him over the side.

The dragonfly flapped its four wings, knocking the noble aside. It rose into the air with Neeva still clutched in its claws. She struggled in vain to pull herself free.

Rikus screamed, "Help her!"

Agis grabbed the female gladiator's legs and locked his own feet around the bridge's handcord.

Sadira fished a piece of silk from her pocket. The sor-

ceress pointed her free hand toward the trees. Flicking
the silk at the dragonfly, she recited her incantation. The
strand disappeared, and a gooey white web appeared on
the insect's wings. The dragonfly tried to force its wings
to beat through the stringy webbing, but it was no use.
The creature and Neeva dropped into the gap.

Grabbing the handcord, Agis braced himself. Neeva
quickly fell the length of the rope connecting her to the
noble, and the suddenness of the rope snapping taut
made the noble groan.

Sadira dropped to the walkway and wrapped her arms
and legs around the vines. Through the thick tangle beneath her face, she could not see what was happening between Neeva and the giant insect.

Rikus stepped over her, reaching for the noble. It was
only then that the second dragonfly appeared above
Agis's head. Its rider leaned over to cast a spell. Sadira
screamed a warning, but she was too late. Agis's eyes flut-
tered, his head tipped back, and he fell into a magical
slumber.

His hold on the bridge gone, the noble slipped over the
edge and plummeted after Neeva. When he'd fallen the
length of the rope connecting him to Sadira, the noose bit
deeply into her flesh. A jolt of sharp pain shot through
her abdomen. Though the impact threatened to rip her
from the bridge, too, the sorceress clutched the walkway
vines and prayed she would have the strength to hang on.

Rikus grabbed the dragonfly hovering overhead by the
wing. There was a loud crackle and a sound like shred-
ding cloth. The mul pulled the creature's wing from its
body and tossed the mangled limb from the bridge.

As the insect screeched its pain, the rider reached for
his dagger. Rikus knocked the halfling senseless, shattering his nose with a casual backfist. The dragonfly raked

its claws across the gladiator's chest, but the mul only gritted his teeth and ripped another wing off the creature.

Rikus dropped both the rider and mount over the side of the bridge, then grabbed the rope and pulled Agis up. The mul passed the noble, still under the thrall of the halfling's sleep spell, to Sadira. She cradled Agis's head in her lap and shouted at him. When that did not work, she slapped him across the cheeks, hard. He remained asleep.

"Typical noble," Rikus grumbled.

Neeva came next, covered head-to-toe with black goo. In her hand, she clutched a dragonfly's head. There was no sign of the rest of its body.

"Are you hurt?" Sadira asked.

The gladiator looked up and wiped the insect's blood from her eyes. "No. Just a few scratches," she answered.

Rikus pulled Neeva to her feet, then took Agis from Sadira. "Good. You carry the noble," he said, placing the sleeping man in her arms.

The mul stepped past Sadira, then cautiously led the way forward. Though they were constantly watching for another of Nok's tests, they reached the end of the bridge without further incident. Rikus immediately went to the tree and reached for the spear.

"Wait," Neeva called, dumping Agis's body on the ground. "Nok's coming."

Sadira and the mul looked back across the gorge. The halfling chief strode across the swaying bridge as if walking down a trail, not even bothering to hold the hand-cords. Behind him, moving somewhat more cautiously, came two dozen halfling warriors. None of them looked happy.

"We've passed enough tests," Rikus said.

The mul gave the spear a mighty tug. When it slipped

out of the tree easily, he stumbled and nearly fell. He stood with the weapon in hand, regarding its balance and shape in awe. At last, he looked up and said, "I feel its power. My hands are tingling!"

Nok stepped off the bridge, cradling Ktandeo's cane in his arms. He regarded the mul with a look of disdain, as if Rikus had offended him. The gladiator returned the scornful expression.

At last, Nok said, "The Heartwood Spear will penetrate any armor. It will defend you from the energies of the body and those of the world—from the Way of the Unseen and from magic. Now that you have this wondrous weapon, what will you do with it?"

"Kill Kalak," Neeva said, taking the spear from Rikus's hands.

The halflings behind Nok gripped their daggers meaningfully. Sensing that she and her companions had not yet passed Nok's most important test, Sadira took the Heartwood Spear from Neeva's hands.

"We swore to offer our bodies and spirits to the forest," she said, facing the halfling chieftain. "It is not ours to decide what should be done to defend it." She held the spear out to Nok, saying, "Please accept this offering."

The halfling smiled and touched his hand to the weapon. "Now you are worthy of the Heartwood Spear," he said. "It is yours to use in the service of my forest."

Sadira passed the spear to Rikus, then fixed her eyes on the cane still cradled in Nok's arm. "If we are worthy of the spear, then perhaps we are also worthy of Ktandeo's cane."

Rikus quickly added, "You were the one who said it would take more than strength to throw the spear."

"If it is a weapon we can use to defeat Kalak and defend the forest, please give it to us," Neeva said. "We have passed your test, but we'll still need every advantage you can provide to defeat the sorcerer-king."

Nok regarded the two gladiators pensively. Finally, he held the cane out to Sadira. "I entrust these to your keeping so that you may protect the forest as you have pledged," he said. "Kill Kalak, and then you must return the weapons to me."

Sadira accepted the cane. "We will not fail. I promise."

SIXTEEN

Endgame

Rikus and his three companions stood in an alley across from Tyr's great stadium, listening to the roar of the crowd thunder over the high walls. Two templars stood in each gateway of the structure, their pole-axes gripped firmly in hand and their short swords dangling at their hips. Outside the gates hundreds of men and women, overcome by drink, heat, or excitement, sat in the streets. These refugees waved fans before their faces or simply held their heads in their hands. They would have fared better returning to their homes, but the mul suspected that they hoped to recover in time for the day's grand finale. Rikus thought they were fools—not the sort of people for whom he wanted to die.

The mul faced his weary companions. After a grueling four-day hike, they had arrived in Tyr last night, only to discover that the ziggurat had been completed and the games were scheduled to begin in the morning.

"This will never work," Rikus said, eyeing the guards at the stadium.

"Do you have a better idea?" Sadira asked.

The half-elf was dressed like a noblewoman, with a silver circlet in her amber hair and a silken cape over her shoulders. On her fingers she wore rings of silver, gold, and copper, and the straps of her sandals were studded with tourmaline. According to their plan, she would find a vantage point in the noble tiers from which she could see both Rikus and the King's Balcony. Just before the mul threw the Heartwood Spear, she would use Ktandeo's cane to destroy the magical shielding that they assumed would be protecting Kalak.

"I haven't thought of anything better—yet," Rikus admitted reluctantly.

"We don't have much time, Rikus," said Agis, looking nervous and uncomfortable in a templar's cassock. "They could close the stadium any minute."

"Let them! Tithian will never join us." Rikus tipped his spear toward the stadium. "If we go through those gates, we'll all be killed before we can assassinate anyone."

"We don't need Tithian to *join* us," Agis said. "We just need him to leave us alone. He's already promised that much. Through Sadira's efforts, he knows where the amulets were hidden. So far, he's kept his word."

Rikus had to admit this much was true. Last night, Agis and Sadira had asked around to see if people still expected the mul and his partner to fight. To their surprise, everyone assumed Rikus and Neeva would be part of the grand finale. Apparently Tithian had honored his promise and kept the escape of his two prize gladiators secret.

Nevertheless, the mul was far from enthused about the crucial role the high templar played in their plans. "Agis, you're asking Tithian to let you attack Kalak from the High Templars' Gallery. If that isn't helping, I don't know what is."

The noble lifted a hand and nodded. "You're right, that is helping. It doesn't matter, though. Tithian will cooperate. Leave him to me."

Rikus shook his head stubbornly. "He can't be trusted, no matter how close you were as boys. There must be another way."

This part of the plan was what made the mul nervous. When Rikus threw the spear, Agis would simultaneously pound Kalak with a psionic barrage. Unfortunately, to make his attack, the noble needed to see the king's face. The only place he could do that from was the High Templars' Gallery. With that in mind, Agis had donned a templar's cassock. He intended to convince Tithian to let him pose as a minor functionary and watch the contest from the gallery.

Neeva had the same fears as Rikus. "Agis, if you're wrong about Tithian, the instant Rikus and I step into the arena, he'll have us killed—and Kalak will survive. I'd feel better if I knew why you're so confident the High Templar of the Games will cooperate."

The noble smiled. "Because Tithian doesn't want to die," Agis said. "When he hears that Kalak wants to become a dragon, and what that will mean to Tyr, the high templar will see that his best chance of survival lies in our success."

"How do you know Tithian will believe you?" Neeva objected. "Or that he won't think Kalak intends to spare him?"

"We don't need to convince Tithian of anything," Agis countered. "He was already frightened when the king told him to lock the stadium. He'll be even more frightened when I tell him the reason."

Before they had left the forest, Nok had revealed everything he knew about dragons. One of the things he had mentioned was that Kalak's incubation would require the life force of tens of thousands of people. Of course, the companions had immediately realized that this was why the king wanted the stadium sealed.

Agis continued, "Besides, there are two more good reasons for me to be close to Tithian. First, if he tries to sound an alarm when you and Rikus take the field, I'll kill him. Even if he does betray us, that might give you enough time to finish Kalak."

"Before the templars kill us," Rikus added. "I still don't like this plan. I'm here to help Sadira and Neeva. I don't care about a mob of citizens who are here because they enjoy watching slaves chop each other up. As far as I'm concerned, the crowd deserves whatever Kalak does to them."

"And what about the rest of Tyr?" Neeva asked. "You heard Nok. Once Kalak becomes a dragon, he isn't going to stop killing once he leaves the stadium. He'll annihilate Tyr and probably the entire valley as well."

"We're not going to save any lives if we die before we have a chance to attack the king," Rikus replied. "On the other hand, we could be certain of saving thousands of lives by spending the afternoon warning those who didn't go to the games."

"Rikus, this is about more than saving lives," Agis said. "It's about liberty—"

"We have our liberty," the mul responded. "That's what matters to me."

"This isn't about liberty either," Sadira interrupted. "It's about evil. If someone had stopped the sorcerer-kings a thousand years ago, Athas wouldn't be the terrible place it is today. If we don't stop Kalak now, who knows what the world will be like tomorrow?"

"I understand that," Rikus answered, "but you and Neeva—and even Agis, I suppose—are more important to me than all of Tyr. I'll help you fight Kalak, but I don't want any part of getting any of you killed."

"Perhaps it won't come to that," Agis said. "That's the other reason I want to be near Tithian when we attack. If anyone can save us after Kalak dies, it will be him."

"That's a nice thought, but I don't see why he would," Neeva said, shaking her head. "After Kalak dies, Tithian will want to hide his part in the assassination. It'll be in his interest to make sure that everyone who knows about his involvement is killed."

"Which is why I'll be nearby," Agis countered. "The threat of an immediate and painful death will persuade Tithian to help us escape—that much I can promise."

"It's better than anything I've thought of," Rikus admitted.

"Good," Sadira said. "Now that we're all happy, let's go." She started toward the stadium before anyone could debate the issue further.

"I didn't say I was happy," Rikus grumbled, laying the spear over his shoulder and starting after her.

Agis stepped to his side. "I'll help you and Neeva get into the stadium," he offered. "As . . . slaves you might have some difficulty. . . ."

"I think they know us here," the mul said with a smile of pride.

The mul motioned to Neeva, then walked across the street to the nearest gate. As the pair of famous gladiators entered the dark passageway, the guards moved aside and tipped their polearms in salute.

* * * * *

Rikus and Neeva stepped into the arena. The crowd's thunder shook even the granite foundations of Tyr's mighty colosseum. The two gladiators paused in the arched entryway to let their eyes adjust to the bright light. The mob roared even louder. Moments later, the matched pair walked toward the center of the fighting arena, leaving behind them the stale stench of wine and sweat that hung close to the stands.

As usual, both gladiators were lightly armored and armed, for they believed in fighting with mobility as well as strength. They were dressed in the emerald-green battle array that Neeva had selected before they came to the stadium. Rikus wore nothing but a breechcloth, leather cuirass, bone skullcap, and spiked cops upon both his knees and elbows. For a weapon, he carried the Heartwood Spear.

Neeva was armed with the steel-bladed trikal Agis had given her. In addition to her breechcloth and chest halter, she wore an ivory-horned helm and a pair of shoulder pauldrons from which hung a winglike cape. Long gauntlets covered her forearms, and a pair of greaves with spiked knee cops protected her shins.

When the pair reached the center of the immense sand field, they stopped and acknowledged their ovation by raising their weapons to the crowd. The stadium was as full as Rikus had ever seen it. In the grandstands, people sat in every available space, completely blocking the aisles and stairs. The balconies overhead were more crowded. Spectators even sat at the edge of the overhang, clinging to the rope railing to keep from being pushed off their precarious perches.

It seemed to Rikus that every person in the stands was yelling or screaming or slapping their palms against the stone seats. He could hear his name being shouted in a thousand places all at once. The mul wondered if any of those showering him with adulation now would try to help him or Neeva when he threw the spear into Kalak's heart.

After acknowledging the crowd's applause, the gladiators bowed to the ziggurat looming over the western end of the arena. Next they faced the High Templars' Gallery, a small seating box protruding from the grandstand balcony. Its back and sides were screened to hide the occupants from the people in the stands, and a yellow canopy hung over it to provide shade. Though the resulting shadows prevented Rikus from seeing into the gallery itself, he hoped that one of the figures watching from the darkness was Agis.

* * * * *

"Tell me, on whom should I place my wager, Rikus or Kalak?" Tithian asked, leaning toward Agis to make himself heard above the din of the stadium.

"Rikus, of course," Agis answered. He looked toward the King's Balcony, where Kalak's wrinkled face could be seen just above the railing. "If you bet on Kalak, you lose—no matter what."

The high templar raised an eyebrow. "Is that so?"

Agis nodded, then leaned closer to Tithian's ear. Speaking just loud enough to make himself heard, the noble reported what they had learned from Nok. There was a small risk that Kalak was magically eavesdropping on their conversation, of course, but Agis suspected the king would have other things on his mind at the moment.

Tithian's face paled, and he slumped back into his well-padded chair. "I suppose I should find this too incredible to believe."

"Do you?" asked the noble.

The high templar shook his head.

"Then you're with us?" Agis asked, leaning close to Tithian's ear.

As a matter of routine, the senator had been searched before being allowed into the gallery and was unarmed. Nevertheless, his command of the Way was always with him. If he did not receive a satisfactory answer from his old friend, Agis was prepared to kill the high templar.

"I never said I would help, only that I wouldn't stand in your way," Tithian answered. "I've kept my word, as is obvious from the fact that you're here and my gladiators are down there." He pointed toward the center of the arena, where Rikus and Neeva still waited his answer to their salute.

"There are no bystanders in this," Agis said. "You're either with us or against us."

Tithian met his friend's menacing gaze evenly. "I'll want something in return."

"What?"

The templar shrugged. "It depends on what you want me to do."

"What we need should be a simple matter for someone of your authority," Agis said. "Just get us out of here after Rikus throws the spear."

Tithian closed his eyes and let an ironic sigh escape his lips. "Agis, I'm not in charge of the security force," he said. "Kalak assigned that responsibility to Larkyn."

*　*　*　*　*

In the center of the field, Rikus was beginning to fear that he had been right not to trust Tithian. At any moment, he expected a detachment of half-giants to rush into the arena, or a pair of magical lightning bolts to streak out of the gallery and destroy both him and Neeva.

He waited. Nothing happened, save that the din in the stands rose to a fevered frenzy. The two gladiators stood motionless in the stifling afternoon heat, the stale odor of the morning's blood and death lingering in the sands.

At last Tithian stepped to the edge of the porch, where Rikus and Neeva could see him. He acknowledged their salute by waving a black scarf. "It's about time," Rikus growled, spinning on his heel to face the eastern end of the arena.

"Don't complain," Neeva countered, also turning. "It looks like Agis was right about Tithian."

This time, the two gladiators faced the Golden Tower, where the King's Balcony overlooked the end of the fighting field. A single pair of half-giant guards stood on each side of the balcony, flanking a huge throne of jade. The throne sat at the front edge of the small box. The pate of Kalak's bald head, his golden diadem, and his dark eyes were barely visible above the balcony's front wall.

"I hope he stands up when I'm ready to throw the spear," Rikus said, dipping his weapon to the king. "Even at half this distance, his head isn't much of a target."

Kalak did not keep them waiting nearly as long as Tithian had. After the formality of a two-second wait, a half-giant bodyguard motioned the pair to a corner of the arena. As they went to their starting positions, Rikus studied the other gladiators on the fighting field.

On each side of the arena stood six matched pairs. Some were full humans or half-elves, rough-looking men and women who had been sold into the pits to pay their debts or as punishment for a crime. There were also sev-

eral representatives of more exotic races, including a set
of hulking baazrags, two purple-scaled nikaals, and a pair
of stooped gith.

Rikus recognized only a few of the other fighters. In
the opposite corner stood Chilo and Felorn, a skilled pair
of tareks. Like muls, tareks were big, musclebound, and
hairless. Their heads, however, were square and big-
boned, with sloping foreheads and massive brow ridges.
They had flat noses with flared nostrils and a domed
muzzle full of sharp teeth. Neither tarek wore armor of
any kind, and each carried two weapons: a steel handfork
that could serve equally well as a parrying tool or a slicing
weapon, and a bone heartpick, a hammerlike weapon
with a serrated pick on the front and a heavy, flat head on
the back.

To Rikus's right stood a hairy half-giant carrying an obsidian axe with a head as large as a dwarf. His partner was
a full-blooded elven woman armed with a whip of bone
and cord. The mul did not know the elf, but the half-
giant was a former guard named Gaanon, whom he had
wounded in a contest a year earlier. For armor, Gaanon
wore a leather hauberk that a normal man could have
used as a tent. The elf wore a bronze pauldron covering
her left shoulder and a spiked gauntlet on her right arm.

Upon noticing that she was being studied, the elf gave
Rikus a twisted smile. The mul did not know whether
she meant the gesture to be polite or intimidating, but it
made him think she was looking forward to battle. He
shrugged and looked away, turning his attention back to
his own partner. "Any sign of Sadira in the noble
booths?"

"Not that I've seen," Neeva replied. "Don't you trust
her charms to get her into position?"

"I trust her charms," Rikus said, giving his fighting

partner a warm grin. "But maybe not as much as I trust your trikal."

"I hope you remember that when this is finished," she returned, giving him a meaningful glance.

A loud creak echoed throughout the stadium, drawing the attention of gladiator and spectator alike to the center of the arena. A great bulge formed in the sand as an immense pair of doors began to open. Excited murmurs of curiosity rustled through the crowd, for those huge doors covered a subterranean staging area where Tithian stored building-sized props. They seldom opened unless some special amusement was being raised into the arena.

Today was no exception. As the doors reached their locked position, a familiar orange shell rose out of the pit. A pair of barbed, arm-length mandibles protruded from the underside of one end of the shell.

*   *   *   *   *

"The gaj!" Sadira whispered, watching the beast rise out of the prop area.

She stood on the terrace above the noble tiers, having spent the last two hours trying in vain to work her way into position. Unfortunately, because the stadium was so crowded, common spectators had been trying to sneak into the lower tiers since early morning. The nobles had complained bitterly, and now the half-giant guards at the top of each row would not allow anyone down the stairs unless someone in a booth vouched for the newcomer.

As Sadira watched the gaj rise out of the pit, she soon saw that it sat atop Kalak's obsidian pyramid. Hoping that the spectacular object would supply the distraction she needed, she worked her way down the terrace until she found a guard who seemed more interested in the arena than in his job. The sorceress took a deep breath, then boldly stepped past the half-giant's hip.

A huge hand descended in front of her. "Where are you going?" demanded a deep voice. The half-giant did not look down to see whom he addressed.

Sadira fixed her eyes on the one vacancy in the throng below, then rapped the guard's knuckles with the pommel of her cane. "To my seat!"

"Oww!" The half-giant pulled his hand away and looked down, astonished.

Sadira started to step past.

"I'm sorry," the half-giant said, fixing his baggy eyes on her face. "I do remember you from—"

The guard furrowed his brow, and Sadira instantly realized that she had problem.

"Pegen!" the half-giant gasped. He latched onto her shoulder. "You're the one who made me look like a fool at the city gate! You killed Pegen!"

"In the name of—" Sadira hissed, cursing her bad luck.

She spun around and swung her cane at the guard's groin, which on a half-giant was at perfect striking level for her. He groaned and released her shoulder, reaching for the bone club he had left leaning against the terrace wall.

Sadira resisted the temptation to use magic, for she was in plain view of much of the stadium. Instead, she slipped past the guard and ran for an exit tunnel. The half-giant followed, yelling orders for her to stop and threatening dire consequences if she did not obey. The scene evoked a few chuckles from those in the immediate vicinity, but the sound of Tithian's magically-augmented voice quickly drew their attention back to the obsidian pyramid.

"The rules of the game are simple: the last pair of gladiators able to stand on the summit of the pyramid will win the contest."

Though Sadira wondered what was happening in the arena, she did not dare pause to look. The half-giant lagged only a few steps behind her.

All around the stadium, loud bangs began to sound from the entryways as the gates came crashing down. Realizing that she was about to be cut off from the streets, the sorceress ducked into the nearest exit. The clatter of chains rang through the rock archway, and the templars at the far end of the tunnel leaped into the street. A huge gate crashed to the ground and blocked the short passageway. Sadira was trapped.

                    *   *   *   *   *

Kalak rose and stepped to the edge of his balcony. "Let the games begin!"

The other gladiators charged toward the pyramid, which a group of templars had levitated into position in front of Kalak's balcony. Neeva started to follow, but Rikus quickly grasped her shoulder.

"Let everyone else fight for a bit. The gaj will keep them from claiming the prize too soon," he said, pointing to the top of the glassy pyramid, where the murderous beast still sat. "Besides, if Kalak stays at the edge of his balcony, we might get a clear throw at him from below."

"What about Agis and Sadira?" Neeva asked. "You can't attack if they're not ready."

"They'd better be watching," Rikus said.

Ahead of them, Gaanon drew first blood by leveling a vicious swing at a dimwitted baazrag. The furry creature blocked with its trident, its sunken eyes betraying its confusion at being attacked. The half-giant's axe snapped the weapon as though it were a twig, then sliced the baazrag's massive torso into separate pieces just below the breast line. A thunderous roar sounded from the stands.

The female baazrag went into a rage. It threw its twin-bladed axe at Gaanon's leg, causing the clumsy half-giant to teeter at the brink of falling. The baazrag raised its massive arms and bared its yellowed fangs, then charged. The half-giant's elven partner suddenly disappeared from Gaanon's side, then reappeared behind the raging baazrag.

"The elf's a teleporter," Rikus noted.

Neeva grunted to let him know she had heard, but seemed otherwise unimpressed.

The elf lashed her whip around the baazrag's legs. The furry beast-woman fell at Gaanon's feet. He quickly beheaded it with another swift stroke of his axe.

"Let's see if we can work our way toward Kalak," Rikus said, leading them toward the general melee.

The seeming chaos of free-for-all combat was actually comprised of many smaller fights between a handful of combatants. Rikus carefully picked his way past these little battles toward the center of the field.

A few yards from the pyramid, two gith moved forward to intercept the mul and his partner. Keeping their bulging eyes fixed on Rikus and Neeva, the hunched lizard-men moved forward in a stooped gait that could not quite be described as scuttling or loping. Each of the scrawny creatures wore a plumed helmet atop its bony, arrow-shaped head. Mekillot-shell plates protected the vulnerable spines on their backs.

"Let's make quick work of these two," Rikus said, bringing his spear to a defensive position. He did not add a warning to watch for psionic tricks, for he and Neeva had fought gith before. She knew their innate abilities as well as he did.

"Don't waste time talking!" she said, stepping to his side. "Just kill them."

The smallest gith led the charge, rushing Rikus with a series of awkward hops. The mul brought the creature to a quick halt by threatening it with his spearpoint. The gaunt lizard-man reluctantly raised its spiked mace to trade blows. The maneuver, Rikus knew, would soon result in its undoing.

The other gith stopped a few yards from Neeva and studied her trikal with a bulging, lidless eye. An instant later, Neeva's weapon slithered to life in her hands.

"The damn thing animated my trikal!"

Without taking his eye off his own foe, Rikus shook his head. "You shouldn't have done that," he said loudly, addressing Neeva's attacker. "It only makes her mad."

*　*　*　*　*

A stout templar with a lined, leathery face stormed into the gallery. The man stopped directly in front of Agis's chair, blocking the noble's view of the fight between his friends and the two gith.

"What's the meaning of this?" demanded the newcomer. He ignored Agis completely and fixed his attention on Tithian.

"The meaning of what, Larkyn?" Tithian asked.

"You closed the gates too soon!" Larkyn said. "Half my templars are locked outside, and the crowd is already growing restless."

"Is that so?" Tithian asked nonchalantly. He gave Agis a knowing glance.

Larkyn looked at the senator and frowned, but showed no sign of recognizing him. This did not surprise the no-

ble, for high templars avoided the Senate as diligently as
senators avoided the High Bureaus. Though their names
were certainly known to each other, Agis doubted that
they had ever been within a hundred feet of one another
before today.

When the noble made no move to rise, Larkyn cleared
his throat forcefully.

A sly grin flashed across Tithian's thin lips, then he
cuffed Agis with the back of his hand. "How dare you sit
while a high templar stands!"

Agis jumped to his feet with all the chagrin of a subordinate who had forgotten his place. "Please forgive me,
High One," he groveled, bowing to Larkyn. "I was absorbed by the contest."

Larkyn dismissed him with a wave of his hand, then sat
in the chair the noble had just vacated. Agis stepped to
the back of the booth and glanced down the stairway. At
the bottom stood a knot of two dozen lower-ranking templars. Though it was impossible to tell Tithian's men
from Larkyn's, Agis could see that one group was blocking the other's access to the gallery.

Admiring the astuteness with which Tithian had ma-
neuvered Larkyn into the chair, Agis stepped close behind it so no one could see what he was doing. He
reached under his robe and withdrew the stiletto Tithian
had given him before Larkyn arrived—the high templar,
of course, being free from any sort of weapons' search.
While the noble would have preferred to use the Way,
leaving Larkyn alive but incapacitated, his old friend had
insisted upon a dagger in the back.

As Agis thrust the blade through the soft chair, a white
light flashed from the gateway into which Sadira had
fled. It was not particularly bright, neither was it long-
lived, nor did it create a peal of thunder. Nevertheless, it

was quite visible, and many curious spectators found their attentions split between the combat in the arena and the mysterious pyrotechnics in the stands.

* * * * *

"Did you see that?" Rikus asked, looking away from the flash he had just seen in the stands. At his feet lay the two gith, dispatched easily and without so much as a scratch to himself or Neeva. On the balcony above, Kalak perched at the edge of his throne, watching the fight with no indication that he was concerned by the flare of light. The mul decided it must have been a templar dispatching an unruly spectator.

"Rikus, pay attention!" Neeva said. "The tareks!"

The mul spun around. The powerful male tarek was so close that his musky odor filled Rikus's nose. The female had already engaged Neeva. The two women were exchanging lightning-fast blows, filling the arena with staccato pops as they blocked and parried.

Chilo swung his heartpick at Rikus, striking for the mul's arm. For his part, Rikus used his spear to block. A sharp crack sounded, then the pick whistled past Rikus's side. The tarek opened his muzzle and bared his white fangs, then slashed at the mul's stomach with the hand-fork. Rikus pulled back. As the sharp blades scraped across his light cuirass, he leveled a side-thrust kick at Chilo's massive chest. As it landed, the tarek flared his cavernous nostrils. Otherwise, he did not flinch. Rikus pushed away, trying to put a little space between himself and Chilo's hulking form.

Felorn slipped between the mul and his partner. To prevent himself from being separated from Neeva, Rikus started to move backward. The dark eyes beneath Chilo's

bony brow flashed. Rikus knew he was doing what his
opponent expected. He caught himself in midstep and returned his foot to the ground. Chilo charged, swinging
both weapons with fully extended arms.

Rikus raised the tip of his spear. "Expecting to intimidate *me* was your last mistake," he said, stepping forward.

Chilo's weapons sliced through the air behind Rikus.
The mul thrust his spear at his enemy's heart. The point
slipped easily into the tarek's densely muscled chest. Chilo's mouth dropped open, his eyes glassed over, and his
charge stopped—but he did not fall or even drop his
weapons. He merely stepped away from the mul and
pulled his body off the spear.

"I hate tareks worse than Asticles wine!" Rikus
growled.

He did not doubt he had struck Chilo a fatal blow. Unfortunately, tareks often continued to fight after death.

Rikus took advantage of Chilo's momentary shock and
threw a glance over his shoulder. Felorn still stood between him and Neeva. The mul stepped backward, slipping the butt-point of his weapon between the female's
ribs. Howling in pain, she futilely tried to pull herself off
the spear.

As Rikus looked back to Chilo, Felorn dropped her
weapons. She thrashed about so wildly that the mul
could barely hold onto the Heartwood Spear.

Chilo staggered forward and swung his heartpick at the
mul. Rikus reached inside the pick's arc and blocked the
attack at the tarek's wrist. The serrated blade flashed over
his shoulder. The mul found himself staring into Chilo's
lifeless gaze. Without looking away, he kicked at Felorn
backward, like a horse, and knocked her free of his spear.
Chilo dropped his heartpick. Grabbing Rikus by the

shoulder, the dead tarek raised his handfork.

One of the things that made Neeva and Rikus a great fighting team was their ability to recognize when they needed help. Now was one of those times. "Neeva!" Rikus shouted calmly.

The handfork started down. Neeva's trikal flashed past Rikus's head. He heard a sharp whack, then the hand holding the fork tumbled to the ground. The stump of Chilo's bloody wrist struck the mul's face, opening a long gash on his cheek.

Rikus reacted quickly, smashing his spiked elbow cop into Chilo's mouth. The lifeless tarek dropped to the ground and made no move to rise. Rikus turned to assist his partner.

At that particular moment, Neeva had no need of his help. The gladiator brought her trikal down on Felorn's neck, separating her head from her shoulders. The tarek's body did not try to fight on.

Rikus glanced up at the King's Balcony. Kalak stood behind the railing, his sunken black eyes fixed on the dead tareks. The mul was tempted to throw the spear at that moment, but he didn't have a clear shot at the ancient king's body.

Neeva caught his arm. "Not yet," she said. "We've got to make sure Agis and Sadira know what you're doing."

"You're right, as usual," Rikus answered, looking back toward the obsidian pyramid.

The field had now been narrowed to three sets of gladiators: Rikus and Neeva; the half-giant, Gaanon, and his elven partner; and a pair of humans. The humans had removed their sandals to climb the glassy pyramid and were about to reach the top. Gaanon and his elven partner were just behind the leaders, climbing along the ridge where two sides of the pyramid met.

"Let's win this contest," Rikus said, retrieving Chilo's fork from the disembodied hand that held it. "On top of the pyramid, I'll have a better shot at Kalak, and Sadira and Agis won't be able to miss what I'm doing."

The mul sliced his sandal thongs. Neeva removed hers with a flick of her trikal's blade. Before Rikus and his partner began to ascend, the two humans reached the apex of the pyramid. As the woman crested the top, the gaj extended its head in a lightning fast blur. It caught her in its pincers, wrapping its tentacles around her brow and arms. She dropped her weapons and screamed.

When her partner tried to help, the gaj slammed its mandibles into him. The man tumbled down the pyramid. As he passed Gaanon, the half-giant hefted his huge axe and sliced off an arm.

Neeva started up the ridge opposite Gaanon and the elf, observing, "It's us and the half-giant."

"And the gaj," Rikus added, following her. The obsidian was so hot he could hardly bear to plant his feet long enough to take the next step.

Rikus and Neeva were about three-quarters of the way up when the gaj released the dead woman. The beast spun around to face Gaanon and the elf.

"Good," Rikus commented. "Let the half-giant take care of it."

Rikus! came a familiar thought-voice. *I have waited to hear your thoughts. I feared you had died below.*

They haven't beaten me yet, Rikus responded, echoing the last words the gaj had said to him. *How did you survive? I thought a spear through the head would kill anything.*

Master Tithian sent a man to care for me. Without his thoughts, I might have been too weak to recover.

You attacked your healer? Rikus asked.

I am like Yarig. I must follow my focus, the gaj replied simply. *Just as you have come here to follow yours.*

Rikus looked up in time to see the elf disappear from the ridge she and Gaanon were climbing. She reappeared behind the gaj. Unfortunately, her whip and spikes were useless against its thick shell. She simply stood looking at the creature. The amused crowd began to heckle her with catcalls.

As Gaanon approached the top, it became apparent to Rikus that the elf's strategy was a sound one. She lashed at the orange shell with her whip, capturing the gaj's attention. It turned slowly to face her, wrapping a tentacle around her arm. The half-elf cried out in pain, then the gaj snapped its pincers closed around her waist.

Gaanon stepped onto the platform behind the creature. "Now, Raffaela!" he boomed.

The elf teleported away, leaving nothing but empty space between the pincers. The gaj screeched, for the tentacle that had been wrapped around the woman's arm also vanished. Raffaela reappeared at the base of the pyramid, writhing in agony as she pulled the tentacle from her arm.

Gaanon stooped over and grabbed the back of the gaj's shell. The half-giant began to lift. The creature's canelike legs shot out and scratched at the glassy surface of the platform.

"This is for the wound you gave me last year, Rikus!" Gaanon boomed.

The mul saw the gaj's head and pincers being forced off the platform directly above him and Neeva. Gaanon's witless face hovered over the top of the beast's rust-colored shell. He was glaring at the mul with a gap-toothed sneer.

A faint hiss sounded from beneath the gaj as it released

its defensive gas. Gaanon looked as though he would retch but kept pushing the beast forward. Suddenly the gaj slid down the glassy pyramid, appearing as little more than an orange streak as it crashed into Neeva. Rikus jumped out of the way. As he landed on the steep slope, his feet shot from beneath him. The mul tumbled head over heels down to the sandy field.

Gaanon's brutal laugh boomed over the fighting field. Rikus leaped to his feet, spear in hand and spitting sand. The half-giant's moronic expression changed to fear when he saw the weapon pointed at him, but Rikus restrained himself from throwing it. Raffaela had no doubt recovered by now. If he threw the spear, she would certainly teleport to him and attack before he could secure another weapon.

Instead, Rikus looked to where the gaj had landed. The beast lay on the ground without moving. Its legs were retracted beneath its carapace, and its head was pointed away from him. The mul heard a muffled scream and saw that Neeva's trikal protruded from beneath the gaj's shell. Without pause, he leaped atop the beast.

"Release her!" he demanded.

Neeva lay directly beneath the gaj, flailing wildly at its head. The creature's tentacles were wrapped around her helmet, frantically trying to remove it.

Release her! Rikus repeated, this time using thought speech.

No, came the reply. *Let me have her or I'll tell the king your true reason for fighting today.*

"Then tell him!" Rikus snarled, plunging his spear deep into the monster's head.

The gaj shuddered and shrieked in pain, but the injury did not prevent it from tearing Neeva's helm from her head. *You should know you can't kill me,* it said. *Go, or I tell the king!*

"Rikus! Get it off!" Neeva yelled. The gaj tried to snake a tentacle around her head, but she blocked with her forearm. As the stalk entwined her wrist, she howled in pain.

"Its body!" Neeva screeched. "Hit its body."

The gaj lashed its free tentacle around her head, and she fell silent. Somehow Neeva found the strength to grasp at the stalk. From his own experience, the mul knew even Neeva could not last long once the thing invaded her mind.

Rikus pulled the Heartwood Spear from the beast's head, then jabbed at its hump. The point passed through the shell as easily as it had penetrated the tareks' bodies. An ear-piercing shriek sounded from the gaj's head. It began to lash about fiercely. Rikus pushed the spear in deeper, twisting the shaft like a butter churn.

The gaj stopped struggling. The stench of its defensive gas filled the air. Rikus pulled his spear free and leaped off the beast.

"What are you waiting for?" Neeva gasped, her voice weak and raspy. "I can't breathe."

Holding his breath so he would not be weakened by the gaj's gas, Rikus flipped the lifeless creature onto its back. Using the spear, he removed the tentacles from Neeva's head and arm. Welts and blisters had already formed where the thing had touched her.

The crowd broke into a horrendous roar. Rikus stepped away from gaj, drawing a deep breath. He saw that Gaanon's elven partner had returned to the pyramid's summit. Both the half-giant and the elf stood at the edge of the platform, staring at him with an air of haughty disdain.

Rikus looked back to Neeva. "Can you fight?"

"I'm still alive, aren't I?" she said, though she had still not risen to her feet.

People in the stands cried Rikus's name, urging him to abandon his partner and attack the pyramid. The mul picked up his spear and looked toward the King's Balcony. Kalak remained at the rail. He leaned over the edge, staring down at the mul and his partner, his lips curling into a sadistic grin.

Neeva grabbed her trikal and tried to stand. Her knees buckled before she was halfway up. "I'm too weak, Rikus," she said. "You'll have to try without me."

"No," the mul said. "We're in this together."

He lifted the spear as if ready to throw it, pointing the tip toward Gaanon. The half-giant took a step backward. A thunderous roar exploded from the stands, with thousands of voices urging the mul to kill his rival.

Rikus let the uproar continue to build, then glanced down at his fighting partner, who lay gasping on the sand. "For you and Sadira," he whispered.

Neeva shook her head. "For freedom and Athas."

With that, Rikus whirled around to face the King's Balcony. Kalak's eyes widened.

At that moment, a deafening explosion shook the stadium. A great silver and gold flash shot out of the lower tiers as Sadira made her attack. The bright flare filled the air with a peculiar stench that reminded Rikus of melting copper. The bolt hit an invisible barrier at the balcony's edge, exploding there into a brilliant cascade of red and blue sparks. The mul glimpsed a magical wall of shimmering force, but it faded away amidst a cacophony of loud sizzles and sharp pops.

Rikus stepped forward. Kalak looked away from the mul, his eyes drawn suddenly to Agis of Asticles in the High Templars' Gallery. Rikus hurled the spear with all his might. As the enchanted weapon sailed toward its target, an image born of Kalak's twisted mind, augmented by his mastery of the Way, appeared over the entire stadium: a dragon, fierce and terrible, rose to the height of the great ziggurat.

The image of the dragon reared back, ready to strike.

It was in that instant that the Heartwood Spear struck Kalak, sorcerer-king of Tyr, squarely in the chest and passed clear through his body. The king's screams filled the stadium, then the entire city. The unearthly cries did not fade as the half-giants grabbed their leader and dragged him into his golden palace.

The Dragon

The stadium remained tense, but calm. Most common-
ers stayed in their seats, too frightened or too stunned to
move, filling the air with the steady drone of their astonished voices. Knots of angry nobles yelled at stony-faced
templars, trying in vain to make them open the sealed
gates. Glowering half-giants stalked the terrace and
aisles, their massive clubs resting over their shoulders
and their red-rimmed eyes scanning the crowd.

It was not the reaction Agis had anticipated. He had
envisioned a thunderous uproar, the stands breaking into
a riot, the frenzied crowd pouring onto the fighting field.
There was none of that. The spectators were too shocked
to do as the noble expected, and Larkyn's half-giants
were too efficient to let them.

The crowd's reaction was not the only thing that had
failed to go as Agis had pictured. The timing of the companions' attack had been perfect, but that was where
their success had ended. As powerful and well-placed as
Rikus's throw had been, it had not killed the king. From
the High Templars' Gallery, the noble had seen Kalak

321

gesturing angrily as his half-giants helped him off the King's Balcony and into the Golden Tower.

Agis turned his attention to the fighting field, where a swarm of templars and half-giants surrounded Rikus and Neeva. The two gladiators were allowing themselves to be escorted toward Tithian's gallery. Agis suspected their complacence was due to their faith in his influence over the high templar, for he knew that Rikus and Neeva would have died fighting rather than suffer the indignity of execution.

When the swarm of guards stopped below the gallery, Tithian stepped to the edge of the porch and regarded the pair with a spiteful glare in his eyes. Rikus and Neeva glared back, their faces betraying distrust and hatred of the high templar. Agis moved forward, so he would no longer be hidden in the shadows below the canopy. Neeva's clenched jaw relaxed, but Rikus's expression merely changed from hatred to defiance.

"Bring your prisoners to the gallery," Tithian said, speaking to the man who had assumed command of the mob.

The templar looked uneasy. "We're assigned directly to the High Templar of the King's Safety," he said. "Larkyn has instructed us to accept orders only from him."

Tithian glanced at the chair where Larkyn's body sat slumped. Though the man's eyes were closed and he was not moving, that was the only visible of evidence of his death. If anyone in the stands could see into the shadows engulfing the gallery, Agis hoped it would appear to them that the high templar was merely sleeping in the chair.

"I'm afraid the attack on our king has left Larkyn indisposed," Tithian said, looking back to the fighting field. "Bring the prisoners to him, and he'll attend to them from his chair."

The templar looked uncomfortable, but nodded his assent. He prodded the two prisoners toward the edge of the arena.

Tithian retreated into the shadows of the canopy. "Now what?" the high templar asked, staring at the king's balcony. "Kalak is a thousand years old. I doubt that he'll do us the favor of dying from his wound."

Agis could only shrug. He was beginning to think Rikus had been right in hesitating to attack without a better plan.

A messenger poked his head into the gallery. "High One, a noblewoman insists upon seeing you."

"What does she want?" Tithian demanded. He looked past the guard and frowned at the partition that screened the gallery from the balcony grandstands behind it. "Who is she?"

"Her name is Sadira of Asticles," he answered. "She—"

"Send her up," Tithian interrupted. He faced Agis and snickered. "Sadira of *Asticles*?"

Agis felt the heat rise to his cheeks. "Not . . . formally, my friend," he said, wondering at the implications of the sorceress's choice of title.

A moment later, Sadira stepped onto the porch, her chest heaving. Her silk cape was tattered and ripped, and the silver circlet was missing from her head. Agis went to her side and took her arm. "What's wrong? Are you hurt?"

"The mob is getting ugly," she answered breathlessly. She stopped just beneath the canopy and braced herself on Ktandeo's cane.

Agis glanced out the front of the gallery. Across the fighting field, the crowd swarmed toward the gates. Fighting had broken out in dozens of places, most of the brawls involving spectators trying to force their way into the locked exit tunnels. Outside the High Templars' Gallery, hundreds of voices were demanding that the gates be opened and that Rikus and Neeva be freed.

Ignoring the tumult erupting in the stands, Tithian stepped to Agis's side. With a sarcastic smile, he took Sadira's hand and said, "*Lady Asticles*, I can't tell you how it pleases me to see you again."

He started to kiss her hand, but Sadira jerked it away. "I assume you're with us," she snapped. "Agis would have killed you by now if you supported Kalak."

Tithian cast an exaggerated look of hurt in Agis's direction, but did not seem surprised or angry. He faced Sadira again and said, "At this point, girl, I'm not against you."

"Open the exits," Sadira demanded. She pointed toward the grandstands across the arena, where Larkyn's half-giants were trying to clear the gateways by smashing spectators with their heavy bone clubs.

"The gates can't be raised," Tithian answered. "Kalak had the chains cut."

Before Sadira could respond, Rikus and Neeva came up the stairs. They were followed by two of Larkyn's templars. Both held short swords pressed against the gladiators' backs. Though Neeva's steps were slow and measured, she seemed to have recovered much of the strength lost in her battle with the gaj.

Agis leaned close to Sadira and whispered, "Keep your dagger ready and follow my lead."

Though she looked confused, the sorceress slipped a hand beneath her cape and nodded.

Tithian led the two gladiators and their guards to the front of the porch. Agis and Sadira followed, taking care to stay behind Larkyn's men.

The leader peered over Rikus's shoulder at the

slouched body of his commander. "High One?"

Tithian said, "He's dead."

Keeping their daggers concealed beneath their robes just in case anyone outside the shady gallery could see what was happening, Agis and Sadira stepped up behind the two templars. They pressed the tips of their weapons to the men's backs.

Tithian said, "You two have a simple choice to make: stay quiet and live, or sound the alarm and die."

"The king will—"

"Probably kill us all," Tithian interrupted. "That has nothing to do with your choice. Drop your weapons or die." When both men let their swords clatter to the floor, the high templar added, "A wise decision. Lest you change your minds, remember that I have just given Rikus and Neeva their freedom. If you so much as move, they'll kill you in the blink of an eye. Given the chaos in the stands, I doubt anyone will notice."

Tithian waved the two templars to the front of the gallery, where they would be easy to watch. Once the templars had done as ordered, Neeva asked, "Agis, what's all this about Larkyn? I thought Tithian was in charge of the games."

Agis described the complication he had run into when he asked Tithian to secure their escape, and explained how they had improvised a solution by luring Larkyn into the gallery and murdering him.

When the noble finished, Tithian said, "At the moment, Larkyn is hardly the issue. What are you going to do about Kalak? I doubt your little pinprick will stop him from proceeding with his plan."

"We'll have to track him down and finish him off," Rikus said coldly.

Neeva regarded the mul with a look of surprise. "Is this

the same man who said he wanted no part in getting his friends killed?"

"I finish what I start. You know that," Rikus replied. "Besides, if we don't destroy Kalak now, he won't rest until he kills us. Let's go."

"The Golden Tower is a big place," Tithian said. "Perhaps it would help if you knew where to find the king before you entered it."

"Of course it would," Agis said. "Are you saying you can help us?"

The high templar nodded. "I'll want something in return."

"Isn't living enough?" Sadira snapped. "Help us or die, it's that simple."

Tithian gave her a condescending smirk. "Nothing is ever that simple."

"It is this time," Rikus said, moving toward the high templar. "No purple caterpillar is going to stop me from killing you now."

Agis stepped between the mul and Tithian. "Let's hear him out."

Rikus shook his head and started to circle around the noble, but Neeva pressed her hand against the mul's chest. "What is it you want, Tithian?" she asked, still watching Larkyn's men from the corner of her eye.

Smiling, the high templar said, "I'm not asking for much, but it occurs to me that after you kill Kalak, Tyr will need a new king."

"Never!" cried Sadira.

Rikus and Neeva added their protests in the form of disgusted snorts, then Agis asked, "Why would we change one tyrant for another?"

"Because without a king, Tyr will fall into chaos," the high templar replied, nonplussed by the objections.

"Someone will have to run the city. Otherwise, it will fall into ruins as surely as if Kalak becomes a dragon. Who better to assume that position than a templar? We've been running the city for a thousand years—"

"And we all know what you've made of it!" Agis objected.

"Then help me make it better," Tithian urged. He almost sounded sincere.

Agis suddenly felt the familiar tingle of life force being pulled from his body. He looked to Sadira.

"I feel it, too," she said. "Something's drawing power from us."

A cacophony of panic erupted in the stadium. Agis stepped to the back of the gallery and pulled aside one of the heavy curtains shielding the porch from the grandstands.

In scattered places, aged men and women clutched at their chests and dropped gasping to the ground. Stronger spectators screamed in anger, attacking half-giants and templars with stones or seats they had pulled from the terraces. They pushed and shoved into the exit tunnels, trying in vain to force the gates open. The mob succeeded only in crushing those who had entered the passageways first. In many places, Larkyn's guards organized counterattacks against the crowd, the templars firing lightning bolts and the half-giants clubbing anyone within reach.

Amidst all the confusion, more than a few hands were pointing toward the summit of the great ziggurat. A small geyser of burgundy flame was shooting from the top of the structure. A moment later, a billowing cloud of yellow smoke replaced the pillar of fire.

Rikus and Neeva asked, "What's happening?"

"Kalak has started his incubation," Sadira answered,

pointing toward the obsidian pyramid. "He's drawing the life out of the spectators."

Agis looked in the direction the sorceress pointed. The air around the pyramid shimmered with raw energy, and waves of flaxen light scintillated over the structure's glassy surface. Deep within the thing's black heart glowed a steady golden light that grew brighter even as the senator watched.

"Well?" Tithian asked. "The longer we delay, the weaker we become and the stronger Kalak grows."

"You *will* have to make Tyr a better place," Agis said. "The first thing will be to free the slaves."

"Of course," Tithian replied. "You have my word on it."

*   *   *   *   *

The Golden Tower was every bit as large as it appeared from the outside. It had a floorplan as twisted as the tangled branches of a faro tree, with dimly lit halls arranged in spiral patterns, gloomy rooms built in warped shapes, and dark nooks that served no apparent purpose except to make a passerby wonder what lurked in them.

Nevertheless, the group had little trouble following Kalak. A trail of black, steaming fluid that Agis took to be blood led the way deeper and deeper into the palace. Every time they rounded a corner, the noble cringed, expecting to meet some hideous beast Kalak kept to guard his home. Tithian, however, moved with the speed and confidence of someone who knew what surprises the palace did and did not contain.

At last, after they had descended to the foundations of the ancient tower, they reached a cavernous, circular vault. It was lit by an alabaster ceiling panel set into a

grid of copper-plated beams. In the shadowy squares between the beams hung carved reliefs of beasts and races
that Agis had never before seen. At the edges of the ceiling, fluted columns of granite, capped with sculpted
leaves and flowers of strange shapes, rose from the floor
to support the rafters. Between these columns stood
dozens of rows of shelving, empty save for a few ancient
steel weapons.

Tithian held a finger to his lips, then led the four companions to the other side of the room. In the shadows
near the wall, the huge bodies of Kalak's two half-giant
guards rested on the floor. The shattered remains of an
obsidian ball were scattered over the area, and two more
globes, still intact, sat nearby. Between the two corpses
lay the dark circle of an open trap door.

As they stopped to inspect the bodies, a voice said,
"Sacha, isn't that your worthy descendant, Tithian of
Mericles?"

Agis and the others brought their weapons to ready defense positions.

"So it is, Wyan," answered another voice. "It is. Such a
handsome fellow, too. Perhaps he could find it in his
heart to open a vein in those half-giants and feed us."

To his astonishment, Agis saw that the voices came
from a pair of heads sitting on a shadowy shelf. He
grabbed a steel sword and started to approach the abomi-
nations, but Tithian laid a hand on the noble's shoulder
and restrained him.

"What are they?" Agis asked.

"Kalak's friends," the high templar answered. "The
last time I was here, they called me a snake-faced runt."

"That was Sacha!" objected Wyan. "I wouldn't blame
you if you left him to starve."

"Ignore them. They're harmless, as long as you don't

get too close." Tithian used his toe to nudge the desiccated body of a half-giant. It fell apart like a wasp's nest. "What caused this?"

Sadira motioned to one of the obsidian globes. "Kalak drained their life away," she said.

Tithian's eyes lit up, and he retrieved one of the ebony balls. "Show me how to use it, and I'll—"

"Not in a hundred years—even if that were the way dragon magic worked," Sadira said.

The templar frowned. "Dragon magic?"

"Obsidian isn't magical, it's just a tool. Like any tool, it's only as powerful as the person using it," the sorceress explained, echoing the words Nok had used to explain the properties of the glassy rock. "To a hunter, it's just a knife or an arrowhead. To a dragon, it's a lens that converts life force into magic—but *you'll* never use it for that."

"Why not?" Tithian demanded, motioning at Sadira's cane. "You are."

The half-elf shook her head. "The spells are in the cane. *It* draws the energy through the pommel, not me," she said, her tone somewhat regretful. "Dragon magic relies on psionics and sorcery together. To use it, you must be a master of pulling energy from your body and a genius at shaping it into spells. It's the most difficult kind of sorcery, but it's also the most powerful."

"And the more time we spend here, the more powerful Kalak becomes," Agis said, unsheathing the ancient sword he had taken from the shelf. "I suggest we get on with it."

Neeva selected a great, steel-bladed axe from the vault's shelves. "I'm ready."

Pointing at the hole in the floor, Tithian noted, "That leads to an obsidian-lined tunnel. The tunnel opens into the lower chamber of the ziggurat. I suspect that's where you'll find Kalak."

"You mean *we*," Rikus said flatly. He took a curved sword from the shelf and handed it to Tithian. "If you're going to be a king, start acting the part."

"Kings don't risk their lives—"

"You'll be a new kind of king," Agis said, prodding the high templar forward.

Rikus gripped the Heartwood Spear; they had found the weapon lying on the King's Balcony, where the half-giants had left it in their hurry to move Kalak into his palace. "I'll take the lead. Nok said the spear would protect me against magic and the Way. Hide behind me, and I'll be your shield."

Neeva went next, followed by Tithian, then Agis, with Sadira behind him. As he dropped into the hole, the senator gasped at the eerily beautiful sight ahead of the group. They stood in a gloomy tunnel lined by bricks of obsidian. A half-dozen paces ahead, a sparkling stream of golden energy poured from an overhead shaft and flowed down the passage with a hiss. At the far end, the light passed upward through another trap door. From that opening shone a vermilion glow threaded with thin wisps of scarlet mist. A horrid, deep-throated growl came from the room above and throbbed down the tunnel.

Holding the Heartwood Spear in both hands, Rikus led the way toward the other end of the passage. He did not even pause before stepping into the golden stream of radiance, an act Agis thought to be a little foolhardy.

As Agis and the others followed Rikus into the light, their skin crawled with a ticklish, pleasant feeling. Tithian's long braid of auburn hair rose into the air and began to writhe in a sort of macabre dance. The noble sensed his own unbound locks doing the same. Otherwise, the companions suffered no ill effects. Agis even felt somewhat invigorated.

They had moved most of the way through the tunnel when Rikus cried, "Look out!" He shifted his grip on the Heartwood Spear, holding it diagonally across his body.

At the far end of the passage, a clawed hand as large as a half-giant's dangled from the open trap door. The gnarled fingers made a series of gestures and pointed at the companions. Without warning, a ball of green flame crackled down the passageway. Neeva and Tithian hid behind Rikus, and Agis huddled as close to them as he could. Sadira pressed her body against his back.

As the fireball washed over him, everything in Agis's vision turned green and warped as if underwater. For a moment it seemed as though they were all trapped in a molten emerald. Then the air itself rushed from Agis's chest, and he could not breathe. Where another person's body did not protect him, he felt as if his skin were being seared over a bed of coals. At last, almost against his will, he drew a long, deep breath. His lungs exploded with scalding pain, making him gag. The fiery air contained a horrible, caustic fume that made his eyes water and burned his stomach as badly as it scorched his lungs.

An instant later, the fireball passed. The hand still dangled from the opening, gesturing in preparation for another spell. Rikus lifted the spear to throw, but stopped when Sadira cried Nok's name and activated her cane.

Agis ducked and pulled Tithian down beside him. Everyone else had sense enough to crouch on their own.

"Mountainbolt!" Sadira cried.

A deafening boom shook the tunnel, and a sapphire flash streaked over Agis's head. It struck the hand and exploded into a dazzling spray of blue-white sparks. Shreds of flesh and bone flew in all directions. An inhuman howl reverberated down the tunnel.

Rikus took off at a sprint, leaving the others standing behind him, astonished at his boldness. As the mul reached the end of the passageway, Kalak reached down with his other hand to grasp the trap door. The hand glowed with bright crimson light, and wet, soft scales covered it.

Before the king could pull the door closed, Rikus thrust the spear through the hand. Another howl, not quite as pained as the last, rolled down the passageway. The hand withdrew, dripping black blood. Kalak sent a cloud of yellow gas billowing through the door. The mul stumbled back to his companions, coughing and gasping for breath. Before the cloud reached the others, it was carried back toward the king by the golden stream of energy coming from the shaft behind Sadira and the others.

"Quick thinking, Rikus," Agis said, still wheezing from the effects of the green fireball. "I don't know what we'd have done if Kalak had closed the door."

The mul acknowledged the compliment with a grunt, then asked, "Anyone hurt? You all look pretty rough."

Agis noticed that the fireball had burned away the robe on his arms and legs. The exposed skin was red, with white blisters forming in several places. Tithian was in much the same condition, as were the two women.

"We're fine, Rikus," Neeva said. "Get on with it."

The mul led the way to the end of the corridor, then looked up at the narrow opening. "We can't all go up at once."

"I'll lead the way," Agis offered, stepping past Tithian and Neeva. "With both hands injured, Kalak won't be casting many spells or fighting with weapons. That leaves the Way, my area of expertise."

Rikus nodded. "You're right," he said, holding the

spear out. "Take this."

Agis shook his head. "We can't afford the risk that I'll lose it," he said. "I can hold him long enough for the next person, even without the spear."

"That makes sense, but—"

"I can do this, Rikus," insisted Agis.

The mul regarded him for a moment, then nodded. "If you say so." He leaned the spear against his shoulder and formed a stirrup with his hands.

Before Agis stepped into it, he felt a warm hand on his shoulder. "Be careful," Sadira said.

Smiling, the nobleman handed Sadira the sword he had taken from Kalak's treasure vault. Rikus gave Agis a boost, and he shot up into the secret chamber.

The room felt as hot as a furnace. Though its intensity did not compare to Kalak's fireball, Agis's lungs ached when he inhaled, and the heat scorched his skin—especially where he had already been burned. The chamber was fairly large, built entirely from glazed brick and filled with whorls of the translucent golden energy that rushed in from the shaft. Dozens of paintings decorated the walls and ceilings, portraying a huge dragon as it ravaged estates, caravans, and even whole cities.

So much dark blood covered the floor that Agis wondered how Kalak could still be alive. The black pools bubbled and steamed, sending wisps of greasy brown vapor to roll along the ceiling until they reached the center of the room, where a shaft rose toward the distant sky like a massive chimney.

Dozens of obsidian globes lay strewn over the floor. They varied in size from that of a small faro fruit to a huge melon. Scattered among the glassy balls were half-a-dozen empty husks, shaped like thick-bodied worms and made of soft, pinkish scales. The smallest of the husks was just over five feet in length, the largest more than ten.

Kalak himself lay on the far side of the room. His serpentine body, now more than twelve feet long, was covered with glowing scales that lit the whole chamber with their fiery radiance. The king paid no attention to Agis, for he was squirming and thrashing about, trying to free himself of his latest husk.

Realizing they had caught Kalak at a particularly vulnerable time, Agis reached through the opening in the floor and motioned for the others to follow. Sadira handed him his sword. As the others climbed into the room, the senator moved toward the king.

He could barely recognize Kalak in the grotesque larva writhing on the floor. The old man's face had flattened into a serpentlike oval, and his ears had disappeared entirely. Reptilian scales now covered his wrinkled head. The golden diadem of Tyr's kingship lay discarded on the floor beside him. While his neck had grown long and sinuous, his arms and legs had all but disappeared. At the moment, they seemed no more than withered and useless vestigial limbs. Boiling black fluid oozed from the spear wound in the dragon larva's chest, from the stump at the end of its right arm, and from the hole in its left hand.

As Agis approached, the larva paid him no attention. It seemed to be in horrible pain, both from its wounds and the process of shedding its skin. It slowly opened its mouth, revealing two rows of jagged teeth. The repulsive beast placed its mouth on an nearby obsidian globe as large as its own head. To the noble's amazement, it swallowed the black ball. A spherical bulge slowly began to work its way down the beast's long throat.

Rikus and the others crept up behind Agis. They studied the gruesome beast for a moment, then Sadira said,

"Let's kill him while we can." She raised her cane and started forward.

The larva stopped writhing and whipped its head around to face them, the dark pits of its eyes flaring with anger. "Kill *me*, foolish girl?" it sneered, puffs of black steam leaking from its mouth. "Perhaps five hundred years ago, but not now."

It fixed its hateful gaze on the sorceress, and Agis realized immediately the dragon-king was about to attack. It had let them come this close only because it intended to use the Way and finish them all at once.

Five battering rams, each carved in the image of a horned dragon's head, appeared in front of the larva. It took Agis an instant to realize that they were mental constructs and not physical, for there was so much energy in the room that they had taken on the appearance of a material form.

The noble knew that he possessed the skill to resist the direct, overwhelming attack the king intended to make, but if his friends were to survive, he would have to try something desperate. Agis visualized a sand dune and opened a pathway from his power nexus to the room itself.

Kalak's rams shot forward. In the same instant, the entire chamber seemed to fill with sand. Three of the king's attacks plowed to a stop instantly. The one in front of Rikus simply disappeared as it approached the Heartwood Spear. Only the ram directed at Sadira forced its way through Agis's psionic sand and hit its target. The sorceress was knocked across the room and slammed into the wall, collapsing into a heap.

A terrible wave of fatigue and dizziness came over Agis. His knees buckled, and he let the defense drop. When he fell to the floor a moment later, he landed in a hot pool of the king's blood.

Rikus rushed to the dragon larva, followed closely by Neeva and Tithian. Using his free arm to shield his face against the heat of the beast's body, the mul stepped toward the head. He motioned the high templar to the midsection and Neeva to the tail.

Kalak did not move as the trio approached, apparently as exhausted by the psionic combat as Agis. But as Rikus lifted the spear, the larva raised its head. "You can't believe I'll let you strike."

"I don't believe you can stop us!" Neeva said, swinging her axe.

She sent a three-foot section of tail skittering across the floor. Kalak roared in pain, then Rikus thrust his spear at the larva's neck. The dragon-king smashed its massive head into the mul's side and knocked him off balance. Before Rikus could recover, the beast sank its sharp teeth deep into his massive chest and lifted him from the ground. The mul screamed and dropped the spear, beating at the king's scale-armored head with his bare fists.

Neeva hefted her axe to strike again, but this time the larva was ready. It slapped what remained of its mighty tail across her face. The blow shattered her nose and sent her tumbling across the floor, unconscious and bleeding.

Tithian's face blanched to the color of alabaster. Without striking a blow, he dropped his curved sword and backed away.

"Coward!" Agis cried, vainly attempting to stand.

"If Rikus and Neeva can't kill it, what do you expect me to do?" the high templar countered, moving toward Neeva's prone form.

Agis took several deep breaths and concentrated on drawing as much power as he could through his energy nexus. He rose to his knees.

At the same time, Tithian picked up Neeva's axe. The gladiator lay unconscious in a pool of her own blood, her chest heaving with quick, shallow breaths. Gripping the ancient weapon, more from fear than from courage, the high templar moved to Sadira's side. She moaned and sat up, holding her head.

Tithian looked from one wounded rebel to another, Rikus's screams echoing off the glazed brick walls, filling his ears. It seemed as though there were a hundred muls in the room, each dying a particularly horrible, painful death.

At last the high templar hefted Neeva's huge weapon. To Agis's surprise, Tithian rushed forward and brought the flat of the axe down on a ball of obsidian. It shattered into a dozen shards. The high templar moved to the next one and smashed it, too.

"What are you doing?" the senator cried weakly.

"There's more than one way to fight," Tithian answered, moving away from the noble. He went to the corner farthest away from the dragon and smashed another black globe.

Agis remained puzzled only a moment longer, for Kalak abruptly tossed the mul's savaged body aside. "Stop!" the king cried. "I command it!"

Tithian smashed another ball. "Why should I?" he shouted. "Will you spare my life? Will you give me control of Tyr when you're gone?"

The king crawled slowly but steadily toward the high templar. "You know better than that," it hissed. "But I will promise you a painless death."

Tithian smashed another sphere, then rushed to a different corner of the room.

"You are a high templar!" the king cried. "You must obey your king's demands!" The beast changed directions and followed Tithian, turning its back to Agis.

The high templar's arms began to tremble so badly that Agis could see the axe shaking. Nevertheless, he brought the heavy axe down upon another obsidian ball. Standing in the center of a scattering of black fragments, Tithian made no move to leave his corner.

Agis forced himself to his feet, fixing his eyes on the Heartwood Spear. He stumbled over to it, whispering over and over to himself that he was not tired, that he had plenty of strength left. He picked up the wooden shaft. It seemed impossibly heavy, at least for muscles still liquid from the effects of psionic exhaustion.

The larva reached Tithian at last. Rising up to its full height, the dragon-king opened its maw. The high templar screamed in terror and let Neeva's axe slip from his hands. Dropping to the floor, he curled into a ball.

Agis braced the spear in both hands and charged just as the thing that was Kalak lowered its head to bite Tithian. The exhausted noble screamed a feral battle cry and thrust the Heartwood Spear into the back of the dragon's head. The oak shaft slid smoothly and easily into the heavy skull, requiring no strength at all. Agis took two more steps forward, driving the point as deeply as possible into the dragon-king's brain.

A shudder ran through the serpentine body. Kalak gave a single thunderous bellow, shaking the room to its foundation and knocking a cascade of loose bricks off the ceiling. The beast's head dropped to the floor at Tithian's feet, one end of the spear protruding from its mouth.

Agis dropped to his knees, trembling and gasping for breath. Tithian took his hands from his face and studied Kalak's vacant eyes. After a moment, when the thought that the dragon-king was dead took root in his mind, the fear washed from the high templar's face and he retrieved

Neeva's axe. Tentatively, he struck the larva's head with
the blade. When it did not flinch, he raised the axe higher
and brought it down on the beast's neck more sharply.
The blow opened only a small wound, but the dragon did
not respond at all.

"The king is dead," he said, dropping the axe.

Agis nodded and also stood. "Tyr is free."

Tithian stepped past the noble. Agis turned to follow
and saw Sadira kneeling at Neeva's side. The sorceress
gently probed the unconscious gladiator's smashed nose
while holding the woman's mouth open so she could
breathe.

Rikus sat a few yards away, grimacing in pain and still
dazed from the mauling Kalak had given him. More than
a dozen wounds were visible on his bulky torso, all ooz-
ing dark red blood. In places, bits of white rib showed
through. He stoically took measure of his injuries and,
tearing strips from his clothes, began to bind them as best
he could.

Tithian passed within an arm's reach of the mul but
did not pay him the slightest attention. Instead, the high
templar went to the wall where Kalak had been molting.
He dropped to his knees and began running his hands
through the steaming pools of dark blood that covered
the floor.

Silently cursing the high templar's callousness, Agis
went to the gladiator's side. The noble began to tear
strips from his own robe, then aided the mul in bandag-
ing his many wounds.

"You killed Kalak," Rikus wheezed. He squeezed the
noble's hand. "Well done."

"No, we killed Kalak," Agis corrected, warmly returning the mul's handclasp. He looked in the direction of
Sadira and Neeva, then added, "We couldn't have done it

without each other."

Near the wall, Tithian rose to his feet, a self-satisfied smirk on his face. In his hands, he held the golden diadem that Kalak had worn for a thousand years. Both the crown and his fingers were stained with black blood.

"Long live the king!" he whispered, placing the circlet on his own head.

Prism Pentad
BOOK TWO
The Crimson Legion
Troy Denning

A dream born from tyranny . . .

After a millennium of sorrow, the city of Tyr cast off the
yoke of the brutal despot who reduced its fields to dust
and its citizens to bondage. The new king, Tithian of
Mericles, has liberated the slaves . . . and plunged the
city into chaos. Only the man-dwarf Rikus, the gladiator slave who sparked the rebellion, can save the city
from the mighty army sent from Urik to destroy it.
February 1992.

Book Three: *The Amber Enchantress*, August 1992.

Our toughest challenge ever, the DARK SUN™ world!

Open the book and discover a shocking, once-verdant world turned barren. Open the game box and enter the deserts of Athas. There lie the scattered city states, each held captive by tyrannical sorcerer-kings. Athas is a land of deadly magic and powerful psionics. It is an unforgiving world, but the riches it offers can be great. Face the fires of Athas and enter one of the most challenging AD&D® game worlds ever!

Also included are two 96-page rule books, two 24-page flip books, two full-color maps, and a short story, "A Little Knowledge," that accompanies the adventure.

B·O·O·K·S

Token of Dragonsblood   Damaris Cole

To Noressa, raised by simple rural folk, a curious prophecy means nothing. She has vowed a lifejourney to answer the summoning that compels her eastward. But from the beginning, the fates are against her. Hunted by demons and possessing a talisman that awakens strange powers within her, Noressa learns that the prophecy means everything. Available now.

The Cloud People   Robert B. Kelly

When a "flying machine" crashes in the mountains, the prince of Fief Karcan goes to investigate. The missing pilot may well be the savior whose coming had been prophesied, the only man who can open a powerful medallion and save both the prince's father and his world from the evil Lord Thyden. October 1991.

Lightning's Daughter   Mary H. Herbert

In this sequel to *Dark Horse*, young Gabria comes to terms with her magical ability and her role as a strong woman leader in a male-dominated world. The magic-blessed outcasts from the horse clans make Gabria their mentor, but before she can become their teacher, she must lead them against a magical creature bent on destroying the Dark Horse Plains. December 1991.